THE
SECRET FAMILY

THE
SECRET FAMILY

A Novel

LAWRENCE RICHETTE

This is a work of fiction. Names, characters, places and incidents either are the product of the author's imagination or are used fictitiously, and any resemblance to any actual persons, living or dead, events, or locales is entirely coincidental.

This book was printed in the United States of America.

To order additional copies of this book, contact:
Xlibris Corporation
1-888-795-4274
www.Xlibris.com
Orders@Xlibris.com
18113

This novel is for my father,
who taught me about secrets and families,
for my mother and all the Aversas living and dead,
and for Cynthia Lynch.

"Man is a creature whose substance is faith. What he believes, he becomes."

—Hindu proverb

"They don't suffer—they don't even speak English."
—George Baer, President of the Reading Railroad, 1905

PART ONE

ONE

There are places on this earth God must regret He ever made. Odysseus, wisest of men, sailed past Calabria to find friendlier land, since from the sea the coast above Italy's heel looks merciless. Dry trees thrust out of stony soil, towns tumble headlong down cliffs, and even the birds seem paralyzed. Houses, piazzas, churches lie stunned by light so harsh that even natives retreat, at noon, to darkened rooms.

Beneath that soil lie martyrs' bones. As soon as Italy unified, Calabria revolted against the Northern King, who ignored the famine it was suffering. In 1861 the Cavour government dispatched troops, while hundreds of young men formed guerrilla bands each week. "They send bullets instead of bread," was their rallying cry. The peasants called the rebels "our honored youth." From March, 1861, to April, 1863, the Army killed or wounded over 7,000 honored youths, proving the Northerners were right: Calabrians were animals who deserved to starve to death. A few stuck to banditry, but the rest of Calabria went back to sleep. In those days they joked that anyone hoping for a better life prayed to God and hanged himself.

The town of San Lorenzo perched over the sea, white houses flung like dice against tan cliffs. Above the town lay fields where olives and wheat grew raggedly. Northerners called Calabria the land time forgot, and San Lorenzo's dirt streets and crumbling church explained their sneer. The Prince possessed the only car, and it rarely appeared. The telegraph office did so little business that its owner threatened to shut it down. And nobody read the local paper, after Father Ugo, the parish priest, denounced it from the pulpit as Socialist.

By 1904 San Lorenzo lost a third of its men to America. Their longing to leave was shattering its history, as longing always does. Those who remained lived, as the saying went, on bread and onions, seasoned with hope, that most dangerous food. The ruling Northerners still taxed the poor so harshly that workers lived no better than beggars. Above them stood the Prince and the Church, who together made visible the unchanging order of things. To inhabit San Lorenzo was to place more faith in angels than in your fellow man, to expect nothing from this life except the same misery your parents endured.

Truth and Justice were words for children and politicians; no adult took them seriously. One Sunday morning an old woman was crossing the church piazza when the Prince's English mastiff, his owner laughing all the while, mauled her and flung her to the ground. Though unhurt, she decided to sue the Prince in the local court, but could find no witness to testify for her. In the end the Prince, through perjury, convinced the court the woman had provoked his dog, at which point the court acquitted him and condemned her to pay the Prince's costs. She died in debtor's prison, and the witnesses who refused to testify for her congratulated themselves on siding with their Prince.

San Lorenzo entered the twentieth century by accident, and seemed prepared to ignore the fact indefinitely. The church bell still tolled its cracked and broken chords, the fishermen still shouted filthy jokes in dialect. Only a handful of gentry aspired to more. One of them, a man of mature years, was leaving his ornate townhouse on this damp October noon, proudly twirling a walking stick ordered all the way from Paris.

Leone Monti, like God on the seventh day, surveyed his creation and found it good. He owned roughly one third of the land encircling his hometown of San Lorenzo, to say nothing of his rented houses and, closest to Leone's heart, those stocks he was amassing on the Rome and Milan exchanges. Unlike God, it had taken Leone Monti forty-seven years to conjure up his world and, also unlike God, he frequently felt disbelief at his own creation. Why should he be spared the starvation that stalked San Lorenzo, all Calabria, indeed most of Italy?

Day and night you could see the dust rising five miles away and you knew they were leaving. Those too poor for a train to the port cities had to walk, sleeping in the parched fields, a silent army retreating from the battle Leone had already won. In those days all of Southern Italy looked to be in full retreat, three thousand men each week, or was it four? Leone knew what they wanted, earthly Paradise, a devilish Socialist notion to which the peasants clung despite all contrary proof. Those who returned told of hellishly foul cities where Italians were called animals and worked accordingly, but how could the truth dispel so intoxicating a dream? Didn't the peasants say of someone whose luck improved that he had found America?

Leone, a secret freethinker, had no patron saint to thank. Let the scum of the earth flee; Italy would prosper without them. Since the Northerners who ruled ignored Southern landowners like himself, their unspoken bargain ensuring neither faction would ever lose a lira. As for San Lorenzo, life would continue here as it had for ten centuries. The dust would settle, the dreamers would disappear. And he would grow as rich as Croesus before his death.

Soon Leone would own as many buildings and farms as his enemy the Prince. That thought caused Leone more than a twinge of disbelief. He, a starving doctor's son, rivaling a Prince whose nobility predated that of the Bourbons! Leone prided himself on building his fortune on the slender foundation of his wife's dowry, not lazily inheriting his family's lands like the Prince, whose paradise was not America but England. At moments Leone dreamed, wildly he knew, of driving the Prince into an English exile. Still, and he thought it often, his success meant he would triumph over history.

Today he walked through the town, accepting the bows and curtsies of his tenants. Leone knew that their homes were worth far less than the uncertain soil above the town, less even than the gaudy shares of railroad stock he kept hidden in his safe. Yet without the steady trickle of rents he could never keep afloat. To combat the Prince, he turned to another enemy, the local priest who acted for the Cardinal in worldly affairs. Father Ugo demanded twice the going rate for mortgages and got it, his smug clerical smile the reason Leone cursed the prelate with the same fervor that his wife prayed for his own health. The Mezzogiorno would die of priests, Leone liked to declare. If only Garibaldi had won, he sighed, and from the Pope down to that greedy Father Ugo every one of them had to work for a living, preferably in a foreign land.

The fields clung to the mountains and the mountains ran down to the town, to the sea. San Lorenzo overlooked the razor-edged blue depths of the Ionian Sea, facing Greece and the lands beyond. Leone's peasants grew wheat and olives, when the weather held, and with his profits from stock speculation he was gradually buying up their fields. More often than not they paid in promises, and he let them, calculating that would prove wiser than the Prince's abrupt foreclosures. The fields clung to the mountains and the peasants clung, poor animals, to their fields.

In the north of Italy men were driving horseless carriages side by side with women shamelessly smoking cigarettes. Leone saw rotogravures and knew he belonged to the old order as surely as the aging Prince, not that he cared. All of them would soon seem absurdly old-fashioned, the peasants, the Prince, himself, but Leone dismissed the thought. Progress was for intellectuals to debate in cafes. Life, his life, the only life he knew, lay in San Lorenzo.

His speculations in Rome and Milan financed new ventures, however often his wife begged him to stop risking their wealth. His money had an independent existence, it seemed, as though the telegraph reports of its rise and fall referred to another battle of Solferino or Custozza. Leone enjoyed bold gambles and indulged in them often, chastised by his wife, who would glance at his flushed cheeks and know he had defied her once again.

From the piazza's edge he glimpsed his two sons, Vittorio

and Francesco, playing soldiers on the beach. Vittorio, the elder, sixteen and vigorous, was leading Francesco in a childish parody of the army drill. Francesco was following with his customary air of bemused tolerance. Leone called out to his sons, but the wind muffled his voice. As he turned away, he heard Vittorio cry "To Adowa! The honor of Italy depends on us!"

Leone took the café chair offered by Signor Amabile, the town's attorney and scribe. A glass of brandy appeared an instant later, compliments of the owner, one of his tenants. Signor Amabile dipped snuff, then sighed deeply.

"What will be left of San Lorenzo now that our young men are all deserting us?"

"Be grateful," Leone said. "If it weren't for the money they send back, you'd all be eating each other." It was his usual line. It also had the advantage of being true.

"With respect, Don Leone, what about the women? Who will marry our daughters?"

These lawyers, Leone thought, always grumbling. "We'll have a fine crop of nuns, and why not? A bride of Christ is a bride, is she not? My own daughter wants nothing better."

"We are impoverished. In twenty years San Lorenzo will be a ghost town."

"Many return, Signor Amabile. Evidently those streets aren't all paved with gold."

"You, Don Leone, you are in a position to help the town— an excellent position."

"Me? I'm a humble landowner. Talk to the Prince."

"Put these men to work, Don Leone. Keep them in San Lorenzo."

"The problems of the town do not concern me. I'm a businessman, Signor Amabile, merely a businessman. I repeat, ask for an audience with the Prince. He also sits in the Parliament, in Rome. He can solve this problem, not I."

"Ah, you are angry. Forgive me, Don Leone. But when the rich close their ears, the poor talk revolution."

"Revolution!" Leone banged down his glass. "And you call

yourself a lawyer. Aren't you sworn to uphold the King's justice? Aren't you?"

"Men with empty bellies have a way of making their own justice . . . with respect."

"I'll buy every one of them a ticket to America!" Leone stood up, trying to look impressive. "That scum dishonors the fatherland. I'll buy them all tickets! Anarchists and malcontents— let them find paradise in America, if America wants them!" Leone strode away from the café table, pleased with himself, believing every word.

Father Ugo, the town priest, lived not in the little whitewashed house behind the village church but, more grandly, in a small palace abandoned by the Prince's younger brother when that bankrupt fled to parts unknown. A Franciscan nun with a mustache formidable enough to silence all gossip let Leone in. He waited in what had been the nobleman's drawing room, the walls and ceilings frescoed with mythological couplings, Atalanta and Meleager on the verge of indecency, Zeus and Danae represented more chastely by a barely clothed nymph standing beneath a shower of gold. The priest's true deity, thought Leone sourly.

He began to pace, and pacing he caught sight of himself in a dusty mirror. That could not be him, could it, that fretful, haggard face, those querulous lips and those watery eyes? Could he have become an old man overnight? Hearing the priest's quick step behind him, Leone turned.

"Tell your housekeeper to keep that mirror dusted," he said, forcing a smile.

"Is the mirror to blame for what it reflects? We grow old, my friend, it cannot be helped."

"I hope you don't plan to give me a sermon."

"Not a sermon, no." Father Ugo grinned, revealing uneven, discolored teeth. "Sit, sit, I pray you." He spoke in the unfamiliar Italian of the Northerners.

Leone sat. The priest made himself elaborately comfortable, tucking his vestments beneath his legs. When the Franciscan nun appeared, twitching her mustache, Leone refused coffee, a liqueur, lunch, choking his impatience with the dawdling priest.

"You sent for me, Father?" he prompted.

"I have offered you my credit and my friendship," the priest began hesitantly. "And it is my friendship which compels me to speak to you today. Have you considered your finances? Have you given thought to the dangerous position you are in? Leone, you have been robbing Peter to pay Paul. In a word, you are overextended. You endanger yourself and, though I would prefer not to say it, you endanger me with your reckless speculations. You act like a rash youth though you are at an age when you must act wisely and prudently."

Leone was struggling to control his temper, if only because this miserable parasite could still ruin him. He told himself to keep calm now no matter what else Father Ugo said, since these clerics loved nothing more than getting a man into their power and then strangling him at a cobra's pace.

"Perhaps you are right, Father. Perhaps I have been foolhardy, only God can say. But remember that you have never lost a single lira because of what you call my recklessness. No, *you* have profited, as one look around you will reveal. Because I chose you and not the Prince as my banker, you live like a nobleman yourself!"

"It is true that I live well," Father Ugo replied, "but I am in no danger. I have the Church to protect me. Who will protect you if those animals whose fields you own stop paying rent? Or if the miserable peasants in the town do the same? Or if, God forbid, you should quarrel with the Prince or, more likely, those stocks and bonds you love to juggle should begin to fall? Who will protect you, Leone?"

"The same God who protects all Christians," shot back Leone, rising to his feet.

"God rules the next world, my friend. Men like the Prince—and me—have power here and now. One blunder, and you will learn that unlike God I act out of interest, not mercy."

"Are you threatening me?" Leone thundered.

"I am warning you not to drag me down with you."

"Go tell the Pope how to run his business, you blood-sucking priest! I'll make you sorry you ever left the seminary!"

Father Ugo rose to his feet. "The Prince is determined to buy your mortgages. For years I've refused, but now I would rather let him assume the risk. Whatever happens, Leone, remember that I warned you. When it comes to money none of us are Christians. But even a bad priest has more scruples than a bad Prince." He stopped, as though waiting for Leone to repent. Then he grimaced and, shrugging, turned away. "Very well, then, destroy yourself."

Leone stared at the priest in mute rage. His brain was calculating quickly, and he needed to act. With a snort of contempt he flung open the door and marched out into the dusty street. The priest's arrogant words and his supercilious drawl echoed mockingly in his ear.

At that same hour of the day, Leone Monti's two sons, Vittorio and Francesco, were tiring of playing soldiers on the beach. Vittorio, the older, as always gave the commands, and his fierce insistence that the Italian Army must avenge the shame of its defeat at Adowa wearied his amiable younger brother Francesco. He doubted that anyone cared much nowadays about Adowa. A new battlefield of iron and steel was taking shape, one he found infinitely more engaging than stealing worthless colonies from African brutes, as Italy had failed to do at Adowa. Everyone except his older brother knew that the days when war meant glory were dead, as dead as chivalry, and would soon seem equally absurd.

He kept such thoughts to himself, though, and the two brothers climbed the rickety steps from the beach to the town arm in arm, looking cheerful enough. Vittorio, as the elder, made the sharper impression. He was just old enough to turn a few young girls' heads, and delighted in the fact. In those days everyone talked of animal magnetism, which even his detractors admitted Vittorio had. Tall for his age, he walked with conscious grace, posing for some as yet uncarved monument. He had his father's blazing eyes and his mother's poised dignity, so that even playing on the sand he suggested a pregnant destiny.

Francesco, the younger, had no wish to impress and could not have if he tried. His expression alternated between playful and meditative, only nobody would have taken his meditative look as a hint of future glory. The only clue to the man he might become was a sudden sternness which burst over his face like summer lightning, and disappeared with equal speed. At those times Francesco looked as much the man of destiny as his older brother, if not more. Indeed, he had more than once frightened his own mother with the determination of his gaze. More often he followed his brother or his playmates down the dead-end streets of boyhood, and looked happy to follow them.

Other boys discovered Francesco was not as passive as he looked. Once, when Vittorio lay on the ground, felled by a well-aimed slingshot, Francesco fought off the gang of young ruffians who panted to finish the job. Bleeding, he carried his elder brother home on his shoulder. From that day on the town knew that while Vittorio talked a good fight, Francesco knew how to win. Vittorio accepted the tribute of his brother's loyalty and, ever after, expected him to serve as defender, no matter how uneven the battle. And it was Francesco's bittersweet pleasure to obey.

"I will be the King's favorite general," Vittorio declaimed, "He'll entrust me with the honor of the Army. You," he added generously, "can be my aide-de-camp."

"Mamma wants you to be a doctor," Francesco said slyly. "She says doctors live longer than generals."

"Women are cowards! If Columbus had listened to his mother he'd never have left Spain."

"But think of the rich women who will want to marry you. Women with dowries . . ."

"And what do you, age eleven, know about women *or* their dowries? Glory, little brother, glory is what counts in this life— and there's no glory in staring at sore throats."

"What do you know, age fifteen, about glory? You think war is fighting with peasant cowards who run the minute we fight back. Better to win glory the way Papa does, owning land and investing in the North. Don't you think Papa has glory when his shares go up, and isn't that better than slaughtering savages?"

"You should be a lawyer, little brother," Vittorio laughed, "Your love for argument grows keener every day."

"Well then, be a general, and I will own the companies that make your guns, and see which one of us gets your stupid glory."

By now they were both laughing. At their ages the future, any future, seemed so unimaginable that talking about it felt ridiculous. All their lives they had strolled the streets of San Lorenzo where nothing in the least ever happened, or ever would. Without quite saying so both brothers knew they would someday leave, as their sister Leonora already had, though she was destined only for a convent hospital. There was nothing in San Lorenzo for them, no glory, and certainly no fortune. Their father, they believed, would have fled himself, had he not fallen into the ancient trap of marriage. They never dared whisper that to one another, not even when Leone railed at his entombment in their dim provincial town.

Vittorio knew he would never make that mistake. Whether on a white horse or in a white coat, for in truth he hardly objected to a rich doctor's life, he would escape San Lorenzo at the first opportunity. Francesco thought less about such matters. When he imagined them at all, he pictured himself behind a vast marble-topped desk, listening with a smile to the entreaties of smaller investors who begged him not to ruin them. My friends, he would say grandly, set your minds at ease, I am stalking far bigger game than you . . .

At that moment Leone was paying a call on some peasants who worked in the fields next to the railroad, tardy tenants named Brunetti whose promises seemed to stretch, like the tracks, out to infinity. Thanks to the priest, Leone knew he needed cash now to shore up his position, especially if that bastard made good his threat and sold the Prince his mortgages. Even a little surplus would hold those bloodsuckers at bay. But when he knocked on the Brunetti's shack, he heard only the sound of metal scraping wood. Pushing his way inside, Leone saw the Brunettis, father and two sons, banging a trunk shut. Every cupboard, every shelf stood as bare as though robbers had just attacked.

"I've come for my back rent," Leone began, hiding his astonishment.

"He's come for his back rent," Brunetti grinned at his two sons, who stood smiling like ruffians.

"Eh, Signor Leone, maybe you should work your fields yourself and make them show a profit."

"What?" Leone felt staggered enough to sink against the filthy wall.

"You can't fill empty mouths with last year's bread, now can you, Signor Leone? Even you know that much. So go work your fields, dry and barren as they are, and God help you. As for us, we're going to America."

"America! You'll starve in the street, all of you!"

"Starve here, starve there—what difference does it make? At least we have a hope in America. Here—" Brunetti spat eloquently. "Here we can't afford hope, let alone rent."

"And what am I supposed to do? I trusted you, like an idiot!"

"Keep piling up those big gold coins you're so fond of, Signor Leone. Someday you'll know what the rest of us know—you'll never pile up as many as the Prince, even if you live a hundred years. You think the Prince would give me six months' grace on my back rent? Only a fool like you, Signor Leone. Only a greedy fool."

"I'll stop you. I'll keep you here, so help me God I will!"

Brunetti grinned again. "Go ahead and try. By the time you get the carabinieri, we'll be halfway to Naples on the train."

Leone desperately tried to reason the matter through. Train fare cost money, which meant Brunetti had at least some cash on hand. Honor would be satisfied by a token payment, however small. He told Brunetti as much.

"Your honor comes cheap," Brunetti remarked. "I'll give you ten lira, no more."

"Twenty."

"You're in no position to bargain. Not now."

"Twenty lira. Last month's rent."

Brunetti stuck a hand in his pocket, then froze. "Why should I give it to you?"

"God only blesses honest men. Even in America."

"And if I don't give a damn about honesty, or God?"

"The carabinieri will meet your train in Naples." Leone allowed himself to smile. "You would take the shortest trip to America in history."

Brunetti's face relaxed somewhat when he handed Leone the cash. "A bargain is a bargain, Signor Leone. My boys deserve a chance in life . . ."

Leone left them tying the trunk with battered rope. He walked directly to the carabinieri post, where he spent five lira assuring himself swift justice. Brunetti and his boys would take the far shorter journey to the jail, while the officers who arrested them enjoyed a drink or a wench. Certainly it would never do to let one tenant defy him. That would lead only to ruin or, in the lawyer Amabile's phrase, revolution, assuming the two were not identical.

TWO

"**You** were a fool, Brunetti," the Prince said complacently. "Only a fool tries to steal from a thief."

"Bless me, your Excellence. Help my family in our time of need."

"Should I help a peasant who forgets to show respect?"

Brunetti seized the Prince's plump white hand and kissed it fervently. "We depend on your mercy, Excellence. My boys and I don't even eat bread, only beans and potatoes, and most of the year we barely eat at all. Show mercy, excellence. Let us work your land."

"You should be whipped for fleeing to America," the Prince said, as if he hadn't heard Brunetti's plea. "I have warned for years, in and out of the Chamber, against this insane emigration. Five million in thirty years, the ruin of Italy! Even that bastard Garibaldi agreed with me. Here in Calabria you would think the plague had killed our men. Nobody wants to work. No obedience, no order, no respect. Is it any wonder the Northerners take our taxes and spit on us?"

"My boys and I want to work," Brunetti repeated. "We will work for you, Excellence—on whatever terms you please."

The Prince blinked like a man startled out of reverie. "Wait outside, Brunetti. And remember, I can easily let all of you starve. If I do not I expect gratitude. Gratitude and respect, damnit!"

Brunetti seized the Prince's hand and kissed it with so much "respect" that the nobleman, for all his grumbling, felt gratified by the peasant's deference. He withdrew his hand and gestured curtly for Brunetti to disappear.

It was almost six, and the aroma of the Prince's dinner wafted into his study from the kitchen below. He thought sadly that food was one of the few pleasures left to him. His bed was cold, not counting the rare mornings he tumbled a chambermaid. And God knew his wealth, his lands, gave him no joy. They paid for the English boarding school where his sons were learning to be gentlemen, they kept the Prince's drafty palace alive with servants and, of course, they supported his title with the only nobility anyone nowadays recognized, the aristocracy of gold. Yet none of that contented him.

Though the Prince would never admit it, he knew that Italy, the Italy his father had helped forge, scarcely needed him at all. And would need his sons still less, even assuming no revolution swept away their titles and their lands. He saw the back-of-the-hand smiles when he addressed the Chamber of Deputies; he knew he was tolerated only for the cash he contributed at election time. Where was the grandeur in irrelevance? The Northerners sneered at him more or less openly, for no factories, no railroads stood on his land, while the Southerners seemed uneasy mouthing his ancient title. The Prince knew that he should have been born in another age, when he could have helped beat back Napoleon or join a crusade. His title would have meant something, then. The peasants would have feared him and the lesser nobles would have clamored to serve his house. His destiny would have soared above the grievances of bankrupt peasants and the greed of arrogant priests, like his dinner guest Father Ugo.

The Prince mistrusted him as an altogether too modern man. Bad enough for a gentleman to juggle numbers, but a servant of Christ? Still, he'd cultivated the black-robed thief so carefully that he knew Leone Monti's debts better than Monti did. When the priest sent word that he was ready to sell Monti's mortgages, the Prince tasted the heady wine of victory; now he would crush that upstart bastard at last. But he knew the priest would want his share of the spoils. The Prince was calculating, as he waited for Father Ugo, just how much he could afford to spend ruining Monti. In this ghastly age, the Prince lamented to himself, we noblemen must share our gold with priests once content to bless it. How different it must have been when honor and not greed ruled Italy!

Involuntarily the Prince glanced at the portraits of his father and grandfather. They hung opposite his desk, silently condemning the business he transacted there. He thought with a twinge of shame how his father remained proudly ignorant of the gold their estates earned, allowing his bailiff to collect it and spend it as he thought fit. The Prince's grandfather refused even to hear such matters discussed, not even when the 1848 uprisings nearly ruined the family. No wonder, the Prince thought, no wonder I feel so unfitted for an age like this. I have a taste for grandeur and a love for gold. And it is impossible, he thought bitterly, to satisfy them both.

An hour later the Prince and Father Ugo sat sipping the tart local wine in the pause between courses. Elaborately baked ziti followed by a school of tiny fish aswim in butter and wine left the two men breathless with polite gluttony.

"Monti was reckless enough to overextend himself," the priest said cheerfully. His features wore the rapt look that talking money to a rich man bestows on those less fortunate. The Prince knew perfectly well that Monti had done nothing to deserve the priest's reproach, but understood this would be the rationale Father Ugo needed for committing what they both knew was the mortal sin of usury.

The butler carried in a saddle of lamb and displayed it with a flourish to both men. The Prince inhaled its gamy perfume with a sigh of bliss, then began carving carefully.

"Monti's land is heavily mortgaged," the priest continued. "And, I might add, at the highest rate of interest the law allows. The deluded fool tried to speculate in stock while piling up property, an ambition quite beyond his means, of course . . . . ah, just a morsel of lamb, your Excellence. Here in town he has perhaps a dozen houses, and they bring in a little every month. Not to mention the two his mistress demanded for her favors, but naturally their income goes to her . . . ."

The Prince, who knew all this better than Father Ugo did, chewed with an expression suggesting that each fact came as startling news. At last he laid down his fork.

"And so, Father, what price would you put on the mortgages—all of them, I mean?'

Father Monti blushed. "I know you admire the English, your Excellence. But must you imitate their bluntness of speech as well?"

The Prince made a show of controlling his impatience. "I await your price, Father.'

"Ah, it is so hard to calculate . . . . perhaps we should discuss these matters another time."

His host gave a mirthless laugh. "You sent word you wanted to sell Monti's mortgages. And as you know, nobody else in San Lorenzo can afford to buy them. Now, Father, state your price."

"You are worse than English. You are American!"

The Prince grimaced. "I am thinking of a number with six digits. The first digit is two."

"Three," Father Ugo said with the same firmness he preached patience to the poor.

"Two-fifty. And remember, if I don't buy, nobody will."

"Two seventy-five . . . . your Excellence."

"Two-fifty. And not a lira more." The Prince resumed carving the lamb.

Father Ugo, like a fish gasping for air, opened and closed his mouth desperately. Meanwhile the Prince chewed majestically, never taking his eyes from the priest's stricken face.

"Two hundred and sixty thousand lira," Father Ugo at last managed to say.

"On one condition." The Prince pointed his fork for emphasis. "A certain Brunetti, a peasant . . . Monti has thrown him off his land. I want Brunetti and his sons to work for you."

"For me?" Father Ugo stammered in bewilderment. "What can they do for a poor parish priest like me?"

"Not so poor as you *should* be." The Prince laughed brutally. "Put them to work counting your money, for a start."

Father Ugo sat stiffly, as though in shock. Clammy sweat trickled down his back and arms. He had tried to outwit the Prince and he had failed, fool that he was. And now the Prince was paying back his insolence with these Brunettis, who would surely steal every lira of his profits, given sufficient time. The Prince was gazing at him with that nobleman's haughtiness that seemed at least half cold contempt. "As your Excellence wishes," said Father Ugo in a strangled voice.

Leone Monti might command his peasants and tenants, he might sway the value of a stock with a cunning ploy, but unlike the Prince he did not rule in his own house. His wife Lucinda, in the time-honored Italian style, granted her husband the illusion of power while keeping firm hold on its reality. Leone blustered; Lucinda smiled tolerantly and did as she thought best. She hired the help, did the household accounts, dealt with tradesmen, decided how much charity Father Ugo's church deserved. If Leone found fault with anything, Lucinda knew how to wait until his temper cooled, after which she continued to act precisely as she had before. Some in the town ascribed her slyness to Leone's flagrant infidelities, though in truth Lucinda was practicing it long before he ever strayed from her bed. A true daughter of Italy, she understood that since the family ruled its members more surely than any King or Pope, a wife faced the bitter choice of dominion or servitude. And even the meek virgin who'd married Leone Monti had no taste for servitude.

Tonight, as every night, she supervised the cook and the scullery maid who served the meal. Leone sat grandly in a chair once used by Murat, quizzing his two sons on their schoolwork. He affected not to notice Carmela, the maid, spooning out the ravioli in the chicken broth that Lucinda considered healthier than rich sauce. Vittorio gave Carmela an appraising stare, making her giggle idiotically and drop the ladle into the soup tureen.

"Clumsy peasant," Leone growled. "Why did you ever hire the cow?"

Lucinda smiled. Yes, there was something slow and bovine about the girl. She'd hired her so that not even the most malicious tongue could couple the girl with Leone. But it seemed she attracted Vittorio instead. Though such seductions were customary, if not encouraged, in well-bred homes, Lucinda would not permit one in hers. She would warn Carmela to flee her son, handsome as he was, handsome as the Devil himself. Let him visit the town brothel instead, Lucinda thought. That will bring the Monti family no scandal, no peasant girl pregnant with his bastard child. She said a quick prayer to the Virgin for such thoughts, then sprinkled grated cheese on the steaming broth.

"And now, Vittorio, your Dante." Leone motioned for silence. "Begin, my boy."

"'When we stood at the upper side of the high riverbank, on the open hill, I said, Master, which way—" Vittorio hesitated, "which way must we go? And he answered, do not fall behind a single step, but keep climbing the mountain behind me until some guide appears.'"

"You are misquoting Dante," Leone snapped. "Is there a greater sin for an Italian who aspires to serve the King? My boy, you should be a doctor, not a general. Stick to broken bones if you want to serve your countrymen."

Though Vittorio's lips were trembling with rage, he kept himself from answering by driving his nails into his palm. Francesco, fearing a scene, began rattling off Roman history to distract their father from saying any more.

"The slave Spartacus rebelled in the year of our Lord 73, leading a skillful army of gladiators and slaves southward from Capua. For over a year they plundered the great estates and fought their way across this very province. Spartacus tried to escape by sea but failed, and after a terrible battle died in Apulia. Six thousand of his brave followers survived. All were mercilessly crucified and their corpses lined the Appian Way . . . ."

"Socialist propaganda!" Leone roared. "What damned Red teaches one of you to butcher Dante and the other to praise a slave revolt?"

"You know very well," his wife put it mildly, "that no Socialist can teach in the Royal Academy."

"Then they're damn sneaky subversives, even worse! Ah, you'll kill me, all of you—you, wife, serving me this slop fit only for Frenchmen and Socialists! Tomorrow night I dine like a man of wealth and position, do you hear? If I wanted to eat like a poor man I would have lived on your pitiful dowry, and not multiplied it a thousandfold!"

"Yes, dear," Lucinda smiled sweetly. Francesco started shooting bread balls at their half-blind dog, a petty cruelty that went unnoticed while Leone denounced the cook, his stockbrokers, Father Ugo, and the Brunetti family, concluding:

"And I will tolerate no Socialists or subversives in this house! Honor your father and honor your King! Ignore troublemakers like that lawyer Amabile with his subversive talk. You, Vittorio, will learn medicine—yes, that is your father's decree. An honorable and ancient art, your grandfather's profession and yours too unless you wish to be disinherited! Francesco is fit only for street brawls, curse the day I sired him. But swear, my sons, swear you'll never be Socialists so long as you bear the Monti name. Swear you'll always be loyal to what you have learned in my house."

Leone's family was too used to his sudden gusts of rage to wonder what provoked this one. In fact the Brunettis' attempted flight, coupled with the lawyer's remarks about a revolution by the poor, had brought his fears to a new pitch of intensity. While Leone knew nothing of Socialist ideas, he dreaded the poor as only a parvenu can, painfully aware he could count on neither the deference owed the Prince nor the grudging respect even a bad priest like Father Ugo could command. Leone had no sure position in San Lorenzo and never would, no matter how much gold he managed to pile up. To the nobility he was an upstart, to the poor a hated predator. Suspended between them, Leone felt the potential prey of both. Abruptly he rose, calling for his derby and his walking stick.

"I must collect some rents," Leone told his wife, whose lips were curling into a mocking smile. "Don't let the boys play cards instead of studying."

"Give my regards," Lucinda drawled, "to the widow Lucenti. Tell her how glad I am that she's finally paying rent."

Husband and wife avoided each other's eyes at such moments, making it easier for Leone to leave his house with a semblance of dignity. No sooner had he departed than Lucinda sent her sons, still gobbling cake during their parents' dialogue, to separate rooms so they could study undisturbed. Then, at last, she permitted herself a harsh, solitary laugh.

After dinner the brothers, postponing their schoolwork as long as possible, shared one of their father's cigars on Vittorio's balcony. In that part of Calabria the early autumn dusk resembles summer turned pleasingly cool, with a fragrance of fallow soil and fading leaves carried by the breeze. The cigar was making Francesco lightheaded, a fact that did not escape Vittorio, who laughed at his ineptitude.

"You'll never make an officer at that rate. The King would take one look at you and reduce you to the ranks!"

"I'd be happier reading about your bravery in the papers," replied Francesco. "One soldier in the family is enough."

"If only the Prince were our father," Vittorio sighed. "I'd be a general and you . . . . what would you be, coward that you are?"

"If the Prince were our father we'd be at school in England, like his sons."

"And the English girls are ugly, flat-chested things. You're right, we're better off than they are, though God knows I have no taste for medicine . . . ."

"Don't worry. When I explore the South Pole you can be the expedition doctor."

"A fine explorer you'd be when you can't even smoke! Anyway, by the time you're old enough the whole world will be mapped as thoroughly as San Lorenzo."

"Since you know everything," Francesco mocked, "do you know where Father went?"

"To collect rent from the peasants," Vittorio said indifferently.

"I know something you don't know," Francesco sang out cunningly.

"Of course I know, you idiot. Only we can't talk about it in case the servants overhear. We have to set an example, after all."

Vittorio tossed the cigar stub down into the chamber pot, reminding Francesco painfully which of them would soon be an adult. He walked to his desk, planted himself firmly in his leather chair, and opened a school edition of the Purgatorio. Stung by the sudden dismissal, Francesco returned to his own room, cursing himself for inhaling that cigar. He took up his mathematics book with a groan. He hated being so young that Vittorio could casually shatter his every dream. If only their sister had been there to puncture his brother's knowing pose as she always did. What a weakling I must be, he thought ruefully . . . .

Francesco, dozing over his hated algebra, suddenly heard an unexpected sound. Someone was tiptoeing down the staircase from the servants' attic, step by muffled step nearing the floor where he and his brother slept. He listened. The slippered footsteps stopped . . . . he heard Vittorio's murmur, then an explosion of giggles which ended as quickly as they began. Francesco listened in shock as the ancient hinge of Vittorio's door slowly, carefully creaked shut.

He thought he could guess who was inside but he had to know, he burned with the ache to know. He raced upstairs to a room his mother used for storing clothes and planted his eye next to a crack in the floor above his brother's room. Francesco felt an excitement that made his pulse race sickeningly, as though he expected to witness some crime. Yes, it was the scullery maid Carmela, wearing only a flimsy blouse and skirt. Vittorio's hand was busily climbing her leg.

"Stop Master, what if Signora Lucinda comes in?"

"You know she won't . . . . now don't resist, open your thighs . . . ."

"What are you doing with that hand? For shame!"

"You can go anytime . . . . do you want to go?"

Francesco felt amazement but no real surprise. He wondered

where Vittorio had learned to act this way, and wanted to find a willing girl so he could do the same. Vittorio had far outstripped him, conquering this world he knew only through schoolboy chatter and baffling jokes. Now he was removing Carmela's skirt.

"No Master, not that. I'm a good girl, I am."

"And I'm to be a doctor, so I need to learn anatomy."

The girl began to struggle, fiercely but silently, while Vittorio tried to wrench her undergarments off. At last he snatched a few coins from his bureau top and displayed them impatiently.

"Here. A gentleman pays for his pleasures."

Carmela gave a weak shake of the head.

"Take them. More than my mother gives you in a week."

Vittorio seized her waist and kissed her with a violence even Francesco seemed to feel.

Carmela tried to wrench free from his embrace, at last defeated by her unequal strength. She began to weep silently as Vittorio bent her over the leather chair face down. Standing behind her, he forced his fingers into her while unbuttoning his trousers at lightning speed. He thrust himself into the girl with such force that she let out a shriek, prompting Vittorio to cover her mouth with his hand. It seemed hours before he finished and, buttoning up his flies, turned his back on the now sobbing girl.

"Master—"

"No more money, whore. You haven't earned it."

"I was a virgin, Master. Look and see. I never thought of this . . . ."

"Be grateful a gentleman had you first, not some peasant with dirty hands."

"A virgin," Carmela repeated, quickly dressing herself. "But who will ever marry me now?"

"Marry a Socialist," Vittorio grinned. "They preach free love. Marry any fool who wants you, only get out, you whore. Or I'll tell my mother to let you go."

Carmela stared at him, her eyes growing colder as he spoke.

"May your family suffer and bleed as I did," she spat out, throwing Vittorio's coins at his feet. "Take your stinking money, you'll need it when your father goes to jail for bankruptcy. And remember who cursed the Monti family."

Francesco watched her dart out of the room and shuddered, believing, as anyone in San Lorenzo would, in the power of Carmela's curse. Unable to breathe, he went to the window for air. The stars shone with a cold brilliance that mocked everything below. God lived up there, didn't he, somewhere? Crossing himself, Francesco made a vow to act with strict justice, no matter how much he craved anything. He came no closer to condemning Vittorio, not even in the silence of his brain.

The moon disappeared behind fleecy clouds. Somewhere nearby the Prince's English mastiff, Milord, began to howl. The beast sounded just as satanic as the children and peasants liked to claim. A mocking male voice begged the Prince to get a louder dog, and then San Lorenzo returned to its deep provincial sleep.

THREE

In the fields above the town, the peasants were celebrating the rites of spring. On a hill they burned a straw man with a grotesquely painted face representing Winter. As the figure burned, a young girl, ample of breast and hip, writhed naked and masked, mating with the stony, uncertain earth to ensure its fertility. The girl moved to the tune of ancient melodies twanged on a mandolin, amidst bawdy shouts in the thick peasant dialect. Then—and to San Lorenzo this seemed most scandalous of all— unmarried lovers renewed the earth in different combinations until dawn.

"Filthy pagans," Father Ugo said spitefully, "I will excommunicate them all, Signora Monti, wait and see. My servant Brunetti is there taking down names even now."

"My husband says they're another race, the peasants, closer to the earth but farther from God."

"Nonsense, nonsense. We are all children of God." Father Ugo gave his guest a searching look. "But Signora, you didn't come here to discuss such matters. Something is troubling you— speak, speak, I pray you."

"You know, Father, how little some husbands confide in their poor wives. Perhaps I am to blame, but these past months Leone tells me nothing at all, though I gather his affairs are going worse and worse . . . ."

"They are," the priest said ambiguously, reluctant to say more.

"Even you know?" Lucinda pressed a handkerchief to her mouth. She lifted her moist eyes and said tonelessly, "The Prince has seized half his farm mortgages and most of his town properties. For six months he's been slowly strangling my husband, so slowly that poor Leone deludes himself he can still buy stock without danger.

"Speak to him," Father Ugo advised. "He will listen to you."

"Not to me." Lucinda smiled bitterly. "To *you*, Father. Tell him to think of our boys, at least. Otherwise, he will be ruined."

"Perhaps you should request an audience with our Prince," the priest said comfortingly. "He is a true aristocrat, noble in heart and blood alike."

"Do you know how to cook frogs?" Lucinda asked with new intensity. "You raise the heat under the frog pot so gradually that they never feel enough pain to jump for their lives. That is how the Prince is killing Leone, now."

"Speak with more respect of our Prince," Father Ugo cried, "remember you are a lady, not some peasant slut . . . ."

"I remember you used to hold these mortgages," Lucinda drawled. "How much did you get for them from the Prince?"

"Remember who I am, Signora Monti. Think to your immortal soul. Defy Jesus' soldier and you defy Jesus himself."

"Forgive me, Father," Lucinda knelt quickly, bowing her head. "I spoke like a fool."

"Yes, yes, you did. Now rise to your feet—"

"I will not rise unless you bless me." Her voice was low yet firm as stone.

Father Ugo blessed her with the pectoral cross, murmuring a Paternoster over her lavender-scented hair. How he hated this business of forgiveness. At times the priest suspected God laughed at this charade, for did any of it matter to sinner or priest an hour later?

"You will intercede for us with the Prince," Lucinda said hopefully.

"I promise nothing, Signora. I will do what I think best."

She stood frozen in the doorway, alternately pleading and

accusing with her reddened eyes. Lucinda felt the recklessness of defeat and would have threatened this hypocrite with exposure of his own avarice, had she thought that would force him to do what Jesus would willingly have done, or for that matter any decent parish priest. The lewd pink frescoes of Father Ugo's house seemed to mock her, fat nymphs and grinning satyrs pursuing them through the blue of an antique sky.

"You must help, Father. One more foreclosure and we will starve, because only worthless properties remain in my husband's hands."

Father Ugo grimaced as he escorted Lucinda into the hall. He felt no remorse, only a vague wonder that the Prince was taking so long to bring Monti down.

"You know the Prince adores everything English," he said with an ironic smile. "Well, his favorite expression is, naturally, English too: *Business is business.* You understand? Worship God but tend to your business, he says. Perhaps you can help your husband do so, Signora. I pray God you can. As for the Prince, I will do what I think best."

Which will be nothing, thought Lucinda with a dull pang. The priest felt loyalty only to himself and to his Church, not to another soul; how then could he know the anxiety that wrung her heart? She feared for Leone and her boys truly more than for herself. She would make any sacrifice to spare them misery, to spare them poverty. What else should a mother do for her flesh and blood? Family was the first reality and the last refuge. Your husband might betray you but you were his eternal bride in the eyes of God. Your sons were your flesh, your hand outstretched into eternity, and you would steal for them, kill for them if need be. These were truths even the peasants, poor animals, understood, the rock stratum under the shifting sands upon which you lived. Lucinda hugged herself and crossed the town square with swifter steps, glancing occasionally at the darkening sky and murmuring fragments of prayer.

The lawyer Amabile rose from his café table to greet her, ending her reverie. She had the awful suspicion that Amabile knew, that everyone knew. Were the villagers looking at her with contempt, or, worse, pity instead? Lucinda stopped at the apothecary's for a dose of salts to clear her head. Through its glass doors she could see San Lorenzo's red and yellow stucco becoming blue-black, the color of the local wine. What would she do, what would Leone do, she wondered, pleading again with Christ to spare her family. Easter week was drawing near, always more sacred to her than Christmas, for Easter meant rebirth and resurrection, and never had Lucinda craved them more. All that remained of her girlhood was her devotion to the Virgin and a deep faith in Our Lady's power to intercede. Lucinda took the salts, laid a coin on the zinc counter and, summoning up all her fortitude, strode into the square.

The few shops which had gaslight were turning on their lamps. Oil wicks illuminated the rest, giving shopkeepers' faces a melancholy glow. Lucinda prayed the Hail Mary with a desperation she would never show another soul. As she walked her lips moved and, with an involuntary tic, she clasped her hands together and unclasped them, incessantly. Men tipped their hats and bowed, but she saw none of them. Only the women who passed her in the almost lightless street recognized Signora Monti's look as fear.

"I have locked your miserable Vittorio in his room," Leone announced before Lucinda had even removed her hat. "He dressed up like a peasant, if you please, and even smeared his boots with horse manure. I caught him sneaking out to that filthy festival and had to drag him upstairs by force."

"I hope you didn't hurt him," Lucinda said mechanically. She was searching for a way to bring up the subject of their finances. Her husband grunted ambiguously. "Did you read our daughter's letter?"

"Yes, yes, the Mother Superior rebuked her. What of it?"

"She rebuked her because you donated half of what you gave last year."

"Are *you* rebuking *me*?" Leone's voice rose dangerously.

"If you would stop paying the widow Lucenti—"

"Silence!" Leone shouted. "You have no right—"

"I am your wife," Lucinda erupted. "If you destroy yourself you destroy me too. Who will lock you in your room to prevent another folly?"

She spoke quickly so Leone could not cut her off. Astonishingly, her words provoked no wrath, so she went on:

"I beg you, darling, be sensible now, you must, you . . . . stop supporting that woman and stop investing in stock. I beg you, think of us. The Prince will ruin you and that will ruin your sons, your innocent boys."

Leone sank into an antique chair, his body sagging, his eyes averted from his wife's. She moved quickly to his side, caressing his hair consolingly. At length he looked up and gave her a weak smile.

"I tried to borrow money today," Leone told her, "and of course I failed. Sometimes it seems I have offended the good Lord himself. My lands, all gone, most of my property . . . . what will I leave my sons? You tell me to forget the stock exchange but I need cash, I need to recoup my losses, and how else can I? As to the widow, I've already told her I can no longer maintain her. Yes, I promise you I have, I am to give her a lump sum so she won't starve in the street and then nothing, nothing—"

His head clapped onto his chest and a low moan escaped his throat. Lucinda felt relief and disgust mingled equally. She left her husband to oversee the evening meal.

Francesco had two surprises that night at table, his father's absence and his mother's granting him permission to forgo schoolwork and attend a debate at the Positivist Society. Vittorio chose to dine in his room, still sulky over his earlier shame, all of which left Francesco wondering what distemper was plaguing everyone. He had no great desire to listen to grown men chatter, only his history teacher was to debate the lawyer Amabile, and Francesco admired his teacher above all other men in San Lorenzo. His name was Achille Lampa, he stood six feet tall, and he spoke the purest Italian the boy had ever heard. Manly and lucid, Lampa could hold his class in rapt attention by describing anything from the 1848 revolution to the Rothchilds' wealth. Francesco half-ran, half-jumped down the narrow cobbled streets.

"History is the will of God who knows my name," Amabile declaimed. "Progress, yes, there has been, there will be progress, but on whose terms—God's, or man's? If we lose faith, if we break the covenant our ancestors made, this new century will be the Devil's century, gentlemen—I promise it. History is the manifest working-out of a divine plan. The French revolution failed, and why, I ask you, why? Because it devoured the godly and the godless alike, because it lost its principles when it rejected Christ. Well, I tell you this new century is in even greater peril. The Jacobins killed a few thousand, but today we can kill that many in a week, a day, perhaps an hour. Only justice under God will prevent a second Reign of Terror, and only under God. Feed the hungry. Clothe the naked. Render unto Caesar—but only if you render unto God." He sat down to fulsome applause. Francesco held his breath until Lampa rose and began to speak.

"I am not about to question the existence of God," he said gently. "Nor will I say that God is not a Royalist or a Catholic—for all I know he is. Yet is it not a fact that the Japanese, that comical race, defeated the Christian Russians in a single sea battle? Was that not also God's will, Signor Amabile? And if it was, what hope will Italy have if war comes, since we have not the guns nor the men to fight the Austrians? I know, you will tell me war is impossible, and we all pray that it is. But history is not made by sleepwalkers, gentlemen. Garibaldi stunned the world by acting without the Pope's blessing, and here we are today, rid of the French, rid of the Spanish. History is made by the will of *men*—ordinary men like you and me. We are all making history, even sitting in this room tonight, oh yes—and we will make history whether we call ourselves Christians or not, just as the Japanese did, as Garibaldi did. For we are free. We invent ourselves in this new century and so we invent our history. Italy suffers because we trust too much in obedience and servitude. It is our curse. We suffer because the English, the French, the Germans take their fate into their hands, while we dawdle, year after year, in pious laziness. We have made a wasteland and call it faith. The peasants who flee to America know better. So should we."

After Lampa sat down again a stunned silence prevailed, during which each man looked at his neighbor to decide how to respond. Even Francesco, though he listened with some confusion, felt a twinge of fear at his teacher's boldness. Did he really believe that man should act as though God did not exist? Was Lampa what his father called a Socialist? The lawyer Amabile rose as the room started to buzz and hum.

"My poor deluded Lampa," he said pityingly. "You really must stop reading those Godless atheists of yours, Schopenhauer and Nietzsche—you see, I too am familiar with their so-called thought. Man in and of himself is worth nothing, a handful of dust, a thinking reed, and no philosopher can turn you or me into a colossus of solitary strength. Without God, nothing. With God, everything. When will you learn that truth does not change with the years? Your shallow nihilism will destroy you, as surely as demons drove that herd of swine Jesus wished to cure into the sea. I beseech you, return to the love of a just God. Have done with these madmen's fever dreams."

The audience applauded Amabile long and hard. Lampa rose to his feet and, shaking his head balefully at the crowd, stalked out, followed by Francesco. The teacher leapt onto his bicycle and pedaled away, his bell ringing shrilly in his wake.

Francesco strolled through the crooked streets, avoiding the amber pools of gaslight the still-open shops shed on the cobblestones. Thanks to Easter's approach San Lorenzo took on a gayer look. Brightly colored statues of local saints crowded shop windows, dispelling for a while the town's usual monotony. The devout hung elaborate vines in their windows, festooning them with grapes and berries rendered forever ripe by some mysterious trick. And even at this late hour music echoed through the town, local folksongs and opera duets or arias, played on zithers, untuned pianos, ancient violins. Puccini and Verdi themselves would have blushed at the result, but what difference did it make, the town was coming to life.

The boy turned a corner and came upon a figure sprawled in the dark, like a broken doll. Though he walked by quickly, wondering who dared offend San Lorenzo's proprieties, the creature groaned and made a noise. When Francesco turned in surprise he recognized Carmela. Nobody mentioned her in the Monti house after Vittorio, making good his threat, persuaded his mother to banish the peasant maid. And now here she was, stupefied in the street, smelling of dirt and cheap wine.

"Come closer," Carmela was saying, "don't you want to look at me, sweetheart?"

He could hear her sharp intake of breath when she recognized his face.

"The little Monti," she said after a pause. "You remember me, don't you?"

"Vittorio—" he began . . . .

She spat out a word no woman should know, let alone speak. "But you're different, you were always good to me . . . . wouldn't you like Carmela to be good to you? I'll make you feel like a real man—"

"No, no," Francesco stammered, as he often did under stress, "my parents are waiting up for me." The thought of touching her was sending an unpleasant shiver down his spine. Carmela caressed his thighs, making him jump back.

"Not like your big brother, eh?" she snickered. "At least he knows what he wants, bastard though he is. What're you made of, eh—holy water?"

"I'll give you money, Carmela, I'll give you everything I have—"

"How you Montis love your money," the girl laughed sardonically. "You think the rest of us should love it too. No, keep it, little boy, keep it. You aren't rich enough to throw your lira around. Not even your father is any more."

Carmela stood up, brushing herself off, and disappeared down an alley, leaving Francesco humiliated and ashamed. He was a coward, oh yes, the girl had that right, why else would he refuse her so timidly? He would never, he thought, trotting home, be half the man Vittorio was, not at this rate, not now, not when a tramp like her could make him feel cowardly . . . .

Before Francesco could see his house he heard some commotion there. As he approached he saw Vittorio wriggling in Brunetti's powerful grasp. Vittorio, dressed like a peasant, was fighting to free himself, while Brunetti mockingly slapped his scarlet face. Francesco began running towards the pair, when with a sudden kick Brunetti forced open the never-locked Monti door, dropping Vittorio deftly onto the floor.

"Peasants lie down with peasants, understand?" Brunetti said. "Be grateful I found you and not your father."

By now Francesco was almost behind Brunetti, who kicked Vittorio's leg for emphasis before departing with a laugh. Francesco went to help his older brother to his feet. Vittorio, panting, ignored his hand and rose with a muttered oath. Francesco burned to tell him about Carmela, though he knew Vittorio would not want to hear of her tonight.

"I had two different peasant girls up there," Vittorio bragged. He would have said more but for their father's step on the stairs. The boys watched in silence while their father, seemingly unaware of them, walked unsteadily upstairs and into his room.

"Let's go to bed," Francesco whispered. "It's very late."

"Two peasant girls," Vittorio whispered back boastfully. "One of them stank like a mule, but never mind. And then Brunetti came, I thought he would strangle me . . . ."

"Do you believe in God, Vittorio?" The brothers were leaning over Vittorio's balcony, half an hour later, dressed for bed. Vittorio laughed, and poked Francesco with his nails.

"Don't trouble your mind with such questions," he replied. "Pay no attention to that Lampa, he'll end up in prison one of these days."

"That's not an answer. Do you believe?"

"I believe some power besides our father and mother created me. Otherwise, I put my faith in myself—in what I can see and touch. And if God helps anyone, he helps those who help themselves."

Francesco did not answer at once. The vision of Carmela forced itself into his mind.

"I saw our old scullery maid tonight, Vittorio."

His brother frowned petulantly. "What devil is in you tonight? First catechism class, and now that whore?"

"She said something I didn't understand . . . . about our father needing money. What did she mean?"

"A drunken slut raves and you take it to heart," said Vittorio uneasily.

"She knows something, doesn't she? And you know too. Nobody will tell me except you," Francesco pleaded. "Please Vittorio, it's awful to be kept ignorant."

"Remember what I said about who God helps?" Vittorio replied at last. "I hope our father will help himself—and that's all I care to say. You're too young to understand business, anyway."

Anger suddenly filled Francesco's heart. "Carmela cursed our family because of you. If anything happens remember what you did to her!"

Vittorio was for once too stunned to speak. Francesco, not trusting his anger to subside, ran back to his own room.

FOUR

At that same moment Leonora Monti was traveling south to San Lorenzo for the Easter holiday, mortifying her flesh by sitting up in an uncomfortable third class car as though she felt as sure of her vocation as when she'd made the reverse journey months before. The train hissed and jolted through black fields, lurching down the peninsula as it stopped inexplicably to take on Bersaglieri, the King's crack troops, and peasants, who often carried squawking hens. Leonora could tell that she would reach San Lorenzo far behind schedule and regretted writing her parents requesting to be met. This modern world, she reflected, not for the first time, was turning out as badly as the medieval Italy it strove to replace.

Leonora fingered her rosary beads with a feeling of unease, even hypocrisy. Before leaving the convent in Rome she had informed the Mother Superior of her desire to delay her final vows. Neither woman said it, but Leonora knew she would never take them now. She was experiencing a crisis deeper than losing her inbred faith, one she couldn't explain to her Mother Superior or, indeed, to anyone at all. Leonora still believed in God but she no longer believed that He ruled this world, if He ever had. That was a fable for children. Another God, or even the Devil, she thought in her darkest hours, held sway over this world. A weak God, yes, who could direct life no better than the conductors of this train, unable as they were to keep it from stopping suddenly in the dark. If she said her rosary she did it to avoid the sin of despair, beside which the temptations of her doubt seemed venial indeed.

She would not become a bride of Christ, that much she knew with certainty. Perhaps you found out what you wanted by learning what you refused. Leonora thought rarely of men or romance, though she supposed that she would marry once she left the convent. Yet whenever she walked the streets of Rome she longed for some grander destiny, something higher than Church or marriage bed could provide. Those women strikers in Turin and Milan or those women embarking for America or North Africa, weren't they afire with passions she'd never known? Leonora had inherited the thirst for glory without knowing it. Other convent girls yearned to imitate Florence Nightingale, but she had no such idol. Leonora preferred to become her own ideal.

What little she saw of life emboldened her, not that she sought to live like a New Woman, smoking cigarettes, taking lovers, an existence quite as mindless as any nun's. No, Leonora wanted to create her own meaning, in that respect faithful to the social gospel her Mother Superior decried. Like her brother Vittorio she wished to strike a blow, if not draw blood. But returning to San Lorenzo always weakened her nerve and made Leonora feel her own feebleness. Between the convent and some arranged marriage, what choice was there? Her father, beloved, ruthless, would tolerate no third alternative, not that she had one to offer.

Leonora sighed, dropping her rosary beads. The curse had begun the day she was born, and if she didn't remove it, it would end only on the day she died. Her poor mother suffered enough for all Monti women, she thought with disdain. What tempted Leonora was the dream of choosing her life, not squeezing into a ready-made cage. Ah, she rebuked herself, you think like a fool, you dream like a silly girl. Only free people, free men, have that choice, and perhaps not even them, given the demonic chaos everyone called God's world.

She knew her train was approaching San Lorenzo when she smelled the lemon trees. By now the sun was climbing the sky, and the cerulean blue overhead lifted her sagging spirit unexpectedly. Along the railroad tracks stood lemon and grapefruit trees, the lemons carefully cultivated while the grapefruit rotted on the vine. Through the trees Leonora caught glimpses of plowed fields awaiting the sowing of that year's seed. The lemon trees gave way to taller, equally fragrant pines, bordering the fields like benign demigods who offered protection to their crops. The pine trees carried telegraph wire, almost invisible in the sun, and began to thin out only when the signs for San Lorenzo started appearing between them on wooden posts. With a great heave and shake, Leonora's train slowed to a stop, its whistle sounding three shrill notes before the conductors shouted, a little wearily, the name of her hometown.

After the porter deposited her bags on the platform, Leonora looked around with anxiety. Had she somehow mistaken her destination? Nobody awaited her, not even her family's familiar old gray horse pulling that pretentious carriage her father liked to claim once belonged to a bankrupt duke. Leonora inhaled the spring flowers blossoming between the rails, mystic roses and wild lilies, comforted a little by their perfume. All around bustled peasant women in headdresses, their men driving painted carts, speaking the dialect she scarcely understood. Leonora felt as always the strangeness of Calabria, of her San Lorenzo, foreign soil now after so many years in Rome.

At last she wearied of scanning these unreadable faces, seamed with dirt and hard work. Leonora opened a parasol against the pitiless sun and, a moment later, heard Francesco repeating her name. He was driving a peasant cart, looking taller and older than she recalled. When he hurried over to shoulder her bags she noticed that he smelled of manly sweat. They embraced briefly. Francesco seated her next to him above the horses and then, with a patient switch of his whip, they began the long drive home down the mountain.

"Papa sold the carriage," Francesco said without preamble. "Business isn't so good right now. I don't mind," he added bravely, "driving this cart one bit, even if Vittorio does—I feel like a real country boy at last."

"Papa used to love that carriage," Leonora said, startled at the news. "What happened to all his land?" She gestured vaguely at the wheat fields passing slowly on either side.

"Mamma will tell you," Francesco evaded her. "Now tell me about Rome, what did you see, where did you go—I've been waiting for weeks to hear about something besides this miserable town."

Leonora told him about the foreigners on the Spanish Steps, the Swiss Guard, the Pope's balcony. Francesco nodded, disappointed, as though he'd really wanted to feel impressed. Then his sister began describing the strikes in Northern Italy, and the part that women no older than herself were playing, the way they stared down Bersaglieri without fear. This interested her brother a little more. He interrupted:

"Those women make Papa mad . . . . he says they're keeping the newspapers from reaching San Lorenzo, though how they could, I don't understand. He calls them dirty Socialists," Francesco added, imitating their father's voice suddenly and explosively. Leonora laughed, then explained in a serious tone that yes, not only the women but the men wanted a general strike to seize all Italy, like the one the year before.

"You should talk to my professor Lampa," Francesco said. "Papa calls him a dirty Socialist too. But he's good to me," he added irrelevantly. "He gave me Thus Spake—Thus Spake Somebody to read, a German wrote it."

Leonora smiled. So the age of suspicion was taking hold even in San Lorenzo, this age of doubt and disobedience she herself was stumbling through. The cart passed heaps of manure taller than her, and women grinding flour at a communal drum, and men playing cards outside cafes with lazy ferocity. Truly, she thought, not even a revolution could shake San Lorenzo out of its idiotic sloth. Francesco waved his whip with casual disdain.

"Vittorio wants to fight in Africa, and I want to leave the way you did. Not to serve God, but—"

Luckily they were reaching the Monti house, which spared Leonora from giving her brother a dishonest reply. That much of what the nuns taught her she still believed.

"Oh, my darling girl! My darling, darling girl!" Leone seized her by the waist and swung her to the ground . . . "I hope you brought some newspapers, thanks to those dirty Socialists I have no Stock Exchange quotes for a week—but look at you, you are so womanly, a real bride for our Savior, a true daughter of the Church!"

"Father . . . ." Leonora embraced him, smelling cigar smoke and French cologne. Out of the corner of her eye she noticed her mother standing nervously some distance away.

Leone gave his daughter one last embrace before disappearing down the street, muttering something about collecting rent, and would she bring her newspapers to the café at noon? Francesco was stolidly unloading baggage from the cart, while her mother stood gazing at her as though uncertain what to say.

"Hasn't there been any news?"

"Not since the strike began." Lucinda gave her daughter an appraising glance. "Dearest, you are too heavy for a girl your height. Look at me, the same size as the day I married your father, and I'm taller—but you couldn't even wear my wedding dress, not that you need to, naturally . . . ."

Leonora could have wept. "Is that how you greet me, Mamma? Would you like me to go back to Rome?"

"Of course not." Lucinda's tone softened a little. "Forgive me if I am sharp, our situation makes me so." She instructed Francesco to carry the newspapers Leone needed to his café, and not waste time reading them himself.

When the two women were sitting in the living room's privacy, Leonora asked about the family "situation." Her mother sketched it with as little detail as possible. Listening, Leonora felt uncomprehending, shocked—like all well-bred girls she found the way one made money far more mysterious than the way one made babies. She must have looked stunned, because Lucinda hastily vowed that the Monti family would not simply survive but, in time, prevail. Alas, Leonora could not return to the convent after Easter, her Mother Superior wrote, could never return unless her father's donations reached their old height . . . .

Leonora nearly laughed at such a neat escape from her dilemma, indeed would have laughed had it not depended on her family's poverty. She told her mother all this came as a horrendous shock, that she needed time to adjust and might she walk down to the beach and pray to the Virgin for strength? Lucinda, apparently relieved by her calm, embraced Leonora and warned her to wear a hat against the breeze.

Francesco was ambling down the twisted cobbled streets, his mood as gay and sunny as the day. Leonora's arrival always lifted his heart, but today he was enjoying the prospect of no schoolwork for a week, and, better, the glances every girl he passed showered on him, glances which signaled his own arrival at manhood's gate. And sometimes now he dreamed not just of girls but of some distant city he couldn't name, which glittered like a steel-girded fairground under a million electric lights. All over Italy, all over Europe, young men were stumbling towards that city, rushing headlong into the wider world.

The newspaper ink smelled of that other world, intoxicating him a little when he placed the stack of newsprint before his father's glass. Then Francesco set off at a run across the square and down to the beach where he saw Leonora twirling her parasol into the wind. Francesco trotted across the sand to where she stood.

Less than an hour later Leone staggered into his house, clutching the newspapers so fiercely that they blackened his hands. Leonora, embroidering quietly, was startled by his sudden arrival and, still more, by his animal cry when she asked what was troubling him. Leone sank as though wounded to his knees and began to pound the carpet with his fists. After a time he stopped and allowed Leonora and the maid to help him upstairs, where he collapsed onto the bed. And for the rest of that day the Monti household pretended not to hear his groans.

Lucinda, without mentioning her husband's collapse, gave her children orders not to visit him nor ask tactless questions about his stocks. And they obeyed. Not even when the family doctor arrived did any of them speak. His habitual grimace reassured them that Leone was suffering from a malady considerably less grave than the ancestral stroke. And so, by Saturday, a queer normalcy was settling upon the children, though their father remained invisible, inaudible, and though their mother still wore the drawn face of catastrophe.

Vittorio and Leonora quarreled, as they always did. They fought so often and over such trifles that Lucinda had to leave her husband's bed to rebuke them both. Leonora sensed her brother knew she no longer loved the Church, all, in his view, a woman of their class was good for if she perversely refused a good marriage. So she took comfort in Francesco's innocent questioning. He wanted to hear what Rome looked like, how tall the Pope was, curiosity she felt comfortable satisfying in long walks on the beach. They read each other's most selfish thoughts, about the money and their future, but they never spoke them.

Easter Sunday dawned crisp and gold, a mellow wind off the ocean perfuming the town. Leone awakened with a cry which Lucinda immediately shushed. Vittorio began dressing for Mass early, rejecting cravats maniacally, while Francesco wolfed down a roll and vanished, still wearing his dirty clothes from yesterday. By the time Leonora sat down to breakfast their mother was worrying about her younger son.

"No, Mamma, I don't know where he went—"

"But he must dress for Mass. Leonora, you will find him, dear, won't you, please?"

One paradox of a town as small as San Lorenzo is that it is easier to disappear in than a great city. Since everyone knew Francesco, nobody paid any mind to the direction in which he walked. What difference did a boy his age make? The town was buzzing about his father, after all, retouching the known facts with the gaudy palette of gossip. Leonora's cheeks flushed when she overheard talk about the widow Lucenti, and had to pray to Saint Theresa for patience. The townspeople, ill-clothed, unkempt, gazed at her mockingly, as if to say, come, come, we know your family shame . . . .

Francesco and his teacher Lampa sprawled on a ruined wall

above the town. Lampa's red hair and freckled cheeks contrasted oddly with Francesco's smooth olive skin, stiffly peaked black hair. They might have been prisoners shackled together, but for the casual intensity with which they spoke.

"Didn't understand the book, well, someday, someday. The main thing's keeping an open mind."

"I wish your German would leave a place for God. Why couldn't he?"

"Don't sound like that fool Amabile, that fine fifteenth-century mind—there's a place for God, but the problem is, he abandoned it long ago."

"Did he?" Francesco sat up, sucking on a sprig of mint. "Where would you go if you left, Professor? Rome seems like a foreign city, and they don't like people from Calabria in Turin or Milan, either . . . ."

"Why stay in this rotting country at all? There's Paris, London, even America. There's the entire world!"

"Why don't you leave Italy, if that's how you feel?"

Lampa grinned like a wolf. "I'd go so far away I'd never return. Why don't you, you're young? Australia, America . . . ."

"Never." Francesco flung the word at him like a rock. "You think I'm a peasant who wants to find streets of gold?"

"No, a hardhead Calabrian who asks for advice and gets angry when he hears it!"

Lampa and Francesco started to laugh. The teacher gave Francesco an affectionate punch on the arm, almost knocking him off the wall, and that was how Leonora found them, laughing in the lemon-scented breeze. Lampa looked her up and down as soon as she spoke, and she had to suppress the desire to blush.

"Our mother wants us all home," Leonora said. Francesco made a face, but got to his feet.

"You're the sister?" Lampa bluntly asked. "The one who's going to be a nun?"

"Introduce me, Francesco," she hissed.

"My history teacher, Professor Lampa. This is my sister Leonora."

Lampa grinned at her, remaining insultingly slouched against the wall. "You're too pretty to be a nun, Signorina. I'm not sure God deserves such a lovely bride."

"You talk that way on Easter Sunday? For shame!" she half-whispered, wondering why she still pretended she would ever be what Lampa mocked. "Francesco, come."

When they reached the Monti house a strange sight awaited them in the downstairs parlor. Leone sat in a stiff-backed chair, wrapped in a shawl, Lucinda standing beside him. Vittorio, twitching nervously, let Leonora and Francesco into the house while Lucinda waited to speak until all three of her children were sitting on low chairs.

"It's time you children understood things," she began haltingly. Leone patted her hand as though to encourage her, and she went on: "Your father has suffered a great, a tremendous loss. It is not his fault—never, ever say that or believe it or hate him in your hearts. Thousands of other investors lost as much or more . . . . the Government wants to build a navy, God only knows what for. And so the gentlemen in Turin will subsidize building ships, ships, ships, and the money that was invested a week ago elsewhere fled to those companies that will be subsidized. That means your father's investments—good investments, all of them—are practically worthless. You understand?"

The children looked at each other, and then at Leonora, slowly nodding. Francesco understood nothing but nodded too.

"From today forward, we will live differently . . . . very differently. I've contacted the Prince and he'll allow your father to buy up our remaining mortgages, so the income will be free and clear. That leaves you children. I have prayed, I have wept over you. Without you there is no Monti family . . . ."

Vittorio half-rose to embrace his mother, but she waved him down. Drawing herself up to full height, Lucinda said as quickly as she could:

"Your father and I have made arrangements. He will explain."

The children shifted their attention to Leone, who stirred

uneasily in his chair. He had been so silent, they'd almost forgotten his presence in the room.

"Vittorio, you will be a doctor," Leone told him in a hoarse voice. "You will go to the University in Naples or Rome as soon as you finish your studies here . . . ."

"On what money?" Vittorio replied incredulously. "Will you pay with worthless stock?"

"Disrespectful boy," Lucinda snapped. "Be grateful your father thinks so much of you."

"Leonora is to remain here," Leone continued, obliviously. "We will have no servants now but you, my dear. I know the nuns have taught you how to serve your parents."

Leonora said nothing. The sour taste of nausea filled her mouth, but she choked it back. Well, an unmarried daughter should embrace her servitude, at least until she traded it for a husband's. Her parents were doing what any family in San Lorenzo would have done.

"We will live more modestly," Lucinda added. "Now we can't waste a lira, and the neighbors will be watching everything we do. And all of you know how vicious they can be. So all of you must help the family."

With some surprise Francesco heard himself saying, "What about me? How am I supposed to help?"

Leone shuddered under his blanket, and gestured for Lucinda to answer. She kept her face frozen and without expression as she did:

"You are the younger son, Francesco. You know our custom, the younger must support the older. Not that I love you less, but all our hopes are for Vittorio. You must leave San Lorenzo. Find work. Send money home. Do what millions of our men are doing—for now you must become a man, my son."

Francesco suddenly felt quite dizzy and, standing up, wobbled a little, so that his brother seized his arm to prevent a fall. The moment was like one of those dreams where you know you are only dreaming, but not surely enough to end the dream. Lucinda stood tall and erect like a warrior queen ordering her sons into battle. For the first time Francesco grasped that a mother could take life as easily as she gave it; how terrible his mother seemed stripped of everything but that. Vittorio and Leonora sat calmly, almost contentedly, and Francesco wanted to scream at them, at everyone, to shatter their calm. Instead he slipped out without a word, out into the bright sunlight, the lemon-scented air.

Cymbals, trumpets, drums blared in the street. Why hadn't they heard the parade earlier, Francesco wondered pointlessly, it must have passed the Monti house by now. Though other towns in Calabria celebrated a full-dress Passion Play, San Lorenzo, for reasons quite unknown, preferred this shrill, monotonous noise, more like a funeral dirge than joyous song . . . . he ran headlong down the beach, squatted on the sand, gazed at the sunlit water clutching a coin. Italy or America, Francesco repeated, America or Italy. He noticed he hadn't once asked God's help so far. Lampa was right, he told himself, feeling utterly alone on the empty beach, on his Calabrian earth. A sob filled his chest and he stifled it. With a shout Francesco hurled the coin straight into the indifferent sun. It seemed to take an eternity to fall back into his hand.

FIVE

Francesco Monti reached America in June 1905. Unlike most immigrants, he never told his version of the national myth, no tales of crossing the Atlantic in steerage, no anecdotes about Ellis Island, called by Italians the Isle of Tears. Francesco seemed bent on making his arrival unimportant, a comma within the complex sentence of his life.

> *Dear Mamma and Papa, I am teaching myself*
> *English, I read Bleak House by Dickens and Leaves*
> *of Grass by Whitman*
> *Dear Mamma and Papa, today I turned fourteen*
> *Dear Mamma and Papa, no, no, I can't send*
> *any more money home unless I starve myself to death*

By 1906 Francesco was working the anthracite mines in Scranton, Pennsylvania. Sixteen hours underground, seven days each week. The company owned everything, even his underwear, and deducted his debts from the company store from his paycheck, down to the penny. One quarter of his wages went for the cabin he shared with nine other men, Slovaks, Russians, Poles, their furniture absurdly overpriced and bought on the installment plan.

Francesco had never seen such snow as fell that first winter. He never forgot it. Or the time his molar became inflamed, and the company doctor demanded ten dollars to pull it, ten-fifty with anesthesia. He was making two dollars each week and sending all but forty cents of it home to Italy. Francesco returned to his cabin and worked the tooth loose with his penknife. His cabin mates stood amazed. He spat out the blood, bought himself a shot of rye, went to work at midnight as usual.

> *Dear Mamma and Papa, tell Vittorio how proud*
> *I am he is graduating*
> > *Dear Mamma and Papa, everyone says I am*
> *starting to talk pretty good English*

How could they understand? Francesco scarcely did himself. The mines were fearfully black, yet they seemed realer to him than the flimsy town above, the tarpaper cabin he and Enrico now shared, the tasteless canned food, the moonshine they drank on Saturday nights waiting to fuck an indifferent whore. At least under the ground his life felt real. In the mine shaft each second could separate him from death, a cave-in, an explosion, so that whenever Francesco surfaced he knew he was alive, if only for a moment. After that the dull ache in his chest started, and he never knew if he was sad or coalsick, and he never cared. Today the pain of his tooth was forcing him awake, tired as he felt, trudging next to Enrico down the rows of identical cabins gray with dust.

> *Dear Mamma and Papa, I hope Vittorio knows*
> *how proud I am of his graduation*
> > *Dear Mamma and Papa, I think of you especially*
> *at Easter time and you are always in my heart*
> > *Dear Mamma and Papa, I am speaking English*
> *now with practically no accent, or so my friend Enrico*
> *says, pretty soon I will sound like everybody else*
> > *Dear Mamma and Papa, I can only write once*
> *a month now, I am too tired to write every week now*
> *that I work sixteen hours every day*

Dear Mamma and Papa, today I am eighteen,
here is a photograph of your son dressed like a real
American

The two men entered their cabin. Francesco had to sleep on
the bottom bunk because he was taller and otherwise his feet
jostled Enrico awake. They had a shard of mirror nailed to the
wall, a wash basin, a deal dresser. There was a privy for them and
ninety-three other miners, so far from their cabin that sometimes
on winter nights their bowels gave way on the path. The mining
company deducted one quarter of their wages each week for the
cabin, as they also sold them food, soap, and drink. Even the
whores had to pay for the right to enter town. Francesco no
longer thought about these conditions; he had long since
concluded it was fruitless. Sixteen hours underground taught you
to conserve energy.

Sometimes in the seconds before he plunged into sleep
Francesco imagined he had never left San Lorenzo, that he'd been
split in two and his other self somehow remained, listening to
the cracked church bells, strolling the beach, smelling that lemony
breeze. Everything that happened in Scranton was only the shadow
of a dream, and soon the two Francescos would become one.
This body would explode like Mr. Krook in Bleak House, leaving
his actual self, unchanged, Italian. Who could say he was wrong?
America was no more than a vast fever dream, the hallucination
of fifty million fools yearning for a country that existed only in
their skulls. Here you dreamed to stay alive, to avoid drowning
in lies. Scranton, Pennsylvania, a lie, a town that showed you its
ass and told you it was its face, sold you canned food and insisted
it was a feast. Scranton, and before that, and before . . . .

They'd quarantined him at Ellis Island, a mistake as it turned
out since, thanks to his mother's cook, he wasn't malnourished
enough for rickets. A tiny room, a cell really, down an endless
corridor smelling strongly of piss. After two weeks made bearable
by books, sudden departure. His name written on a cardboard
tag. His suitcase lost, no explanation, it could cross the ocean but

not a corridor. Out into the tangy ocean air, across the bay, his money clutched in a rag and the rag hidden in his pocket. Shivering, thinking America is cold, why didn't anyone tell me how cold?

Voices barking Italian at him, real Italian. He hadn't heard it since the steerage hold; he tried not to think about those three weeks without sunlight or air. Never, never would he talk about them. The voices were shouting a strange word, Filladelllfia, turn left for there, turn right for New York. Francesco knew what happened to boys in New York, Chinamen bought and sold them and fed them to dogs. Probably not true, but it frightened him, though he wasn't sure what a Chinaman actually looked like. Voices shouted insults: idiots, peasants, come on, can't get rich playing with yourselves, and so he turned unthinkingly left, towards the cars for Filladelllfia.

Inside the car, chill turned to humid heat, thanks to a hundred bodies shoehorned into half as many seats. Francesco sat clutching his coins so hard that his hand grew numb. Finally the train groaned into motion. As it gathered speed, rising steeply up a hill, the other passengers' cries nearly deafened him, their fearful moans and their false laughter. The train slowed at a siding, and everyone fell silent. New York City came into view, like a conjurer's trick, its ten thousand towers gleaming with jeweled light that made the sun seem a pale copy, immaterial. The city seduced and menaced in a single glance, as though it was watching Francesco in disdain. Soon it will be too late to escape, he thought, rising, wanting to jump off. At that moment the train lurched into a dark tunnel, forcing him down, accelerating into America.

Enrico lay on the bottom bunk and played his harmonica. In a few hours they would go down into the mine again, time enough for a little sleep if his friend ever stopped wailing out what passed for music in America.

"Enough," Francesco said. "The Devil himself can't listen to your 'blues.'"

Enrico blew one last sour note. "How long have we been in Scranton now?"

"Almost five years for me, you a little less. You ask me this every goddamn day—"

"It's time to leave, Francesco. We'll die in that mine like rats."

"Where can we go? Don't tell me you think you play that thing well enough to earn a living?"

"We just leave. We get paid and go to Pittsburgh—the steel mills pay better, you heard that man in the saloon."

"Go to Pittsburgh, since you trust that Irish liar. Only give me your rent money before you leave."

"And you, you aren't staying here until you die? Your brother's a doctor, isn't he, by now?"

"Oh yes." Francesco tried unsuccessfully to picture Vittorio with a white coat, a kindly air. "I expect to leave. But I will be sure of my destination when I do."

"Eh, you always want to be 'sure.' Go back to Italy, you want to be so sure of things."

A month later he and Enrico left for Philadelphia, reasoning that they would find work easily where there were other Italians. They left Scranton at night since the midnight train cost less. The empty cars rattled across a moonless countryside where, from time to time, a tree, a barn, a church would suddenly flash into sight and suddenly disappear. It was like a journey in a dream, and Francesco felt the sharp loneliness of those dreams in which nothing is familiar, everything seems ominously charged. He felt a heightened version of the dull daily twinge in his chest, as though his heart was being hollowed out vein by vein. He tried to accustom himself, but always failed, to the ache of knowing that in America he had no home, no family, nobody even to bury him if he died. Always, even in dreams, he could feel the cold anxiety of being thrown into this world alone, of having to travel it alone, forbidden even to speak his pain, since who in America would understand or care?

Dear Mamma and Papa, I think of you always
but especially at Easter time, and I weep.
Dear Mamma and Papa, tell my sister how pretty

she looks in her convent photograph, her eyes are too
serious though.

In 1907 he was seventeen years old, already almost six feet tall, an unusual height in that America. Because of his blue eyes he was rarely taken for an Italian. Francesco spoke English well enough to avoid the immigrant's telltale habit of repeating the few phrases which had to cover all occasions. His blue eyes looked out calmly on the country he had chosen and on the city, Philadelphia, self-proclaimed workshop of the world, which seemed to have chosen him. Francesco walked down the stinking streets where Italians, Jews, Negroes crowded into one-story houses. He was still childish in his thoughts, though less and less every day thanks to the schooling his new land administered. Here only the strong survived, or so Francesco heard, and saw that in fact strength could be measured in dollars, in property, far more accurately than in San Lorenzo. He half-despised the poor who thronged his neighborhood streets, as he half-despised himself, for lacking any strength at all. He knew he would acquire it, find shelter from the hurricane force America brought to bear against his kind, naked upon the earth and whimpering in the storm.

Yes, only the strong survived, it was the gospel of the age. Professor Lampa would get no argument, not even from the magnates who owned steel and railroads and banks, not from the penny pamphlets boys sold everywhere. RAGS TO RICHES, PENNIES MAKE DOLLARS, EVERY MAN A J.P. MORGAN. In the saloons the slow gay music called ragtime tinkled beneath shouted conversations, all about money, how to get it, save it, spend it. Why not? What else had Francesco, had all of them, come here for?

His boss, one John B. Carney, paid him six dollars a week for working half the hours he had in the mine. He laughed and joked with Francesco, buying him tall drafts of beer after work, offering to take him to a sporting house. Carney winked lasciviously. Brothels appealed to Francesco but he doubted the propriety of whoring with his boss. He wanted a woman, of course. In Scranton the mining company's whores had disgusted him, with their reek of gin and cheap perfume. Francesco yearned for something better and he knew he would find it someday, though perhaps not in one of the sporting houses Carney so lovingly described: all red plush and featherbeds and clean white girls.

Francesco liked Philadelphia and roamed it, on his free nights, long past midnight. In fact the city was no more one place than Italy was. He walked through Chinatown, inspecting suckling pigs and upside-down ducks roasting slowly, wondering at the sounds streaming out of those unreadable yellow faces. A little further on lived Negroes, silent, sullen, a few picking out mournful songs on instruments he'd never seen. Their wealthier brothers lived miles away, respectable in stiff collars, praising the Lord vehemently. Then came the Slovaks and the Russians. They grappled in the street, then fell weeping into one another's arms, only to end by sharing a dirty bottle of fruit brandy. Least of all Francesco understood the Jews, conscious of their difference and haughty despite their poverty. On Friday nights prayer candles quavered in the windows of their synagogue, and a chant so doleful as to make the Negro music sound gay rose like a cloud from the swaying, sweating men.

But the Irish, ah, them he thought he understood: Carney, his boss, genial, always had a joke or an impression of Teddy Roosevelt. Francesco had been a guest in his home, had met Mrs. Carney and his three daughters, all slender and dark though he supposed childbearing would make them as stout as their mother. Carney took a shine, as he said, to Francesco when he discovered a way to point brick in almost half the previous time. By God we'll build this fuckin' Quaker City into something grand, Frank. He called Francesco Frank. I'd make ye' a partner but for your lack o' capital, Carney added with a pitying look. But Francesco's method became the preferred one and he received doubled pay. In return, Carney told him, he was signing Francesco up as a dues-paying member of the Democratic Party. Let the blueblood

Republicans keep you and me out, we'll get our revenge. You mark my words, Roosevelt will rip up his party yet, that cowboy fool. All we got to do is wait.

Francesco liked the energetic smile the President showed the cameras. It could almost have been a face he passed on a midnight walk, the face of a brawling immigrant. Carney admitted that Roosevelt was doing a fine thing, attacking those malefactors of great wealth. And malefactors they are, look at the palaces they've built right here on Rittenhouse Square. Our poor Irish girls have to tote hot water bottles up and down six flights of stairs whenever some fine lady gets a case of the vapors. And, he added significantly, those bloodsuckers won't give John B. Carney a contract to fix their brick, oh no, they want an old American firm, like I'm not as good an American as any of them! They hate my guts, Frank, and I hate them. Take all the hate in Philadelphia and put a match to it, we'd blow halfway to the moon.

If the city seethed with hatred, Francesco thought, he could feel none of it. If anything, Philadelphia seemed, for all its factories and sweatshops and railroad switching yards, far less mad than the Chicago and New York he glimpsed at the nickelodeon. Perhaps Carney was right and the aristocrats, if you could call them that, still wielded too much control. But the city Francesco saw diffused its energies by scattering its neighborhoods, so that each miniature San Lorenzo seemed complacently self-contained. When he rode the trolley to Germantown or across the Schuylkill, Francesco felt transported to the countryside, and when he and the Carneys explored Fairmount Park they fled the city with exuberant cries. As it expanded the city would need more housing, as Carney pedantically explained, but it would expand slowly, carefully, not so much the workshop of the world as its corridor. Francesco liked the city's marriage of this century and the last. America might be ruthless but it didn't move, thank God, at a uniform headlong speed. So in some way Philadelphia reached out to that part of him, the other Francesco, who still lived in a provincial town. And Francesco would listen to Carney's declamations ironically, certain he knew Philadelphia better than the voluble Irishman.

Everyone was making money, it seemed, more money than avarice could dream. The first sign of what Americans called a slump came in April, when Carney, with no contracts for the generally busy spring months, dismissed half his workmen. Francesco was by now hardened to this custom, having seen it even in the mines. He scarcely spoke when Carney told him about his competitors, who were also letting men go. Business would right itself, Carney said, it always did.

Even now the brickyard worked at an infernal pace. Through dust clouds you could glimpse men running relay between kilns and storage sheds, tossing bricks onto ziggurats while exchanging insults, gossip, bawdy jokes. In the morning Carney oversaw them, a flask of brandy in his waistcoat, cursing whenever one of the workmen broke rhythm. Francesco thought of him as kindly, yet now that the brickyard was selling less and less Carney nipped often at his flask and cursed louder over small mistakes.

Francesco walked the neighborhoods at night and dreamed of how they might look, tenements replaced by fine brick houses, sewage-fouled streets paved and rumbling with motorcars. It had to happen, Carney was right about that. But sometimes he felt the bile of impatience fill his chest when he contemplated that glistening future. He was rich as immigrants as immigrants measured wealth, no matter how much he sent home, and yet he was still so dreadfully far from the Carneys, the self-made men everyone in America worshipped so noisily. He needed luck and luck came unbidden, or not at all.

One night Francesco walked a different route, along Spruce Street, the Babylon of Philadelphia, the newspapers called it. Half-naked women leaned out of windows, dice games filled the air with frenzied cries, and the smell of opium floated down like an invitation to sail some Pacific of the mind. Francesco could feel himself becoming a child again. Now that he was old enough to understand these transactions he found himself unable to ignore them. To that day he hadn't had a woman, not out of principle or fear but because he was waiting for luck to place one in his hands. He walked the narrow sidewalk listening to the painted ladies laughing, smelling their soap and flowers and harshly sweet perfume. Whenever one called out Francesco walked even faster, thinking what a coward he was to walk through Babylon like a priest making a parish call.

When he thought of himself as the Frank Monti who'd doubled Carney's business he tasted the grandeur awaiting him; that world he yearned for became realer than his narrow iron bed four flights up in a boardinghouse he'd selected for its clean cheap rooms. That bed could have been his magic carpet, so instantly did it transport him away from his four walls, the scent of tomato sauce, his married neighbors strenuously enjoying their conjugal rights. Francesco would leap over all that. Carney gave him a book called *The Shame of the Cities* and suggested he read it with an eye to politics. It made less of an impression than Dickens; he had seen too much by then to believe this law or that would change more than the name under which money ruled. He tried explaining that to Carney, who laughed and said, I'll never make a good citizen out of ye, Frank, never! Francesco told him of San Lorenzo, about the Prince and Father Ugo, but Carney cut him off. Everything's dead there, isn't it, why else would you be in America, in your country they're just cutting up the corpse.

But the letters that crossed the Atlantic painted another scene. Leonora wrote him more regularly than their mother, filling pages with her stiff convent script. She retailed San Lorenzo's gossip or told him of their family's small victories, and neither now seemed altogether real. He had lost the power to summon that landscape except in dreams. Vittorio, thanks to his monthly stipends, was studying medicine in Rome; Leonora commented that he liked the poet D'Annunzio better than anatomy. Their parents were getting by. They ate meat only on Sundays, complained Leonora, exactly like peasants. Professor Lampa she mentioned rarely. Francesco wrote more than once to ask for news of him but received the terse reply that he was still teaching and writing articles for the newspapers in the North. Of their father Leonora gave a sketch, perhaps mocking, describing his daily visits to his tenants and the quarrels that ensued, followed by his scrutiny of bankbooks and papers, a long study ended only by the dinner bell. The body was still alive, Francesco decided, no matter how feeble. Vittorio would infuse it with his high spirits, while Leonora would no doubt find a worthy husband finally. He refused to believe his sacrifices, all their sacrifices, would count for nothing in the end. The Montis had been, the Montis were, the Montis would be. That much of his childhood Francesco still believed. The family would not just survive, it would flourish: as the old Calabrians said, not every wound proves mortal to the one who suffers it.

His father had shaken the family but not wrecked it. Very well, then, it was up to him and Vittorio and Leonora to restore the Montis, and at the moment he, Francesco, was of the three doing best. But soon Vittorio would become a doctor, perhaps in Rome, tending to Papal Counts and politicians rich enough to make his fortune. Leonora could hope only for marriage, and now she was putting even that at risk. Soon Francesco would be working for himself, and though the thought made him a trifle guilty, he yearned for the day when he could buy himself a meal at one of those rose-marble hotels on Broad Street or ride in a hansom cab through Fairmount Park at dusk, his arm around some girl, some prize for his selflessness.

The Italians in his neighborhood approved of him, even pointed to Francesco as an example of how their sons should conduct themselves in this vale of tears they called La Merica. His probity and continence were legendary, as was his invention of a successful process Carney adopted just as the Irishman had more or less adopted him. In the streets men twice his age nodded to him, called him Signor Monti as though he were not a boy of eighteen. All this gave Francesco a grave look as he walked to Carney's every morning. He knew he had a reputation to uphold, odd as that seemed. He was beginning to understand his father's mania for appearance. The immigrant quarter was San Lorenzo built out of bricks, not stones, with only a handful of

mispronounced English words sprinkled randomly into the
dialect. Was it any wonder that the Americans, as Carney called
the native-born, mistrusted Francesco and his kind, that the papers
called them organ grinders at best and murderers at worst? His
neighbors wanted only as much of America as they could grasp,
and that seemed so little that Francesco despaired of his people
ever leaving the villages of their souls to join him in the city
surrounding them. They were like the Jews without their stiff-
necked pride, he thought, and without that the Italians would
never accept their apartness or thrive in La Merica, let alone
America.

Carney, like his Irish brothers, had no such qualms. He
confessed to Francesco that he aimed at a ward leader's seat, and
spent hours each week paying court to Democratic satraps. But
then as his business slowed he found himself unable to contribute
lavishly. Francesco saw that Carney, too proud to become a mere
hanger-on, was searching for a cheaper way to curry favor with
those plump, waist coated men who spat cigar butts into gilt-
bottomed cuspidors. Through all of May and June the would-be
ward leader paid only perfunctory calls on them, and just before
July Fourth he announced a scheme to Francesco by which they
would build a new Democratic clubhouse in Carney's ward. If
the bosses liked the result, Carney would build its twin in every
ward. That night Carney presented his scheme to its judges and
received a tentative yes, encouragement enough for him to start
work instantly.

Francesco supervised. Carney paid his workmen irregularly,
so that the clubhouse rose at an equally erratic pace. Though
Francesco remonstrated, Carney insisted on employing ward
heelers and unemployed relatives of the party bosses; their
incompetence and sloth held construction back still more. More
than once Francesco found himself chin to chin with some jeering
man, older and stronger, who laughed at a demand to stop
drinking beer. He despaired of ever finishing, especially when
Mrs. Carney and her daughters began visiting the worksite and
bandying coy phrases with the men. Finally Francesco took to

policing the site every morning to prevent anyone from starting work with a bucket of beer in hand.

After the heat broke in September the men worked a little faster. Three stories of Carney's best brick rose from the filthy site, made even filthier by the men relieving themselves anywhere they pleased. He reported to Carney that by the end of October all the windows and plumbing should be complete, and for this news Carney gave him thanks. And in fact Francesco would have met his schedule but for the run on the banks that began two weeks earlier. The jittery nerves of New York, usually confined west of the Hudson, frightened even phlegmatic Philadelphia. If the rock-solid Knickerbocker Bank could fail, why not their smaller ones? Some workmen failed to return the day after two Philadelphia banks shut down, while those who did demanded to be paid in advance. Francesco stared down the men and sent for Carney, who never came.

Hours later he found him in a bar, newspapers spread before him like a losing hand of cards. The country's finished, he said without preamble. They'll have to sell Lady Liberty for scrap, Frank. Wearily Carney went on: Wall Street in a panic, banks failing between there and Montana, even the giant Trust Company of America threatening to fold . . . . Francesco understood nothing, wondering, where is Montana? It struck him that he should guard the clubhouse site in case one of their workmen came back angrily drunk. Carney smiled. You're a good man, Frank, but don't worry, my boys would never do such a thing. Let me buy you a black and tan and you'll feel better . . . .

Francesco walked his boss home, feeling considerably worse. He bought a roast hen from a vendor and walked home chewing joylessly, listening to telegraph runners shouting new calamities. On impulse he detoured to the clubhouse site; as Carney expected it stood perfectly unharmed. What a fool I am, he thought, walking away. Without warning he was flung painfully up against a brick house front. That little shitheel, shouted a raucous voice, we ought to string the little dago up!

When his eyes focused he saw three of the men from Carney's

crew. They dragged him back to the clubhouse by his hair, taking turns kicking and punching him on the way. At the site they hurled him up the stairs, onto the unfinished second floor. Then came a long ominous silence: Francesco felt too afraid to breathe. As he descended he heard the men smashing the windows, splintering the doors. And then he smelled an acrid odor, something harsh and metallic that hurt his nose. Francesco heard rather than saw a bottle crash into the front room, tumbling through what was left of the window frame.

Something inside the bottle, the source of that smell, leapt into flame, a small red tongue licking along the wooden floor. Without conscious thought Francesco dove for it, throwing it back out into the street, where the flame turned blue and orange, shattering the bottle with a hiss. The men had fled; Francesco stood watching the fire, breathless but somehow calm. The street was filling up with neighbors carrying infants in their arms, shouting and cursing about the fire.

He waited until firemen arrived. Their horses bucked and reared; water spurted onto the now blackened street. Francesco wanted to slip away unnoticed, but Carney and his wife appeared, dazed and sleepy, then loudly grateful when they learned the facts. After that, of course, Francesco had to go home with them, and eat, and tell them everything, everything, one more time. He went, feeling a little numbed. Already his adventure seemed to have happened to someone else.

SIX

Vittorio's train rattled up a hill, jolting him out of sleep and forcing his eyes open. Flashes of intense blue glittered below at intervals, glimpses of the Ionian Sea which was so much darker, as Homer sang, than any other in the world. With a yawn he straightened up. Vittorio could smell the disinfectant on his fingers from the operation he'd helped perform the night before, his first. The disinfectant smell brought back all his excitement the same way, he thought, that the scent of a woman did. Already the hours under those harsh lights assumed a terrible gravity. How strange that at last he felt a doctor's vocation, now that he was returning to San Lorenzo to inspect the ruin of the father who'd made him one.

The damp smell of mud, mingled with narcissus and mint, reminded him it was spring. The seasons ran together now, especially in Rome where he never had time to stroll, as he once liked, in the gardens of the Villa Borghese. For amusement he and his fellow interns chased working-class girls in Trastevere, or sat in the smoky darkness of a cinema hoping to pick one up. They had gone after the operation, despite Vittorio's complaint that it was too fine to sit inside, and sure enough the newsreel depicted America, its cities and vast plains, huge iceboats slicing across vast frozen lakes, New York crowds hurtling across streets wider than the piazza of the Vatican. And of course he thought of his brother Francesco.

His few letters told Vittorio too little and too much. Bad enough to leave Italy, of course, no matter the circumstance, but far worse to put down roots in that mad, electric, artificial soil. And Francesco was doing worse than that, since he seemed happy to remain there for life. For death? Vittorio shuddered. The idea of a Monti working with his hands appalled him. And in a brickyard—could anything be more vulgar, less gentlemanly? It was as if Francesco had reverted to the peasant outlook their family had long since lost, or perhaps the Italians in Philadelphia were dragging him down to their level. Either way his brother was disgracing them all.

Vittorio felt the bite of ingratitude whenever he thought that way. He knew how much he owed his little brother, he had reckoned it down to the lira, and vowed he would pay him back. Nevertheless, he reasoned, there must have been other ways and means for his brother to earn what was, in American terms, not really very much. Francesco had never, he knew now, felt the slightest sense of honor, not even playing soldiers on the beach. He seemed aloof from their duty to the Monti name, to Italy, as though such burdens meant nothing to him. Let him stay in America, Vittorio thought with sudden heat, let him slave in those hellish cities where a babel of tongues rose from the rat-trap slums. Let him stay. In that way we shall divide the world in two, separating it as a surgeon separated health from disease. America had the monstrous vitality of a plague city and like a plague it had infected Francesco, making him unfit for the Italy he'd left.

Another gradient, another rattling. Now Vittorio recognized this countryside. Peasants stood threshing in the stony fields, where orange poppies burst through the April mud. Again that mint smell, so pleasing after the long trip, the hours of smoke and stale sweat. Suddenly the train swerved thirty degrees, hugging the edge of the cliff now, unfurling the bright rug of ocean below, and Vittorio felt his heart leap with joy.

Halfway down the cliff below the tracks, Leonora and Achille Lampa lay facing one another on a blanket that softened the sharp stone. They were still at that stage of love where each other's company suffused them with a vague delirium, the illusion of an eternity of hours like this one, an illusion all the more potent for the difficulties they found first in stealing such hours and then in keeping desire from becoming the one forbidden act, illusion's final, fatal gift.

"The Naples train," Lampa said. "Your brother is on it?"

"That one or the next, I guess." Leonora didn't want to discuss Vittorio and by implication the family crisis calling him home. "What kind of nun would I have made, you think?"

Lampa laughed. "An unhappy one."

"Are you happy teaching your idiots?"

"Life's not about happiness. Only children and Americans think it is."

"Why do you want to marry me then, Achille? To share your suffering?"

"Read Marx, read Engels, read Kautsky. The final struggle is near. We must fight together on the same barricade—don't you understand that by now?"

"I still think about God," Leonora said wistfully.

"Naturally." Lampa hurled a large pebble into the vast expanse of sea. "I hope you don't think about Him the way the nuns taught you to . . . ."

"I'm becoming a Manichean, I fear. Look at this world, Achille, what else can you be if you still believe at all? Isn't everything we see a war between evil and good?"

"I see evil but as for good . . . . good people yes, but I'm sorry, on this earth the real struggle hasn't begun. The Devil rules this world, or maybe a God too weak to fight him, I don't know. Take the Prince. He's in the Devil's party, just like that miserable priest who blesses his every crime . . . ."

"Don't give me a speech," Leonora laughed mockingly. "Save it for your Socialists in Naples . . . ."

"I'll have to go next week," Lampa said wearily. "They called a meeting to discuss our position on these new elections . . . ."

Though she believed Lampa was faithful to her in Naples,

the news gave Leonora a twinge of anxiety. He was a man, after all, and though he loved her he would feel tempted to stray, as her father had strayed, as all men did. Lampa had told her enough of his life before San Lorenzo to make her certain he was capable of that. And so every time she knew he would leave she debated whether she should give herself to him, a token and pledge, a way of preventing the casual betrayals men found so impossible to resist. Leonora read novels in French which pictured wanton conduct, invariably punished by suicide or syphilis, and while she knew fiction was false she feared surrender. In her convent she had known a so-called fallen woman, taken in adultery, as the Gospel put it, a lovely woman who wore a look of perpetual regret. She had given herself and lost. Ever since she'd come home, Leonora felt something growing inside her, a new self, neither Leone Monti's daughter who had to leave her convent nor the household drudge rolling out pasta for the family supper. She felt that somehow she had become herself, thanks perhaps to Lampa, or rather to her freedom in loving him. That was her true and lasting fear, that she would lose the Leonora flowering within her as vividly as the wild mint and thyme she could smell blossoming around them now.

"You're afraid of me," Lampa said, piercing her thoughts as he sometimes could. "You think I want a wife like your mother, a sacrificial victim . . . . don't you know me by now? Don't you understand my ideals?"

"Ideals, Achille? The workers' revolution, the dictatorship of the proletariat, those ideals?"

"Don't be a fool." He sat up, brushing himself off impatiently. "I need a wife who will be my comrade, my friend. My equal, Leonora—you know that's what I want."

"What you want," she murmured. "An Italian Socialist but still an Italian man who dictates, aren't you?"

"If that's what you think, what are you doing here?" he demanded.

"Oh, Achille, please . . . ." Leonora felt herself soften, as she always did. "Don't," she said weakly, "spoil this beautiful afternoon."

"If only we lived in a real place," he said despairingly. "Anywhere but here . . . ."

"People change their skies but not themselves," she quoted Horace in her convent Latin.

"Horace was an ass," Achille said. "He lived on the Emperor's patronage and he wrote silly little poems about how vulgar money was, the hypocrite. Give me Juvenal any day."

"Juvenal hated women," Leonora said, just to vex him.

"Juvenal hated corruption," he corrected her pedantically. "That was his greatness and his strength."

"Why don't you become another Juvenal, then?"

"Oh, I tried, I did . . . . but I haven't enough talent even to be mediocre." Lampa forced a laugh of self-deprecation. "Italy has enough bad poets, we could fill an ocean liner with them. So I chose action instead . . . ."

"Is that what a Socialist is?" Leonora smiled. "A failed poet?"

"That's what the world is. A failed poem." Lampa snapped his fingers. "My God, I've made an epigram! Thanks to you."

Leonora stood up, massaging her stiff legs. "You can take the credit."

"But who could I tell in this miserable town? Even the lawyer Amabile finds my conversation troublesome."

They began folding the blanket and clearing their refuge of evidence that they'd spent an hour together there. "Amabile has daughters," Leonora teased him, "why don't you woo one of them? They're rich," she added quickly so as not to offend, "but not yet corrupt, so far as I know."

Lampa said, "You hurt me most when you think you're humorous," and marched off down the trail to town, leaving her baffled and trembling on the verge of tears.

At that moment Leonora's mother, having met her son's train and escorted him home, was walking across the piazza, head down, as quickly as her aging feet would take her. She wanted to pray in church, not in the uneasy quiet of her home, and so she found a pew far from the altar and began to say her rosary. As she fingered the blue onyx beads her lips moved in a murmur inaudible five feet away. She was praying, she knew, for the impossible or at least the highly unlikely, that Leone's condition would prove as temporary as a scratch, and since even her God rarely worked miracles she prayed as feverishly as she and Leone had, long ago, made love. Gradually she lost sight of the church's Baroque decor, its altarpiece depicting Saint Lawrence sizzling gruesomely on his grill, oblivious finally, so intensely did she pray, to the scent that rose from the banks of tapers between the altar and the pews. And after a time she prayed too for herself.

Examining his father, Vittorio felt the satisfaction that competence, even mastery, brought. Leone sat propped up in bed, a shawl draping his shoulders, one eye half-closed. His son spread out instruments on the sheet and poked the old man as gently as he knew how. One side of his father's body looked paralyzed, while the drooping eye confirmed his initial suspicion of a stroke. From his mother's description he had guessed as much, but seeing the frozen flesh, the sightless eye, gave him a queer tremor. Suddenly Leone's other eye blinked.

"Is it you, Francesco?"

"It's me, Father. Vittorio. It's me."

"Quit making bricks, son, it's no trade for gentlemen. Become a banker instead."

"Father, it's Vittorio—"

"Shut up! You're a child, you know nothing of this world . . . ."

Vittorio gritted his teeth and continued to examine his father, who fell silent again. The nerves in his body's left side registered nothing, nothing at all. The left eye confirmed paralysis. Leone's face, though, still moved as fiercely as ever, making his son wonder what damage the old man's brain could have suffered. A little, perhaps, no more. Vittorio knew cases, and not only in textbooks, where the brain survived more or less intact, a cruel joke on the useless body attached to it . . . . his father was talking again, calling him by his brother's name, but now he ignored it, palpating his limp hand, prodding his good arm with a silver probe, tapping his knees so that he could test the reflex. His father grew angry at this and tried to box his ears.

"You have no respect," the old man cried when Vittorio continued. "You are not my son, America has ruined you, I feared it would! You must come home, yes, home . . . ."

"Try not to speak," Vittorio forced himself to be calm. "You're upsetting yourself."

"I may be old and weak but I am still head of this house and you, you must respect me, you *will* respect me or—"

"Be quiet, old man!" Vittorio couldn't help bursting out. "Lie there in peace, you're only making yourself sick." His father began to weep silently, and Vittorio had to flee.

Just after four the rain began. From her room Leonora listened to her mother and Vittorio's voices rising and falling, sometimes angrily, sometimes merely aggrieved. Of course, she thought, who of the Montis would not feel aggrieved, cheated by fate's wheel of the glittering chips once within their reach? After a time the rain started beating steadily on the roof. Vittorio's voice faded out, while her mother rattled a few possessions palpable enough that Leonora could feel it one floor away.

She went down to the kitchen, knowing she should make dinner but feeling no desire to cook. Through the rear windows she watched the rain darken the sky; the downpour was gathering intensity. It occurred to her that the peasants had been warning of a torrent all week, not that anyone with a clean collar ever paid them any mind. But as she watched the water fall so fast its drops became invisible, Leonora felt a shudder of fear. In Calabria any disaster seemed possible, even likely. Unlike the Northern towns, San Lorenzo never invested in a system of staggered drains to break this water she could see, coursing downhill faster than any river did.

Vittorio came in, still downcast from their mother's words. She told him of the semiannual flooding, but he gave her a passive shrug. They both stood watching as the rain carried away saplings, flower beds, their neighbors' eggplant and waterlogged tomato plants.

"It's like the flood," Leonora said in a low voice, as though speaking any louder would enrage the wind and the water they were staring at with horrified interest.

"The house will be safe," Vittorio replied. "Don't we have stone foundations?"

With a tearing sound the rain leapt the property line and poured into their kitchen. Leonora and Vittorio almost hugged each other in fear. Water was filling the kitchen, so quickly that Leonora had no time to think of saving the silver or the Baccarat. Instead she stood frozen, her feet soaked, listening to the screams of horses, who by instinct feared a flood the way their owners feared a fire.

Vittorio shouted, "We must see to Father, we can't stay here—"

Leonora backed out of the kitchen, water now splashing her legs to the knees, into the drawing room, where the flood hadn't yet reached. She found a crucifix her mother swore belonged to Saint Catherine and hid it in her apron, not that she could have explained why. She heard Vittorio call her name and she bolted upstairs, water squishing from her shoes, only to find him trying to lift their father out of bed.

"Go see," he panted, "how far the flood is rising, and how fast."

Leonora and her mother both tried to get a look. By now the whole drawing room, except for the tall Napoleonic clock, was stained black by the flood. Ottomans floated crazily in the dark stream filling the whole ground floor, encroaching on the stairs to the second floor. Leonora's mother made the Sign of the Cross, mumbling a prayer.

"God is punishing us," she said in an old woman's distant voice.

Leonora entered her parents' room, intending to help Vittorio. But he was carrying their father on his back like, she thought, Aeneas carrying Father Anchises out of the Sack of Troy. The women followed him down the staircase and out the door, warped and ajar. Leonora could heard her father muttering, "Let me die, let me die, I've lived long enough . . . ."

Vittorio and their mother began climbing San Lorenzo's main street in search of safe high ground. They needed Leonora, it seemed, not at all. And her first thought was of Achille Lampa, her beloved, of his miserable shack further downhill. Sudden panic filled her; she began running towards it. The water hindered her, and she progressed at an agonizingly slow pace. At last she reached Lampa's shack and found it bare, as though its owner had received advance warning of the flood, giving him time to pack books and papers, before his prudent escape. Leonora felt glad that her beloved had fled, and furious at his absence. All San Lorenzo was fleeing uphill now, in carts pulled by mules whose owners cursed them colorfully, in carriages moving to the balky rhythm of scared horses, in little knots of shouting folk climbing the hill on foot.

Lampa is my family now, she thought with the cold force of revelation. Mother and Father and Vittorio didn't stop to see whether I lived or died, wretches that they are. Lampa always preached the worthlessness of families such as hers; here was the proof. Vittorio should have let my father drown, she thought wildly, all of them might as well drown, for all the good any of them will ever do me or anyone else . . . . Leonora began climbing the hill, scraping through mud with her hands, scrambling to the summit where, improbably, the peasants were burning ricks to light the townspeoples' way. How stupid, she thought, but at least the peasants still feel pity, no matter what they suffer or how much they hate . . . .

When Leonora reached the summit, she gathered up her soaked skirts, trying to look not too bedraggled. That man Brunetti, once her father's tenant and now Father Ugo's retainer, greeted her with a cry of relief. Her parents and brother were not far, he told her, and her father was, blessed be God, weathering the storm like a second Garibaldi. She wanted to laugh at him, instead asked politely where the schoolmaster Achille Lampa might be holing up. Brunetti made a face. He's probably preaching sedition, he said, and spat a thick jet of tobacco juice at the ground.

Another hour passed while Leonora inspected every group, however small. At last she couldn't control her tears and lay down on a flat rock, sobbing into the slow trickle of rain. Below her, San Lorenzo lay prostrate, and if she raised her head slightly she could make out the family house, still brightly lit as for some party that would never, now, take place. Leonora felt a hand clasp the back of her neck. It was Lampa. In the firelight his red hair made him look devilish, but what matter, she told herself, he was alive and in her arms, and that was all she wanted, tonight or ever, world without end, amen. He kissed her fiercely. His mouth tasted of cheap wine, garlic, and something else. It must be destiny, Leonora thought, closing her eyes to kiss him back.

SEVEN

"**Welcome,** welcome, Signor Monti. We were not expecting you tonight."

Or any night, Francesco said to himself ironically. The Calabrian Club was quite happy to accept his dues and dispense with his presence, since he made the members uneasily aware of how far he had surpassed them. The American, they called him, and the name wasn't a compliment. Francesco spoke more English every day then these men did in a month. He was a citizen, wasn't he, a graduate of the Americanization School and now owner of a green passport the precise shade of the currency. And now he and Carney owned the building company even-steven, as Carney said, making him altogether too successful for the men who nodded warily at him through the blue smoke of their cigars.

"Eh, Francesco I gotta joke for you," said Enrico, his tailor, his only friend in the stuffy room. Outside ice glittered in the mud of Ninth Street and the wind whistled past bins of burning trash. Winter, another winter, why did time accelerate faster and faster every year? He felt a premonition of old age when he walked the neighborhood, sniffing burned coffee and the herbs these peasants grew. Thank God Enrico reminded him of his youth, of the time before his life swirled like a shaken kaleidoscope: Enrico made him laugh.

"What's the difference between an Italian with hope and one without?" His friend paused for effect. Francesco shrugged, "Italian boys with hope stay home and pray God for mercy. The rest of us come to America."

Enrico worked seventy hours each week bent over his needle and dreamed of an anarchist paradise even he knew was more distant than the moon. And so he made little jokes, irony one measure of the distance between fact and desire, and came to the Calabrian Society to preach the gospel so many Italians wanted to believe. But it was 1912, Francesco insisted, and their world spun so rapidly that no compass could point true north. Enrico laughed and called him an American, meaning an Italian who believed only in the color green.

At last the meeting dawdled into order. The president, that Pisano who'd greeted Francesco so unctuously, announced that the Society was feeding three hundred and forty families in Philadelphia to supplement the soup kitchens and the breadlines run by the Church. Swift arithmetic told Francesco that represented perhaps five percent of the newly-created poor, another product America produced faster than Italy ever could. He stood up and offered jobs for skilled laborers.

"But do you truly have work, Signor Monti?" Pisano asked diffidently.

"Not much, now. But they can work when spring comes."

"Hungry men can't eat promises," Enrico interjected. "Up in Lawrence they're striking, Italians like us are, but us—we bleat like sheep."

"Why don't you go on strike against yourself?" someone said acidly.

Enrico slapped his thigh in exasperation. "No wonder the Americans treat us like dumb animals! Two Italians, Ettor and Giovannitti—"

"Terrorist thugs," Pisano said, more firmly than before. "Let them and their kind rot in jail."

"They acted legally, Signor Pisano, and now they are charged with murder—and you say let them rot? They never even touched a gun but they are going to jail or the death house. And all because those fine Yankee capitalists saw what power we have, Italians like us, once we stop sitting on our immigrant asses, and they got scared!"

"Let's get back to our own city," Francesco interrupted. Enrico could speechify for an hour and tonight he had neither time nor patience to hear him out. "I offer jobs in one month, when the winter ends. Until then I will increase your efforts and surely do better than you can now."

Pisano stiffened. "Signor Monti, you are a mere twenty years old. It is true, you and Carney are partners, it is true you make a good living. But now you have grown arrogant. I am the president here and I will decide such matters, I alone. You cannot buy me or my members, though God knows you would if you could. Go start you own society, Monti. Go."

Francesco smiled, not altogether startled by Pisano's words. Goddamn America, he thought, and goddamn these Italians for hating me, envying me. He could feel their resentment as he rose to his feet, pulled on his ulster and his hat, and left the hall without a word. Goddamn America. You could hate the place in one breath and lust after it in the next, and somehow only the lust felt real. Even a woman was safer; you could want a woman and have her without losing yourself. He shook his head and walked north, faster than before, out of the Italian quarter and toward his most tangible dream.

He could see her lights burning, his lone beacon in the winter dark. As he neared Delancey Street, the heart of Society Hill, that aristocratic enclave on the city's eastern flank, Francesco thought that the longest journey possible was not from San Lorenzo to Philadelphia, but in fact from the streets where immigrants burned trash on unpaved streets, to Laura's house on this block of granite and brick. I have made that journey, he told himself triumphantly, climbing the servants' staircase and pausing to inhale her room's perpetual scent of flowers, incense, and cigarettes. He tapped lightly on the door. Instantly Laura was encircling him with her thin arms, pulling him inside and onto the ottoman.

When they sat up an hour later, still dizzied by passion's force,

Francesco saw that Laura's servants had laid out a late supper, cold meats, oysters, and he reached for a slice of beef. She laughed.

"What appetites you have! Are you never satisfied, Frank?"

"This is good," he said between bites. "Open a restaurant if you're ever broke."

"Money—is that all you can talk about?" she nibbled his ear. "You're as bad as Teddy, I swear. Six of one and half dozen of the other, men . . . ."

Teddy was the husband Laura had sent packing shortly after their wedding night, when she discovered he practiced the so-called English vice of flagellation. Though this might have interested Laura had she read it in one of those novels she studied for clues to life, it hardly pleased her as marital reality. Since Teddy had luckily not given her a child, a discreet Philadelphia divorce was limping sluggishly along, and until the decree Laura retained the house and servants he'd gotten her. She considered herself an emancipated woman, eyes forced open by unhappiness, so that when she met Francesco at a Democratic Party function she was already half persuaded that she deserved to take a lover.

Laura's parents lived in Connecticut, comfortably far away, leaving her free from any pious interference. Her women friends concurred. Wasn't it a time for them to shoot Niagara Falls, smash saloons, preach anarchy or at least the right to vote? With contempt Laura described her mother's life to Francesco, that endless round of childbirths and charity balls; that angel in the house unable to sign a check or venture out alone. Everywhere women were marching for freedom. Her dear friend Alice Paul was abandoning stuffy Philadelphia for New York and suffragettes, while she wasted her days dickering with Teddy over property!

Laura's revolt led her to the Progressive Club, a tent of good intentions under which respectable folk could perform a tame circus of protest. In this presidential year the Progressives were growing so fast that even Carney and his friends wanted them to join that even larger circus, the Democratic Party. So Laura Warrington went to meet the enemies of good government one night, those corrupt men her idol Lincoln Steffens mercilessly exposed, and came away with the memory of a quiet, blue-eyed Italian who made her laugh as Teddy never could. Soon enough she found a pretext to visit Carney's, and after a decent hesitation she let the first love of her life blossom into flesh.

Francesco understood her hesitation, or thought he did: by sleeping with him Laura was violating several social codes of the day. Ladies from her class might commit adultery, might wander dreamily from man to man (and Laura told him of women whose names he read in the papers who were doing both), but they would have found sleeping with an immigrant unthinkable, the sort of slumming that simply *was not done*. Philadelphia had a well-oiled social machine precisely because all classes kept proper distance from each other, kept their extramarital frolics within circles they knew.

What Laura and Francesco were doing broke that rule. It was a transgression, really, since Laura's act expelled her from the state of grace her husband's income and her Society Hill house provided her, a sin, in fact, against Philadelphia's iron law that the only people suitable to know were people you already knew, including rakes and lotharios. To choose an immigrant not ten years off the boat was to suggest he had a sexual appeal beyond any of the Rittenhouse Square gentlemen with their polo ponies and their proven skill at adultery, their apartments on side streets where nobody spent the night, their self-satisfied lips curved in a perpetual smile at a woman like Laura Warrington. If those men or their wives ever learned of Francesco, society would pronounce its verdict, from which they both knew there was no appeal.

"You're gaining weight," she said slyly to him.

"I'm walking less with this cold, dear. Am I as fat as President Taft?"

"Ever since you bought half of Carney's business—"

"I thought we weren't talking about money, dear?"

"Oh, I hate the thought of it . . . . if only Teddy would die or disappear, and set me free."

Though this new theme startled Francesco he tried not to let her see it. Instead he caressed her thin shoulders and neck as soothingly as he knew how.

"I tried to be a big shot tonight but it didn't go over good," he told her.

"That's too bad," Laura said. He could tell she wanted to talk about her own troubles, so he took the bait and asked what Teddy had done to deserve the death sentence.

"His lawyers told mine they're going to fight the divorce. Meanwhile Teddy wants me to pay him rent for living here— *rent*, Frank, can you imagine such an ungentlemanly thing?"

"He wants to hurt you."

"I know that," she said, suddenly not his lover but an exasperated society lady faced with a stupid clerk. "I deserve *some* happiness after my boring silly life. And I intend to find it, if I have to spend a hundred years in court. With you, Frank, of course with you—only don't, please infuriate me by telling me things I already know!"

"Then I'll tell you what happened tonight before I came to you."

"Only if it's amusing, Frank."

And Laura curled up on her bed, childishly draping a bank of goose feather pillows with her glowing hair. Francesco began to act out the Calabrian Society's characters, pompous Pisano and feckless Enrico, turning the scene into comedy as he impersonated each in turn, those grave Italian voices now foolish American ones. His beloved laughed as a proper lady should, tittering until she had to cover her mouth lest a guffaw escape.

"Oh, darling, come and kiss me." He kissed her. She gazed lovingly. "You Italians are so—theatrical."

Francesco shrugged. "At least our women don't smash up saloons."

"You don't believe in temperance? Are you that cynical?

"What does 'cynical' mean?"

"Morally low,—someone who thinks evil of everyone. Someone without hope."

"I have hope, yes. But you Americans are the theatrical ones, always shouting about making a better world. Shouting and doing nothing for anybody else."

"Don't attack me, Frank. You know I would help everyone if I could."

Laura was wearing her most endearing face and he kissed her, drawn as always by her look of wounded helplessness. How little he knew, Francesco thought, how stupid to think he could ever make her do anything, this steel-willed child who'd dismissed her husband from her bed, then coolly set in motion a divorce. Laura had a woman's bravery quite equal, he suspected, to his own. And like Francesco she wanted victory, not the sullen truce most human beings settled for. Their hot kiss metamorphosed into a kiss between their limbs. Laura broke it long enough to dim the lamp, then sank back against the pillows with a sigh.

Laura had an unspoken fear that one of her husband's servants would meet him face to face, and so he kissed her sleepy mouth and stole out of the mansion, pausing to detect approaching feet. There were none. In the street Francesco felt that peculiar emptiness that seized him when he made love to her, an emptiness that filled him more utterly than the richest meal, as though she nourished him and drained him all at once. Despite the night chill he took the long way home. He worried that Laura was wearying of his embraces, weary enough to find another Teddy, who had ordinary tastes in bed and smiled on suffragettes. Francesco loved her without hope, precisely as she had said Laura thought she deserved happiness, and happiness had temporarily assumed his form.

Francesco was pondering these thoughts, almost savoring the pain they caused, as he turned onto Spruce Street. Despite the midnight hour and the cold, the sweet painted ladies were still posturing in windows. Two of them called down to him, hey big man, whaddya say, five bucks for both of us. The proposition would have stupefied him six months ago, but it now only made him laugh and sing a chorus of "Oh, You Beautiful Doll." The girls laughed and blew kisses. He turned off Spruce at Ninth and walked faster, smelling that indefinable aroma of the poor, boiled cabbage, dirty linens, and outhouses compounded into a single stench. On South Street the smell grew overpowering, for here the poorest families crammed the tenements like a mass grave. A few dogs, so underfed that their ribs stuck out, trotted up to Francesco, beseeching a bite of food. Inside the houses men cursed, women bent over oil lamps doing piece work, children bawled. Francesco could make out a dozen languages, all speaking the dialect of misery.

A little boy ran out and seized his hand. He's as old as I was when I got here, Francesco thought. The child would not let go. His hair stank of the carbolic soap used ineffectually to ward off lice. He had stiff black hair, black eyes, a face so dusty that Francesco could scarcely make out whether he was black or white. At last the boy said something that sounded Russian or maybe Polish. Pani, pani. Francesco led him back to the house he'd run out of. A woman sat stitching a shoe, muttering under her breath.

Francesco was about to give money when the woman ran over to the boy, beating him with the shoe she'd been working on. The boy began to scream but made no effort to escape. God help him, Francesco thought helplessly. He found a half-dollar and handed it over. She paused long enough to take the coin and bite it to verify it was real. Then she grabbed the boy by his shirt and dragged him inside. Francesco hesitated, unwilling to depart. But the boy's cries were silenced and so he left, walking away as quickly as he could escape.

"Never give them money," Carney said more sharply than Francesco had ever heard him speak. "A woman can afford a soft heart, Frank, but not us, not men like us. Did anyone give you anything for nothing? Or me? And look at us. Look around you, son. Carney and Monti Brickworks and Construction. A business, by Christ, a going concern."

"We could give them jobs. You said so yesterday."

"You don't give a man a job, he earns one. I don't know about you but I'm here makin' money, not saving souls. Leave that to the parish priest. You didn't come to the U S of A to perform corporal acts of mercy, unless I miss my guess."

The lunchtime whistle blew. Francesco stood up, hoping Carney would for once let him dine alone, but instead his partner accompanied him to the corner saloon. Carney could never resist the buffet that a nickel's worth of beer purchased. Solemnly he worked his way down the spread, plucking a herring here, a slab of corned beef there, while Francesco, who had no appetite, took a single hard-boiled egg. Upstairs, Francesco took a swig of bittersweet ale, warning Carney wordlessly not to say more. It was useless, since the Irishman could never halt a speech once he began.

"Frank, let me tell you, even if you emptied your pockets, what could you do? You'd be pissin' in the ocean—you see that, don't you? Even our lord Jesus said that we always have the poor, didn't he?"

"You trying to convince me or yourself?"

"Damnit, man, it's this American folderol that's turnin' your head, that Whitman and Emerson and the Lord knows what. Nobody believes that tripe today!"

"Eat your food, Carney, before some poor bastard takes it away from you." Carney laughed, or rather his mouth did. His eyes remained a chilly blue.

"Carney and Monti is a business," he said after he chewed a bit. "What do you think America is, Frank? This isn't a country, it's a business. And the same goddamn rules apply. Fuck or be fucked."

"All right," Francesco said, weary of his partner's voice. "From now on I'll be all business, OK? Only don't ask me to like it."

"You're thinkin' of your father, aren't you? But you're your own man, Frank. You haven't ruined yourself or your family, dammit, you're my partner and I'm proud you are."

"I've been thinking." Francesco hesitated, then plunged. "Maybe we should sell the patent on my brick-pointing. We could use the money, couldn't we? Then we could bid on those new land parcels outside the city limits, pick some up cheap."

"Now there's my boy!" Carney beamed, "But lease the patent, not sell it, Frank. You don't sell the goose that lays your golden fuckin' eggs."

"That land won't stay cheap forever, though. Already they're calling it the Main Line—"

"You been listenin' to the fancy gents all right." Carney gave him a shrewd glance. "You wouldn't be speculatin' on behalf of a certain lady whose name shall never pass my lips?"

Francesco reddened. He had long suspected that Carney knew about Laura Warrington. Philadelphia was less a city than a collection of villages, some of which often overlapped. That night at the Bellevue when he shook Laura's hand, dazzled by her mischievous green eyes, Carney had surely noticed; casual gossip could fill out the tale. She had pledged him to secrecy, and he had failed. Now he merely shook his head. To say anything would only confirm his partner's guess.

At about five he heard the workmen shouting his name, and glimpsed his friend Enrico at the gate. As he approached, summoning up a joke for his friend, the tailor held up a telegram, touching it up warily as though somehow it might explode. Enrico waited a moment for Francesco to speak. Then he said in Italian that he would help in any way he could. Francesco nodded.

When the yard closed at six Francesco wished he could stay overnight, so comforting was the smell of brick dust and fenced-in material. He forced himself to bid Carney good night amiably, and then he slowly began to walk. Later it seemed to him he must have walked the city's length. Francesco walked to the Delaware with its steamships, massively white in the dying light of the winter day, then all the way to the Schuylkill, where rowers sculled the icy currents and lovers lay on blankets, casually entwined.

The sight gave him a pang. Although by now his feet were telling him to sit down, he kept walking, kept a steady pace backwards, into the web of streets east of Broad, dead ends, alleyways, sniffing stews and soups simmering in their kitchens, walking faster as he neared Society Hill. A block from Delancey Street he hesitated, for a moment. No, he had no choice now. When Francesco reached Laura Warrington's house he let himself in, taking the stairs two at a time until he stood at her door.

From inside her music box was playing a slow waltz. Then came the noise of something thudding to the floor, and Laura's voice uttering an exasperated oath. So she was alone. He thanked God for that and pushed open her door.

I wasn't expecting—she began, but Francesco put his hand up. As he did a tattered telegraph form fluttered onto the Persian rug. He sank onto the bed. Laura reached up to caress his thick brown hair, and at that instant he began to shake. Francesco began weeping noiselessly. Laura sat frozen for a second, fearful of the stranger who had invaded her room, until she noticed the tattered paper and, plucking it from the rug, read aloud: FATHER DIED SEVEN P.M. STOP POINTLESS YOU RETURN FOR FUNERAL STOP WILL ADVISE FURTHER DETAILS VITTORIO. At some point Francesco's tears became sobs, neither loud nor soft, and when she finished she embraced him with a fierce tenderness she had never shown. Francesco could barely feel her thin arms embracing him. Now I am a man, he thought, mechanically. Now I am finally a man.

EIGHT

The Calabrian soil, brittle as glass under an early frost, yielded reluctantly to the gravediggers. Far below the cemetery glittered the Ionian Sea, its surface hard and brilliant as a diamond, topped by quick-moving clouds. The Montis stood listening to Father Ugo, now so stooped he resembled a hunchback, reciting Latin prayers for Leone's soul. Their faces revealed nothing, not even grief. Vittorio glanced back and forth for a flicker of sentiment, found none, and reflected that for Southerners death held no more terror than birth. How different a Roman funeral was, with its elaborate show of loss, its pretense that mourning was but the display of manners by other means. Father Ugo flung a sacred medal into the grave and then the ceremony came to an end.

He would die gloriously, Vittorio swore fiercely to himself, he would lie in a marble tomb. Better to do great things than to believe petty ones. The soul, now, his father's soul, allegedly in the hands of God: what man who had dissected a cadaver believed such rot? The body reeked and rotted and once its coffin collapsed, it joined the earth, an indifferent heap of cells. And if Leone Monti had ever had a soul, he kept it hidden from his eldest son. All foolishness, Vittorio decided, helping his mother and sister into the rented coach.

The lawyer Amabile was waiting for them at his door. Since his elevation to King's Counsel he wore the finest suits in San

Lorenzo, prompting the envious to complain he wanted to outdo the Prince himself. His eyes gleamed behind a pince-nez with a sentiment Lucinda took for sympathy.

"How good you are, Signor Amabile, how kind a heart you have to set aside the King's business for this poor widow . . . ."

Amabile bent over her hand, murmuring the sentiments appropriate to her grief, while Vittorio and his sister exchanged a glance. Neither had broached the subject of a will to their mother and hence neither knew what to expect. When they were drinking liqueur in Amabile's parlor he began to speak:

"I fear that Signor Monti left his estate in a rather unclear shape. He wrote several wills, but the most recent one shows such a confused mind, forgive me, Signora, it is not even signed or dated. I hope I make myself plain?"

The three survivors, none of whom understood, nodded.

"What does this mean?" Amabile addressed some unseen court. "What does it signify? When a man dies in such a legal tangle, his estate passes to his nearest relative. And in this case that means you, Signora."

"It can't be worth much anyway," Vittorio said.

Amabile gave him a sly smile. "Shall I surprise you? Those shares your father held on to have tripled in value since he bought them, thanks to the wise policies of our Prime Minister Giolitti. And even the properties in San Lorenzo are reliable. Your father was reckless, perhaps, but he was certainly no fool."

"Please explain," Lucinda said, her hand plucking nervously at her throat. "Was Leone hiding his profits from me? Why?"

"Ah, Signora, between a man and his wife only God can judge right or wrong. Perhaps he was piling up gold for your old age—who knows?"

Vittorio laughed. "He was a greedy peasant when you scratched him hard enough. Greedy and stupid—and now I have to beg for my birthright."

"You're forgetting Francesco," Leonora said sharply. "He deserves the largest share of all. He sacrificed his youth for you, and you don't even mention his name."

"Yes, poor Francesco," snorted Vittorio. "He's found Paradise in America. Making bricks, Signor Amabile, how's that for a noble trade?"

"Better than seducing peasant girls," Leonora snapped.

Lucinda made a shocked noise. "Children, children, this is not the time . . . ."

"Yes it is," Vittorio interrupted. "I need cash. I want to start a practice in Rome and I can't do that otherwise, it isn't possible. It isn't fair. I was always a good son, Mother, wasn't I?"

Leonora laughed at him spitefully. Her brother shot her a poisonous look.

"None of this is material," Amabile said smoothly. He was used to these family scenes after funerals and considered them as inevitable as rain. "Signora Monti, you control nearly four hundred thousand lira in stocks, bonds, and property. I advise you to consider thoroughly how to dispose of it. Remember that Francesco's interests must, under the law, be protected. In distributing your husband's estate you must include your youngest son."

Lucinda did not reply. When she finally spoke, her voice sounded as chilly as the hill where her husband lay.

"I will distribute nothing. My husband would not have wanted it. Neither do I."

Vittorio began to protest, but one look from his sister shut his mouth.

"My daughter needs a dowry. She must marry well. And my Francesco will survive, no, he will flourish. But I must live. For many years, perhaps—my family is long lived and I shall follow them, if it is the will of God. So the money will remain with me. My husband would have wanted it."

"But my medical practice—"

"You can practice in San Lorenzo. I will make that possible."

"I hate you!" Vittorio burst out. "You've never wanted me to be free of this hellhole, you want me to die here of boredom or malaria! Let me tell you, mother," he said with sarcasm, "I'll never practice one day here, not for all my father's loot. I was born to be a great doctor, not a provincial nobody!"

The women looked quickly at Signor Amabile to see if he'd taken offense at this. But his face revealed nothing. Vittorio poured himself another liqueur, then flung the glass into the hardwood fire.

"Keep your money for Leonora's dowry," he told them. "The strongest man is he who stands alone."

Vittorio turned to go. The three others watched him leave, impassive, unimpressed. Then they spent an hour discussing the formalities necessary to transfer Leone's estate to his widow. Amabile escorted Lucinda and her daughter out to the hired coach, promising he would make sure the King's court would act with all possible speed, since in such matters haste was impossible.

As soon as Leonora and her mother got home each went to her room without saying a word. Leonora's room had grown untidy during the past weeks, clothing flung on chairs, books heaped in piles, and now that disorder filled her with disgust. How far from the convent life she'd come, how far from the days when she prided herself on the homely virtues, despair held at bay by the small disciplines. Now she felt naked before her enemy and her enemy was herself.

Had she loved her father? Pitied him, yes, and nursed him better, though she would never say so, than her half-distraught mother had, though always her heart was breaking not for him but for Lampa. Of course she told nobody. What else did it mean to be a daughter? She never mentioned Lampa's name, and never ceased to think of him, not even in sleep, not even her dreams could set her free. The first man you live for, she'd read in a French novel. And so when Lampa had lost his job, after he had offended the Prince himself by organizing his sharecroppers, he packed his bag and told her he was leaving town. She said nothing. He urged her to join him, leave San Lorenzo for Rome or Turin or the Lord knew where, and still she said nothing.

The greatest sin was betrayal, she still believed that, despite those German nihilists Lampa made her read, and if her ethics were (as he scoffed) slave morality, then Leonora chose to remain in bondage. Let Vittorio strut his freedom. She had her duty, and duty, if you examined it carefully, was all a woman could ever have. Someday she might have a duty to herself, but not yet, not yet, and how she resented Lampa for forcing her to choose. He could wait; if he loved her he would. And so she didn't run, though when his letter came from Naples the day after her father died, when every nerve in her body, every cell, screamed for him. Leonora couldn't have explained why. Duty, perhaps, pity for her mother, so lost and feeble now, or was it the knowledge that Vittorio would be no help? It didn't matter. She expected Lampa to wait and he was waiting, and she would see how long he would; that would be his test. She had never given her body to him and now that refusal seemed a safeguard of his love.

Leonora's room darkened as wan winter light leaked from the sky. She lit a lamp and lay across her bed, trying to empty her heart of its turbulence. On the opposite wall hung a large map of the world. When Francesco moved to Philadelphia Leonora stuck a pin into the dot representing his new home, wondering why he hadn't chosen New York, seemingly the apex of America's energy. Philadelphia looked nowhere in particular, neither on the ocean nor inland, and even the vivid letters her brother sent home sketched no more definite place. Leonora read them as a child gobbles sweets, savoring the details yet feeling somehow hungry— for what, she could not say. She guessed Francesco was carrying on a love affair since he mentioned no women. American love, what would that be like? At such moments she grew jealous, thinking meanly, at least he got out, at least Francesco managed to escape.

He must be twenty one now, think of that. Would any of us recognize him if he appeared in San Lorenzo? His money was coming in much larger sums now, though their mother still refused to hire servants or resume the life they'd once so proudly led. Francesco no doubt imagined her unchanged, all of them the same. You left home and home froze in your heart, wasn't that what old folks said? But of course none of them were now what they'd once been. Their mother was growing old, shocking even Leonora who saw her daily, as though her burden of cares had broken her suddenly down. Even before Leone's illness she began spending hours alone, pretending to stitch embroidery, gazing glassily out at the sea, that sea she never bathed in, that gray-green void impervious to human life. Still Leonora wrote to America in her old lighthearted tones, rattling on about Vittorio's success in school and the petty gossip of San Lorenzo, which scarcely altered from year to year. Francesco replied, explaining his brick pointing method, and although she saw that it meant wealth, she understood little else. She could never picture her baby brother commanding workmen, no matter how often she tried.

The ormolu Empire clock downstairs began to chime. Leonora got up, shaking the indolence from her limbs, and descended to the kitchen. None of them except Vittorio had much appetite nowadays, so she began preparing a risotto for him while boiling two plates of soup from the ever-present stockpot. As Leonora was chopping onion she heard a scratching noise come from the kitchen window. She knew it was her lover before she even glimpsed his face.

"You can't come in, Achille," she said through the half-open window. "My mother—"

"Damn your mother. I walked all the way from the train."

"Later," she replied weakly. "Wait an hour or two."

For answer he forced open the kitchen door. Leonora recoiled a little and he stepped forward, encircling her in his arms. He kissed her, a long fervent kiss that would have lasted all eternity had she not pulled away.

"Why did you come? Why couldn't you wait, as you said you would?"

"You know why." He tightened his arms around her waist. "I can't wait forever."

"We just buried my father, Achille. It is impossible."

"Still the little convent girl?" Lampa smiled ironically. "I want you to marry me, darling. I want us never to be apart."

"But how will we live?" she almost wailed. "And how can I leave my mother now?"

"You want to be her kitchen maid all your life? Because she'll never let you go."

"Oh, Achille," she murmured. "You know I want that too, only I can't . . . ."

"The train for Naples leaves in three hours. If you aren't with me, you'll never see me again."

They glared at each other like enemies. The soup was boiling over and Leonora turned aside to tend it. She heard Lampa's footsteps recede, and his whistle. She recognized the tune, a tenor aria from Puccini he adored. *And the stars were shining . . . .* it had always been his message of love for her, and with a sob she heard his whistling, too, disappear.

Father Ugo was noisily devouring a steaming heap of pasta seasoned with fennel and fresh sardines. The portion, Vittorio observed bitterly, would have fed his family twice over. Some shadow of that thought must have crossed his face, because the priest offered him a plate. Vittorio shook his head.

"Of course, of course, you still mourn. Death is a comfort, but not the death of one we love."

"Why didn't the Prince have that bastard Lampa put in jail?"

The priest blinked. "Our Prince is merciful. When that fool Socialist began agitating the sharecroppers, I warned him he might end in jail. But no, the Prince said. Prisons make martyrs. Better to throw him out on his Red ass." Father Ugo laughed. A piece of pasta stuck in his throat, making him cough.

"Breathe in," Vittorio instructed. "Hold your breath, then drink some water . . . . water, not wine."

Vittorio watched the priest, wincing uncomfortably, follow his advice. After a moment Father Ugo smiled.

"I've lost my appetite," he exclaimed. "Thank you, my son. I thought I would choke to death."

Vittorio shrugged to say he would have done the same for anyone foolish enough to eat greedily. The priest poured him a glass of wine, pushing it across the snowy tablecloth.

"I spoke to Amabile," he began.

"Yes, I thought you'd know all about that," Vittorio said, to cut him off.

"Your mother is behaving shockingly," Father Ugo continued, unwilling to lose the chance to criticize one Monti to another. "You must feel yourself ill-treated. Any son would."

The priest gave Vittorio a sly, complicit look. He forced himself to smile radiantly. He swore he would, unlike his father, win this priest's favor, no matter how hard he had to bite his tongue.

"What a fine young man you are, and so brilliant," Father Ugo sighed. "And what a pity you'll never make your own way in this world, as your brother has."

Vittorio took a sip of wine, forcing enough calm to ask in a level voice what the priest meant. Father Ugo sighed again, theatrically.

"Unless your mother relents you must stay here. And San Lorenzo is no place for a man of intellect."

"I will join the King's Army," Vittorio said. "I will travel, I will fight."

"Ah, the Army." The priest smiled knowingly. "But that takes cash, first to buy a commission and then to equip yourself. And you have none."

Vittorio laughed. "Why didn't you bury me next to my father while you were at it?"

"It's a pity you had no vocation for the church," Father Ugo said musingly. "You would have gone far, farther than I perhaps."

"God made me a doctor, as you know. And this is the age of science, Father, not the age of faith. We will force nature to disclose her every secret. We will cure every disease."

"You are no atheist, I hope?" Father Ugo barked. "Our beloved Pope has stated that the Church respects all science which venerates God . . . . not that infidel Darwin, of course, but I know you have not learned his heresies."

The whole world has, Vittorio thought. Soon all the priests and cardinals and that toy Pope he'd seen gesturing from his balcony would seem as silly as witches did, once people stopped believing in them. He said respectfully, "I came to seek your help, Father. I am a true son of the Church and of Italy—please, help me in my hour of despair . . . ."

"Despair is a sin against the Holy Ghost," Father Ugo replied mechanically. He took a bite of pasta, swallowing gingerly, then gazed intently at Vittorio. "Stand up, my son. Extend your arms. Come closer, my son."

When Vittorio was standing next to him Father Ugo reached out and encircled his arm with a parchment-thin hand. The priest squeezed once, and then exhaled slowly, as though he were in pain. Vittorio suppressed a grin. Men of Father Ugo's kind had made more explicit overtures, especially in the Roman streets at night. He considered them sick men whom science would someday cure, perhaps by injecting hormones into their brains. Father Ugo startled him by running his hand down Vittorio's thigh.

"A sin against the Holy Ghost," the priest repeated in a distant voice.

Vittorio sat down again. "There is something else for me here, perhaps."

The priest began eating again in earnest. "Yes, yes, and what is that?"

"Our Prince lacks a personal physician," Vittorio said carefully. "Isn't that risky at his age?"

"He is in perfect health, as the world knows," Father Ugo declared.

"With respect, Father, he suffers from angina attacks so bad that he must stay in bed for days—"

Father Ugo half-rose in rage. "Shame, shame on you for repeating servants' chatter!"

"It's true, then?"

The priest lifted his hands heavenward, a gesture somehow conveying fatalism, hope, and doubt all at once. It emboldened Vittorio enough to say:

"Then he needs me. I specialized in heart disease. I know the latest methods, the new treatments."

Father Ugo stared at him. "You have thought carefully, I see. You know what you want. But then the Montis always do—but getting it is usually too much for you."

"If you would recommend me, Father. Your word carries great weight with our Prince, I know . . . ."

"And why should I? Other than Christian charity?"

Vittorio gave the priest as abject a look as he could bring himself to feign. Oh, how I will make him pay, this pig of a cleric, how I will make them all pay, my mother for betraying me, most of all . . . . Father Ugo's features relaxed. He smiled in a rictus of glee, and proposed that Vittorio join him in a toast to the health of their great and merciful Prince. "Which you, my son, will preserve and protect, if God wills it." God, Vittorio knew, had long since abandoned San Lorenzo to His enemies. Now Father Ugo and the Prince ruled, and he must find a way to make himself indispensable to them.

NINE

Though it was a mild March night Laura insisted on wearing an ankle-length fox coat with a white mink collar, as if she felt a chill no thermometer could register. The opaque veil attached to her picture hat prevented, Francesco knew, anyone from noticing that Laura Warrington was on his arm. The veil screened her face not only from nosy strangers but from him, and he found it disconcerting to recognize his mistress only by her voice.

"And now he's cut my allowance again, the rotter, the cad . . . . he wants to blackmail me into taking him back and I won't, I won't—oh, if only I knew how to make money, if only they'd taught me something useful instead of needlepoint and how to entertain . . . . And my family, those hypocrites, they'll never stick up for me, never make Teddy do what's right . . . . God, how I hate being a woman, Frank!"

She talks far too much about herself, Francesco thought. It was like listening over and over to the strains of a music box he could neither shatter nor escape. Laura patted his cheek with a gloved hand and gave him her sad, bewitching smile. All at once something in his blood sang, the insistent chord of desire. Looking up Francesco saw that they were passing the Continental Hotel, and, over her protests, he steered Laura to the registration desk. Pocketing his bribe, the desk clerk gave them a key and suggested they dine at the Palm Room, where the dance orchestra was already tuning up discordantly. It sounded like the overture to some awful Wagner, in three dissonant chords. Francesco ignored it and led Laura to the elevator. She was wearing a look of surprise he knew masked either anger or a lust equal to his.

Their room overlooked the white electricity of Chestnut Street, where streetcars jolted up and down and the voices of pretzel vendors, piercing and hoarse, formed a strange counterpoint to their solitude.

Laura pulled the drapes instantly. She faced him with a quizzical smile which faded into a pout when he approached her, tugging off her coat and her hat so that he could see and touch her at last. They made love, not in the oversized bed rented for that, but against the mauve wall, their bodies pink and flushed atop its elaborate wallpaper of fauns and nymphs disporting in Arcadia. Francesco's passion was half anger, so that he cared little about Laura's comfort and pleasure, and thrust into her with a mechanical rhythm that made him think he was a sort of streetcar running unstoppably along her body's tracks. When his breathing grew heavier, Laura wrenched herself free and with a grin finished him with her hand, his white spray staining the Continental Hotel's wall, leaving a dribble of his posterity across the nude buttocks of one mass-production nymph.

Inevitably he felt a certain sadness after they made love, yet tonight his heart ached, he was melancholy, he felt fragile. He lay on the bed half-naked while Laura bustled into the bath to rinse her inmost parts. More and more nowadays she shattered his mood by carefully cleansing his sperm. She had announced that she hoped to buy a pessary, an illegal contraceptive device unmentionable in Society Hill or even at the Progressive Club. He wondered just what Laura sought from fucking, wondering if she knew herself.

In his darkest hours, struggling to fall asleep, he tortured himself with the thought that to Laura nothing they did meant more than the contract bridge she played with the young matrons of Washington Square. If love was merely another of her games it would extend itself indefinitely, pointlessly, perhaps forever, so long as the loser kept playing with sufficient desperation. But he did not wholly believe that, unless he had drunk himself into despair. Laura loved him enough to risk disgrace, ostracism, divorce. He knew that. That knowledge would have to satisfy him, and most of the time it did.

Now she was dressing quickly, quietly. Her brisk movements reminded him of all the hours they spent apart, all the tasks she carried out, furnishing Teddy's house, feeding the poor in her best Methodist style. Laura could function without him beautifully and did, he knew, though when he recognized her self-sufficiency it gave him a deep pang of uselessness. He wanted her to belong only to him, to live for him, and she never would, not this New Woman who read Emma Goldman and John Reed and felt herself a secret rebel against the velvet cage into which she had been pushed. Ah, how he wished he could leave her, find a more pliant woman in the streets he walked where Italian and Yiddish filled the sooty air. Francesco knew he would never leave Laura; he suspected she knew it too.

"Why don't you write that novel you were telling me about?" he surprised himself by saying as she stood before the mirror repairing the damage to her hair.

"I don't know . . . . do you think I should? A satire on this stuffy provincial town?"

"I thought of your title," Francesco said caressing her shoulders. "Nobody's Fault."

"Oh, it's a silly dream, that's all . . . . and novels don't make money nowadays."

"I'll give you my patent," he said slowly. "That keeps raking in the bucks."

"I couldn't do that," she said sounding shocked. "I'd be a kept woman."

"My friend Enrico says all wives are kept women—all bourgeois wives."

"The anarchist? Did he ever get up to Paterson?"

"Better than that. He got himself arrested . . . . suspended sentence, thank God."

"Oh, I wish I'd gone, before things quieted down. John Reed

said it was like a war." Laura looked at him with shining eyes. "He said your people are very brave."

"They have nothing to lose," Francesco told her, wishing they could talk about something more personal. "It's easy to be brave then, and foolish too."

"You're so cold," Laura murmured. "What will it take to move you, Frank, a massacre?"

"Stop it," he said, more sharply than he intended to. "You know I did what I could last year when they put those Italians on trial. I sent money to Lawrence, I did everything I could—"

"You sound guilty, Frank," Laura announced, turning to him with a superior smile.

He uttered a profane oath. "That's not an answer," she said. "Besides, I have to get to the Progressive Club any minute. Your friend Giovannitti, the hero of the Lawrence frame-up, will have plenty to say. A wonderful poet—*and* a fine figure of a man," she said teasingly.

"You don't win a strike talking to rich wives," Francesco remarked, opening the door. Laura swept past him into an elevator, and he had to run to catch it too. In the cab they sat in that awkward silence charged with negative energy, when even an innocent word might stir argument. The cab rolled through a lavender dusk, past Reading Station and around the scaffolded City Hall. Starlings chirped madly in its eaves, putting Francesco in mind of an aviary made of gloomy stone. At last they reached the Progressive Club.

Francesco started to escort Laura from the cab, but she squeezed his hand painfully hard and said, in a low voice made all the more harsh because he could not see her eyes, "Tonight you treated me like a whore. I'm going to make you pay for that, Frank."

He remembered her involuntary spasm, her languid sigh. "But you liked it."

"That's why I'm going to make you pay. You won't see me unless I send for you."

And Laura stepped swiftly onto Sansom Street, hurrying into

the safety of a brightly lit room visible through Gothic windows. Francesco watched for a moment but then, when she failed to appear, paid the driver and got out himself, determined to follow her inside. Then he heard a familiar Italian accent call out his name, and knew without turning that it was Enrico. He accepted his friend's noisy greeting with a sensation of having been rescued from something unnamable.

Refusing to answer questions, Enrico led him to the side door of a saloon so dimly lit any passer-by would think it closed. In the back of a long room sat three men, unmistakably Italian, two of them flanking the third, who gazed at Enrico and Francesco with a dreamy smile. It was Giovannitti. To Francesco's eye he resembled a musician or poet of the last century, not the dangerous agitator whose blood the papers were baying for. His long fingers swirled arabesques in the air. When Enrico made the introductions, Giovannitti's eyes were grave, even though a half-smile still lingered on his lips.

"Sit down," he said in Italian. "I take refuge here because my enemies are in the street, eager to finish the job the fine Yankee gentlemen in Lawrence botched. You don't believe me, Signor Monti? I had many letters warning me to stay out of this City of Brotherly Love." Giovannitti smiled to show he was serious. "Your city seems almost as hospitable as Paterson, where all of us sleep with one eye open, in a different bed every night."

"This isn't a bad place," Francesco said feebly.

"If we didn't need money for our strikers I'd never have come. I learned in Lawrence, Signor Monti, how dangerous Americans can be."

"Francesco gave to your defense fund," Enrico said. "And generously."

"Thank you, thank you," Giovannitti said, clapping his hands together comically. Francesco had the sense that this man was always acting a part; at any moment he would make him the straight man for a vaudeville gag. Instead Giovannitti grew serious, asking Francesco questions about himself. When he learned that he ran a brickyard he leaned forward as if stunned.

"And your business is profitable, Signor Monti, you will need more men?"

"Probably. Yes." Francesco felt baffled by this sudden interest in his business.

"Then I have men for you, good Italian men, hard workers, honest too."

At last Francesco understood. "Strikers? From Paterson?"

"They will learn your trade quickly, I'm sure."

Francesco glanced at Enrico before answering. His friend's face wore a rapt expression, as though he felt blessed by Giovannitti's presence. The other men were grinning, perhaps expecting jobs.

"With respect, Signor Giovannitti, your men are not skilled bricklayers. They worked in a silk factory, so . . . ." Francesco indicated his helplessness.

Giovannitti scowled. "You are refusing to help my men?"

"Not at all." Francesco removed his checkbook from an inside pocket. "I can support your strike with money; it's only right. We Italians have only each other—"

"Money." Giovannitti sighed deeply. "This strike could last until the summer. It's a miracle my men and women haven't surrendered yet. They are heroes, Signor Monti! They are placing their bodies on the machine, on the vile American machine, and they are saying no—no to the hectic glow of this world which loves only cash."

"Heroes and heroines have to eat," Francesco said lightly. "I can give you five hundred now and the same every month the strike goes on. As far as the hectic glow, I don't think Walt Whitman would consider the I.W.W. a solution."

"The I.W.W. will win," Giovannitti shot back. "History is marching down our path. Nobody can defeat us now, if we don't lose faith."

"Five hundred dollars, Signor Giovannitti. To keep your troops fed on your glory road."

Suddenly Giovannitti guffawed like an American. "Of course I'll take your money—I may be a poet but I'm practical too." He reached for Francesco's hand and pumped it effusively. "You're a young man, Signor Monti. You must be very ambitious man to win such fortune at your age, eh? And of course you want to go farther, like any good American?"

"If I can," Francesco said carefully. "I came here to support my family when I was a boy, and since then I've been—"

"Lucky, were you going to say?" Giovannitti released Francesco's hand. "There is no such think as luck. A peasant superstition, nothing more. But certainly there is fate, *Il destino.* Some men have a destiny, Signor Monti, and perhaps you are one."

Enrico said excitedly, "He's the child of fortune, our Francesco, money sticks to his fingers. Another J.P. Morgan . . . ." Giovannitti talked over him:

"When I was sitting in that jail up in Lawrence, when it looked as though the State of Massachusetts was going to murder me legally and judicially, I said to myself, Arturo, *you* must seize your fate. You must seize your destiny, I told myself. And I did. I organized a public campaign that reached all the way to the King of Italy! Millions of ordinary people rose up and said, no! You must not murder this man and his associates! And I wrote that poem, the one they compare to Oscar Wilde's, and so, Francesco, I grasped my fate with both hands, I spoke to that jury of one hundred percent Americans—and here I am. Alive." Giovannitti gave them his most dazzling smile. Francesco felt the electric jolt of a personality stronger than his own.

"You were brave," he murmured reluctantly.

"And you were brave too—coming to this mad country alone, a little boy, with no English and no friends. Was that not courage, my friends?" The other men grunted assent.

Now Francesco glimpsed the other's purpose. "If you're trying to change my mind about hiring your men—"

Giovannitti waved disdainfully. "Not at all, not at all. But perhaps you could increase your contribution to our strike fund?"

"I will give you what I said, no more, no less." Francesco tried to sound firm.

"Spoken like a capitalist." Giovannitti grinned wolfishly. "I hope, Signor Monti, that you will remember that we are your brothers and sisters, not men you do business with."

"I have a family of flesh and blood," Francesco replied. "The rest is sentimental shit, politics. You said that two weeks ago, didn't you, Arturo?"

"Let me tell you about America, Signor Monti. I have lived here longer and, of course, I have been a prisoner in its highly democratic jails. This is a nation that thrives on the blood of men like you. Young, ambitious blood. To keep the wheels of its machinery greased. Which leaves a man like *you* with a choice." Giovannitti paused for dramatic effect. "You can become an American. Or you can remain a human being."

Francesco wanted to laugh into Giovannitti's face. Impatiently he scribbled a check and handed it to Giovannitti, who stuffed it into a side pocket and rose to leave. His men filed downstairs after him, leaving Francesco needing something, he didn't know quite what. First Laura had rejected him and now this unsatisfactory scene, both leaving him feeling hollow, uncentered, without a self.

He stood drinking straight whisky at the saloon counter, paying triple since Pennsylvania blue laws didn't allow that on a Sunday night, until he felt the whirl of thoughts and images, his brain's magic lantern show, slow down. Without thinking Francesco walked back to the Progressive Club.

He stood outside, his nose pressed to the window of that bright, high-ceilinged room where Giovannitti stood addressing those one hundred percent Americans from a high lectern. Francesco tried to find Laura's face in the blurred oval of attentive faces and could not.

With an involuntary, groan he sank into a horse cab, thinking bitterly, I never should have come here, I never should have left San Lorenzo, those two painful thoughts alternating until he reached his neighborhood. A police barrier reminded him that the festa was still taking place, how stupid of him to have forget, and he would have turned on his heel to leave except that he was finally, unavoidably home.

The procession must have ended some time ago. The statue

of the Madonna stood in front of St. Nicholas' Church, guarded by the vestrymen who'd carried it. The Madonna's body was covered with dollar bills pinned to it while it travelled through the streets. Francesco found these rituals tasteless, contriving when possible to avoid the monstrous sight of his fellow countrymen and their piety. Now he walked past the statue, wondering what Giovannitti would have said to inspire these sons of Mother Church to seek salvation in this world instead. Francesco still felt the whiskey humming in his nerves, but not enough, so he bought a bottle of homemade wine from the grocer before going home. It was that rare night when he wanted to drown his consciousness in one hundred percent American style.

That year he occupied the upper two floors of a house Carney found for him at a sheriff's sale. He rented out the undesirable downstairs to Calabrians whose child had the croup and sometimes screamed himself to sleep. Even while he cursed the noise Francesco felt a certain tenderness for the miserable infant, accompanied by a twinge of shame when he thought of what Laura had said to him not long after their affair began.

They had just made love and she sat up, brushing her hair quickly, impatiently. What's the matter, he asked, are we going out?

There's something you ought to know, Laura said, glancing into his eyes and then away. If you ever give me a baby I'll have it taken care of. I want you to know that.

At first he didn't understand. And then when he did he felt too stunned to register the insult to himself. How can you say that, Laura?

It's what I want, she answered in her chilliest tone, still evading his eyes. And you shouldn't act surprised, I never said I wanted to marry you.

Is it because of me?

It's because of *me*, she said, her voice softening a little.

He had admitted this American bitch into his life and she had overturned it, capsized it, as if he were her mortal enemy and not her "beloved Frank," as though they were fighting a terrible battle that could end only with death or flight.

In some way he had never quite defined, perhaps never wanted to, he saw Laura as America, *his* America. Walt Whitman said America was himself, but Francesco lacked that majestic arrogance. No, Laura was the nation he lived in, she was the source of Whitman's hectic glow, or perhaps she was the glow itself. And he could never possess her, any more than he could possess this vast indifferent land, never marry her and never give her a child. And he admitted at times like this that so long as he loved her he lost San Lorenzo, would always lose it if he yearned for any connection deeper than what they already had.

Laura could break his heart as casually as this country would. She could dissolve the man Francesco hoped and believed himself to be, so that by loving her, he was doomed to lose himself. Francesco knew all this and told himself he did not. Sober in the daytime, his self delusion often succeeded. But when night came, and he was alone, he sometimes felt an indescribable fear, like the boy in the Calabrian fairy tale who lost his own shadow.

Then who am I, he wondered? The avid young immigrant who piles dollar upon dollar, the dutiful son who sends those dollars home to the family who sentenced me to this fate, or the baffled lover of Laura Warrington, my sweet prison, my proxy America? I drift, he told himself, like a little boat bobbing along great waves and hoping for safety, hoping not to drown. A man should be in charge of his life, in command of it, and am I in command of mine? In daylight, yes, at Carney's brickyard and in the streets where strangers knew his name, and yet at night, in Laura's arms, he became as helpless as the sick infant downstairs. He bawled for her attention, and sometimes she even granted it. She has unmanned me, he thought: she has made me a man and less than a man.

The electric light discolored a row of family photographs. Already he was forgetting the voices of those he loved, those he had left behind. His memories, his dreams were straying farther and farther from Italy, becoming almost absurd, almost American.

Even so, to recall San Lorenzo Francesco had only to shut his eyes. He could hear those cracked church bells, smell that ocean-sour air, only now when he returned in his mind, he felt a sadness potent enough to ache his heart. And he felt an exile, and remembered Dante's sad lines about the exiled heart.

Yet he knew that he would some day return, though not permanently as so many of his fellow countrymen were scheming to do. How petty and mean that seemed to Francesco, acting as if America had less claim on one's heart than Italy and so could be abandoned like some drunken sailor whose pocket you'd picked . . . . ah, Laura, Laura, when you let me go I'll know who I am again, Francesco said aloud, startling himself.

He snapped off the light and finished the heavy, sweet wine in the dark, emptying his heart of its turbulence until only the image of her face—delicate and disdainful—remained to trouble him. Then sleep, blessed sleep, transported him out of America and Italy both.

TEN

"**Call** me Abe," said the balding little man, extending his hand toward Francesco and Carney. His lips smiled but the cold eyes behind his pince-nez kept measuring them. "Anyone calls me Mister Greenglass, it's either a rabbi or a bank president," he continued in a genial tone. The men shook Abner Greenglass' hand and sat in the deep leather armchairs opposite his antique desk. "You've got a funny look on your face, Mister Carney—somethin' eating you?"

"I never shook hands with thirty million bucks before," Carney replied. "I was hopin' some of your luck would rub off."

"No such thing as luck," Abner Greenglass barked. "There's opportunity and there's brains. And when they meet ignorant people call it luck. Now take you, Mister Monti."

Francesco gave him his self-deprecating immigrant's smile. Calabria had taught him that the gods punished the proud, and so he pretended to be unimpressed by his own success. Abner Greenglass offered a brief sketch of Francesco's career, ending with the observation that he'd done pretty well for a man without connections.

"But connections," he told them, "are everything in Philadelphia. It's not what you know, it's *who* you know. You're either on the inside looking out or on the outside looking in. And you two are still on the outside, am I right?"

"Compared to you practically everybody is," Carney replied. Greenglass smiled again, then grew thoughtful. He swiveled his chair to glance out the enormous window. Sunlight was bursting through a gray sky departing rain clouds had left behind. From this height, Broad Street and the city below looked as frenzied as an anthill.

"Look down there," he instructed them. "There's only two kinds of men in this world: players and spectators. Players make things happen and spectators watch, simple as that. You two are small-time players, very small-time. But you have one big-time advantage."

"My brick-pointing process," Francesco said.

Greenglass sat forward in startled response. "How did you know I meant that?"

"You researched me, I researched you. In 1908 you started investing in West Philadelphia. Mostly residential. You've been waiting for the right time to sell your properties and you think this is it. Only they look like hell. The brickwork especially. Which is where my process comes in."

Greenglass sighed. "Sometimes I forget I'm not the only smart man in this town. Yes, I want your process. I'll buy it outright. I'm offering ten thousand dollars. Cash." He smiled thinly. "Which is the best way to do business nowadays with Uncle Sam breathing down our necks."

"You're a Republican all right." Carney grinned. Both men watched Francesco for his response. He sat deliberating, absolutely still, expressionless. Finally he said: "You can have it for nothing."

Greenglass and Carney both erupted into passionate, puzzled speech. He gestured for silence. "For nothing, on condition that Carney and Monti does all the work and for our usual price. Plus ten percent of the resale."

Greenglass' mouth puckered as though he had bitten a lemon. "There's nothing to stop me from stealing your process, you know," he said threateningly.

Francesco smiled. "Sure there is. I applied for the patent on it this morning."

"Good boy, Frank!" Carney slapped him on the back. Both men faced Greenglass triumphantly, though they'd won nothing from him yet. He drummed his fingers irritably on the desk as though that might conjure a solution from its ornate depths.

"We have a deal," Abner Greenglass said as though the words offended him.

"While we're at it, I'd like to invest in some of that property myself."

"The smallest parcel," Greenglass replied coldly to Francesco, "costs five thousand. Expected return, four to five hundred percent profit."

Francesco nodded, smiling, thinking how different his life would be if he had the five thousand. Abner Greenglass made money for everyone who invested with him. It was the source of his reputation, the fount of his power, of his "connections." How often he listened to Carney denounce Greenglass and all the Jews for their clannish ways, for making money just a little too fast for his Irish taste. And then, confronted with the enemy himself, Carney toadied, the way people in San Lorenzo used to act towards the Prince. All sorts of power resembled each other, Francesco thought, at least in their effect on the powerless. Though this reflection pleased him, his lack of the needed cash rankled when he and Carney rode Greenglass' private elevator to the street.

"I thought you were givin' away the store, Frank," Carney exclaimed, bustling him into the sun-splattered air. "Thank God you didn't. It's a wonder you can put on your drawers without losin' your dick."

"We'll make a fortune with Greenglass," Francesco said, in a mild voice.

"Ah, but that's only me business, Frank, not my heart. Politics, Frank, now . . ."

"Politics won't feed your men. Greenglass will."

"Will ye listen to me? Now you know I been anglin' for the ward leader job and many's the year, too. Well . . . . I been promised it. What d'ye think of that?"

Over beer and pig's feet Carney excitedly explained. His gift of clubhouses to the Democratic Party had finally paid off "in spades redoubled." As Boss Greer always said, the Irish were born to rule, politics flowed in their veins, and soon enough, pray Christ, all City Hall would fall into their hands. He, Carney, was rising because he had spunk enough to help Boss Greer, and best of all he'd done it on the strict up and up. Once he became ward leader for Schuylkill, Carney aimed to outdo his colleagues who handed out Thanksgiving turkeys, Christmas hams. Carney planned to give every man old enough to vote the straight Democratic ticket all the bricks and mortar he desired.

Francesco laughed. "You'll ruin yourself, Carney. And anyway, half those bricks belong to me."

"But that's the beauty of it. We'll be partners all the way, Frank—better than wastin' money on that sheeny and his fucked-up schemes, I swear. Now I've spoken to Boss Greer about you and he sees you're the comin' man among the Eyetalians. His idea is you should build up a little machine, a local one, see, from the Jews and Eyetalians in your ward. Especially the ones that don't speak the language yet; they don't vote regular. You do that, Frank, and before long you and me will both be ward leaders. What do you say?"

"I don't like making trouble in my neighborhood," Francesco demurred.

"You don't have to. Be a friend to everyone. Hand out cheap cigars if the fancy takes you. But help them all get naturalized. It'll be grand. Thank God we got a Democrat in the White House, there'll be patronage finally—even a Princeton professor knows that much. Why, his top man Tumulty is an Irishman like me!"

Francesco frowned. "Why should I bother? I'm busy enough, as it is—"

"Think of the future, Frank. Someday we'll be callin' the shots, God grant me breath and life to see the day. These Republican shitheels will all die off, and then who'll have the clout? Opportunity knocks once and when she does you have to grab her with both fuckin' hands." Carney paused. "Besides, I *need* you, Frank. Us Irish are too weak alone, we'll lose a straight fight without your people and the Jews. Together we can run this town, maybe run the fuckin' country someday too."

"But they're talking about keeping Italian immigrants out. What's your President Wilson going to do for us?"

"He knows his duty, Frank. He's got 1916 to think of and maybe, just maybe, 1920 too." Carney paused, studying Francesco's face. "Now, you could find jobs at the Navy Yard for your Italian mechanics. I got the OK from Greer to promise you that."

"I'm twenty-three." Francesco hesitated. "You think I have what it takes?"

Carney knew he'd made a sale. He grinned, "Teddy Roosevelt got famous for riding up some goddamn hill. You think he was smarter than you are? All Teddy had was that fuckin' horse."

Despite the August heat Francesco decided to walk home, refusing Carney's invitation to a home-cooked meal, more talk of politics. It was Friday. The streets bustled with chattering girls who avoided his eyes, blushing as they passed. In the humid heat every building seemed coated with sooty light. Francesco tried to imagine what his life might be with a wife and a child, but failed. Worse, if he thought of San Lorenzo his spirits sank. There he had known who he was. In this city he had become, he sometimes thought, too many things too fast. His selves did not contradict each other so much as they failed to touch. His days consisted of work, Laura, and the dreams sleep brought. He dreamed of San Lorenzo, and on those mornings he woke up dispirited.

Now that Teddy had cut off support, he had become Laura's protector. Her family sent hardly enough to pay the servants, showing, as Laura bitterly said, tacit hope that husband and wife would end their "scandalous" breach.

Francesco reflected that so far his dollars had bought him little more than the use of the front door. She still preferred not to appear with him publicly, except at political meetings where their presence together could be explained. When you are in love, she liked to say, you thrive, on difficult circumstance. And so he did. That was the dream, that the Laura in his arms would be his eternally, a dream they conjured up together if not perhaps in precisely the same way. Francesco gave her pleasure, he know, she said so, the pleasure every woman craved, and yet when they lay panting side by side he felt their joy evaporate like steam on a windowpane. She loved him, or so she said, but what was it worth to be loved like that, without a future and without a past, loving only the hour their bodies were locked in that combat, that caress? How alone he felt at night, leaving Delancey Street since he preferred not to skulk out at dawn, how solitary he became once he shut her door and entered that other world, the world he inhabited alone.

She was waiting for him in the twilight, a pitcher of iced tea the only sign that she expected company. Francesco told her of Carney's plan, as by now he told her nearly everything that might appall or amuse her.

Listening, Laura smiled distantly. "You won't do it, will you?"

"Not now." Francesco added, "I won't let you down. You know that."

"You'll be letting yourself down, darling. Boss Greer is an awful man."

"Not like President Wilson, you mean?" He liked to tease Laura for her Presidential passion. Wilson had occupied the White House nearly two years and to Francesco's eye had done no more than pontificate, reminding him of a taller and thinner Father Ugo.

Don't, Frank. And don't talk like that tonight at the Progressive Club."

He made a face. "Are we supposed to go? Don't Progressives take summer vacation?"

"There's trouble in Europe and we're to hear a talk," Laura replied frigidly.

"I saw the papers. Nothing more serious than usual, dear— not worth a trip to Rittenhouse Square."

"Jack Reed will be there," she said angrily. "You don't have to come since you already know all about him from the yellow press your Eyetalians read."

He stared at her, trying not to lose his temper. How often

she had used that haughty tone before. "What's bothering you? Is it your, what do you call it, your *curse*?"

"No, it is *not*," she answered, each word a hard pebble flung at his head.

"Then let's drink some of your good iced tea and pretend we never said any of this shit."

"We aren't going on holiday, Frank." Laura's face tightened. "I know you wanted to, and it might have been fun, but we simply can't."

"Holiday? I said that only once last week. But if you can't go . . . ."

"I can't." She paused. Suddenly her features softened. "My parents have written, Frank. They want me home in Connecticut for a month or two."

"No, they want you to take Teddy back, and now . . . ."

"Regardless," she interrupted, "I have no choice. I can't quarrel with everyone, can I. And I can't let you pay my way from now on. If I play my cards right Father will give me funds."

Francesco stared at her. "You had this all planned, didn't you?"

"You're a man, you earn your living. What can I do but compromise, a little, anyway? Besides, how long can I count on *you* to stand by me, Frank? Would *you* marry me?"

"Laura," he said, shocked, stunned. "Don't you love me even a little bit?"

"That isn't the point," she said impatiently.

He wanted to slap her, shout at her, make her moan. Francesco tugged at her dress and at first she resisted. Then she began gravely, silently, to strip. He pulled off his own clothes and stood naked before her in the fading light. Laura closed the curtains and they faced each other, beginning to kiss, to clutch, to couple in the only way possible for them, with all the heat and impermanence of a guttering flame.

"Oh God how I love you," she said, trembling in his arms. "Don't you know that, Frank?"

"Then don't go tonight. Stay here with me."

She sat up, brushing her hair back from her flushed face. "I wish I could, darling, you know I do . . . ."

Francesco's thoughts were racing almost as wildly as at the moment of orgasm. He seized one, examined it briefly, held it out to her, a playing card . . . .

"Atlantic City?" she cried. "How?"

"The trains leave all night. We just go. *Tonight*, Laura." He grinned. "Your penance for Connecticut."

"Idiot!" She tried to look stern, and failed, helplessly beginning to laugh. They both giggled like children, Laura collapsing onto Francesco's naked chest in mirth.

"All right," she gasped. "But what about the Progressive Club?"

Francesco made a rude gesture. Laura laughed again and stood up. She turned on the gaslight to arrange her hair at the Tiffany mirror. "It'll take me a little while to pack," she said, not turning around. "Why don't you meet me at the train? In an hour?"

"Two hours," Francesco said lazily, beginning to dress. "I have to stop by the brickyard."

Laura groaned. "I pray we don't see anyone I know."

"Your friends are too rich to take the train."

"No," she grinned. "They'll all be at the Progressive Club."

"Thank God for the Progressive Club," Francesco smiled.

He kissed Laura goodbye and skipped down her stairs gaily, three steps at a time. On Spruce Street he hailed a hansom cab and told the driver to take him to Carney and Monti's fast, then wait while he went inside.

Francesco's sole indulgence was his flat, built next to his office, where a Murphy bed folded down from his wall and freshly pressed clothes hung in a lacquered chest. He packed quickly, tossing articles into a gladstone bag, picturing Laura radiant by the sea. The sound of footsteps approaching froze him suddenly. He took out a derringer from his chest, wondering if he'd forgotten to lock the brickyard gate.

"Put your toy gun away, wop." The deep American voice was just behind him. Francesco turned to face a tall man, beefily built, standing in the office door. "This isn't one of your dago brawls. Besides, I've got one too." The man displayed a long-barreled revolver he held awkwardly.

"I have a cab waiting," Francesco heard himself say. What an imbecile I am, he thought.

"Not now you don't." The man smiled. "Still don't know who I am?"

Francesco shook his head. Names he forgot, sometimes, faces never. Could this be one of Carney's enemies?

"Theodore Warrington, at your service," the man said sardonically. When Francesco studied his face he saw a coarsened, thickened version of the single photograph Laura had so reluctantly let him see. "Laura's husband, in case you've forgotten who I am . . . ."

"Why did you come here? Your wife isn't here."

"Oh, I know where she is." Warrington nodded sagely. "And I know where you're going, tonight, like a pair of fucking animals . . . ."

"You can't stop her," Francesco said, more bravely than he felt. "Or me."

"I can't?" Warrington approached him and he drew back. "Relax, son, I'm not here to hurt you. If I wanted that you'd have been dead long ago. But get rid of you, oh yes, I can and I will. By God I will! Laura's maid's given us evidence enough, but not quite what I need for a divorce. Go to Atlantic City, though—" he chuckled, "and I'll have detectives get me pictures even a whore wouldn't show her customers. And I'll divorce Laura quicker than the wind from a duck's ass." He chuckled again.

"You'd do that to your wife?"

"It's no worse than what she's done to me—you and her both, you little wop."

"How did you know about our trip?"

"Hire a servant and you hire a spy. Now what do you intend to do, greaseball?"

Warrington must have talked to her, Francesco thought. She was never going to Connecticut, I should have smelled something phony about that tale. Women lied as easily as men drew breath . . . . but if Warrington had Laura by the throat, why did he need him now?

"I don't want a divorce," Warrington said. Abruptly he belched. Drunk, Francesco thought, or halfway there. "I want Laura back. The way we were before."

"Including the horsewhip?"

Warrington laughed. "With her imagination she ought to write dime novels. Laura doesn't want a child, Monti, that was always the real problem. Too bad she lied to you, but there it is. She's a little loony, but she's mine, wop, mine . . . ."

Against his will Francesco found himself half-pitying this drunken child. One hundred percent Americans never became men, stumbling from immaturity to old age. He and Enrico often spoke of it.

"You spoke to her?"

Warrington nodded. His hands trembled uncontrollably.

"And she'll take you back?"

"That's about the size of it. After tonight you two are going to be strangers. Not even strangers, because I'm taking Laura to Africa."

"Then why bother me?" Francesco was confused.

"Because we can't stay away forever. Call it a down payment against our marriage. Call it whatever the hell you want."

"I don't need your goddamn money," Francesco said quickly.

"Everyone needs money, son. This is America. I've checked around and your money's tied up in this brick shithouse, so take my cash and say thank you very much, sir."

Warrington casually tossed Francesco a roll of bills.

"Five thousand smackaroos," Warrington said. "Isn't she worth that much to you?" he added jeeringly.

Francesco held the money, afraid to look at it. Warrington laughed, an ugly laugh.

"She gave me a letter," Warrington added. "Maybe it'll help you understand."

My dear, I want you to see I had no choice and please, please don't hate me, I cannot be your wife ever, alas, you know it's true, and what kind of life could we have loving each other on the sly? You would end up hating me if we went on like that. Teddy and I are leaving, I'm sure he told you. Maybe we'll come back, probably not, it's all indefinite. I say this not to hurt you but so you'll get on with your life, make a real success for yourself without me holding you back as we both know deep down I would. So, my darling, become rich, become a great man if you can, and forget you ever knew me.

There was no signature except the scent of violets.

By the time he looked up Warrington had disappeared. Something raged in Francesco's heart, some helpless protest. Only bad operas ended so stupidly, not life, not his life, ... Stupefied, he pulled out the Murphy bed and lay down on its camphor-smelling sheets. He closed his eyes and Laura's face, Laura's body, her secret places, danced drunkenly, broken shards of time, of love, danced in his mind.

Never to touch them again, touch her, kiss her, was it possible? Francesco felt a great woe contract his chest and suddenly stood up. He thrust Warrington's money into the bedroom safe, averting his eyes as he did. Then he left the brickyard, locking up mechanically, beginning to walk cross-town in the darkening August night. The sounds of the city never reached his ears.

Francesco must have walked for hours, circling Delancey Street without daring a closer look, seeing nothing but the figures in his mind, until at last he reached the red light district, Spruce Street, its smell of cheap perfume and opium; they forced him back to consciousness.

Francesco looked at the painted ladies and told himself: you're no better, the only difference is your price. He found the thought so painful that he tried to laugh.

He laughed so wildly that the girl watching him from above decided he was drunk enough to roll. She signaled the doorkeeper. Francesco entered the whorehouse like a vaudeville clown making a surprise entrance. He entered a mauve parlor where a player piano was tinkling gaily. Drunken men in suspenders turned tipsy faces to him the way sick plants tilt toward the light. "There's

going to be a hot time in the old town tonight," a girl sang
somewhere, out of sight, in a sweet, flat voice. My God, Francesco
thought, how long it took to discover America.

PART TWO

ONE

Sundays, Leonora worked a half day at the munitions factory. Her day of rest coincided, by tacit entente, with Lampa's day at Socialist headquarters, so that the two encountered only each other when exhausted. Lampa, too, worked in the munitions factory, a floor boss in charge of a hundred women and the few men who, like him, avoided the war in exchange for Industrial Service To The State. And by late summer 1917 the State lay bleeding, as pitifully wounded as any soldier left to die on the retreat from Caporetto. All that inspired Lampa, all that gave him hope, was the Russian Revolution, now lurching toward the Bolsheviks' triumph. Leonora found it hard to care about such distant events, imagining sometimes when she read the papers that they were fictional. Her own life—their life together—was difficult enough; she tried not to think about it so that fear wouldn't paralyze her utterly.

Turin, alas, still seemed foreign, forbidding. The natives spoke a dialect resembling French, so her Calabrian accent made her sound a peasant and a fool. And then the dark, dense streets, lined with buildings too tall for them, dead-ending in the infernally noisy, infernally dark factory yards, these streets would never feel like home, she knew. Leonora still dreamed of San Lorenzo, of its brightest, most sparkling days, and when she did she could smell the lemon trees, the Adriatic on the breeze. True, she'd left home before, yet Turin frightened her more than Rome ever had;

it felt so modern, so brutally functional, so entirely dedicated to practical ugliness. Turin entered the twentieth century willingly, greedily, and that made her wonder whether she would ever feel at home in her time. Its Duomo, at least, belonged to an earlier age, and when she prayed there, she felt consoled by Baroque excess, enough to hope God would overlook what she and Lampa were doing: out of principle (his), they remained stubbornly unwed.

Leonora had too much pride to beg Lampa for marriage and he, having decided the issue, never reconsidered it. Their Socialist comrades echoed talk against bourgeois morals, all except Comrade Gramsci. Perhaps that was why Leonora liked him best. Certainly not his manner, unemotional, at times severe, nor his looks: he had a hunchback and seemed overly conscious that he lacked Lampa's charms. Still, Gramsci spoke gently to her, and since his Sardinian accent was even thicker than her Calabrian, Leonora saw him as a fellow outsider.

She found herself quoting Comrade Gramsci in her weekly letters home. Still the dutiful daughter, Leonora never let Sunday pass without writing to her mother, though by now she considered herself enough of a Socialist that she preached the gospel beside reports of household trivia. Her mother, predictably, ignored her talk of politics. Leonora had led her to believe she was married and so she asked incessantly why her daughter was working and not bearing a child. Answering these impatient questions required all Leonora's ingenuity. She doubted she could ever return to San Lorenzo; it would be far harder to sustain the lie in person. The dutiful daughter, she thought ruefully, had become a hardened liar, and for the best of reasons.

On Sunday nights, laying down her pen, Leonora found herself wondering at the strangeness of her life. She, who feared nothing would ever happen to her if she returned to San Lorenzo, was living out a romantic adventure! Not that there was anything glamorous about assembling shell casings in a munitions factory, or boiling dried beans on a coal stove, but when she compared her life to what it might have been—bitter spinsterhood under her mother's scrutiny—she felt a thrill of release, like a convict who has escaped the prison where he expected to die. And the Socialism they all lived and breathed thrilled Leonora too. If Russia could build an earthly Paradise then so could Italy. The war would destroy all unjust authority, even their King with his silly calf's eyes and his corrupt ministers.

And yet she wondered, what would it truly change, this revolution that Lampa and Gramsci preached? These same satanic mills would roar and belch, these same workers would shuffle out when the whistles blew, all in the same deathlike trance, except now they would own their own torture instruments. Was that progress? Some nights Leonora dreamed an explosion so vast it levelled Turin, leaving the factories a rubble of broken glass and steel, and after such dreams she woke happy. That would be true revolution, Leonora told herself, almost afraid of the thought. We must destroy this iron cage and then build something better, something more humane.

But destruction proved far pleasanter to admire in theory than in fact. All summer long Turin was growing tense, a violin played pizzicato so long the sound unnerved her ear. The fall of the hated Czar intoxicated the factory hands, so that Lampa spent the hot nights cooling their hopes, while the soldiers arrogantly patrolling the streets offered an enemy more hateful even than the shopkeepers who, overnight, had no bread to sell.

One August morning Leonora and Lampa woke early, uncertain whether they had heard the sound of gunfire. Why today of all days, Lampa said, listening to scattered bursts from the center of town. Ignoring Leonora's pleas to wait until the shooting stopped, he hurried out; in a frenzy she dressed and followed as quickly as she could. She trailed a hundred yards behind until she lost sight of him at Piazza Cavour.

The streets were impassable, thanks to grim-faced workers dragging fallen trees and derailed streetcars into the crosswalks. They dug in behind these makeshift barricades, occasionally firing at troops who tried to pass. Both sides fought dreamily, like bored children killing time, until the workers surged over their barricades to smash store windows, dancing on broken glass, stuffing their rucksacks with cheap wine. Others were overturning cars, setting them on fire, rolling them downhill to disperse the cavalry who sat waiting, sabers drawn, until the flaming wrecks forced them back.

With a sickening certainty Leonora knew Lampa was going to die. She saw herself alone in this city she hated, this city now plunging gleefully into civil war. Suddenly the cavalry regrouped and, leaping over the burning cars, charged up the narrow streets. The horses' hooves clattered like doom as they broke through the barricades. The few workers with guns fired so ineptly that they missed the troops, who slashed through them, sabers bright with Socialist blood. Leonora thought she would faint when she saw a lancer hack a worker down, hearing his scream and seeing his arm fly off like a broken doll's. Desperate to find Lampa, she ran blindly on.

One man was looting a pet shop, killing caged cats and birds with a pocketknife. The creatures' cries froze Leonora as she passed. Their killer seemed scarcely human himself, as though some witch had given him a pig's eyes and jowls. With blind fury he stared at Leonora for a moment. Too stunned to speak, she wrung her hands imploringly. He ignored her and began slashing at a cockatoo.

Following behind the shots, Leonora rounded a corner, and nearly collided with Lampa. Blood ran down his forehead from what she thanked God was a superficial wound. He shouted at a crowd to disperse before the Army arrived. "You are defying Party discipline," he kept repeating in his grandest voice. "You will accomplish nothing except give our enemies an excuse to proclaim martial law." One of the men spat into Lampa's eye. He flinched, but wiped the spittle away patiently with his sleeve while continuing to plead for retreat.

The men turned back to the task of massing streetcars into a barricade. "Listen to that," Lampa exclaimed, when a fusillade erupted in the next street. He cried out to the men that the Army would gun them down, this wasn't Russia, the King's soldiers were well armed . . . . they shot him looks and gestures of contempt. "Come, come, my love," said Leonora, leading him away. "You can do nothing with these fools." She started to tell him about the man slaughtering pets but Lampa's eyes were faraway, gauging the distance of the machine guns.

Leonora and Lampa searched the barricades for their comrades and, finding almost none, looked instead for Gramsci and the Socialists in authority. All the while Leonora reflected that she had seen for the first time history, if not History, men making their destiny under conditions not of their choice yet making it, however foolishly, even suicidally. For by midday the soldiers were sweeping aside the piled-up streetcars, chaining the rebels by their feet, shooting those who continued to resist. History meant chaos, disorder, everything the books and the Socialists pretended would not float in the wake of even the smallest wave. All her life, Leonora had thought of herself as too far from the crest of the wave to witness it, as though history took place forever elsewhere, forever distant from her daily pettiness. Now it had arrived like a cold wind in her face.

Three months later the true revolution seized Russia, Lenin's lightning bolt startling all of them except Gramsci. "What intelligent eyes," he murmured as they all watched the newsreels, smoking and talking. Suddenly the war in the East was over and the hated Germans looked ready to chase the Western Powers into the sea. Only Gramsci, serene, hunchbacked, welcomed the rout. "There will be two, three, five workers' revolutions before the snow. Lenin has lit the fuse now, and now—" Now millions of men were deserting, millions more were ready to lay down their arms, and even if the Germans won they would find a Europe whipped into the anarchy of despair. How quickly, she thought, the impossible becomes yesterday's news. How quickly we accept a new map of the world, a new constellation by which to steer. And yet the year ended without revolts, with the Western armies holding fast. In Turin the sullen workers punched out shells for troops who perversely would not desert. The newsreels stopped

showing Russia and pictured instead angels guarding the trench
lines, where even the sandbags looked ready to collapse.

But, miraculously, nothing collapsed. The fearsome Germans
were weary, too, and sank into the Somme mud seemingly
overnight. Everyone said the Americans made the miracle and
for once everyone was right. Those barbarians, unbloodied, almost
untrained, fought with a savage joy fierce enough to drive the
Germans reeling back. By the end of October even the
outnumbered Italians were driving Austria into retreat, thanks to
the evilly precise bombs their planes rained down. Italy,
spellbound, watched Austria's first defeat in fifty years. And then
peace came, though it felt more like the continent collapsing
with fatigue, with disgust at the long insanity.

Lampa began spending more nights at home or in the card
rooms, sometimes earning a week's pay at the bridge table, excited
enough when he did to tell Leonora he loved her with a heat he
hadn't shown since San Lorenzo. She spent more time at Party
headquarters than he did, now that the factory had let her go, so
that she knew the Socialists' gossip; though when she repeated it
to him he shrugged indifferently.

"Master Spirit of the Universe," Lampa would pray aloud,
sardonically, "deliver me from the petty squabbles of intellectuals
who think talk is a form of action. Their balls are dried up, their
blood runs thin. Give me a peasant who knows where to aim his
rifle any day instead . . . ."

More and more often Leonora daydreamed about her convent
years. She recalled the placid, monotonous rhythm of that life,
the days indistinguishable from one another, broken only by the
liturgical calendar of feasts and fasts. She thought too of how
she'd adored the Blessed Mother in those days, how she had prayed
to Her and not to Jesus or the saints, since she felt herself under
the Virgin's special protection. High grilles separated the nuns at
prayer from ordinary churchgoers. Occasionally some lewd man
would hiss salaciously at her, and Leonora would lift her eyes
heavenward, as Mary did during her Son's Passion. Otherwise
her world consisted of prayer, kitchen duties, school, ending each

dusk in that narrow iron bed so uncomfortable it seemed designed to torture her. And the Roman dawn, tawny yellow even in winter, awakened her with the sharp clanging of the bells, always the bells, like the voice of Mother Superior become solid brass, and when Leonora awoke she felt calm pleasure at beginning another day like all the rest. She had been happy there, or too ignorant not to be.

It was not on Sundays that Leonora thought back to those days, not even after the Armistice when she lost her extra shifts at the factory and she could lie half-awake listening to the Cathedral bells and the smaller bells echoing them through the Turin sky. Fridays, instead, left her wistful when she wandered home through streets made melancholy by winter twilight and a haze of tulle fog. She longed then for the country, for the bright San Lorenzo landscape of sea and stone. I will go back, Leonora vowed to herself, I will, even if Lampa says no. If she closed her eyes it all came back so sharply it made her wince, the razor-edged sunlight, the lemon trees, the houses unbearably white against those sun-bleached hills. She would go back, she knew. The people in Turin took her, by now, for one of them, something Leonora knew she would never be. She might learn their accent, the way they dressed, their anxious step from one ugly building to the next (even the Cathedral was ugly here) but never would she feel at home.

Lampa sensed her mood. Now that he too was working less, they began spending Saturdays in the country, or what bit of countryside the trolley line could reach. They read Leopardi aloud to one another, thrilling to "Saturday in the Village" and "To Silvia," luxuriating in their languid world-weariness. "What would Comrade Gramsci say?" Leonora teased him, and Lampa flushed like a boy eating stolen sweets. At such moments he would remember his Party chores and scribble a leader about the Versailles Peace Conference or Prime Minister Giolitti's latest crime . . . . and Leonora, watching his seriousness, wondered what had become of the laughing young man she'd loved in San Lorenzo. Was that Lampa as dead as the convent girl he had seduced? Did any trace remain of your lover once he no longer had to woo you with honeyed words?

She never asked herself that on the days Lampa packed a blanket, giving her a secret smile. They went a bit further into the countryside, searching in silence for a deserted stretch of grass or woods. When, by unspoken accord, they found one, Lampa spread the blanket carefully on the ground, and they undressed. He covered her mouth with scalding kisses. His hands caressed her breasts. Leonora was learning all the many ways she could make love to him. Sometimes she made him lie naked on his back while she licked down his body, biting his nipples, tickling his skin with her lips until she reached his manhood, when Lampa would sigh as though he were about to die. He liked her to rest her secret part on his mouth while he worried it with his tongue and teeth until she nearly swooned from the sensations he taught her to call *orgasms*. After that, they paused a moment. Leonora liked to climb astride him (the position he told her the Latin poets adored), until he moaned with pleasure, and stars burst behind her eyes, on a very good day both at the same instant.

One Friday afternoon Leonora paused in the street, hearing an unfamiliar sound, a hammering and scraping all at once. She followed it to the side courtyard of a great house. Through its half-open door she saw a woman her mother's age chiseling an angel out of sea-green stone. Leonora could tell it was an angel because it had one finished wing. The woman, tall and somehow elegant despite her dusty smock, carved angrily, as though impatient with the stone.

"Come in, then," she said, without looking up.

Embarrassed, Leonora closed the door behind her, timidly approaching the table where the angel shook under the chisel blows.

"If I am disturbing you, Madame . . . ."

"Stop chattering . . . . this work is lonely, I enjoy company." The woman glanced at Leonora. "Factory girl, eh?" Embarrassed again, Leonora nodded. "And probably a Socialist," the woman said with a grin, briskly shaving a ribbon of stone onto the floor.

"Ah, well—I am a Duchess, but as you see I too work with my hands."

Deciding not to curtsy, she introduced herself, extending her hand as a proper New Woman should. The Duchess smiled a little but kept carving.

"For my war dead," she said finally. "My brother and my son . . . . both fell at Caporetto."

"I am so sorry," Leonora gasped.

"They did their duty, I suppose," the Duchess said contemptuously. "But they died for what? Do *you* know? I ask and ask but nobody can say . . . . now the fools in Paris want territory, territory, I ask you! Little bits of land, is that worth dying for? Patriotism, they call it—my son enlisted and I wept, I wept . . . ."

All this time the Duchess carved with, if possible, greater ferocity. Leonora stood mute, uncertain how to reply.

"Perhaps you lost someone and I've offended you," the Duchess said. "But my heart is so bitter, I cannot hold my tongue. All I can do is carve these memorials. You, as a Socialist, disapprove of me?"

"No, no," Leonora stammered out. "How could I?"

"It's sad to be a woman, my dear—you'll learn that too. Because we survive. Our men die but we must go on. Yes, a bitter fate."

Nearby a churchbell tolled the hour. Leonora mumbled that she had to leave.

"Come back if you like," the Duchess said, "The Palazzo Bondini, in case you lose your way." And she bent dismissively over the stone.

I won't tell Lampa, Leonora thought, stepping into the street. He wouldn't believe me if I did. In theory Lampa and his comrades knew that aristocrats existed, as they knew of Chinamen and crocodiles, never expecting to encounter one. Aristocrats were enemies and should be treated with scorn and disdain. That was another reason not to tell: she had failed in her duty to the class struggle.

As it happened the poet D'Annunzio invaded the port of Fiume that same week, displacing all subjects lovers might discuss. Lampa admired the boldness the occupation showed, the heroism (however mad) of acting while diplomats and politicians blathered impotently. Leonora began to see why the Duchess's son and brother had marched off so happily to war. Even Lampa, who should know better, yearned for the supreme thrill battle offered men. What foolishness, she thought but did not say, what a childish way to prove you are a man. And she thought too of the Duchess's words. Thank God, Leonora told herself, I'll never have to wait for word of my man, never have to hate some unknown enemy or mourn in bitter loneliness. For if the War had made nothing certain it had at least proved that Europe couldn't afford another bloodletting. On that point even Duchesses and Socialists could agree . . . .

She wrote all that, or tried to, in her monthly letter to America. Wasn't her brother Francesco as brave, no, braver, than any soldier with a gun—leaping headfirst into this America which sounded, when she read his letters, as frightening as any battlefield? Alone, too, not flanked by comrades, not led by generals. Leonora knew she could never have done that. Why, he was still a child, really, when he left home. He'd sacrificed his youth for their family, that was the truth—something she herself had almost done, and would have if Lampa hadn't rescued her. Was it any wonder that she alone of their family properly estimated Francesco's worth?

When she tried to tell the Duchess all that, she got only a quizzical smile. "You're a believer, aren't you?" the Duchess asked. Haltingly Leonora told of her convent days and how far behind she'd left their certainties. "I've begun to doubt, too," the Duchess said confidingly. "I wake in the middle of the night and I'm cold with terror . . . . I think sometimes that God is losing the battle. That the Devil is winning, and this chaos we see everywhere is only the Devil's plan, the Devil's world."

Leonora stammered that she couldn't agree. "What else," the Duchess said passionately, "can explain this catastrophe—twenty million dead, ancient empires vanishing like smoke, mobs sacking palaces? Oh, I see Satan everywhere. And then I tell myself such thoughts are sinful, and they disappear. But look around you, my dear, and ask yourself if this is truly the world God made." The Duchess raised her chisel and began carving again, prompting Leonora to ask why she bothered with the stone angels at all. The Duchess smiled ironically. "I still believe. I have never lost my faith. I only wonder, has God abandoned us? But without despair, my dear, always without despair."

Such feelings were a luxury for the rich, thought Leonora, hurrying down the arcades of Via Roma as light drained from the smoky sky. No poor woman ever had the leisure to challenge God, let alone feel despair. Leonora laughed aloud at herself for thinking like a Socialist. That broke the rhythm of her steps, so that she stumbled and nearly fell but for the stream of women who righted her, as the wind keeps a sail aloft. They are my people, aren't they, she asked herself, only why can't I feel our kinship the way Lampa does? She must not have purged the Monti snobbery from her soul, not yet. Lampa was right: she had changed everything but her mind.

At intervals down the arcade stood crippled war veterans proudly begging their daily bread. Leonora knew them individually, just as they knew her, and greeted her as she hurried by. The only one she could not face had neither arms nor legs. He squatted on a filthy pillow, onto which passers-by tossed coins. Once Leonora had looked into his eyes, cold and ice-blue, suggesting he had some final knowledge denied to her. How can he live, she thought, if I were that wounded I'd kill myself . . . . his lips jerked into an uncanny smile, as though he could read her mind. Could suicide be a sin for a man without arms or legs? Surely God understood, she thought, remembering Christ's cry of betrayal on the Cross; if God understood he didn't sympathize, and left his only begotten son to hang bleeding as a sign that we too must suffer blindly, like animals, in a world indifferent to our pain, a world of pedestrians who hurry by without a glance.

When the arcade ended, at that dreary Piazza Castello which

fronted the gloom and soot of the railway terminus, Leonora felt her soul sink helplessly, as though she were melting into the Turin dusk. Oh, to escape, she told herself, to flee this prison of bleak streets, blank walls—how delicious, to leave without a backward glance. And then go where, demanded the sensible adult who vied for her heart with the dreamy yearning girl? Where, indeed, Leonora wondered, making her way home in a trance, remembering to buy the venison Lampa loved, since at day's end the butchers sold it for half price . . . .

"Your Duchess sounds a bit mad," Lampa said. "Imagine carving angels to honor her weakling God!"

"It's grief," Leonora replied. "Still, I see how she can believe all that, yes, and don't make fun of me. When she said it I understood her perfectly."

"Still the little convent girl, I see." Lampa was smiling, not a kindly smile. "Haven't I taught you anything, haven't you left the Dark Ages yet? I expect a titled idiot to believe fairy tales, but you—claiming to be a Socialist, saying you want what the International wants, what every thinking person wants—"

"But I do," Leonora interjected. "You know I want everything you do."

"Then understand, once and for all: *we* make this world, not her Devil and certainly not her impotent God. The Kingdom of Heaven will happen here, on this earth, or not at all. What else are we fighting for? To make a paradise on earth, man's paradise, not God's."

"But how can we live without grace? What will we live for until your Paradise is built?"

"For justice," Lampa shot back. "For a just world, where nobody needs your useless 'grace.' Which would a peasant or a worker rather have—our justice or your grace?"

"They are the same," she murmured.

"You think so? Then you don't belong with me."

"Why can't I believe in both?" she burst out vehemently. "Surely your workers and your peasants don't stop praying when they get their Party cards."

Lampa nodded, slumping in his chair. "That's what Gramsci says—though he won't dare write it in our paper. But if you're right people will never change in this stinking Italy, and they'll be no use if the Party rises up someday. We'll end up like Rosa Luxembourg did, outnumbered, slaughtered, tossed into a ditch."

"You don't mean the Socialists are planning an uprising here?" she asked, trying not to sound afraid.

"Oh, no." Lampa grinned sourly. "We talk, we argue, we debate—me most of all. But listen: the time is coming, and soon, when the factory workers will rise up with or without us. I say we organize a national strike, I say it every week, and none of them listen any more. They're my comrades, but damn them for timid sheep."

"Why haven't you told me this before?"

Lampa shrugged, that eloquently ambiguous shrug which could mean anything from *it's no use* to *what fools these mortals be*. Leonora knew he would fall silent, would clear the table with that opaque look meant to silence her. And so he did. Hours later, she was almost asleep when Lampa said very quietly, "It would be better if you were my comrade in everything." Leonora didn't know what to say. At last, in the uneasy silence, she drifted off, ignoring the hand he had placed tentatively on her breast.

TWO

Three mornings each week, Vittorio shined his Army boots. He would have shined them daily for the pleasure of recalling his life's heroic phase if it would not hasten their demise. To be pedantically precise, something Vittorio liked being except when it came to himself, they were the boots of a cavalry officer, not an infantryman: they reached thigh-high and had hobnails, the better to command a skittish horse. But, luckily, nobody in San Lorenzo, not even the ex-soldiers he led, ever mocked Vittorio's pretensions to higher rank. He loved striding through town, jodhpurs tucked into his boots, a natural aristocrat, he told himself, unlike that bloated syphilitic the Prince. But when his soldiers railed at the Prince for monopolizing the land and thus the wealth, Vittorio carefully said nothing an informer could report. All San Lorenzo knew how the Prince had built a shiny new clinic where Vittorio dispensed medicines the older folk called witchcraft—a suspicion which hindered nobody from swallowing his pills, or lining up for inoculations, injections, invasions of the flesh Father Ugo sanctioned in sermons by pointing to Jesus Christ Our Lord's medical expertise. How many village doctors had Mother Church and the town nobleman both beating the drums for them?

The recipient of their good will felt none in return. Indeed, Vittorio lost himself, between patients, in vivid daydreams of flaying Father Ugo the way his company once flayed an Austrian officer. How delicious, to remove the fat priest's skin bit by bit, to listen to him shriek. As for the Prince, Vittorio could not deny his envy for the rogue, mingled with the old resentment over his father's ruin. Age had loosened none of the Prince's grip. Forever demanding Vittorio cure the ailment both pretended wasn't syphilis, gorging all day on his favorite foods, the Prince still knew where every blade of wheat fell in San Lorenzo, and how much the soil it fell upon was worth. That bastard, Vittorio thought, will die with an abacus in his hand . . . .

Such thoughts, however, never darkened his mood when he shined his boots. Instead Vittorio recalled glorious days and nights driving the Austrians out of Italy, the mighty Hapsburg Empire shattering like old bones, like the skeleton of an extinct mastodon. And unavoidably he thought of the defeat that followed victory, that thin-lipped eunuch Woodrow Wilson piously cheating Italy of her promised spoils, so that every soldier had to ask, what did we fight for, why did so many of us die . . . . at this point the chamois cloth would be flying through Vittorio's hands, and if he was drilling his ex-soldiers that night he would drill them extra hard.

On this particular morning Vittorio's mother knocked timidly, knowing how her son loathed being interrupted during the ceremony of his boots.

"Forward," he said, using his soldier's voice.

"My son, excuse me but . . . . Father Ugo is downstairs."

"Somebody die last night?" asked Vittorio, grinning at his own joke.

"He has come to take you to the Prince . . . ."

"That's queer." Vittorio placed his boots on the chair sacred to them, then followed his mother to the drawing room. Father Ugo was sipping coffee and eyeing the furniture, probably, Vittorio thought, wondering when he could get it cheap.

"The Prince is waiting," said the priest, clattering his cup and saucer down on the table, which began to shake.

"Is something wrong?"

Father Ugo's face remained as neutral as Switzerland. "That is for the Prince to say. Not I."

Now that the Prince had no strength to conduct business downstairs, he spent untold lira transforming an upstairs room into a study vulgarly ornate. A fresco painter from Naples worked months on its trompe-l'oeil walls and the ceiling littered with blushing nudes. The Prince even installed a window, just large enough to see the sun. If meant to convince visitors of his health, it failed entirely.

Before Vittorio and the priest could speak, the Prince brought his fist down on his Empire desk.

"The scum of the earth, the scum of the goddamn earth!"

"Forgive me, Excellency, I don't understand—"

"Those pals of yours, the ones you dress up and play soldiers with—scum, all of them!" The Prince glared at Vittorio. "The war's over," he roared, "been over for years, in case you don't know—and that scum of yours dare to make trouble, dare to harass my bailiffs, and then say they answer only to you! You know, Father," he glanced sardonically toward the priest, "how many times have I said these new ideas will destroy Italy? Just look at Milan and Turin—factories calling themselves Soviets, the countryside teeming with Reds—but not here, dammit! Here I will have order, and no mistake—and no goddamn troublemakers on my land, or I'll have every shit-ass beggar of them shot—" Out of breath, the Prince slumped in his high-backed chair.

In that instant Vittorio knew why he despised the Prince and Father Ugo. They were dead, as dead as Austria, only they still had life enough to strangle him, his men, everyone in San Lorenzo. These useless old men, why didn't someone purge the town of them? They were nothing but corpses, rotting, stinking corpses . . . .

"I will look into this at once, Excellency."

"Look into it! He says he'll look into it!" The Prince's imitation of Vittorio made Father Ugo titter like a girl.

"Father, tell this young fool what you will do at Sunday Mass—"

"It is well founded in Church doctrine that civil authorities must be obeyed," the priest intoned. "These ex-soldiers risk mortal sin if they do not—"

"Mortal sin, Father?" Vittorio burst out helplessly. "Those men—like me—fought and bled for this country, and then your so-called civil authorities sold us out at Versailles! With respect, Excellency, they are not scum, they are patriots—they destroyed the Austrian Empire, the oldest in Europe, our historic foe—"

"Shall I tell you Italy's historic foe?" The Prince nearly screeched. "Our own people, dammit! Scum like your toy soldiers, that's our enemy! Illiterate, every one of them, I'll bet, no religion, no respect for law, waiting for another Garibaldi, aren't they—*that's* our enemy, our people and their endless goddamn stupidity!"

"Ignorance is not stupidity," Vittorio said, as mildly as he could.

"You told me yourself the people call you a sorcerer," Father Ugo put in.

"Because they know no better. Do your Church schools teach physics or biology?"

"You quibble like schoolboys, both of you!" The Prince gripped the carved lions' heads adorning his chair. "The fact is plain—our people are stupid, easily misled, and thus dangerous. I give you Russia as an instance of what can happen here—and will happen, Doctor, *if* authority weakens. I can't control Turin, or Milan, but I damn well control San Lorenzo. In this place, at this time, I am authority—do I make myself understood?"

"Not entirely," Vittorio said, feeling himself inching toward a precipice. "I vowed to investigate the incident—isn't that enough?"

"Away from your pills and powders you are lost," the Prince observed coldly. "Did you think me a fool like you, wearing an officer's boots and taken in by your pretense yourself?"

"You want me to disband the regiment?"

"I want you to disband the regiment," the Prince said slowly, acidly, "and I want you to turn the guilty men over for punishment."

"I will turn over men only if I am satisfied they *are* guilty," replied Vittorio, still stung by the Prince's taunt about his boots.

"You are no lawyer and certainly no judge," Father Ugo said quickly. "Let the Prince decide, he renders justice in San Lorenzo."

"The police and the prosecutor," Vittorio said, "are they no longer your civil authority? When did the Prince replace the law itself?"

"Answer me this, dear Doctor?" the Prince drawled sarcastically, "Why such loyalty to this scum? Are you fool enough to think them your equals, when you are part of San Lorenzo's upper class?"

"They are my comrades," stammered Vittorio, taken aback.

Father Ugo raised his palms heavenward, the local gesture of surprise. "But you are their leader, superior in every way. Why defend these villains so stubbornly?"

Vittorio smiled. "The priest," he quoted, "was what you found instead of what you would have wished . . . ." Father Ugo recognized the line from Manzoni's *The Betrothed* and, in spite of himself, flushed at the jest.

"You will turn the criminals over by noon or I will padlock your clinic," the Prince declared in his grandest voice.

"I will turn any *suspects*," Vittorio stressed the noun, "over to the police prefect alone."

"Then let the sick suffer for your stubbornness!"

Vittorio sketched an ironic bow before racing downstairs and into the brutal morning light. It raised his spirits that nearly everyone in the street saluted him, some of the elderly pestering him for healing on the spot; these villagers admired him, didn't they? He sauntered down to the beach where, smoking a cheroot, he watched the fishermen, like children at games, tossing and catching sparkling nets. The Prince won't dare touch my clinic, Vittorio told himself, not right away . . . . wildly he thought of tracking down his men. Impossible—they were still scattered across fifteen miles.

The clinic was padlocked before ten, despite the wails of old women lined up to see Doctor Vittorio. By the time he arrived not a soul remained, and he felt free to curse aloud. Vittorio kept most of his instruments and all his medicines there, so he would most likely be able to treat only the mildest cases at home. Damn that Prince for a murderer, he all but shouted when he found the windows nailed tightly shut.

Vittorio spent the day composing a petition to the King, along with less temperate letters to Senators known to be anti-aristocrats. He drafted a report to the Health Commissioner in Rome, describing San Lorenzo as a town of invalids, sure his exaggeration would fetch an inspector speedily. Then, after telling his mother a version of the facts, Vittorio rode a skittish mule above the town where his mistress Peppina and her family lived.

He guessed she had worked as one of the town prostitutes during the war; the dirty jokes of his regiment suggested it. Before they began relations he examined her with care and, finding no disease, told her sincerely she was good enough for him, sincerely because Vittorio, after three years at the front, was inured to whores who serviced a hundred men a day. Peppina might have been twenty, she might have been twenty five, but her lank black hair and expressionless eyes gave little of her soul away. Yet she came alive after the act, repeating all the town gossip and pleading for a gold bracelet "just like the one the Prince's woman has."

Tonight Peppina was waiting for him with her face set grimly, uncharacteristically, in a frown. "They're waiting for you in the shack," she said curtly, before marching off ahead of a puzzled Vittorio.

Peppina stood with her arms crossed while two of his ex-soldiers offered to turn themselves in to the Prince. "Were you the ones who attacked his bailiffs?" The men exchanged an uneasy glance. "No, Doctor, but what difference does that make? We don't want you to be in trouble on our account." Vittorio, enraged, actually stamped his foot. "This goddamn Prince wants to ruin all of you," he bellowed, "he'll see through you, and then where will we be?" "But your clinic," one of the men began, "we know how you care for that . . . ." "Go ahead, but it will do not a bit of good." The men shook hands ceremoniously, like soldiers departing for a suicide march.

As soon as they left, Peppina, irate, demanded to know how those men knew about her and him, did they take her for a slut? Vittorio soothed her, assuring her that nobody knew of his visits. Relieved, Peppina began to grin in her old salacious way, and dashed into the shack they used for lovemaking, shedding her garments as she neared the door. Vittorio followed her inside, where they mingled the four elements of water, fire, earth, and air so late that the jackals who raided the town dump at midnight became audible.

"What will you do about the Prince," Peppina said. "He forced himself on me, I was twelve years old, that fat stinking bastard forced himself on me and I struggled, I shrieked, he had to have two of his servants hold me down. And then he threw his money in my face, that fat stinking bastard."

"You never told me," Vittorio said.

"What difference would it have made?"

"Girls like you will be safe, in the Italy we will build."

Peppina grinned. "Italy? What Italy? There's only men and women and parents so poor they sell their little girls, and none of that will ever change, not ever."

Abashed, Vittorio fumbled for the one lira he gave her every time he came. He handed her the note and reached for a farewell kiss, feeling how tense Peppina's little body was, how tautly strung.

"I won't give in, my love, I swear."

She shrugged. "Not unless you absolutely have to, anyway."

He patted her shoulder and walked into the moonless night. And all the way down the mountain Vittorio couldn't tear that picture out of his mind, the gross body of the Prince crushing the child Peppina's, her screams, his groans of pleasure, and all the while the manservants helping their master ruin her. Yes, they must purge such vultures, such parasites—wasn't that reason enough to keep his regiment alive?

Yet the matter seemed far cloudier when Vittorio's men assembled, early the next morning, shuffling back and forth in front of the Monti house. Vittorio stepped onto the terrace, briskly ordering his regiment to fall in. The two men who'd offered themselves as sacrifice were moving, he noticed, far slower than the rest.

"You two," he barked, "what's the matter, your wives wearing you out?"

A grimace twisted their impassive faces. One man's body abruptly sagged, as though weighted down.

"What's wrong with you?" Vittorio cried; no response. "Isn't anyone going to tell me what you all seem to know?"

The other "volunteer" stepped gingerly forward, saluting even though the gesture made him wince. "We went to the Prince's house. He sent for that animal Brunetti and his boys, and that was when we knew we were in for shit—and sure enough, Brunetti's brats tied us to the stable wall so that pig, that draft dodger, could flog us, thirty lashes each."

"Take off your tunic and let me see your back."

The blood was already scabbing into purple welts, deep abrasions that crisscrossed the spine. Some blood oozed from the wounds, not much; Brunetti had been brutally precise. The rest of the regiment looked on impassively. Vittorio thought how profoundly fatalistic Southerners were; whenever he glimpsed their resignation it chilled him to the bone. What could you do with men who thought justice was a luxury for the rich? Silently, the man buttoned up his shirt.

"And the clinic?" Vittorio managed to ask.

"Still padlocked," replied the man who hadn't shown his back. "The Prince wants you to—"

"Disband the regiment," Vittorio cut in. "Well, what do you men say? You saw your comrade's back, what do you say?"

The men shuffled uneasily; none of them spoke.

"I ask you—did we smash the Austrians so we'd have to kiss this Prince's stinking ass?"

"With respect," a man said, stepping forward, "how will you be our doctor any other way? The Prince, he'll be dead in a year or two, and then . . . ."

"So you want to disband?" Vittorio made himself smile as he spoke. "Why don't we take a vote? All in favor, right hands up—"

All but a few fists shot into the air. Vittorio forced an indifferent shrug.

"So now you can have a little peace of mind!" he said, using the local dialect. The men dribbled off in twos and threes, except for the Prince's victims, whom Vittorio led inside to salve and disinfect. He insisted they take his unguent and told them how often to rub it on. After the men left Vittorio sank, suddenly spent, into a chair. A moment later, his mother appeared before him, hovering like a bad painter's notion of Saint Anne.

"Rest easy, I won't be playing soldiers any more—"

"And you'll go humbly—humbly, my son,—to see the Prince?"

"I haven't made up my mind."

"And breakfast?"

Vittorio laughed at the maternal leap from grave to trivial.

"Then we'll talk now," she said, seating herself next to him. "No mother wants her son to ruin himself."

"Mother, please," Vittorio tried to interrupt.

"Ruin yourself, yes. Exactly the way your father did. In those days you were too young to understand, and of course we didn't talk business to the children, the way these vulgar upstarts do nowadays. But your father ruined himself and you're following in his path. Your father thought he could outwit the Devil himself."

"We're not alike, since I don't believe in such foolishness."

"The Devil is strongest when we are sure he can't exist," she snapped. "Oh, you are like your father—so puffed up with pride you're in a state of sin. But you'll learn, oh yes, and I hope you won't need disaster to teach you humility . . . . you want to keep your clinic open, I know you do," she said in an imploring tone quite unlike her sharpness a moment before, "and where else in Italy can you practice medicine as you do here? God gave you this chance, my son, don't throw it so thoughtlessly away! Don't make your father's mistake and fall into Satanic pride!"

Vittorio smiled. "You should start writing Father Ugo's sermons, honestly."

"Please, please, my son . . . . talk to the Prince. Say whatever he wants to hear. And then go treat your patients, do the work God intends for you. We all sacrificed so much for you—"

"You didn't sacrifice, my brother did." Vittorio stood up.

"We all sacrificed, your sister too," she replied in a steady tone.

"Oh yes! If not for me, she would have been a Bride of Christ! She should thank me for sparing her such a fate!"

"Save your vulgarity for that peasant girl," his mother said, gazing up firmly into his face. "You will see the Prince today, Vittorio."

"Certainly—if his syphilis flares up."

At last he'd managed to make her gasp. At least he'd accomplished that, he thought, striding into the kitchen where, ignoring the maid and cook who stood agog at what they'd overheard, he poured himself a large brandy—French, not Italian, patriotism only went so far—and then another, savoring the fire that sizzled from his stomach up to his reeling head. Still, even with the brandy in his veins, he tasted the sour flavor of defeat. In the end he would submit, he knew, hating himself. Would Peppina hate him too? To hell with her, Vittorio told himself, he could find another girl. But where would he find another regiment? How feeble his life would be, how unmanly, how dishonorable. The two kitchen wenches stared at him. Pouring another brandy he saluted them, grinningly. Perhaps, he thought, perhaps the time had come to consider Francesco's offer . . . . and dammit, whether it had or not, he owed the boy a letter. Writing might take this taste of old metal from his mouth . . . .

THREE

"**You're** wastin' your time and you're wastin' your money," Carney said. "In the first place—"

"He's my friend," Francesco spoke quietly, trying not to let their secretary hear.

"*I'm* your friend and I'm tellin' you, Frank, he ain't worth your trouble."

"He was the first friend I had here. We worked the mines together, we came to Philadelphia together."

"But you didn't get rich together, dammit! Show a little respect, Frank, listen to your partner's good advice."

"Then tell me, you like this nonsense now, this Red Scare?"

The papers called it a Scare, which sounded cute, not this hysteria of making foreigners kiss the flag and arresting strikers and anarchists who, if they'd really built those bombs that fizzled out so laughably, would have spent their family's food money for a month. War propaganda, like cocaine, had left American nerves too taut to relax yet. Deport the foreign bastards, cried the Attorney General, A. Mitchell Palmer, Pennsylvania's native son who claimed that one out of every four adults was plotting treason just as Lenin had. Shoot them or ship them off, before they overthrow America!

"It's a lot of shit, but business is business, Frank . . . . And I don't want any asshole pointin' at my partner and sayin' he has a soft spot for Reds—not with government contracts in our hands."

"He's an anarchist, not a Red. And you worry too much. For God's sake, people call us war profiteers—should we give our money back to shut them up?"

"You've a reckless streak, Frank Monti, and that worries me more. Tyin' up with that Warrington quiff was bad enough—"

Francesco shot Carney a look that froze him into silence. He slowly, deliberately began dressing for the street, donning his tailored overcoat of gray tweed with black velvet lapels, glancing into the mirror to check the angle of his bowler hat.

"Don't do it," Carney said just before Francesco stepped through the private door into the street. "Let him sink or swim on his own, the way you did."

Francesco laughed. "I'm not American enough for that."

His car took too many minutes to warm up, so that Francesco steered through the streets with numbed hands. It was the violet hour, when the shadows of naked trees lengthened eerily, and men walked fast, heads bent against the wind, towards brightly lit houses where women and children huddled in front of kitchen stoves. After a time he crossed into the moneyed precincts, their houses dazzlingly electrified, their sidewalks swept clean of last night's snow. Against his will he thought of Laura, her snug Delancey Street bedroom with its Japanese prints, its fire crackling behind an ornamental screen; and he thought of Laura herself (damn Carney for uttering her name), still able to taste the trace of peppermint in her kiss, to feel the soft pressure of her breasts . . . . no, stop that, Francesco commanded his memory. A moment of weakness had cost him his bearings, and through the dense air, darker every second, he could spot no landmark or street sign. Cursing, he parked and started searching for the house on foot.

1339 Spruce Street, an address every Philadelphian knew, proved so nondescript that at first Francesco felt certain he'd lost his way. Nothing about the house of U.S. Senator Boies Penrose betrayed its owner's grandeur, or even identified the premises as his. He climbed the steps, uncertain whether to knock, when the judas hole opened with a snap. A sonorous Negro voice requested his name.

Senator Penrose must have liked greenhouses, for his house secreted the damp, sticky heat orchids require, a shock after the icy night. The Negro servant ushered Francesco into the parlor where a fireplace, mercifully unlit, stood flanked by twin busts of some laurel-crowned ancient sage; above it hung the portrait of an American, dressed with stiff formality. From a nearby room floated the rich smell of cooking. Francesco noticed a table set with silver and crystal for one. He wondered whether he'd gotten the date or the hour wrong; surely the Negro would have made his arrival known by now. Then, without warning, two white manservants bustled in to set an array of covered plates down on the table. The scent they wafted made Francesco hungry, too: oyster stew and a roast turkey. Did the Senator feed his guests before doing business with them?

From the hallway sounded a deep, contemptuous voice:

"Hell's bells, Jim, the man's never gotten drunk in his life—or maybe even laid—and I can't do business with a Puritan—"

Unsteadily supported by a Malacca cane, the Senior Senator from Pennsylvania lurched into the drawing room with a grunt animal enough to evoke his nickname, Big Grizzly. Boies Penrose sat his girth down with a crash that upset the wine glasses, which a small man entering in his wake deftly caught, like a parlor trick.

"All Puritans want reform, that last refuge of scoundrels—who said so, Jim?"

"Martin Van Buren?"

"He could have but he didn't. Hell, these damn reformers won't be happy until every single human pleasure's unconstitutional, like they did with booze . . . ."

At last the other man noticed Francesco; his smile grew genial and he shook his hand with two of his own. "Senator James McNichol, and you are—?"

"You made his appointment for tonight," Penrose said, "or maybe that slipped your mind?"

"Oh, my heavens yes, Mr. Frank Monti of Monti and Carney—"

"And that's why you'll never go any further than Harrisburg."

Penrose gave the little man a sardonic smile, which bared his teeth alarmingly. "Jesus Christ himself couldn't get you to Capitol Hill."

"You wish Senator Penrose to sponsor a man for citizenship, I believe?"

"He knows what he wants, Jim." Penrose eyed Francesco curiously. "You don't dress like a dago, I'll say that for you. That suit must have cost you a nice piece of change."

"Your office in Washington has my friend's file—" Francesco began nervously.

Penrose interrupted: "You vouch for this man, do you? He don't drink or screw or have fun in any manner of means, because that's un-American?"

Francesco stammered that Enrico was a happily married man who worked hard at his trade. Penrose laughed. "He sounds like another goddamn Puritan, don't he, Jim?"

As he spoke, Penrose tugged on a satin cord. His Negro led in a steward who swiftly poured the Senator three different wines. The servant ladled Penrose a bowl of oyster stew; its buttery aroma filled the room. After Penrose took a few spoonfuls, he smiled cheerfully.

"As you see, I live quite modestly. Nowadays the only thing I can handle's a good dinner—a woman would kill me faster than my cancer will."

"The Senator lives for the people of this great Commonwealth," McNichol said worshipfully.

"You and your flapdoodle!—No wonder they call you Strawberry Jim, you make everything sweet as pie! The people, so called, don't deserve an aristocrat like me, and never will. But the Grand Old Party—now there's something to live for! My crowning glory will be putting a Republican in the White House this year . . . ."

"Senator Harding," Francesco said. The thought of Penrose as kingmaker excited even Democrats; Pennsylvania would again hold the balance of power, and who could sneer at that?

"Damn right, Harding," the kingmaker replied. "He *looks*

like a President, and nowadays that's all that counts. You happen to know what the word Americanism means, either of you?" Both shook their heads.

"It don't mean a goddamn thing," Penrose grinned, "but that word will make Senator Harding President."

"I have the, ah, check for his campaign—" Francesco said tentatively.

"For the figure you and Strawberry Shortcake here discussed?" Penrose cut in.

"Yes, sir." Francesco hesitated; should he talk dollars to a Senator?

"One thousand now, one thousand later," Penrose said, reaching for a turkey leg. "Money's the mother's milk of politics . . . ."

"We'll contact you after Labor Day." Strawberry Jim seized the check Francesco took out; with a cry Penrose stopped his ally from pocketing it.

"Forgive me, Senator, I thought, since you were dining . . . ."

"I can pocket a check and eat at the same time, you idiot!"

Involuntarily Francesco pictured Enrico and his wife feeding their children on Christian Street. His friend would never believe him if he described this scene, and why should he? Francesco wouldn't have credited it himself. He watched a different servant place a canvasback duck stuffed with mushrooms before Penrose and pour a large glass of blood-red claret.

"They say I eat sloppily," Penrose scowled, making his thin lips disappear. "You think I eat sloppily, Strawberry?"

Penrose was swiftly tearing the duck apart, sucking flesh off its bones so violently that his cheeks turned red. Bits of skin and fat clung to his mouth, like debris from some fatal accident.

"The Bellevue Hotel," Penrose said bitterly, "got so many complaints, they made me eat behind a screen! What impudence! But—" he sighed, "their stuffed lobsters were so good, I couldn't stay away."

"Great men are never appreciated in their own time," orated Strawberry Jim, sententiously.

"No, no, you're wrong. After my death I'll just be a name under some bad portrait," Penrose gestured at the canvas over his head, "like poor Van Buren up there. Not that I really give a damn. But I'll tell you both a secret." Penrose smiled wistfully. "I'm glad I'll soon be gone. Yes. Because this city isn't mine any more, let alone the country. Look at Mr. Monti here, a millionaire—aren't you?—and I bet you don't own a single book in English, not a one." That mocking smile again: *You don't dress like a dago, I'll say that for you.*

Before he could catch himself, Francesco said, "You're wrong, Senator. I read Emerson."

Penrose smiled sardonically again. "I'm sure you do." The two politicians looked at one another and laughed. Stung, Francesco pulled a small leatherette volume from his coat.

"Self-Reliance and Other Essays," Penrose read the cover aloud.

"I'm sorry, Senator, it's not your city any more. It belongs to anyone strong enough to take a piece of it. *That's* Americanism, isn't it?"

"It is now," Penrose sighed. "And I'm glad I won't be around to see what men like you do to it."

He nodded to Strawberry Jim, who ushered Francesco out and shook his hand in the hallway. In the street a high wind was scattering snow so briskly it seemed to be falling once again. Francesco drove carefully, hunched over the steering wheel, out of the neighborhood where the patricians lived, into the slums where their inheritors crowded into tenements. Enrico came down to meet him in the street.

"You're safe," Francesco said in Italian, his face expressionless.

Enrico embraced him fervently, as though Francesco were Christ himself. "How can I thank you? What can I ever do?"

"I'll think of something, don't worry . . . ."

"What did the fat Senator say? Did he give his word?"

Francesco nodded, knowing the lie would reassure. "And he said men like me and you will inherit America."

"Men like *you*, Francesco. Men like *you*."

Another evening, another week, later that winter of 1920. Francesco strode carefully through the dirty Broad Street snow, reaching the Calabrian Club and scraping his galoshes on its front step. Contending voices floated out to him:

"—way he avoids his people, is he ashamed of us?"

"Idiot, didn't Monti save our bank, isn't he giving mortgages—"

"Sucking our blood, you call that loyalty?"

"He's an American—he wants to make a buck." Whoever spoke mimicked a native, so broadly that most of the room guffawed.

"No, no, gentlemen, this Monti is a true son of Italy—patient, dignified, never plays the fool . . . ."

"Eh, Salandria, he gave you a mortgage with nothing down!"

Francesco was learning that it was no easier for a rich man to relax than for a poor man to stop worrying. Take those Calabrians: in theory, he knew the men inside resented him, but hearing them say so made him squirm. Why did they matter? Because he hoped to build his empire here in South Philadelphia, providing for his kind as Greenglass—his partner, his mentor—had done for the Jews. But what if their resentment proved implacable? He felt naked as a baby, standing there in the snow, at the mercy of men without his cunning and his cash, men who laid bricks, carved stone, paved roads, who now (and thank God they didn't know) had the power to checkmate his grandest scheme: to build new houses, whole streets filled with shining stone and brick, to move them out of their cold-water walkups into Paradise, or as close to one as Carney and Monti could build . . . .

No, he relished his good fortune rarely at best. He had too many decisions, contracts, overdrafts to approve: he had to gobble lunch at his desk, hunched over columns of figures. At some instant (what month, which day?) Francesco Monti transformed himself, or was transformed, from an ordinary man to an exemplary figure, a man with a biography. Now he did business for himself, not to send dollars home; he was a man on the make, as the saying went, licensed to think only of himself and—so remarkable was his rise—worth studying for the secret propelling him to such heights. Not quite fifteen years in America and already he had a million! All he wanted now was one day free of the fretful daily strain to which a million dollars—if you wanted to double them—sentenced you.

"Gentlemen, gentlemen, where is our Italian pride?"

"He isn't one of us, fool—Monti prefers the damn Irish and the dirty Jews, those Christ-killers."

"They're his partners, donkey head."

"He was smart, getting those Navy contracts. Very smart."

"He was lucky, shitbrain."

"The Christ-killer Jew made money with him, and that was luck?"

"Goddamn it, let's confess it, we're so jealous it's eating our guts!"

"Sure, I wish I had Monti's head for deals, like those houses for veterans . . . ."

"*I'm* not jealous. Fate catches up with moneygrubbers who get too much, too fast."

"Not jealous! Your face is as green as all the dollars you haven't got!"

And after listening to that, Francesco needed long nips at his brandy flask before he could go inside to describe the new houses he wanted his countrymen to buy. In his coat pocket, at all times, he kept his Emerson; he silently chanted the great man's hymns to self-invention on streetcars, in waiting rooms of men he had to do business with, until he knew the words as well as the Lord's Prayer. Francesco liked to think he was living as Emerson prescribed, a free agent, guiding his destiny into the glorious unknown.

He awakened in the winter dark certain he was still working the mine, almost smelling the pungent anthracite in his room. Working the mine, in his dreams, dirty with dust, terrified of a cave-in, anxious to send his pay home to San Lorenzo and thus anxious to work six days a week for whatever the pit boss would pay. Now Francesco knew how unhappy he'd been then, knew it from the way his heart tensed whenever he awakened thinking he was still there. And now, am I happy, am I pursuing happiness? Life's not for that, he would quickly answer himself: a man does his duty, rises or falls by his own sweat, and none of that has a damn thing to do with happiness. Children can be happy, Francesco thought, they have no duties and they sweat only at games . . . .

And yet, despite his worries, came a new pleasure in himself, in the novel thrill of being a successful man. The boy who'd pressed his nose to the windows of the Bellevue Hotel watching men in frock coats and women in diamonds waltzing between the palms—that boy had finally disappeared. Now Francesco could walk into the Bellevue himself, could waltz, could light up any woman he desired with jewels like a Christmas tree. That was what money meant, the freedom to waste it showily. Oh, he knew that boy still trembled somewhere in him, but the world instead saw Frank Monti, pleasingly modest for all his wealth, who neither waltzed nor kept a showgirl draped in jewels; the model young millionaire, thrifty, sober, untainted by vanity. He had at last become a man in his own eyes, and therefore in others' eyes.

The proof was that his two partners, Carney and Greenglass, had begun to treat him as a near-equal. It was men, Francesco thought, who gave you your manhood, women gave you something else entirely—an end to your boyhood, perhaps, which was scarcely the same as becoming a man among men.

"What d'ye think, Frank," Carney often asked nowadays— gone were the blunt assertions he expected Francesco to swallow, like pills, just because they were good for him. What caused his new deference was Francesco's connection to Abner Greenglass. Carney regarded his partner as a sort of con artist who'd "put one over" on the richest Jew in town. And in fact, that five thousand invested with Greenglass had multiplied to fifty thousand when the Armistice came. After that, there was no telling how much

Greenglass would make on the veterans: HOMES FOR HEROES, his company advertised, the slogan flanked by the stars and stripes. Already the doughboys were snapping up houses, any houses, even fake cottages near Fairmount Park, so Francesco's fifty thousand could easily double by 1921.

The war made anyone with dollars rich, or vastly richer if, like Abner Greenglass, he had real money at its start. Thanks to the blessed sacrament of patronage, only loyal Democrats like Carney and Monti won contracts at the Navy Yard—contracts so fat Francesco wondered if it wouldn't be cheaper merely to buy the Germans off. Their brickyard grossed six million before the Armistice, and even with the new income tax Carney cursed, the two men shared profits fat enough to choke a horse. All the while Greenglass was paying cash for Francesco's patent, to say nothing of the housing boom he and his partners milked. Even Carney set aside his habitual sneers, praising Greenglass as the smartest man in town—screw the one hundred percent Americans, their day was done. The three men had a photograph taken just after the Armistice, in front of that bastion of the patricians, the Union League, all three grinning into the camera lens, teeth bared, Darwinian predators hungry for any profits the aristocrats were dumb enough to miss. Francesco kept the picture on his desk.

One other sight consoled him: his image in the full-length mirror he hung at the brickyard. Not that Francesco thought himself a Valentino, no; it was his clothing, not his face, that reassured. In those days businessmen still dressed as they would have in 1910; the young men looked as drab and dispirited as underpaid clerks. But Francesco had other ideas. With an Italian tailor he chose rich fabrics for suits whose cut registered his subtle protest against such tyranny. Other men wore three-piece gray gabardine; Francesco exuded discreet opulence in green herringbone. As for his shoes, he refused to wear the monstrosities New England produced, and ordered English oxfords and brogues. So that when Francesco gazed into his mirror he saw a man of wealth and taste, his own taste, mind you, not the American preference for dull uniform.

Abner Greenglass took a liking to him, in his cautious way, seeing Francesco—correctly—as that rarest of self-made men, one unimpressed by his own success. Greenglass suggested that his partner, imitating his own career, purchase an immigrant bank; then he could issue mortgages and create his own capital. Already Francesco was dreaming of a fiefdom in real estate downtown, among his own people, so Greenglass merely confirmed his private hunch. By now, like all successful men, he had to fight off suitors vying to make him even wealthier. He chose a banker who sold him forty percent of the Calabrian Bank on Seventh Street, plus a share of the brokerage business run on the same premises. Even before the easy money of '21, his Calabrian Bank issued three thousand mortgages. And he profited from every stock his brokers sold, since the plungers borrowed Calabrian Bank money to speculate on margin. Dollars, dollars, how could he possibly lose?

Now he received the polite applause of the Calabrian Club, pausing to sip water before the howitzers began firing questions. Most of them he anticipated; based as they were on fear and not on hope, he could easily calm his audience.

No, they needed no collateral to buy a house, just a down payment of ten percent.

Yes, Abner Greenglass and he would form a partnership to build, but the bank and the money belonged to him.

Of course the tenements are unsanitary, we all know that, look how sick your babies get—

Yes, you can give up your house in sixty days and get every single dollar back.

No, the Jew, as they called him, was not in charge; Francesco was. But he was proud to call Abner Greenglass his friend—

Finally he could stand the stifling room, the sweaty faces, not a second more. The questions were dying down, so he excused himself, thanked the members of the club, gave out his glossy prospectus (GRACIOUS LIVING AT GARIBALDI HOMES), printed in Italian, before bowing and taking his leave. A hard sell, Carney would have called it. Hard, yes, but not impossible; these men—at least some of them—would buy. They had wives who yearned to escape their rat-infested walkups, daughters who burned to be as American as their schoolmates; and American meant you owned. An Englishman's home was his castle, but an American's was his fort. Secure inside, he fought off the perils of this mad country, keeping his family at his side, playing whist, lotto, the new contract bridge, singing Puccini to a player piano, one family under a Catholic God, indivisible. That was how one hundred percent Americans lived, wasn't it? So he knew at least half of these men would sidle into the Calabrian Bank, not Monday or Tuesday perhaps, but soon enough, to inquire anxiously how many lots were still for sale . . . .

Every so often—once a month, perhaps—Carney would ask him why he worked so hard, what was driving him on, and Francesco had to hide his irritation at the question.

"It's fun," he might say. "I like the work."

"Fun, when you're working sixteen hours a day? Don't bullshit a bullshitter, Frank."

"Are we partners?"

"Goddamn right we are."

"Are we making money on the Navy Yard, Greenglass, my houses going up?"

"Does Senator Penrose shit in a gold commode?"

"Then shut up and work as hard as I do, for one day—"

But Francesco knew the answer and had no intention of ever letting Carney too. In his heart he was not Frank Monti, millionaire, maybe would never be; in his heart, he was that little boy who vomited in the steerage hold from Naples to New York, the one who stared frozen with terror at the sooty towers and hell-black mines of his exile's land. Some part of him still felt that fear, still dreamed of San Lorenzo (orange trees, the salt breeze, those three pines you saw when the train accelerated achingly away) and made him wake up in childish tears.

Perhaps that explained his rescue of Enrico: he was keeping faith with the child he'd been, the child in the mines. Francesco shunned that sort of examen of conscience, associating it with priests and penitential rites, with awkward answers in the confessional; he knew, too, that it made no difference what his motives, or for that matter Carney's, were. His partner sought to rise politically. He wanted something else. What did he want? To bury that fearful child, he would have said, had he trusted anyone with the truth. He would have told Laura, of course, but now she was more distant than San Lorenzo.

Luckily he had a woman closer to hand, an Italian, who understood the look of homesickness sometimes shrouding his eyes. Rosita Parenti had worse troubles of her own: the influenza scourge had killed first her husband, a master carpenter, and then their baby boy, so that by the time Francesco met her in 1919— absurdly, on a horsecar that fell into a rut—Rosita lived with sorrow as poor women live with want, constantly shadowed by it, forbidden to forget.

Timidly she approached Francesco, without a dime's collateral, for the money to start a flower shop in an "American" neighborhood. He startled her by advancing the loan personally. Then, little by little, after three months of visits to her shop, Rosita began inviting him for home-baked cookies and real espresso; which led to a five-course Calabrian dinner that made him secretly loosen his belt; and finally, inevitably, to Rosita Parenti's matrimonial bed. By now the affair ran as smoothly as the brickworks, and profitably too, since Rosita passed on the downtown gossip that was helping him sell the Garibaldi Estates.

Rosita needed love, he'd smelled that on her the day they met. Italian girls, right up to the honeymoons, moved under the watchful eye of both parents, not that Francesco lusted after those silly virgins anyway. Rosita, though, repaid his kindnesses with passion far outstripping Laura's cautious embrace. She knew what she wanted and, while she never said a word, she used him as a plaything, much to his delight, and hers.

He installed a brass bed in Rosita's flat, since her favorite gambit was to ride his body like a horsewoman, posting and jockeying while he gripped the strong metal headboard. At such moments broken syllables, hoarse cries, fluttered from her throat. For the first time, Francesco savored the new sweets of passivity. First with her mouth, then with her grateful crotch, Rosita mastered him and mastered him again. And if he lost his self-control and spilled his seed between her lips, she laughed and licked it with a greedy joy that made him want her all over again.

Rosita lived in the second floor flat of a building Francesco, by pure chance, managed on South Broad Street. All night the trolleys rattled past, and in warm weather the Mummers, fantastically dressed and drunk, practiced their New Year's Day dances until dawn. Rosita grumbled, praying to Saint Jude for one quiet night, not that the noise disturbed Francesco, who worked amid worse clangor every day. He offered to find her a better place, but she demurred, not wanting, he guessed, to become his kept woman. The flower shop showed enough profit for her to pay bills and buy food and clothes, a fact that delighted Francesco: what a good bargain I made, he thought, compared to the businessmen notorious for keeping rapacious Floradora chorines.

Now Rosita was serving him fishermen's rice, vivid with pink shrimp, mother-of-pearl clams, and squid black with its own ink. While Francesco quickly emptied his bowl, she repeated the local gossip: his Garibaldi Houses were not popular, since the Italians feared that buying them would mean never going home; and wasn't Francesco Monti too young for such a grand scheme anyway? Rosita suggested he use a different slogan, maybe something to reassure what she called "the greasers." Moving on, she canvassed the fish stores where she'd shopped and announced all but one was too dirty for anyone but the Irish, who as everyone knew ate the cheap fish on Fridays, as the Church prescribed. "I saw poor Doctor Gioia," she exclaimed, "he can't marry off that ugly daughter of his for love or money, and God knows he has plenty of cash . . ." Francesco politely asked who the hell she was talking about.

"Don't you know Doctor Gioia?" Rosita exclaimed, pleased at her momentary advantage over him. "You know, that huge house four blocks from here, with his doctor's office in front, why, it's almost a mansion, it's so big.

"What kind of doctor is this Gioia, with a daughter nobody wants to fuck?"

Rosita blushed. "Don't be vulgar, dear. Well, I think Doctor Gioia started out as an everything doctor, you know, the kind who'll treat a child or a dying man, no difference, only now he's choosier. He only sees people who have cancer or heart disease or anything that's costly to treat. She waved her hand sadly: "My poor Carlo, he wanted Doctor Gioia, but who had the cash for a miracle?"

"And how old would this Gioia be?" Francesco was trying to feign disinterest; Vittorio's letter expressing (at last) a desire to join him in Philadelphia had made him eager. He even stopped eating the fishermen's rice.

"Fifty or fifty-five," said Rosita indifferently. "He's got more money than God, invests in land and stocks and I don't know what. Still he can't buy a pretty face for that horse of a daughter, that Bellina, what a name for her!" Rosita snickered nastily.

"Good God, how ugly can the girl be?"

Rosita grinned. "You'd have to turn the lights out, get drunk, cover her face, and your flesh would still go on strike."

"But if the father is as rich as you say, he'll pay to marry her off, won't he?"

"He's failed so far. And his Bellina gets older and uglier every day." Rosita looked at him, horrified. "You don't want to marry her yourself?"

Francesco laughed. "I'm not that greedy, yet."

FOUR

Carney and Monti surpassed themselves with the model houses for the Garibaldi Homes. They planted rose gardens on the side plots and bright green perennials out front, to say nothing of red horns to ward off the Evil Eye—something Francesco scoffed at but his prospective buyers certainly did not. The front steps, made of the finest brick Carney could kiln, displayed a miniature Italian flag, the tricolor so cheerful it verged on bad taste, or what Francesco and his family liked to call 'cafonita'—meaning peasant taste. All this splendor, alas, came at a price, and it proved too high for Francesco to bear alone. In the end his bank, reeling from the costs—in 1920 half of Philadelphia was under scaffolds, driving up even a box of nails to twice its pre-war price—had to do the very thing Francesco vowed he never would. He went to Abner Greenglass for more capital.

Not that he disliked Greenglass or mistrusted him; no, Francesco wanted to profit completely from the Garibaldi Homes. Which was only fair and just, since hadn't he bought the land, hired the architects, approved the designs, sold the first dozen houses personally? Wasn't he the one the Italians knew?

"Siddown, Frank, siddown. And stop looking itchy, I been expecting you."

"You got my proposal?"

"Your proposition, you mean. Sure. Some proposition—I

should lend you money two points below the banks? Are you kidding with this? Tell me it's just a joke."

"It's not a joke."

Greenglass laughed so hard he started to wheeze. "My people got a word, we call this *chutzpah*. Your people got a word for somebody who has the balls to bleed a friend?"

"You can say no any time, Abe, any time you want."

"You worry me." Greenglass leaned back in his high leather chair, then rocked forward with a sudden squeak. "You want things. Money. Success, they call it. But you want these things too much. You're in over your head now, and you want charity."

"It's a straight business loan like any—"

"What the fuck do I look like to you, Frank, Santa Claus? This ain't a loan, it's a giveaway. I wouldn't do it for my own damn brother, not that any of my brothers would be stupid enough to get screwed like you did."

"Then what do I do, Abe?" Francesco was fighting to stay calm. If Greenglass said no, if he had to go to a commercial bank, he'd sign his ownership away. He wanted to scream at the sky, shout twenty stories down into the street: I *must* have everything, the money and the houses and all of it, I *will* have everything!

"It never occurred to you, now you're my competition?"

"You don't own an outhouse in my neighborhood."

"In principle, my boy, in principle. And in case you ain't heard, Macy's don't tell Gimbel's."

"All right, I get your drift. The answer's no." Francesco rose.

"The answer ain't no, smartass. Siddown, siddown."

"I thought you weren't doing me any favors."

"I'm not." Greenglass leaned forward, his eyes narrowing to a squint. "You got something I want and you don't even know it."

"Everything I own, mortgaged or outright, it's on that sheet."

"You got two serious assets and that's all—your share of Carney and Monti and the patent I pay you too damn much money for every month. The rest is chickenshit."

"The land for the Garibaldi Homes? My Reading Railroad bonds?"

"Everyone in this town has Reading Bonds, they come free with the soft pretzels."

"You want my patent, that it?"

"I'll even let you use the process for free, now ain't that generous? And you're young, you'll make your way without the thing, look at me, all I had was a head for figures and I did all right."

"More than all right, Abe."

"Pretty goddamn good, and I ain't dead yet."

"What—" Francesco hesitated, "what would you give me in exchange?"

"Just the loan you came in here askin' for. That straight business loan you were so hot for a minute ago."

"You aren't serious?" The room swam for a moment in front of Francesco; he reached for a cigarette.

"You're thinking I'm a dirty Jew, ain't you? What you goyim always think, when you run to us for cash. Well, my money ain't dirty, and if you don't take it you'll wind up working for the Girard Bank, you like that better? You take it, Frank, and maybe you'll make so much on those houses you can buy your patent back someday."

"I wasn't thinking you were a dirty Jew. I was thinking I'm an idiot, Abe, and that's the truth."

"No, you ain't. I don't let no idiots in here to waste my time, so cut the crap. Think it over, Frank. And don't forget I'm your friend. I got a heart, more than you can say for any goddamn bank."

Of course, as Francesco knew perfectly well, nobody in business had a heart, not even Carney, his partner and another self-proclaimed friend. Nowadays the two confined their talk to their business and the daily paper's scandalous 'facts.' Francesco scarcely missed their lunches in saloons, so frenzied was his day now that the Garibaldi Homes were vexing him. From eight until six he helped run the brickyard while rushing back and

forth crosstown to the model houses. There Enrico, now attired
(under protest) in a frock coat, tried to sell lots to those Italians
who ambled unwarily in. Half the day Francesco spent on the
telephone, so that he felt a permanent ache from cradling the
earpiece between shoulder and neck; on the telephone and, often
enough, in a rage. His builders and his carpenters seemed
determined to foist their shoddiest work on him, as though the
immigrants who would—with luck—buy his houses deserved
no more. Francesco's foreman, a laconic Welshman, took a
perverse joy in calling with bad news just when he couldn't come
to the site, and Enrico, for all his anarchist creed of equality,
accused the workmen of dawdling and so stealing bread from
Francesco's mouth. And yet, despite these obstacles, Francesco
never regretted the pain turning his dreams into wood, plaster,
and brick entailed; like Jacob with the angel, he would struggle
until his blessing came.

It felt absurd, almost insane, to be a paper millionaire without
the cash he needed the way a soldier needs bullets, without which
he must either surrender or be killed. He had other ways to raise
it, none of them practical: he could sell his half of the brickyard,
but how long would it take to find a buyer even if Carney agreed?
Those Reading Railroad bonds Greenglass mocked might bring
him something, though scarcely enough. The worst alternative
was selling the patent. He had created it with his young man's
blood, in that time he could never recapture; selling to Greenglass
was selling himself cheap. If he consulted Carney his partner would
say goddamn it, no; let the fuckin' houses wait. But they couldn't
wait: the boom everyone said was coming made that unthinkable.
You could hear its underground rumble if you listened closely,
even in South Philadelphia.

Without a doubt that neighborhood legend, Doctor Gioia,
could hear its sound. Gioia spent most of his day in and out of
banks, brokerage houses, anyplace he might hear a tip. His patients
meanwhile waited, half dead, tubes running from their arms,
noses, genitals. Doctor Gioia would inspect them hastily between
trips to research a new stock. It depressed Francesco how much

he and Gioia were alike; he vowed that by the time he reached that age he would have lost the avidity they shared. He would never be such a spectacle, running from office to office like a fool, sitting next to his chauffeur to keep him driving so recklessly that encounters with the police usually cost Gioia more money than whatever tips he heard brought in. Francesco pitied Vittorio in advance for such a father-in-law. Indeed, he pitied himself for the endless evenings he'd already endured: if Doctor Gioia was a pig, his wife Grazia and his daughter Bellina were swinish too in their own female ways.

The first thing you noticed, entering the Gioia house, was that you couldn't see six feet before your face. A ten watt bulb lit every room, and if a guest arrived the Doctor grumblingly turned on a lamp, so that Francesco found himself eating dinners in a long, dark room reminiscent of the anthracite pit. Grazia Gioia held herself like an actress, Duse or Sarah Bernhardt; she spoke in the swooping notes she imagined such divas employed. A life-sized photograph of Duse hung in the front hallway, kept so dim that on Francesco's first visit he thought a live woman was toppling into him, and nearly screamed. A cardboard woman would have made him happier than Bellina, Bellina the unmarriageable, whose lips leaked sentences so insipid, so banal, they almost made him cancel her betrothal to Vittorio. When Francesco showed photos of his brother in uniform (this was early days, and negotiations with the Doctor hadn't begun) Bellina gazed at Vittorio's profile and sighed, "What a brave fighter for our beloved Fatherland!" And she looked at Francesco with the smile of a moron, or a child. What dowry could make any man happy with a woman who smiled like that?

Meanwhile, his hagglings with Doctor Gioia were more annoying than his brother's hypothetical misery. Not only did the Doctor consider Bellina lovely, he disliked the idea of any dowry beyond setting Vittorio up in a modest practice and buying a "little house," as he repeated, driving Francesco to despair. For God's sake, he thought, this vast mausoleum we're sitting in could house every Carney and Monti employee! Yet the Doctor affected poverty, groaning about the income tax, the losses on his land, his stocks, even his Italian war bonds.

"Doctor," Francesco began impatiently, "your land in the northeast quadrant lies across the proposed railroad tracks, doesn't it?"

"And if it does?" Gioia shot back. "You haven't been in America long enough, young man! These projects are castles in the air, mere fantasies! And even if the Railroad buys my land, does that make me a Rockefeller?"

"Not Rockefeller," Francesco said with a smile. "But not a beggar either, am I right? In fact you own three-quarters of the land the Railroad will buy in Philadelphia. I had your title checked, Doctor, so let's not argue over facts."

"I leave such trivia to clerks."

"If the Railroad pays you the market value, your land will sell for six million at least. Surely *that* number you know?"

"Six million or six thousand, it's all a fairy tale until I sell! They say you're a clever man, so understand: we live expensively. Bellina and my wife deserve only the best." Francesco kept himself from laughing in the doctor's face. "We have a large house at the shore, we keep servants, we entertain. To say nothing of the Catholic charities we support, the opera, the orchestra . . . ."

"Bellina, I know, desires a family of her own. And what better husband than a war hero, decorated by the King, and a brilliant doctor like yourself?"

"If he's so brilliant, your brother will prosper here as I did. I'll give him a practice and a little house, no more."

"Doctor, when the sale goes through your land will be worth millions! Be generous, Doctor. And think of Bellina—she has lived in luxury, so why make her start married life like a poor immigrant?"

Doctor Gioia grunted. "Eh, you like to talk, young man. Now I must rest, in the arms of Morpheus, as the divine Ovid says, after a long day of curing the sick. You know your way out, Monti, I believe."

And Gioia stood up, joints creaking under the weight of his

belly, so round and fat that he resembled an overripe fruit about to rot. Francesco could never connect the bloated miser with his giant daughter and her silly smile; Rosita called Bellina God's judgment on the doctor for his avarice. He shook Gioia's pink flipper of a hand, repulsed by its damp flabbiness, and made his way carefully out of the darkened house. If God punished parents with their children, what did that make Vittorio, Leonora, or himself? It was nonsense, he decided, like all talk about God . . . .

That night Rosita put a pink candle in her window to warn him that she was, as every month, indisposed. On such nights he slept alone in the house he'd built near his building site, or maybe went to a brothel and had a girl; tonight neither pleased him. He lingered in the street so long that a scarlet runabout, its white wheels vivid against the night, tootled by so quickly that it almost ran him down. Francesco began to walk.

The August humidity left Philadelphia drained of energy. Here and there Italians waited patiently for the horsecar, nibbling at peaches they carried in paper sacks, talking loudly over the noise of trucks which clattered by. Taxi horns sounded, agreeably blue like saxophones. Francesco glanced up at the skyline, reflexively; it was his North Star, that cast-iron ladder to heaven; he navigated by its frozen light. Now, over the Finance Building, a thin wisp of steam floated into the lights, gleaming like a silver ribbon as it rose toward the sky. And from the dance halls and speakeasies sizzled the hot jazz everybody played nowadays.

Francesco was drinking these details in as though for the first time, as though tonight everything he saw or heard was new. What a disaster he'd made, his houses almost lost and Bellina not yet pledged to Vittorio; without the Doctor's money, everything would slip away, everything he wanted so horribly. Greenglass was right, he wanted things too much, but what other way could he want anything? He remembered his father, as he'd been before and as he was after he'd lost what he wanted for himself—for himself, yes, the rest of the family hadn't meant a thing to him. He saw his father's face the day his mother told him to leave home: white, drawn, the face of a gambler too poor to bet. Do I look that way tonight? Francesco wondered. No. Because I haven't lost everything yet . . .

Next day he woke late, decided to skip the office and the Homes, and drifted over to Ninth Street, the heart of Little Italy. Francesco felt aimless, a way he never felt, a kite waiting for one strong breeze to lift him toward the sun. In truth Francesco was waiting for his mind to present him with a plan. Like Houdini, whom he and Rosita gaped at whenever the escape artist came to town, he would rescue himself, break out of this trap he'd locked himself into . . . .

Ninth Street smelled of fresh herbs and imported cheese in the shop windows, and vegetables that reminded him of home, hot peppers and plump artichokes; but Ninth Street was his home now, it had to be, with vendors greeting him and priests soliciting funds; here he knew who Francesco Monti was, because he had invented him. Invented, yes, and he would not let his invention die. Francesco left Ninth Street and walked to Dr. Gioia's house. He walked so intently he never felt the heat of the day on his face.

As he'd guessed, only the women were home. Signora Gioia greeted him warmly and sent the maid to fetch Bellina. Francesco noted with delight that the Gioias had framed Vittorio's photograph and placed it prominently beside a bust of Mazzini. The fiancé and the liberator, he thought ironically. And who's worth more, a poor country or a rich wife?

"Signor Monti, what a coincidence!" Bellina swept into the room as gracefully as her legs would allow. "Just this moment I was writing a letter to your brother, it is the hand of God!"

"Save your ink, Signorina. I have bad news."

Bellina and her mother exchanged a look. "Your brother is not remaining in Italy?" asked Mrs. Gioia in her swooping tones.

"Ah, no. He wishes to break his engagement to your daughter."

"Break! His! Engagement!" Bellina shrieked each word separately.

"Please, Signorina Gioia, calm yourself. Surely you are not surprised?"

"*I* certainly am!" Sarah Bernhardt suddenly became an Italian mother awful in her wrath. "Last night you said nothing, nothing at all!"

"I received his letter in the early mail. I regret to say, Signora, he sounds quite definite."

"What—" Bellina was stammering, "What reason does Vittorio give?"

"I fear I will be indelicate—"

"Speak, Signor Monti. You are among friends." Signora Gioia drew herself up quite straight, to meet the blow. "I beg you, tell us what you know."

"Your father refuses to give a proper dowry. He says Vittorio must make his own way, that you two must live on a small income because he has expenses like the opera and the orchestra. I protested, but he is adamant. And my brother refuses to give up a certain future as our town doctor, supported fully by our Prince, only to eat bread and onions in America."

"But my wedding dress! It's already being sewn," Bellina wailed.

"Shut up, girl." Signora Gioia clasped her hands in unfeigned despair: "Who on earth will marry my Bellina now? Tell me, Signor Monti, who? She'll die an old maid, this house will go to her, the one in New Jersey, the stocks, the bonds, the land her father owns . . . . and our blood will stop with her. An only daughter carries the family future in her womb!"

Bellina was sobbing noisily. She looked like a defeated giantess in some fairy tale, inconsolable, her head shaking spasmodically.

"I think my husband's lost his mind," Signora Gioia spat. "You wanted a larger dowry? And that caused this breach?"

"As I have said," Francesco repeated carefully, "my brother will never live like a common immigrant in America. A decorated veteran, Signora, a University of Rome graduate? With respect, Vittorio deserves better and so does Bellina. But your husband prefers the orchestra." He shrugged.

"You have something in mind?" replied Signora Gioia cunningly.

"His land," Francesco said after a discreet pause. "Even a hundred acres will be worth a great deal soon. He could transfer the deed to me in care of Vittorio, and of course promise to buy them a large house, hire servants, all the rest. Not to speak of helping Vittorio open his own practice. Bellina is worth every cent, isn't she?"

"You are right, of course!" Signora Gioia declared. "Yes, I will speak to the Doctor this very night. Money comes and goes but our blood, our blood must survive." Her Sarah Bernhardt voice was back; Signora Gioia had regained self-control. Bellina hadn't, yet.

"Please, Signor Monti, help me, I'm just a poor girl in love."

"Love without money is even crueler than money without love," Francesco told her pitilessly. He rose and bid his farewells, even asking for Vittorio's photos back, which sent Bellina into paroxysms of grief. With a show of reluctance, he let her keep them all.

Francesco endured the next twenty-four hours with the aid of cigarettes and coffee. Carney got him drunk in a speakeasy filled with whores so young and clean they looked virginal. Take one of 'em upstairs, his partner said, and so Francesco did; but for once he could do nothing, no matter how the girl helped. He paid her double, mortified, and hurried home shivering, despite the heat. It's a goddamn omen, he thought, I'm through—I can't even fuck.

Francesco slept not at all that night. He lay smoking, watching the sun rise over the Garibaldi Homes; the sky glinted with the dull silver of summer dawn. Trolley bells sounded and the paper boys cried words he couldn't understand. The rhythm of their voices soothed Francesco, and he began to drowse. From far away, it seemed, he heard a knocking on his door. The bell rang three times, jerkily. He wrenched himself awake and dashed downstairs, where Doctor and Mrs. Gioia stood on the steps.

"You are a scoundrel, Monti, a blackmailer! Do you know that Bellina, my precious Bellina, has not eaten a crumb since you left my house, all she can do is sleep and weep—"

"You fool, the whole neighborhood will hear!" Signora Gioia hissed.

Francesco gestured them inside. With a stupefied expression, Doctor Gioia eased his bulk into Francesco's chair; it squeaked helplessly as he made himself comfortable.

"I have one child, Monti, and she is lovesick because of you! I tell you, if Bellina gets any worse, I'll make you sorry you ever heard of her!"

"Who is the blackmailer now, Doctor—you or me?"

"Shut up, fools," Signora Gioia snapped. "She is *my* daughter and I know what she needs—a husband, like every woman on earth! A house of her own and children of her own! But you, her father, would sell her birthright for an opera seat!" She glared at Francesco. "And you—playing with my poor Bellina's heart, leading her on with photographs and war stories—then crushing her! You, Monti, you have no pity, you are a block of ice. But *I* have a mother's heart." She paused triumphantly: "I will settle this marriage despite your male stupidity. I will arrange everything myself."

"The question of the dowry, Signora, remains . . . . troublesome."

Doctor Gioia squirmed; the chair squeaked under him like a mouse. "Blackmail. Blackmail."

"I shall speak reason," Signora Gioia cried, "since neither of you men can! Bellina's dowry will include one hundred acres of the land the Railroad wants. Now, Monti, are you satisfied? Now will you give Bellina back her heart?"

"Two hundred acres would make an even finer gift."

"One hundred and that's all," Doctor Gioia said painfully, as though each acre were a blood relative. "After the wedding, I might settle some property on Bellina—on *her*, you understand?"

Francesco smiled. He had no need to push, now that the Gioias had surrendered the first and most crucial battle. He accepted the land title Signora Gioia had in her purse, embracing his future in-laws, and escorted them downstairs to their Packard while spouting proverbs about marital happiness. Back in the house, he shaved quickly, adding and subtracting in his head. Yes, he could do it, with one lucky play; he would escape like Houdini, who never needed luck. He called his broker, silently begging his patron saints to protect him one more day.

FIVE

The Palazzo Bondini's drawing room looked as though no sunshine had violated its gloom since the War. Dust frosted the porcelain and crystal, once fashionable, now reduced to bric-a-brac; and even the furniture seemed in mourning, its gold varnish turned gray in what light leaked through the drapes. In a stillness broken only by the distant clock, Leonora and the Duchess sat sipping English tea. Family portraits stood sentry, the Bondini counts, from their expressions, martyred by hemorrhoids.

"That fool of a butler made our tea too weak."

"No, no, I like it very much."

"Your revolution failed," the Duchess said, without changing her tone. "Your heroic workers left the factories."

"They occupied them, didn't they?"

"They left without firing a shot. Even a bad opera makes its chorus sing. I thank God Verdi is dead and can't see this."

"Next time—"

"Leonora, there'll be no 'next time'. What do you think they discuss at my husband's club every day? They want order, and they'll find someone who promises it. Those men believe each other's silly talk."

"Then everything good and vital here will die."

"How can something die that was never born? You come from the South, has anything ever changed down there? Here, yes, they build factories, but did that alter one blessed thing? We are still a hundred years behind Germany!"

"You really hate Italy that much?"

"There is no Italy. There are only Italians—you and me, my husband and yours, and this butler who can't make tea properly." The Duchess smiled to show she was serious.

I liked it better when she blamed the Devil, thought Leonora. The Devil was such a comfortable enemy. If he won, it affirmed the need to keep fighting him, and if by chance he lost (or seemed to, his trickery made such conclusions dangerous) not only God but mankind won the victory. Why couldn't the Duchess return to her mystical flights, since now Leonora would gladly agree? The workers' failure made more sense as a satanic plot than as class suicide. Yes, go back to mysticism, Duchess, let's have some fun . . . .

"I am sick of Turin, sick of these politics, if they deserve the name. I have decided to leave for Paris, in two weeks."

"Paris . . . ." Here was the most practical mysticism of all, since for Leonora the city glittered more brilliantly than any diamond sold in Via Cavour. Paris, the capital of freedom, beauty, art—no other city could intoxicate her with its name.

"Just for the winter," the Duchess said. "Winters in Turin are so hideous, you know. I will take a house in the Bois, and study sculpture—I can't live here, filled with disappointment and disgust. Carving my stone angels kept me alive a while, but now . . . . Would you like to come, my dear? Keep an old woman company?"

"Oh, heavens, how could I leave my husband?"

"Don't be so conventional! Aren't we free women, you and I?"

"But I still work, Duchess, and he depends on what I bring in . . . ." She felt so vulgar talking that way in a palazzo, so petit-bourgeois. But the Duchess seemed not to hear.

"I don't hate Italy, as you said. But in Paris one can breathe. Here . . . . slow suffocation, the sickness unto death . . . ."

It was October now, and the dappled leaves made Turin more attractive than usual; still, every worker's face reminded Leonora,

after she left the palazzo, of the factory occupations, of their
fervent days and nights in the FIAT plant, of the looks of
bewilderment and helpless rage on Lampa's face, on Gramsci's,
when the workers came shuffling out of the steel battlefields
they'd seized. Of course everyone had an explanation; defeat, as
her father liked to say, inspired the true Italian gift for blame and
argument. Gramsci and Lampa quarreled fiercely, the hunchback
insisting that the Socialist left split off and become Communists,
shock troops of the proletarians who needed leadership, while
Lampa laughed at such fantasies, saying neither the workers nor
the owners would tolerate Communists. For him, the workers
could have held out if other rebellions had begun, a general strike
maybe or at least a peasant uprising. But alone, Lampa insisted,
even the most militant workers were doomed to lose their nerve.
Both he and Gramsci pointed to Russia, drawing, of course,
opposite conclusions from Lenin's success. Leonora wondered
whether they understood Italy any better; and yet she felt drawn
to Lampa's cool realism, supporting him in the Party debates.

"You don't like me," Gramsci said to her one night.

"We disagree, Comrade, that's all . . . ."

"You don't, I know. How the hell can I build a Communist
Party when a woman like you finds me so unappealing?"

"You might cut your hair, Comrade. All the factory workers
noticed how long it is."

"I wish you would be sincere," Gramsci replied bitterly.

What strange Socialists he and the others made: some, boys
posing as men, some, like Gramsci, paralyzed by self-
consciousness; and then the scrappers like her Lampa, who ran
his engine on espresso and cigarettes, always keen to dispute history
or tactics or strategy. Perhaps the Duchess was right: no revolution
led by this crew would succeed. Yet, failure didn't prove
damnation any more than a success like Francesco's proved God's
grace. He was still sending her money orders she left uncashed in
the bank, saving them for that day everyone foresaw, when the
Socialists might be forced underground. For now the plump
Prime Minister treated them like irritating gnats, swatting their

factory occupations away easily, without violence. But all that could change: thugs loyal to the Socialist Mussolini roamed the country, and who knew when the signal to attack would come from that strutting renegade?

Paris, Leonora thought, shopping for dinner, Paris. Only she knew that Lampa would not leave, not at the instant in history when Gramsci was splitting the Party into meek Socialists and bloodthirsty Communists, not when he hadn't decided yet which way he would jump himself. The great defeats made history move, Lampa told her that over and over, citing the English Chartists and the Paris Commune, associating Turin unconvincingly with those grandiose failures of the Revolution. Paris, yes. But did she have the courage to go alone?

Impulsively she stopped at the Church of St. Teresa. Five-o'clock Mass was ending; the last Latin words were still echoing. High above, candles behind red glass shed a flickering light on the nave. Leonora knelt and prayed as she hadn't done for months. In the next pew an old woman mumbled over her rosary, reminding Leonora of the convent chapel where she could never pray without the company of a wrinkled nun. Still, she prayed the prayers learned in childhood, and little by little she grew less anxious. Give me the wisdom to decide properly, Leonora finished, and dipped her fingers in the ice-blue water of the stoup. Shivering, she made the sign of the cross, quickly genuflected, then walked out into the darkening dusk.

It was absolution she craved, she knew herself well enough to know that: for fleeing San Lorenzo without a word or a letter to her mother, for living in sin with Lampa, for avoiding pregnancy thanks to the pessaries she bought clandestinely. Leonora knew no penance could ever wash all those sins away. Here it was almost 1921—she mocked herself—and she still thought like a peasant girl pulling radishes from the dirt . . . .

When she reached their apartment Leonora heard an unfamiliar thumping sound, like someone pounding on a wall. Opening the door, she saw Lampa dragging the enormous trunk they had brought north with them from San Lorenzo years before, its brass studs bouncing off the floorboards as he pulled it into the living room. He looked up at her, face flushed, and smiled like a surprised child.

"I should have told you not to shop for dinner," he said. "We're leaving on the eight o'clock train."

"Leaving? To go where?" Suddenly dizzy, Leonora dropped her groceries.

"Bressanone. The Party needs an organizer there.'

"For God's sake, that's nearly Austria! We can't go there like gypsies, overnight . . . ."

"That bastard Mussolini's stronger in the country, you read the papers. If we organize now, at least we have a prayer of stopping him—"

Leonora laughed. "Prayer? Is that a Socialist tactic now?"

"Don't be a fool. It must be done."

"When were you going to ask if I wanted to go? In Bressanone?"

Lampa sighed. "I thought you loved me so much I didn't need to ask."

"Oh, that's a good line. It's also ridiculous."

"Why? Because you'd rather hobnob with your crazy Duchess than help stuff envelopes at headquarters?"

"You knew I wouldn't go. Not like this."

"Whither thou goest, I shall go. Book of Ruth."

"First prayer and now the Old Testament! Strange sort of Socialist you've become!"

"Laugh if you want, as long as you come with me." Lampa stared at her. "Leonora . . . . please. I need you."

"Is this why you didn't want a baby? Because the Party has other plans?"

"We can have a baby when we've hung Mussolini by his balls."

"And if I came, what good could either of us do in a place we've never seen?"

"So you want Mussolini to win, is that it?"

"I am not in personal charge of Italian history—are you?"

"So you don't give a damn about saving Italy?"

"I can't touch Italy, I can't make love to it. I can touch you and make love to you. And if that makes me a traitor to the Party, all right then I am. I don't care, don't you understand? If Mussolini wins it won't be because you didn't go to Bressanone."

Lampa's face darkened. "You're saying you'd rather keep me with you even if I'm miserable?"

"Oh, for God's sake. Did you like the sound of gunfire so much you want more? That's what they're sending you to, your sacred Party. Did they give you a gun or are you just supposed to wave Das Kapital?"

"You have a tongue like a snake—mocking me, mocking my comrades. I'd rather drink Mussolini's castor oil than listen to you."

"Then go." Leonora threw herself into his arms. "No, don't go, don't go."

"Come with me, you must come, you must," he was murmuring into the nape of her neck. "I still love you, Leonora, I love you more than the day we met, only you don't believe it now . . . ."

Silently she began to weep. The hot tears streamed down her face, into the crevice between her breasts. "I believe it, I do."

"Then you must come." He faced her again, hope fluttering in his eyes like a trapped bird ready to soar. "We can take the ten o'clock local if you need time to pack."

"My dear, my dear." She was holding his hands in hers. "Don't you see? I won't go, and I won't let you leave."

The trapped bird abruptly folded its wings: something in Lampa's eyes grew hard and old. He removed his hands from her.

"I'm going," he said coldly, bending over the trunk again.

"You'll die there, you know, in those miserable Alps."

"Then be glad," he snapped, "that I didn't leave you with a child."

"You're really going? For a Party that couldn't keep the factories occupied two months?"

"You know what they say about Mussolini, that his wife's

such a shrew that he went into politics to get away from her? I never believed it until now."

"Oh, shut up about politics, Italy, those noble alibis—you want some excitement, that's all, a little guerrilla warfare in the daytime and me waiting with soup at dinnertime. Some revolutionary! Why don't you ask your mother to come instead?"

Lampa's hand jerked up to slap her. At the last instant he stopped himself. "You're a real Monti, you know that? Just like your stupid grasping father and your brother who thinks he's found Paradise in a country where they hang Negroes from trees. You can't see farther than your ass, that's your problem. You left the convent but in your heart you still believe their rules—bathe twice a day, count your money, and ignore your neighbor because loving him is too inconvenient. The only Socialist thing you ever swallowed was my prick."

With a struggle, he got his suitcase shut. They faced each other like boxers too weary for another round.

"Please don't go."

"I'm sorry for what I said."

That meant he was leaving nevertheless. She gave him a last embrace; he shook it off. Halfway out the door, he said: "If you want to write, Party headquarters will know where." She began weeping again, loudly now, her chest racked with pain she'd never known before, as though someone were slowly and painfully stabbing her heart.

She went to the Socialist Party headquarters the next day, after work, with some vague notion of getting Lampa's address and joining him. The comrades were milling around in tense knots, squabbling over the local elections a week away. At last she found Gramsci, who greeted her in his editor's cubbyhole with a harried smile.

"Lampa left alone?" he inquired.

Leonora nodded, humiliated at the memory of their fight. "His address . . . ."

"If you don't have it, Signora, how should I?"

"But he told me . . . ." And she broke down, trying to wipe

her tears away as quickly as they fell. "Maybe," she said, grasping at reason, "maybe he'll send you word when he gets there? Is that possible?"

"By then I'll be purged as a Communist," Gramsci grinned. "If you only knew how *sick* I am—"

"Of politics? Who isn't? Even Lampa, or he would have stayed and fought instead of going north. Here in Turin we are at the eye of the hurricane. If our workers are crushed the whole country will be."

"Yes, I read your editorial last week, Comrade."

"You know why Lampa left? We spend more time fighting each other than we do fighting for votes. It's like breathing poison gas, here. The pettiness, the spitefulness. It'll choke me too."

"Then leave, if you're so unhappy," Leonora's impatience made her almost scream. "Go back to Sardinia—that's your province, isn't it?" Lampa, all those months, must have been feeling the same way—and hadn't said a word. That hurt almost as much as his departure had.

"Sardinia," Gramsci sighed. "In my old age I shall retire there and write down our folktales. After the revolution, of course," he added sardonically. "Like my favorite folktale, 'Brother Antonio.' I will use it for my editorial next week. You don't have to read it, if you want to hear it now."

Leonora shrugged. She felt irrationally safe here, in the office where Lampa had spent so many years.

"Once upon a time a monk named Brother Antonio had to beg for food for his monastery every day. He preferred begging from the poor since whatever they gave, they gave cheerfully. But he avoided a certain rich banker named Franchino, a stingy soul who bled the poor. Franchino, offended, went to Brother Antonio's prior and complained, 'I am no criminal, but an important man—make Brother Antonio accept my charity.' That night, the prior told Brother Antonio to stop offending the banker from now on. And Brother Antonio bowed in obedient silence to this command.

"Next morning he went to Franchino's house, where the

banker loaded his knapsacks with all the good food money could buy. Brother Antonio hoisted the sacks onto his back and set off for his monastery. But at the first step he took, a drop of blood stained his cassock, and then another, and another. People saw the sacks dripping blood and said, 'Well, well, Brother Antonio, meat today for you monks! The banker has given you a feast!'

"When Brother Antonio reached his monastery, the other monks cried that nobody had ever donated so much meat. They grabbed the knapsacks and opened them, but there was nothing inside. 'Is the Devil at work?' they shouted, terrified. 'Where did the blood come from?' 'Don't be afraid, brothers,' Brother Antonio replied. 'That is the blood of all the poor people the banker has robbed.'"

"Trust you to find a Marxist folktale," Leonora laughed.

"Everything in Italy is just a family spat, and then we all sit down for a nice plate of spaghetti. But we refuse to be bribed with a family dinner, we Socialists, and that's why we scare everyone. Even the poor!"

"My father used to say Italians are all either cops or criminals."

"Not even. Not this bunch in here."

"And you, which are you? I can't picture you with a gun."

"It doesn't matter." Gramsci imitated a saint, comically rolling his eyes to Heaven. "I'll end my life in a jail cell, I know, it's my destiny. At least with you Lampa had a house and a bed to share . . . ."

His flirting tone was unmistakable. Not that Gramsci wanted anything so vulgar as a tumble in her bed, she knew: he wanted someone to worship him the way he imagined she worshipped Lampa once. She could scarcely recall that time herself.

"My younger brother in America has sent me cash. I would like to wire it to Lampa in the North."

"He won't want it, Signora." Gramsci smiled gently. "I think it would hurt his pride."

"Even if I sent it through the Party?"

"If you give it to these men, it might never reach Lampa at all. Not that they're thieves, but we're losing everywhere, and they're getting desperate."

She had nothing left to say. Leonora allowed Gramsci to escort her out, through rooms full of men interrupting each other angrily. She promised him she would return another day, for coffee perhaps. Gramsci bowed, smiled, and disappeared back into history.

SIX

It took Leonora weeks in San Lorenzo to know she'd changed, and how much. The woman who'd felt the gray weight of Turin crushing her had disappeared, by then. She now loved San Lorenzo in a way she hadn't since childhood. She walked its crooked lanes gaily, greeting neighbors, blithe as a convict accidentally set free. The Leonora of Turin was alchemized into the smiling clear-eyed woman who faced her each morning in her bedroom mirror.

Her mother accepted the lie Leonora still spun to excuse Lampa's absence, seemingly clearly more concerned with her first grandchild. And Vittorio, became maniacally medical, feeding her vitamins, examining her when morning sickness struck like daily doom. So this is what a family does, she thought with real wonder. For the Montis had never protected or consoled each other before. How long she had seen her parents, even Vittorio, as implacable and harsh, when now they seemed allies or comforters.

Except for the breakfast when her mother declared:

"Of course you will name the child after my poor Leone."

"But if it's a girl?"

"Girls don't matter. Call her anything, a saint's name, maybe."

"Oh, Mamma, what a dinosaur you are!" Leonora cried.

"Girls love their fathers," her mother replied placidly. "Boys are devoted to their mother. Look at Francesco and the liras he sends me. Girls leave home and good riddance, if you ask me."

Vittorio's face took on a comically pathetic air, like Charlie Chaplin about to eat his shoe. He let his chin drop to the edge of the breakfast table and began to wail in an infant's coo, "Mamma, Mamma, can I please have my breast feeding now?"

"Quit clowning," their mother commanded. "Save that for the peasants you prefer to decent folk."

"Which peasants? The ones your sainted Leone cheated out of land?"

"Your father never cheated anyone, poor soul!—Why do you think he lost everything he had?"

"Then my brother Francesco must be a big crook, with all *he's* got."

"Isn't he finding you a rich wife?" Leonora taunted him. "Don't you want to marry a lady of means, as D'Annunzio would say?"

"No," said Vittorio gloomily, "I take whatever gifts God places before me. Only sometimes a gift is a trap, you know, a pit into which you blindly fall. Like the Prince's clinic! I should never have agreed to it!"

"You're talking nonsense," their mother said with her maddening calm. "Where else could you have learned so much so fast? And stayed at home to take care of me, and now your sister?"

"A trap," Vittorio muttered again. Then he posed his daily questions to Leonora, how hungry was she, how much did she urinate, while noting her answers in the ledger he'd labeled LEONORA'S PROGENY, 1921. His show of expertise changed the family mood to expectant joy, so much so that Lucinda started rattling off baby names in case a girl arrived. Perhaps today, Leonora thought, I should finally tell everyone the truth, Lampa too . . . .

Each day at four, Leonora and her mother drank afternoon coffee, which inevitably reminded her of the Duchess' tea. The second mail arrived a bit earlier, and so one afternoon Leonora found herself studying an elaborate itinerary of Francesco's return.

The words AMERICAN EXPRESS glittered at its top in gilt sans-serif.

"Isn't it wonderful, the family united again?" her mother asked gleefully.

"Wonderful. But then my brothers will go to America?"

"Let them go. I will take care of my grandchild. I don't need them for that."

"I was looking at Francesco's photograph . . . ." Leonora let the sentence trail.

"Go on."

"Don't you ever . . . . regret sending him to America?"

"Never. I never look back. Neither should you. Regrets are for fools."

Outside the Monti house, San Lorenzo offered pleasure, pure. The life of the town moved as slowly and predictably as a carousel; after the Turin frenzy, monotony soothed Leonora's nerves. Only her mother's demand that she attend daily Mass curdled her joy. Naturally she kept the secret that she and Lampa still hadn't wed; the shock would have killed her mother, after those letters Leonora tried not to think of as lies. And so she attended Mass, made novenas, said rosaries, even confessed every venial sin to Father Ugo while omitting the mortal ones. Peasants bore children out of wedlock. The gentry never. Shuddering at the thought, she knelt in the dank church and told herself, told God, her child's soul was worth her daily fraud.

Little by little, Leonora made a few acquaintances. Lampa's successor, a mild bespectacled science teacher, came to call, bearing the Turin and Milan newspapers from a few weeks back. But he was dull and awkward. She preferred the daughters of the lawyer Amabile, once a village shyster, now the King's Counsel and intent on rising higher yet. Her mother said acidly Amabile was and always would be a café wrangler, quite out of his depth in the Roman politics he hoped to enter soon.

Yet Leonora liked him, laughed with him at the strange blend of feudal and modern times Italy remained. Amabile loaned her

books, above all his idol Pareto, Italy's answer to the Germans
Max Weber and Durkheim. The King's Counsel had the tact not
to mention her own Socialism when they discussed Pareto's views.
Amabile found his grim vision of the State congenial, perhaps,
Leonora guessed, because he hoped to be someday one of its
mandarins.

Such talk scarcely substituted for real friendship. That Leonora
found in Amabile's own house, with Teresa, his eldest child. Five
years younger than she, Teresa Amabile radiated the cheery sunshine
of their town; her small white teeth were always, it seemed, parted
in a laugh. Leonora envied her slim figure, envious of the younger
woman's perfect, doll-like build, jealous too of her imperturbable
grin.

"Tell me, is marriage wonderful, Leonora?"

"Wonderful."

Teresa sighed yearningly. "What about the kissing and all of
that? You know."

"Heavenly. If you love the man."

"Oooh, I wish I were married right now! It's so dull listening
to Father talking about politics, I'd rather have a husband who'd
talk to me . . . ."

"But you seem so happy as you are."

"But a girl should marry. All my sisters already did."

"And are they happier as wives?"

Teresa giggled, covering her mouth. "Of course not. But *I'll*
be, I know. I'll marry for love, not because Father makes a useful
alliance. My sisters ended up married to help Father's political
career . . . . do I shock you, Leonora? Talking this way?"

"Of course not. We can talk openly." Leonora paused,
wondering how much truth Teresa Amabile could bear to hear.
"But it's just as hard when you're in love. Everything changes
once you have to shop for him, cook for him—"

"I know *that*," Teresa said sunnily. "I think I would adore
ironing my husband's clothes!"

Leonora laughed. "You think so now, when your maid presses your own."

"I know it! I've wanted it ever since I read Jane Eyre when I was twelve."

"You'll marry a man, you know, not some Mr. Rochester."

"Isn't your marriage good? You sound as though I should be afraid, Leonora, it's not so comforting . . . ."

"Life is full of strange twists and surprises. Look at me, having a baby here by myself! I didn't expect that, want that, but here I am—do you see what I mean?"

"Of course," Teresa frowned. "Isn't your brother treating our Prince?"

("Third degree syphilis," Vittorio told her the day she arrived. "If I weren't his doctor I'd put a bullet through his brain.")

"The Prince is taking an awfully long time to die," Teresa continued. "And my father was counting on a new appointment from the King, but that's all impossible until he does . . . ."

"It won't be long," Leonora said. "He screams all afternoon, even with morphine. He sees his life playing back slowly in his head, like a movie show. Isn't that peculiar?"

"He led a sinful life," Teresa observed primly. "The Prince is dying from that disease you get from bad women, isn't he? I know he is, my father said he's had every whore in Calabria. Not to mention the peasant girls. Oh, I wish he'd die soon, tonight even!"

"It's a sin to wish for someone else's death."

"Oh, we prayed for the Austrians to die during the war." Teresa shrugged. "It can't be much of a sin, if you ask me. Anyway I want to touch your stomach, can you feel the baby yet?"

"Just once, in the middle of the night—it woke me up."

"Ooh, how divine! Did it hurt?"

"Not really. It was like my stomach turning inside out."

"How marvelous! Of course you wrote your husband the wonderful news!"

Of course, she hadn't. The day after Leonora felt the kick she received this letter from the Italian Alps:

"My sweet turtledove,
        I never thought I would envy you San Lorenzo, but here I am, surrounded by dreary, foggy valleys and lakes. Bressanone is a town of perhaps 12,000 souls (as the old folks say) where nothing of any importance has happened since Henry IV summoned a council to depose Pope Hildebrand. That was eight centuries ago! Today the valley offers only boredom unless you ski. Since this is summer, dullness reigns. The closer we Italians live to Germans and Austrians the more like them we become: stolid, beer-swilling—in short, idiots. The local doctor told me when I arrived: "If you're born up here you're out of luck. You either become an accomplice or a rebel, there's nothing in between." And those who rebel get out, mostly to Germany or our factories. Which leaves behind the sort of dullards who make you question history's inevitable, upward path.
        "Men have grown no wiser since the days of Socrates or the days of Galileo; they've only grown more petty." So says Alexander Herzen (whose memoirs I read myself to sleep with at night). Though a Russian noble and a critic of Marx, he had clear eyes and a manly heart. I read Herzen and I weep for what we have lost, those simple and above all *real* human contacts, friendships, even friction, the men of 1848 thrived on—while we, in our time, seem unable to act like true comrades for one day. Where is the human warmth which should make us act? Where indeed, when our Gramsci (I see in the paper that came today) has left us! To build his Communist party,

abandoning our hacks and backstabbers! It may be necessary to bring on the revolution by sabotaging the Socialist Party!

Do you recall those Sunday afternoons in Turin when we lay on the grass reading love poetry to each other? I do, and often. I wanted those afternoons never to end. Never did you seem more radiantly beautiful to me, never did my heart yearn more for you. Our souls would softly swoon together at the loveliness of the Leopardi we spoke, half embarrassed at recognizing our own stirrings in his verse. You must remember, too.

Here I am lonely, so much so that I cry into the empty air just to hear my voice echo from the ravines. The great Ovid must have felt just as lonely in his exile, even more, all he could do was write elegies— I at least organize a few more Socialists every day. The people up north are, as I say, stolid, but they suffered badly during the Great War, which means they hear the Party's message and don't sneer at our dreams. Absentee landlords own most of their lands and it's easier to hate the unseen than the seen; as one convert said, "My landlord doesn't even know I exist, so how can he have any rights over me?"

I'm amazed and of course happy that your family suspects nothing. Your story that I am teaching Catholic school in Turin and so can't afford your confinement is really inspired! And in any case you've been away from San Lorenzo long enough to return now, like so many Italian girls who give birth in the cradle of their families. Just don't mention that I'm a paid Socialist organizer unless you want a riot on your hands—your miserable town is a century behind the rest of Italy. At least!

Enough squalid practicality. Know that I love

you, that I dream of you every night. For some
reason you always wear blue in my dreams—
perhaps I should consult that Dr. Freud in Vienna,
since he's not too far away? As for the child's name:
if it's a boy Carlo and Federico are my first choices
(after Marx and Engels, of course)—if it's a girl,
how about Rosa or Eleonora (after Luxembourg,
or Marx's daughter)? But I'll let you decide, since
after all in this division of labor you are
contributing far more than me. I'm only half
joking. It really astonishes me that a single sperm
of mine may produce a Carlo Lampa, nine months
after an embrace neither of us knew would have
such a destiny!

   With all my love, my kisses, my fondest
memories . . . ."

Leonora sat reading Lampa's letter on the sea wall, the dull
booming of the surf a counterpoint to his words. After a time
she stood up and gazed out into the azure mist. Greece lay over
the horizon, invisibly; thousands of years ago its settlers had
colonized Calabria, calling it Greater Greece. Presumably they'd
displaced the original tribes, of whom no record remained, no
tomb paintings like the Etruscans' to mark glory before the
invaders killed them off. That was all history meant to Italy,
wave after wave of massacres by conquerors, the Arabs, the French
and Germans, mingling their blood with the women they
enslaved, so that even in San Lorenzo you saw a pair of blue eyes
under blond hair, or a nose that could only be Saracen. No wonder
Italy couldn't take the idea of a nation seriously. For three thousand
years it had been drinking the blood of foreigners foolish enough
to imagine they would conquer it permanently.

   The Duchess was right: there was no Italy. There was San
Lorenzo and Turin and Bressanone and of course Rome. What
would it take to forge a nation from such anarchy? Socialism
offered brotherhood, but the very land mocked its rhetoric. And

only poets believed in brotherhood. Calabria, all rock and sand, taught suspicion, wariness. A true Calabrian would never leave home, or at least would never feel sure anyplace else would prove less treacherous. You survived by doubting even God's mercy, since it was invisible. Which made Francesco and his ilk renegades, traitors to the folk wisdom, guilty of too much hope. And she too, hadn't she left on a whim with Lampa, and wasn't she humbled by her return?

No, she decided, I feel joy. At the azure infinity of the sea, the shouts of fishermen hauling in their catch, joy even at the twisting streets, around whose every turning lurked a hag ready to give Leonora a fishy look that unsettled her. There was your home and then there was the world. In that sense Leonora knew she was no Socialist, since she dreaded the ways the new century would change San Lorenzo, the displaced persons it would create. Progress, so called, pleased only politicians, who needed proof of their indispensability.

She passed the clinic on her way home and saw Vittorio, for once sitting alone. He gestured her in. The Prince's cry of agony roared out of the palace, one hundred feet away.

"Isn't there something you can do for him?"

"You mean put him out of his misery?" he grinned.

"I don't know . . . . more morphine? Would that help?"

"More morphine," Vittorio grinned, "would kill our Prince instantly. And since I am waiting for his heir to return from inspecting his Argentina lands, I prefer he find a live Prince, if possible."

"In other words, you're keeping the poor man alive?"

"Certainly." Vittorio grinned. "Let him suffer the way our father did when the Prince ruined him. The way I did when he made my veterans disband.'

"That isn't Christian," Leonora stammered.

"I didn't invent pain. If Christ wants to cure syphilis he can, any time it pleases Him."

"But the Hippocratic Oath—"

"Says, first do no harm. If I give him morphine and he dies,

I would certainly do harm, and there would be questions—serious questions."

Leonora shook her head. "It all seems so dreadfully cruel to me."

"Women never understand anything," he smirked.

"I've lived through strikes and riots, and I understand more than you think."

Vittorio frowned. "So do I, Leonora. So do I."

"And what does that mean?" She recklessly flung the dice.

"It means *you* are a *liar*. Lampa isn't teaching Catholic school up north—a fine tale to throw dust in our mother's eyes! In fact he hasn't taught a day since you and he left here."

"Of course he's teaching. Why else would I have come back?"

"He's a Socialist agitator. Isn't he?"

"I won't sit and listen to your slanders—"

"Leonora," he said wearily, "I belong to an organization which keeps a close watch on these Bolsheviks. I know where Lampa is. And I know why."

"Don't tell our mother," Leonora blurted out. "She mustn't know, please, promise me you won't—"

"I'm not as cruel as you seem to think." Vittorio rocked in his chair, studying her like a patient afflicted with some obscure disease. "I know his type, he abandoned you. Did he bother to marry you first?"

In the rare moments Leonora had to tell a sizable lie, she knew she could, and so she nodded casually, as though the question scarcely deserved a reply. Meanwhile, the gold ring she always wore told its own untruth.

"That's something, I suppose." Her brother stood up, cracking his knuckles noisily. "Don't worry. I won't upset our mother. But I want you to know, I hate men like Lampa the way priests hate atheists. If they get their way Italy will have civil war. He didn't fight the Austrians, so he understands nothing. Life is war, and peace comes only after death, if then. And you fight or you die, simple as that. But Lampa's kind think they can declare all men are brothers and that will make it true. Men aren't brothers, Leonora, men are killers, and they kill whenever, whomever they damn well please. You can't make men brothers just because a dead German Jew said they are."

"I don't believe that," Leonora said. "I don't."

SEVEN

Years later, when he was about to die in America, Francesco
Monti murmured, "The three pine trees, the three pine trees . . . ."
As none of his children had yet seen San Lorenzo, his words
made no sense to them at all. But when he returned in the summer
of 1921, the first glimpse Francesco got of his hometown were
those three trees. They stood atop a pyramid of rocky soil, above
the railroad tracks at the very point where the train began slowing
into the station a mile ahead. They stood (until they were chopped
down and the hill leveled after the Second War for a road
mockingly known as 'The German Highway') like proud sentries
patiently watching for the intruders every small town knows may
someday arrive to disrupt its sleep.

They were dry and brittle fingers, three fingers of the same
gaunt hand. Thirsty for rain after a summer of sun and wind
from Africa, their leaves gray and silver, they offered the traveller
no refuge from the long trip south. The three trees chanted the
proverbs everyone in San Lorenzo knew: life is a struggle, only
death brings peace, all else is pain and toil. It was scarcely the
wisdom of the America Francesco inhabited. What an exile misses
is not the beauty of his homeland. Its familiar harshness, its
bitterness can ache him like a missing limb. And so the three
pines outside San Lorenzo, those gray-green, silvery-green pine
trees, imprinted them forever on Francesco's heart.

On the day of his homecoming, though, they seemed an

irrelevant detail, one daub of color in the bright fresco of his Odyssean return. As the train neared San Lorenzo he heard a brass band warming up, which made him wonder whether he had perhaps arrived on some holiday, a commemoration of the bloodbath he'd been spared by leaving Italy? But no, the brass band was for him. The train wheezed to a halt, and they began to mangle first Italy's and then America's national anthems.

His brother hoisted him onto the platform, snatching his bags, his trunk, his briefcase, handing them to two men who ran to an open touring car where, Francesco saw, his mother and sister sat waving at him from a flower-bedecked back seat. Vittorio wore side whiskers and a Garibaldian moustache and, worse, reeked of a violet eau de cologne. A slight stoop to his shoulders, a vague bitterness in the way his lips curved down, made Vittorio seem a bit strange to him. Only his authoritarian eyes, intent on commanding as ever, recalled the brother of Francesco's childhood. At last the brass band switched to a medley of heroic Verdi choruses, a cue for Vittorio and Francesco to walk in the pitiless sun to the car, for the returning son to enfold himself in a sister's kisses and a mother's tears.

Francesco had long since hardened himself to the thought that his mother would grow old and weak. Now he saw how wrong he was. Signora Monti was older, of course, but no more helpless than when he'd left; she seemed stronger, in fact, as though her husband's death had released some hidden strength. Francesco didn't expect to recoil from this new matriarch, but he did, and feeling a traitor to his blood he embraced her over and over as though the gesture would force him to feel, he believed, as he ought to feel. It did not. He was no longer the child who adored her, she was no longer the mother who doted on him, if either of them had ever played those roles.

To add to his sense of displacement, San Lorenzo scarcely corresponded to his memories. As the touring car rattled down the cobblestones, Francesco glanced out, stunned by colors he had forgotten, houses of blood-red stone, blue doorways, tile the precise green of seawater. He had played on all these streets, but not one of them brought back a cozy glow. Now that he'd lived more than half his life in America it made sense, he thought, for San Lorenzo to look alien. The family car might have been crossing a town in Africa, or Samarkand. Either this town that mocked his memories truly existed, or he did. And if Francesco Monti did not exist, then who sat stiffly on the hot leather of the car seat? Who'd crossed the Atlantic and whizzed down the peninsula on a sparkling silver train?

He couldn't prove he existed, here. That boy of 1905 had died, leaving behind only photographs and dissolving memories. No, he thought, stepping out of the car behind his pregnant, uncomfortable sister, I no longer exist. He smiled at Leonora and helped her into the family house, wondering if she could see that he was now a ghost.

EIGHT

"I don't like this Bellina Gioia's face," Vittorio said, throwing her photograph onto the breakfast table. It was the morning after Francesco's return, and the two brothers hadn't yet discussed the marriage he'd arranged. "Her eyes are so far apart, she looks like a fat sheep."

Francesco and his mother exchanged a glance, while Leonora listlessly spooned up her cream of rice. "She's no beauty," Francesco began, cautiously, "but she's a sweet girl. And she worships you."

"Worships me! She's never met me, for Christ's sake!"

"Don't swear," his mother snapped. "Drink more coffee, all of you—I ordered it specially for this occasion, this Ethiopian."

"Bellina will make you a fine wife," Francesco continued. "She's obedient, and polite. Besides," he added slyly, "she's an only child and her father's worth millions. Beauty fades, Vittorio, but money multiplies. Forever."

Leonora finally raised her head. "You're both disgusting! This is 1921, for heaven's sake! Who arranges marriages nowadays?"

"*I* should have arranged *yours*," Signora Monti said in her sharpest tone.

Vittorio frowned. "More important, what kind of medical practice will I get? I'm sick of treating this town's scum for everything that ails them. I want to treat children only."

Leonora and her mother stared at him, shocked. They'd never heard this plan before and, considering Vittorio's lack of patience, the thought of him ministering to screaming babies seemed an unlikely one.

He smiled wolfishly. "I know what *you* think: I haven't got the temperament. But you're wrong. I happen to be quite good with infants, even those brats in the clinic who crap all over my chairs."

Francesco said quickly, "Doctor Gioia will set you up in any practice you want. He promised me."

"You have a smooth answer for everything! I see how you sold all those houses!" Vittorio grinned, disclosing through beard and whiskers the mischievous scamp Francesco remembered from their youth.

"Then it's definite? You'll marry Bellina?"

"Certainly." Vittorio grinned again. "What do her looks matter—all cats are gray in the dark, aren't they, mommy dear?"

"Don't talk smut," his mother hissed.

"How many months are you—advanced?" Francesco asked Leonora.

"Almost five," she said tonelessly. A moment later, she was dashing from the table to vomit up the Ethiopian coffee and the breakfast rolls.

"I thank God he didn't make *me* a woman," Vittorio observed. "Just think of all the diseases women get that we don't, the thousand illnesses their sex exposes them to. Why, their private parts alone—"

"Vittorio, enough!" his mother cried.

"Require constant attention and care, unlike ours, not to mention the ebb and flow of their hormones every month! It's quite unhealthy to be a woman, no doubt of it."

"Then why, fool, do we live longer than you do?" his mother snapped.

"Because none of you work," said Vittorio triumphantly. "If women worked ten or twelve hours a day, you'd all drop dead sooner than us!"

Francesco smiled at the exasperated look his mother wore. "How did I raise such a simpleton?" she implored God. "At least my other son has common sense!"

"And why haven't *you* married, little brother? Too much common sense?"

"Too busy," Francesco replied evasively. He prayed his mother and Vittorio would remain incurious about his life. Not that he could have told them about Laura; he wouldn't have known how to describe a day spent shuttling between brickworks, building site, and bed.

"American women are all ugly, they look like men, they all have short hair and hard faces," Signora Monti declared. "No wonder you haven't found a bride. Make your fortune first, my son."

"Bellina Gioia doesn't look like *that*," Vittorio quibbled.

"A fine, honorable daughter of Italy," his mother said in a voice appropriate for dedicating a monument. "And Francesco is right. She will make you a fine wife. Not like those American girls who aren't even virgins on their wedding night. Why, I read about school parties where every girl kisses every boy! Disgusting! Infamous! A sin!"

"They are more adventurous than Italian girls," Vittorio observed. "Voltaire says marriage is the sole adventure open to the cowardly."

"Your Voltaire was a blasphemer and a sodomite," Signora Monti declared. "If anyone is burning in Hell, it's him."

"You believe in Hell, Francesco?" his brother asked suddenly.

Francesco pondered the question. Once he had listened to Laura claim that this world was some other planet's Hell, so much suffering and misery did life on earth entail, and she'd almost persuaded him. But Laura was an Anglican and knew nothing of sin. Hell certainly existed: the only doubt remaining for him was its location. It might be a state of continual self-torment, inward agony, or it might be what the priests said, an actual place of punishment. Yet if physical Hell existed, why should Extreme Unction, that deathbed confession even Voltaire craved, save sinners from its flames?

"I don't know," Francesco smiled. "I don't think about religion much."

"Curse your America!" his mother exclaimed, "It's so Protestant it's making you one too. Soon you'll think you earned God's grace by your own merit, the way those animals do, those *heretics*. Tell me, is it true that they have preachers on that box, that talking box—"

"The radio, Mamma," Francesco said quietly.

"Yes, yes, the radio. Preaching to millions of Protestants, don't they, telling them they can be saved by jumping into swimming pools?"

"It isn't quite like that."

"I'll never live there, believe you me, I'd rather survive another war—At least here people understand what sin is."

"What is it, anyway?" Vittorio taunted her. "I've never understood?"

"You of all my children need to ask? Look into your heart, examine your conscience—look how puffed up with pride and arrogance you've become. Thinking you are the Lord himself! A devilish idea your Voltaire and his infidels taught Europe. Sin is what drove Adam and Eve to set themselves against the good Lord and eat the fruit he forbade them to bite . . . ."

"That old wives tale!" Vittorio snickered.

"It is *God's truth*," his mother answered firmly but flatly.

Eager to forestall an argument, Francesco quoted Emerson: "God offers every mind a choice between truth and repose. Take which you want, but you can never have both."

"At least I have one son who understands," Signora Monti smiled, misunderstanding Francesco utterly.

"He's rich, of course *he* believes!" Vittorio leaned forward in his chair. "But what of a poor man, a veteran, what should they believe? They are fools to believe in a kindly God. I saw the face of God at Caporetto and God is a butcher. Like a bad general. He throws thousands of us into the machine guns and then ignores our screams. If there's a God, he's a thoughtless God, indifferent . . . ."

"That Satanic pride of yours! Calling God indifferent when he spared your life on the battlefield! Go, go, do penance for such thoughts!" Signora Monti was almost livid now.

Vittorio stood up. "I'm going to check on Leonora. That God of yours won't keep her healthy. I have to do the job."

After his older brother sauntered out, Francesco and his mother found almost nothing to say. Francesco began babbling about his brickworks, until she cut him off.

"I know what's in your heart," she said quietly. "I sent you away, and that you cannot forget."

"But I know you had to—" Francesco began.

"Understand, Francesco. Your father ruined me. All of us. Even now when I think of him my blood still boils . . . . I had no choice, no. Vittorio needed schooling. But do not hate me, please. I know I sacrificed you, but look how well you've done in that crazy America! You redeemed yourself, you redeemed us all. You saved this family, yes."

"Mother . . . ."

"If you hate me at least hate me for what I did. I had to do it. I never stopped loving you, thinking of you, praying for you. I kept all your letters, all those years of letters! Do you think I stopped being your mother the day you left San Lorenzo?"

"But I don't hate you. I never did. I swear."

"I used to think of you working those dreadful mines—we saw pictures of Italian boys like you down there, I saw them and I wept, I wept. But you were so good, never a reproach, never a complaint."

"I didn't have to stay long, Mamma. My friend Enrico—I wrote you about him?—he and I came to Philadelphia. We made our way. It's not a bad country, really. The people are crude but you can't help liking them, they don't know what *we* know, they don't know what is not possible. And so they do the impossible. I haven't been unhappy, I swear to you."

"And what about you? Did you do the impossible?"

Francesco couldn't help thinking of Doctor Gioia's land. He smiled modestly.

"I've been lucky, very lucky. The war made a lot of people rich. And my partner, Carney, he helps me, he treats me like a brother. So—yes, lucky."

"I don't believe in luck," Signora Monti said decisively. "Your father, God help him, did, and look where luck got him. In the gutter."

"You make your own luck. I got my chance because I was in the right place at the right time, but I didn't land there by accident. I worked! You'll never know how hard! You don't want to know. But the days I sweated, they're over now, thank God. Now I'm the boss. I say build, and my workmen build—and that's the way it'll be from now on. No more sweating for anybody else."

"You mean you don't want me to pity you?"

"Nobody wants pity, Mamma. *You* know that."

"Women do. Men, sometimes."

"But I'm a success, so why pity me? Pity the poor Italians eating bread and onions, the *cafoni*."

"Success, you call yourself. Yes, I suppose. But what did you have to sacrifice? Your home, your family, your country. Nobody ever sacrificed more, my son. You didn't have a real childhood. You had to be mother and father both to yourself. I hope the money is enough to pay you back for that."

"Do you feel guilty, Mamma? Is that it?"

"No . . . . at night I missed you, especially after your father died. I couldn't picture you, couldn't picture your eyes, your face, anything. I kept thinking of you down that coal mine or lugging red-hot bricks. And I wondered, did I really do right? Did he really have to go to America? And I always answered yes, Francesco had to go, or else what would have happened to all of us? But what happened to you? I don't know, because you won't tell me. Maybe you can't."

"I grew up, that's all. I would have grown up here, you know, I would have fought in the war just like Vittorio. I might even have been killed. America was less dangerous." Francesco was trying to make himself smile.

Signora Monti rose from her chair with a grand gesture dismissing the subject and Francesco at the same time. He stood alone in the dining room, listening to the muffled ticking of the clock, suddenly oppressed by the house which seemed to entrap him in its noise of time. Grabbing a boater hat Francesco skipped out the door and down to the beach, where he walked barefoot on the sand, smelling the sexual aroma of the low tide on the inlet's shore.

How close the landscape of memory lies, in the end, to the moonscape of dreams. Francesco remembered San Lorenzo with utter precision and (of course) utter inaccuracy. For years, falling asleep in America, he'd glimpse that stand of pine trees above the train tracks, the family house, the Prince's palace, except now he saw that in truth he had imagined it all. Those pine trees were smaller than his mind had painted them, stunted from lack of water in that stony soil, though they were still the first thing he glimpsed as the train neared his town. And his family home, the *casa* he recalled with such nostalgia, it too seemed quite alien from the one he thought he knew. Now, its antique carpets breathed the dust of neglect, and the family portraits his father had hired a Catanzaro dauber to fake looked vulgar, laughably so. Even its staircase seemed less imposing than the one he and Vittorio skittered up and down so many years ago.

With a pang Francesco felt himself beginning to regret coming home, for now he felt his heart had no home at all. Through the dining room windows he gazed down at the Adriatic, livid blue in the white noontime light. He felt a stranger here, in his town, to this Italy. Catching sight of himself in the drawing room mirror he felt startled, strange even to his own eye, a swarthy man in an American suit. When Francesco first began seeing Laura Warrington she liked to quote Emerson to him: love is the bright foreigner, the foreign self. Now he was the foreigner here, and it chilled him to the bone.

Strolling down the narrow streets of San Lorenzo in search of Vittorio, he had a double sense, of belonging, as he knew he could never belong in America, and utter strangeness, as though he had become a spy in his own birthplace. For one thing, nobody recognized him. That disconcerted him until he recalled that he had grown almost ten inches and resembled the boy who'd left in 1905 not at all. The longest journey for an immigrant is not from his native land to America but from its style of feeling to whatever American style he invents for himself. Francesco couldn't have explained that then, perhaps ever, but what was driving him in 1921 owed nothing to the easy torpor of Calabria, its Prince and its priests and its piazza full of (or so it seemed) the very loungers who occupied the café's chairs sixteen years earlier.

He felt it in his nerves, this secret treason. He was a *ritornato*, as the townspeople called a native son of San Lorenzo who bothered to come home, and yet as he drank in the sights that had filled his distorted dreams, he sensed they meant more to him asleep than they ever would awake. To leave San Lorenzo was well and good, but to feel alien on the day after his return— what home could he have, what cemetery, if not this town? The secret treason was that to leave Italy he amputated too much of his soul ever to return. Thank God, he thought, America taught me to smile like a toothpaste ad, and so he did, greeting the few gossips who knew his face, or guessed at his identity.

Small waves hurtled themselves at the sand, crashing near where Francesco stood before receding with a hissing suck back into the vast azure of the Adriatic Sea. He thought of the gray-white Atlantic lashing the New Jersey shore, its ferocious violence; Carney once told him that each year the Atlantic ate away a foot or two of beach. These waves were mild. They wore the casual, anarchic look of everything Italian, from the railroad conductor whose buttons needed a shine to the bald tires on his mother's touring car. They'll never change, Francesco thought, and thank God for that! Americans bustled and hustled and generally ate each other alive, not even for money so much as petty prestige. Italians sat back and laughed at such frenetic fools. Look at these waves, he mused, they can't even reach my new shoes, they can't even race far enough up the sand to ruin them. And the Adriatic sparkled innocently, indolently.

Then the wind came up, the African wind. It tasted of salt and soil: the sirocco carried its own provenance, as in one of those antique Neapolitan canvases of Neptune summoning all the winds from each corner of the earth. Now the beach seemed almost unfriendly as the waves slashed farther and farther up the sand, until he could feel their tangy scent fill his nose and mouth. He began walking toward the sea wall.

Overhanging it was a sort of cliff, neither steep nor sharp nor forbidding; and from its crags dangled wild berries of the sort parents forbade children to munch. Also wildflowers, roses not quite pink and not virginal white, roses no decent San Lorenzo matron would allow into her house on the grounds of taste alone. Francesco saw they had all been clipped. Someone was tending the wild outgrowth of that cliff as carefully as the Prince did his English hedge.

Approaching the sea wall came a young girl in a fashionable white crinoline, trimmed in black, appropriate to summer. In her left hand she held a basket out of which brimmed a pair of clippers and a pruning hook. The girl was slim, her hips pleasingly rounded, her breasts modestly concealed. Her white dress gave her the air of a vision: Our Lady of San Lorenzo, Francesco wryly thought.

Her small features had their own perfection, giving her the ideal proportions of a doll. Unreal too was the calm way she walked and sat, as though she were the only human being for miles around, and could count on making her way in the world undisturbed. The girl's hair, tightened into a bun, seemed dark enough to be an Oriental's, one of those exotic creatures Francesco eyed when he passed a Chinatown opium den. He had to confess she bedazzled him, in her quiet way; he felt, thank God, none of the anxious commotion Laura used to cause. Despite himself, Francesco approached her on the wall.

"You're tending the roses?" he abruptly asked. "Is it you?"

She smiled. Playfully perhaps. "Aren't you Italian? You speak so hesitantly."

"I live in the United States, but this is my native town."

"I know you." Her smile brightened mischievously. "You're Leonora's brother. The *ritornato*."

"That's right." He introduced himself formally, with a bow: "Francesco Monti, and you are . . . ."

"The rose gardener." Again that mischievous grin. "Names are so *dreary*, don't you think?"

"Yes—I have two names, Francesco here and Frank there, and I dislike them both."

"I wish I were named after an empress or a queen—Theodora or Cleopatra or Semiramis! Now those are names, they are poetry!"

"Don't mind my asking, but why trouble yourself with these wildflowers?"

"Oh, I don't know." She spread her fingers self-consciously on the sea wall, dangling her feet above the onrushing tide. "But they *are* lovely. My mother won't even let me decorate our house with them, isn't that ridiculous?"

Francesco caught himself staring and tried to stop, but he could not. What was it about this girl that made him want to crush her in his arms? She was pretty enough, if no beauty—it was, he decided, animal magnetism, the cant phrase of 1921. This girl exuded a force that was holding him, yes, like a magnet made especially for him, ignorant of her own power even while she deftly wielded it . . . .

"You have a funny look on your face. Are you all right?"

"Yes, yes." Francesco stepped closer to her though he had meant to move further away. "Let me guess your name, would you like me to?"

"Oh, I adore games!" She clapped her hands. "Begin!"

"Not Maria, too common, you could never be a Maria."

She shrugged: a lucky guess, not a winning one.

"Carmela?"

A contemptuous smile. "Do better than that, *ritornato!*"

"Teresa?"

She flinched. He'd guessed right but she wouldn't acknowledge it.

"Isn't that right? You're called Teresa?"

"And if I am?"

"Then I've won. And I claim my victor's prize." And Francesco bent over to kiss her on the lips. Her breath tasted fragrant, as though she also grew wild from a cliff above the sea.

"Francesco Monti, you are no gentleman," Teresa whispered angrily.

"I'm sorry." He wanted to rip the dress from her shoulders and gaze at her young breasts—where, he asked himself, stupefied, where on earth did such lust come from?

"No. I wanted to kiss you too," she said, startling him one more time.

Teresa led him to the rose vine next to the sea wall and clipped him a buttonhole, inserting it with the lightest of fingers into his lapel. Then their eyes met and he knew he had to kiss her again. This time she kissed him back, gently, her eyes closed, her body relaxed against his. Francesco knew she'd been kissed before; real innocence never responded so easily. Now he wanted to hold her, protect her, not ravish her as he had a moment earlier. *Darling, darling, I want to put you in my pocket*, echoing a song they sang at the Italian theater in South Philadelphia. *I want to hold you this way all day, smelling this rose, this sea, feeling this sunlight on my face and tasting this salt on the sirocco . . . .*

"My name is Teresa Amabile. I know your sister Leonora well."

"Ah." He felt like an idiot. What was new? He was one.

"My father wants to meet you, to hear about America. He was going to invite you after you'd been home a few more days. He's the King's Counsel, you know. A very important man."

"And you? Do *you* want to invite me?" He teased her affably.

She gave him a serious smile, like a nun teaching her favorite child. "Come for dinner tomorrow night? Bring a good appetite, our cook is Sicilian, you know how well those people cook, and she makes seven course dinners when we have company." On this mundane note, she began to walk away. "Oh—and what do you know of the philosopher Vico?"

"Nothing, I'm afraid."

She grinned. "Wonderful. My father can lecture you. Tomorrow night. At seven," she called, strolling away.

"Teresa!" Francesco called out, "I liked kissing you very much."

She said nothing, but danced a demure little jig as she skittered away.

NINE

Though, as a rule, nothing happened in San Lorenzo, in the week following Francesco's return his hometown received several shocks, as though by returning he'd unleashed its hidden energies. At long last the Prince expired, before his heir could return from inspecting the family's Argentina lands. Several days of confusion ensued while Father Ugo and the lawyer Amabile wrangled over the Prince's will, above all its insulting provision that he be buried not in San Lorenzo but in a Roman crypt reserved for Senators. Father Ugo tried to set aside the will on the entirely specious grounds that the Prince was enfeebled when he dictated it. Amabile, true to the law, insisted on obeying it to the syllable. The dispute was still boiling when, a few nights after the Prince's death, there came a robbery.

Years before, the peasant Brunetti went to work for Father Ugo as part of a cut-throat deal the Prince foisted on the priest. Brunetti, still wifeless, had three sons whom he could scarcely support on the few lira Father Ugo deigned to pay him every month. He began blustering in the taverns. He would revenge himself on priest and Prince alike, but who heeds the ravings of a drunk? Now his threats became fact: Brunetti and his two sons, who'd always hankered after America, had the nerve to strip the Prince's house of all portable property the second night after his death. Fortunately the noble corpse was at the undertaker and thus could not be defiled too.

Neither Father Ugo nor Amabile, the King's Counsel, could foresee such villainy. Nevertheless, they were responsible to his heir for such now-vanished items as the Prince's small Della Robbias (how could the Brunettis have known their value?), his gold and ruby crucifix, his chairs and divan covered with Napoleonic bees, his silver and crystal shipped from Paris decades before the railroad reached the town, his vast collection of English clocks, his large Caravaggio of St. John and Salome facing each other before Herod (everyone knew *its* value, alas), his Neapolitan Baroque sculptures depicting nymphs in quite indecent postures, and finally his cache of jewels—rings and chains, family heirlooms all—the gems nobody ever saw but everyone knew were hidden somewhere in the palace, and now scattered like beach sand.

Francesco didn't give a damn about the Prince's death except that Amabile sent a note cancelling Teresa's invitation "in this grievous circumstance." And when the Brunettis robbed the dead man's palace, Amabile went into such a splenetic rage that, like a good Italian hypochondriac, he took to his bed. All this nonsense delayed Francesco's formal introduction to the family, frustrating him painfully since he had decided (though he told nobody yet) that he planned to marry Teresa Amabile.

If Vittorio ignored such longing, as he ignored most of his brother's moods, his mother and sister noticed the change in him. Signora Monti wrongly ascribed Francesco's new dreaminess to coming home. San Lorenzo, she hoped, would be a tonic for the ills America inflicted on him. Leonora knew better. She let Francesco ramble on about the charms of Italian girls versus the hard masculinity of their American contemporaries, speeches which inevitably ended by his interrogating her about Teresa, about her boyfriends, her thoughts on marriage, children, love . . . .

He walked every day with Teresa, up the hills, to the farms, or along the beach, and they talked about everything in the world except their sentiments.

"Those Brunettis will surely go to America," she exclaimed the day after the crime.

"Somebody will kill them for their loot before that."

"Is it true that in America criminals stalk the streets and shoot off guns anytime they wish?"

Francesco laughed. "In the movies, yes."

"But I read that this Prohibition is making wine and beer illegal, so isn't everyone who drinks criminal?"

"Only those who sell. You can drink, but you can't run a saloon."

"But that makes no sense! How can such a law ever be enforced? My father could write a better law than that!"

"Is he still sick in bed?"

Teresa smiled. "He isn't really sick. He just doesn't want to be bothered with Father Ugo and all this folderol."

"Very clever. Maybe I'll do that when I get home, myself."

"There—you said it again."

"Said what, Teresa?"

"*Home*. As if America was your home, not San Lorenzo."

"I guess it is now. I've lived there so long," Francesco laughed. "I'm a man of substance in America. I even bribed a Senator once."

"That's nothing to boast of! Why did you do such a terrible thing?"

"For my friend, Enrico. After the war ended Americans got scared, with the Bolsheviks in Russia, went crazy in fact, and they wanted to deport foreign radicals. So Enrico was in danger, and I went to see our Senator. He understood, especially when I paid him what he asked."

"That was a Christian act," Teresa nodded approvingly. "But you need a family of your own. *Your* blood. Helping a stranger isn't the same."

"He isn't a stranger, he's my oldest friend—we worked the mines together."

"Still, he's not your blood. What can he do to show gratitude? The loyalty you need is your family, they'll be with you long after your 'friends' have disappeared! You know I'm right, Francesco, you know. Look at all the lira you sent your family."

"That's why *they* sent *me* to America," Francesco said shortly, wishing Teresa would exhaust this subject soon.

"Look at the Prince. With no family, he died like a dog and now his palace has been robbed! He thought he could do without *his* blood, my father says. But nobody can, Francesco! Without your blood you're a lost soul, not even a Christian." Teresa used the term *Christian* in the custom of their province, to signify *human being*. "Don't you know the proverb, 'A man who abandons the old ways knows what he is losing but not what he will find?'"

"So why haven't you started a family of your own?"

"Who would I marry? One of Brunetti's brats?"

They both laughed, but Francesco was calculating his odds: so she wanted a family, but hadn't found a husband worthy of her yet. Oh, these daughters of the gentry, either they ran off scandalously like Leonora had or folded their hands and waited for Sir Lancelot to arrive! Teresa Amabile dreamed of love, he knew that much: she told him of the English romances she adored, the French novels in yellow paperback, even the spicy stories of Boccaccio. Besides, it was 1921, and nobody's innocence had survived the War. The local papers now luridly retailed rapes and infanticides which would never have been printed in Francesco's youth. No, he felt sure, Teresa longed for love. She might not know its operative meaning, but she wanted it. He was certain she did.

Another walk, another day, the same landscape:

"What is this business of yours that made you so *blessed*?"

"You really want to know? It's dull, Teresa—brickworking, making houses look beautiful without rebuilding them. I invented a process to do that. It's lucrative."

"I see." She walked in silence for a while. "Do you know Thomas Edison?"

Francesco laughed in surprise. "No, no, he's a great man. And he lives in New Jersey. Why do you ask?"

"My father says he's the greatest American alive."

"Maybe he is. But there are so many, Henry Ford, D.W. Griffith—"

"Oh, I adore movies, don't you? I wish Italy made as many as America. That Griffith, he must be a wonderful man, so sensitive!"

"You know his movie INTOLERANCE? The Babylon he shows was built by Italians who came to America specially."

"Oh, now I love America! Hiring Italians to build ancient Babylon! That's almost as funny as you bribing that Senator to keep an Italian radical in America!"

Francesco was being mocked, and he knew it. Her eyebrows arched ironically, punctuation marks putting his folly firmly in its place. She's intelligent, yes, he mused, but I kissed her before I even knew her name. Heat would always call to heat, not to intelligence. It was a law of nature, Francesco knew.

Yet when he returned home the thought of her made him anxious. He found Leonora in the drawing room, sipping tea, and sat down for another guarded chat. Instead, he confessed everything.

"I don't know if she loves me," Francesco said bitterly. "I don't know anything."

"I could ask her, if you want . . . ."

"God, no!" Francesco sat upright as though electrically shocked. "What if she says she'll never marry me? What if she lies about how she feels?"

"She's very young," Leonora said gently. "Young girls like that—"

"She's older than you were when you ran away." He was tempted to boast of their first kiss to Leonora but he thought better of it.

"Her father spoils her, you know. If she wants a book he sends that day to Rome for it; when she refused to learn cooking, he told her she is too *good* to cook."

"I see." Francesco saw nothing. Teresa didn't seem 'spoiled,' whatever that meant, but then how could he know for sure? "Maybe you should ask her something, not directly, though."

"Ask her yourself at dinner." Leonora smilingly produced an invitation sealed in the old style by wax and a signet ring. Francesco ripped it open to find a summons from the King's Counsel

Amabile to dinner at eight o'clock the evening after next. He burst out laughing. "You had this in waiting for me all along?"

Leonora nodded. She was now so pregnant that her belly formed a perfect arc between chest and waist. With Francesco's help, she shifted position on the divan, and when she was comfortable she said: "One thing, little brother. Teresa told me you kissed her the day you met. Bravo—except this one needs a seduction, not a rape. You understand? And the first thing is to deal with her father."

"I'll deal with him."

"You may have forgotten, but an Italian father thinks he's Pope, King, and Prime Minister rolled into one. God knows ours did."

"You're in a sour mood! I'll handle Amabile so well *he'll* ask *me* to marry her."

"You've lived in America too long, little brother! Those mannish girls Mother talks about have ruined you, so independent, so aggressive!"

"Maybe they have," Francesco said gloomily. "I was in love with one of them."

"Yes, you so carefully avoided mentioning women when you wrote me I was sure you were. Do you want to tell me about her?"

"What's there to tell? Every unhappy love story is the same. Only the happy ones count. Like yours."

"Happy, unhappy . . . . the wrong words for marriage, I think. You have a good day and then a bad day—now, is that happiness or misery?"

"I don't know. But love without marriage, *that's* misery, because what do you really have? The woman's body, sure, but nothing more. In America all the Socialists talk about free love, and I always laugh, because if there's anything in the world that isn't free, can't be, God knows it's love!"

"They mean sex," Leonora mildly observed.

"*Sex?* You're a Socialist, do you believe in free sex?"

"Some women need it, Francesco. So many get married as

virgins and then suffer when their husbands treat them like whores—they need to find out about that side of life so they won't suffer more."

"Does our mother know you advocate free sex?"

"I advocate nothing," Leonora said, annoyed. "You're the one who said love can't be free. You sound like you want a woman to own, like those Garibaldi Estates you're so proud of. Any woman worth loving won't give you all of herself, she can't. If that's what you want forget Teresa, because she's her own woman and God bless her, she always will be."

"Does that mean she can't love me?"

"It means *you* can't own *her*. There's a part of every woman she keeps for herself. And if you love her you won't trespass on it."

"Trespass!" Francesco felt primed to explode, but deliberately lowered his voice. "The truth is, you women are liars, all of you, you trick us and you keep your hearts hidden from us—and then you talk about free love as though it's progress! All that will happen men will be more confused, and women will be resentful at having to play new games. Instead of virgins men will marry liars and actresses, and who will benefit from that? Divorce lawyers," he concluded bitterly.

"You're not speaking from experience?"

"You wanted to hear my story, here it is! I met a woman, an American, not one of our people. Beautiful and clever. And bad. She tricked me into supporting her by swearing her marriage was all over except for the divorce. And when she'd squeezed me dry like a lemon, when I had nothing left to give, she went back to him. Free love, you call it? Slavery, I say, only this time the women will control the men—and women have *no* idea of honor, any man knows that."

"Have you told Teresa your view of emancipated womanhood?"

"Of course not." Francesco felt suddenly sick of his own voice. "It doesn't apply to her. I'm talking about Americans. They broke up saloons with axes when all they wanted was to make their men miserable."

"You sound bitter, little brother." Leonora grinned. "Maybe you shouldn't marry at all if you feel this way. Because you'll take Teresa with you to America, and what will she be then? An American."

"She isn't like that now."

"Wait until you see Teresa with an axe in one of your saloons!"

And Leonora's joke, for some reason, made both of them guffaw. At that moment Vittorio ran in shouting he had news, amazing news! "In here," Francesco said, and their older brother marched into the drawing room, trembling with excitement. All the news in San Lorenzo, as long as anyone could remember, was always bad, Francesco thought sardonically.

"They captured Brunetti's youngest son! In Naples, where else could those thieves sell the Prince's stuff? The police set a trap at a pawnshop, and when the boy came back with a silver plate they grabbed him—what do you think of that?" Nobody replied. "And here's the cream of the jest—all Brunetti could sell was a bit of jewelry, enough to buy tickets to America. His boy led the police back to a shack where everything else, even the Caravaggio, was perfectly unharmed! No art dealer wanted to deal with a peasant, however fine his merchandise might be! Who says there isn't justice, sometimes, anyway?" Francesco asked what became of the other thieves. "Oh, they took a ship as soon as the kid was pinched. Good riddance to them! Empty-handed, after stealing billions of lira worth of art! Justice, I tell you!"

"The Prince's son will be pleased," Leonora said indifferently.

"That wastrel!" Vittorio scowled. "He hasn't spent a month here since he came of age. It's a disgrace for him to decide whether my clinic remains open."

"But I thought you were coming back with me?" Francesco asked anxiously. The idea of Vittorio breaking the marriage contract, leaving him disgraced and impoverished after repaying the dowry of Dr. Gioia, whirled madly in his brain.

"Of course, of course. Calm down." Vittorio gave his brother his most winning smile. "But my clinic may not survive, if this wastrel says he's closing it."

"Notice he doesn't say a word about his poor patients," observed Leonora sarcastically. "You'd think the clinic was a castle our heroic brother built with his bare hands."

"I care for my patients, as everyone in San Lorenzo knows! And I am modern enough to say the State should take care of them, not some aristocrat, so called, who speaks English better than his native tongue!"

"Watch out," Leonora teased, "you're halfway to Socialism. Better run to Father Ugo and get a dose of holy water before it spreads. Didn't our Lord Jesus say, the poor ye have always with ye?"

"The poor ye have always with ye," intoned the lawyer Amabile, ladling himself a large portion of green lasagna stuffed with meatballs, wild mushrooms, tomato sauce, cream sauce, and prosciutto ham. "The trouble with Italy is we have far too many poor. And the trouble with poor people is they have no capital."

Francesco glanced around the table for Teresa's reactions to such idiocy, but if anyone else wanted to laugh he saw no evidence. She daintily spooned up escarole soup, the first course, after announcing that she would eat no lasagna, a gesture towards her figure, perhaps, which Francesco took as a covert signal to him. Signora Amabile said nothing, glancing around the table anxiously to supervise the maids who served pasta, filled glasses, and generally got in each other's way.

"You know our great sage Giambattista Vico, naturally, Signor Monti?"

Francesco had, with a degree of pain, struggled through the "New Science" to prepare for this dinner and so was honestly able to say yes.

"Vico divided history into cycles which repeat themselves, until time finally has a stop. Far more sensible than the German sauerkraut Marx and Hegel sell. For them, history moves in a straight line toward some Teutonic goal." Amabile smiled ironically. "Oh, I too believed in progress once upon a time—I even debated it with your brother-in-law, Lampa, before the War. In those days I too felt certain history was moving like a freight train towards prosperity and enlightenment. What idiot believes such fantasies nowadays?"

"In America," Francesco began tentatively, "progress is our religion. Emerson says America will create a new Adam, free of Europe's sins—"

"But we know better, you and I." Amabile interrupted, drawing Francesco into complicity with a cynical smile.

"I wonder. Look what they've done with that empty continent! That's progress, isn't it, Signore?"

"Vico says no. He'd tell you that without Europe and its sciences, America would still belong to the savages." Amabile signalled the maid for more wine. "His three cycles of history are first that of the gods, then the heroic age, and finally one of men—*democracy*, we call it today. But that great thinker gave human beings far too much credit for intelligence. He claimed our age would encourage reason and discipline. The War ended that illusion for Europe, let me say!"

"Still, Italy seems prosperous—perhaps not San Lorenzo, yet—"

"Italy might prosper *someday*!" Amabile's face turned alarmingly red. "But with criminals like Brunetti roaming the streets we'll always be hostage to our scum. The War let every mad Italian loose—adventurers like D'Annunzio, these Fascist blackshirts, even the so-called Catholic party who thinks singing hymns will fix everything! To say nothing of the godless Socialists in Milan arming for revolt . . . . Signor Monti, forgive me, I am an old man and so I speak plain: when a peasant like Brunetti dares to rob a Prince, is chaos far away? Since the War no three Italians can agree on what to do—and that opens the gates to Mussolini or the Socialists, goddamn them both!"

"My sister says Mussolini no longer even leads his blackshirts," Francesco observed."

"Don't you believe it." Amabile was munching joylessly. "That bastard's like a bull, most dangerous when he's almost dead. He'll come back, and why shouldn't he when even our Prime Minister makes daily overtures to his thugs? Imagine an Italy ruled by Brunettis, that's what we'll get—common criminals, the scum of the earth!"

"Enough politics," Teresa reproached. "You know it always gives you gas."

"Yes, yes," Amabile agreed. "Tell me about America, Signor Monti. Tell me something that won't give me gas, if you can . . . ."

So Francesco painted pretty pictures. He left out the coal mines, Senator Penrose, the infants in the slums. Instead he described the Pennsylvania land, scarlet in autumn, golden in summertime. He made Philadelphia sound like a city out of the Arabian Nights, where wizards like Greenglass magically made fortunes overnight, where cars and trolleys carried you to alabaster skyscrapers. In the back of his mind was his need to take Teresa there, and whatever he told her father, he knew, might help Amabile consent.

"And you are bringing your brother back with you, aren't you?" the King's Counsel asked.

"Oh, yes, Signor Amabile. I have found him a rich bride."

"With more money than beauty, to hear Vittorio talk." Amabile laughed with an abrupt sound, like a seal's bark.

"You know San Lorenzo is no place for secrets," Teresa said soothingly, seeing a shocked look cover Francesco's face.

"And our Italians? Are they treated as badly as our papers say?"

"Not badly—no worse than the rest. We have been there such a short time, and we must wait our turn. That seems to be the American way."

"*You* didn't wait, did you?" Amabile gazed at him shrewdly. "I hear you've made a fortune in America. Teresa tells me you invented a process for bricks, is that correct?"

"Yes," Francesco said modestly. "And I also build houses and own a small bank our Italians patronize."

"Remarkable—and at such a young age! Your poor father would be proud, proud of you!"

"Many are richer than I, like my friend Greenglass. It is a place for those who will work hard enough to rise. Because that's possible."

"Yes, yes." Amabile stared at Francesco steadily. "And still you have no wife, no family?"

Here was the moment Francesco had been dreading for two days. No Italian man was rich, no matter how much cash he banked, without children of his own. Taking a deep breath, he explained he'd been too busy supporting his relatives over here to marry in America.

"No wife," Amabile repeated. "Perhaps," he added slyly, "you may find one here in your hometown."

He knows, Francesco thought, Teresa has told him everything! He glanced at her to confirm his guess and, indeed, she was blushing down at the tablecloth. Could she be flushing at her father's words? Francesco decided to plunge:

"I have found one, Signor Amabile. As you no doubt already know."

Teresa's head jerked up, startled and stunned. This was not the way Sir Lancelot would come for her, the way he came in her fantasies: Francesco was conducting himself like a *cafone*, not a gallant Italian, let alone her shining knight. The disapproval was visible in her pursed lips.

"I wish to marry your daughter Teresa," he said, his voice steady. "I ask you formally for her hand."

"You would take her back to America?" Amabile's voice sounded oddly hoarse.

"Yes, of course."

"Then my answer is no, and it is final!" The King's Counsel rose from his chair with a grunt. "Teresa will never live in such a barbarous place. Oh, you tried to fool me, Monti, but I am too clever for your tricks. I know the life she would lead with you there, surrounded by enemies—I'll never sentence my child to exile, I'm not as hardhearted as your parents were."

"Papa, please—" Teresa began.

"Silence, child!" For the first time Teresa's mother spoke. "Your father decides these things, not you."

Teresa began to sob. Her bosom rose and fell rhythmically to the music of her pain, until she uttered a groan and ran out of the dining room.

"You see?" said Amabile triumphantly. "Already you bring my daughter pain."

"Teresa loves me, Signore. I can make her happy in America."

"Love? Happiness? A marriage doesn't depend on such things. If people married for love the world would be filled with lunatics."

"With respect, Signore, please reconsider. Teresa herself says she will marry no one here."

"Get out of my house, go back to America!" Amabile roared. "Brunetti stole jewels but you wish to steal something more precious than any jewel!"

"Yes, go," Signora Amabile added quietly. "This is not the time or the place to discuss." In the local parlance, *discuss* was a tactful way to say *argue*. Francesco left, his stomach twisting and his pulse fluttering.

After that night Teresa's father forbade her from leaving his house. Her walks on the beach, her pruning the wild roses ceased, leaving Francesco lonely enough to weep. For consolation he had only the reports Leonora brought daily after visiting her imprisoned friend. Teresa took to her bed, refusing food, sleeping day and night and sobbing bitterly when she did not sleep. She lost so much weight that her family summoned Vittorio, who could found no organic cause but did persuade her to drink beef tea, to avert collapse.

On the eighth day after he asked for Teresa's hand, Francesco knocked on her front door at dinnertime. He had no real expectation of entering, but after the nervous maid announced him, she came back and said, "The Signore wishes to see you."

Amabile greeted him with a melancholy sigh. "I think my daughter wants to kill herself, Signor Monti. Are you happy now? Are you certain of her love? Never one sign of disobedience, and now this—this insanity. Yes, you know how to make Teresa happy, asking her to marry you when you knew I would never allow you to!"

"I was hoping you would decide otherwise."

"Because my daughter's acting like a coquette in one of those French novels she loves? I'd rather have her dead than married to you, a man who doesn't even show respect by offering to stay here."

"My life is in America now. My brother Vittorio will come back with me, so both of us are choosing the same fate."

"What difference does that make? All you Montis are fools, your father before you was a fool. But we Amabiles are a different house, and in this house we do not seduce peasant girls, or marry Socialists, or cross the ocean to work with our hands like a sharecropper!"

Francesco said as coolly as he could," Is that all you wanted to tell me, sir?"

"Yes, damn you! Now leave my house!"

"I have something to say too." Amabile scowled at him through the gloom, which gave Francesco the heart to say: "I no longer seek to marry Teresa. Since you, her father, oppose our union, it will not take place. And I promise that she will never receive so much as a postcard from America. Not from me. So far as she is concerned, I do not exist. And I wish all felicity for Teresa with the man you choose, if you can find one in Italy she thinks worthy of her."

Rudely, Amabile turned away. Francesco strode out of the house, leaving the battlefield as boldly as though he'd won.

TEN

The heir to the Principality of San Lorenzo nearly missed his father's funeral. He sauntered into the church during Father Ugo's hour-long eulogy, a pale youth dressed, despite the heat, in English tweeds and riding boots. At the gravesite he scarcely looked into the hole his father would soon occupy, gazing instead at the goats stumbling over a nearby hill.

Late the next morning, after an English breakfast of ham and eggs, he summoned the King's Counsel Amabile to his father's study, where the two spoke for exactly seventeen minutes (so the servants later agreed) before the King's Counsel was dismissed. The town speedily learned that its new Prince was selling the family lands, the palace, everything Brunetti had tried to steal, and planned to resettle in Argentina. "That's the future," the heir told Amabile. "Italy is a desert in comparison. Argentina will feed the world with its cattle and its sheep!" San Lorenzo couldn't comprehend such perversity, but, bowing to necessity, accepted it. For the first time in a thousand years, the town would have no Prince and, now, no Senator. The townspeople were transformed overnight from children without a father to bastards without a name.

Then Amabile announced his candidacy for the dead Prince's Senate seat, a move which surprised everyone. His party, the ruling Liberals, notoriously demanded millions of lira from its candidates. Leonora told Francesco that Amabile expected the local gentry to bankroll him: how else could he raise such funds? The answer proved both more and less logical than her shrewd guess.

Throughout this time Francesco, glumly keeping his word, had avoided Teresa and even her rose bushes. He thought of her, of course, continually, except now that he had no hope she seemed dead, frozen, the portrait of love rather than its living face. So when he received an invitation to lunch from her parents it reached him like a chime from some distant bell. Already his heart had sailed back to America.

His first surprise came when Teresa greeted him, not Amabile. She looked too pale for her pink flowered dress, squeezing his hand with a limp palm before sinking into an armchair, smiling wanly up at him.

"I have been unwell," Teresa said.

"Yes, Leonora said. I was concerned."

"But I feel better, seeing you finally."

"Your wild roses need tending. They're all overgrown."

"You never went," Teresa said mournfully. "I wonder whether I ever will myself."

"Don't talk that way. You'll marry, someday. Don't act so sad . . . ."

"I want to marry you!" She said the word *marry* in such a way that a stronger desire burned through her voice. "You, and *only* you, Francesco! It must be you!"

"Dearest, I know, but it isn't up to me."

"If you were a real man you would carry me off, like a medieval knight." Teresa smiled to show she wasn't serious.

"Your father would call out the Army, the Navy, and the Cavalry, and when they caught me he would personally chop off my head and send it to the King."

"But we would have been married for a while, at least!"

They laughed like children until Amabile appeared, wearing a business suit. He greeted Francesco with a friendly smile and escorted the pair onto the terrace beside the house, where a luncheon table waited under the grape arbor.

"A true Calabrian terrace," Amabile said, "look at the tiles, real Roman style. In the Roman Empire this region was known for grapes and gods—the finest wine, and the hills teeming with divinities. They said Calabria was so holy you could find a god as easily as a man."

"Those gods weren't real, Father, were they?" Teresa asked.

"No," replied Amabile cautiously—for who knew where the old gods had vanished to after Christ conquered Constantine?— "still, they were *aspects* of the true God, like Apollo who raised the dead or Isis, so much like our Blessed Virgin."

The fool can pontificate on any subject, Francesco thought sourly, wondering why he'd been invited at all. A butler announced lunch.

The three servant girls appeared, as clumsy as before, plopping down baskets of olives, bread, and farmer cheese. Amabile scolded them for not first serving wine, and they scuttled inside for it. The King's Counsel cleared his throat and said, as though painfully:

"Signor Monti, you know I have declared for our Prince's Senate seat. My daughter says she will not leave San Lorenzo if I go to Rome, and of course my wife must accompany me, so she will be alone. Now I am no fool—" he glanced at Teresa, then back into Francesco's eyes, "—and I know my daughter is in love with you. I thought she was only infatuated, but now I see her feelings won't change. No, no. And I do not wish her to suffer, I want her happiness, only that, even if she pictures it quite differently than I did. What I am saying is that I am now ready to consent to this marriage. Her love has convinced me that you may bring Teresa joy."

Teresa gasped, then boldly seized Francesco's hand, as though ready for a church ceremony that second. Francesco broke into a smile even he knew must look like a fool's beatitude.

"Signor Amabile, Teresa is the consummation of my life. I swear I will never harm your daughter in any way, I will be loyal, loving, devoted until death . . . ."

"Yes, yes, of course." Amabile was tapping his fingers

nervously on the tablecloth. "Teresa my dear, would you excuse us, please?"

As soon as Teresa went inside—not before squeezing Francesco's hand joyfully—her father's uneasiness disappeared. He bent forward, speaking in a more confidential tone, man of the world to his counterpart.

"Our Liberal Party will defend Italy against our enemies, Socialist and Fascist alike. But for that we need money. My party has asked all the candidates to donate—" he hesitated, "two million lira. A great deal, I know, but how can any of us put a price on Italy's future?"

The figure equalled one hundred thousand dollars, more or less. Francesco calculated rapidly: yes, he could probably raise that much without ruining himself. But he hated the thought of buying Teresa, not that either man would ever dare to speak that verb. What would his mother say, or Leonora? Was it a love match when the father sold his daughter's virginity? And then it struck him like a blow to the chest: the Gioias must have felt this way, or worse, when they knew I tricked them out of the land. Somehow they've been revenged, Francesco thought. And in that case I must accept whatever conditions Amabile places, accept every blow to my pride, every kick. Because if I don't, I will never see Teresa again, and haven't I lost enough love for this lifetime?

"Say no more," he told the King's Counsel. "You shall have the money you need."

"I knew you were a true son of Italy! When you and Teresa reach America you will both sleep easier knowing I am in Rome, fighting to keep Italy free. Oh, I am sacrificing my daughter to save our Fatherland! What an opera our great Verdi could have made of this!"

Francesco smiled, instead of laughing in the King's Counsel's face. Verdi indeed! As if selling Teresa for the Senate seat were a noble act! Any man, he knew, could shield his motives from himself, so that he never had to face the truth of a given act. Francesco wondered yet again if lying to yourself wasn't worse than all the other lies you had to tell. Nobody would ever know why you did this or that, because only the results lived on. Yet life was more than deeds and facts. Your actions sprang from sentiments, not always noble ones. He knew his own heart, knew how bitter it would look in a hostile light: what point then in judging Amabile? The man was a patriot, God knew. Was it his fault that patriotism had grown expensive in Italy? Now you are a man, he told himself. You're as corrupt as this world is, because you finally accept that this world must be corrupt.

Francesco returned home to announce his news. Vittorio clapped him on the back, shouting the brothers should have a double wedding in Philadelphia. Leonora and his mother burst into joyous tears. He joked with the women, asking what they had to cry about, but got only a fugue of sobs for reply. Then one of the Amabile maids knocked at the door and asked Vittorio to follow her to her master's house.

"Can't you see I'm with my family? What's the matter there?"

"Our master had a dizzy spell after your brother left. He fainted away before my eyes, Doctor Monti! I was so scared, I thought he died!"

"All right, I'll go, since we're to be in-laws."

"Vittorio, please tell my Teresa what her father said—I'm not sure she knows."

"You want me to heal the sick and play Cupid too, you rogue!"

Three hours later Vittorio returned. He told his anxious brother that Teresa knew of her father's consent, and handed him a bouquet of wild roses "for Mamma and Leonora, your fiancé said." Her father, though, was seriously ill.

"You know how overweight he is," Vittorio began.

"And since when is that an illness?" his mother asked skeptically.

"We know obesity affects circulation of the blood. This is modern physiology, Mother, not a guess. So Amabile's heart and brain don't work as efficiently as mine or yours—the fat blocks his heart from working properly. That's why he fainted, I'm certain of it. He must have stood up suddenly, and that caused a dizzy spell."

"Foolishness," Signora Monti sniffed. "Our men have been heavy in middle age for years. And now you say that's a malady!"

"Heart disease kills most men here. What do you think weakens the heart of a fat man if not fat?"

"You turn everything into argument," Leonora said to him. "I pity this Bellina you're marrying, she'll say it's raining out and you'll say no, it's only condensed vapor that resembles rain." Everyone laughed at that, even Vittorio.

The next day by the sea wall, Teresa and Francesco met. Now they could kiss openly, caress, hold hands, according to the custom of their town, and so they never stopped touching one another.

"The Madonna heard my prayers," Teresa proclaimed joyfully. "I prayed ten times a day for my father to change his mind.'

Francesco asked whether she wanted a wedding in San Lorenzo, and she said of course, "but not a pretentious one, no huge ceremony—something small and elegant." She gave Francesco an accusing look. "My parents believe you're an atheist."

"Me? What have I done to deserve that?"

"You haven't been to Mass once since you returned to San Lorenzo, let alone to Confession. I know you're not an atheist— I would never love you if you were!—but I know you are also not in a state of grace."

"I'll go to Mass tonight."

Teresa laughed. "You've forgotten! You'll have to go to Confession, my darling, if you want Father Ugo to marry us."

"Confession? Do I? I always hated telling that priest my sins."

"Oh, you'll be absolved. Father Ugo gave the Prince Extreme Unction, didn't he? When he was dying from you-know-what?"

"Very well." Francesco smiled at his beloved imp, thinking this was only the second sacrifice he had to make for her, wondering how many more lay in store. "I'll go this very day."

Two hours later, kneeling inside the confession box, Francesco was starting to feel anxious and trapped. No light was seeping in, not even from the banked mass of votive candles flanking the rear of both pews. He knelt on the painful wooden bench, worn smooth and indented by decades of repentant sinners, wishing he'd kept his remorse to himself. Then Father Ugo slid, snakelike, into the opposite side. Francesco could smell the altar wine and costly English soap and that odor peculiar to the celibate, a dryness like that of a corpse, a musty aroma of unlife and unlove.

Nervously Francesco recited the Latin formula, hoping he recalled the words with precision. Father Ugo interrupted him, asking in Italian how long it had been since he had last confessed his sins.

"A long time, Father."

"Don't you go to church in that barbarous place?"

"Not often, Father."

"Well, well . . . . confess your sins, my son. God is everywhere, even in America. He knows all of your sins."

"I—I have had relations with a married woman. Several married women . . . ."

Francesco could hear a sharp intake of breath. "Continue," Father Ugo said brusquely.

"That's all, Father."

"All?" Father Ugo's voice rose on the word. "You shameless creature! You corrupt married women and you expect easy absolution from the Holy Mother Church! Such sins are mortal, not venial, *mortal* . . . ." the priest broke off in rage.

"I am an honest man, Father. I help the poor. I help other Calabrians."

"You are a whoremonger, a menace to decent Christians and their wives!"

Francesco shifted uneasily on the wooden bench. He weighed the prudence of responding with equal heat that he seduced no virgins, unlike the Prince and the local Cardinal, whose debaucheries were the stuff of San Lorenzo legend, not to mention Vittorio, whose life seemed driven by his penis even when he was a boy. Francesco couldn't see himself as bound for Hell, not yet, not until he committed some sin so grave no eunuch priest could absolve him.

"You will make a novena," Father Ugo said dramatically, stage-whispering like a messenger in Verdi who delivers news of some offstage calamity. "A novena will cleanse your soul, and of course a contribution to this church, in dollars, if you please, liras are worthless nowadays . . . ."

"A novena," Francesco repeated.

"And of course you must vow to remain chaste, like a true son of Christ, until your wedding night. That goes without saying! Chaste, pure, continent!"

Francesco began laughing. Those three adjectives struck him as the height of absurdity, and so his laughter rose from barely suppressed giggles and became a hoot, a childish sound which filled the narrow confessional, echoing against its Baroque screen. Father Ugo banged against the grate dividing priest from sinner, enraged at this Monti who showed no fear for his immortal soul.

Francesco caught himself. The laugh died on his lips, while the priest kept rapping on the grate. Francesco asked Father Ugo's absolution in his humblest voice, and when the priest began a new tirade, rose abruptly and walked into the church's cool dark, then out into the scorching afternoon sunlight.

That evening another of Amabile's clumsy maids summoned Vittorio. He was eating dinner and regaling his family with war stories, which everyone except Francesco had heard often enough to recite word perfect.

"What disaster has befallen our King's Counsel tonight?"

"A disaster, that's the word for it," the girl sobbed. "A few hours ago Signor Amabile was sitting in his leather chair and all of a sudden he cried out to me, he said, come quick Marietta, I have such an awful headache the Devil must be plaguing me! So I brought aspirin pills and brandy, that's what my master always takes, and I went away. Ten minutes later I heard a cry, and I ran into his study, and he was passed out in his chair, he hadn't even touched the brandy, he was dead but he was alive," she said significantly. "The other girls and I managed to get him into bed. But now he won't wake up. Poor Signora Amabile's beside herself, she shouts into his ear and he doesn't flinch. And we know he's alive because his breath steams up the mirror," she concluded, alluding to the time-honored San Lorenzo method of determining death.

"A coma, perhaps," mused Vittorio aloud.

"What's that?" demanded Francesco, envisioning another barrier to marrying Teresa. She was turning out to be more troublesome than finishing the Garibaldi Homes, and like them he loved her far too much to give her up.

"A kind of sleep. From what this creature says, Amabile may have had a brain hemorrhage—first headache, and then coma. Yes, that would explain things." He began to eat again.

"You aren't going to let him stay like that?" his mother cried.

"Is there anything I can do to wake him up?"

"Your duty requires you to see what is possible!"

Amabile's maid listened by swivelling her head back and forth quickly between mother and son. Francesco stood up, uneasily aware that Teresa would judge him by whatever Vittorio did or failed to do. "We're going there," he told Vittorio. "I paid for your training, so I have a right to request that you put it to use. Let's go."

The King's Counsel Amabile, paterfamilias and National Liberal candidate for the Prince of San Lorenzo's Senate seat, lay like a tomb effigy of a knight. Vittorio instructed Signora Amabile and the three clumsy maids to shift his position in bed at intervals, to banish all possible light and noise, to keep his face and lips moist and thereby avoid dehydration. Signora Amabile querulously demanded how long this horror would last. Vittorio replied that her husband could revive at any time. Of course, he might have suffered severe damage, so recovery would require months in bed. In any case, he stressed, nobody could predict anything: the greatest doctors often saw coma victims spring startlingly back to consciousness. Teresa stood listening, holding her mother's hands, her face rigidly composed. Francesco assumed she was in shock. How lucky I was, he thought, that Father died after I left San Lorenzo and I didn't have to watch the star I always steered by plummet from my private sky . . . .

Within a day Signora Amabile, now calm, called on Signora

Monti. She wished, she announced, their children to marry not in San Lorenzo but elsewhere in the province, and quietly, since a celebration at this time would seem tasteless, not to say dishonorable. Signora Monti suggested the seaside chapel in Santa Caterina, sixty kilometers distant, far enough away that the news could be kept from reaching their town. She understood and even admired the other woman's hypocrisy, or, as both called it, care for appearances. In San Lorenzo you existed only as your reflection in a thousand eyes, something her poor husband never understood. The crucial point, both mothers knew, was to maintain your position on the social chessboard of the town; their children would leave for America, but they still had to look their neighbors in the eye.

And so Francesco married Teresa furtively. They left the wedding chapel without a parting glance at Calabria, taking the express to Rome with Vittorio, who sat with them all the way up the peninsula, telling war stories and boring Teresa so thoroughly that she fell asleep before the train crossed the Abruzzi hills.

They honeymooned in Venice, to satisfy Teresa's lifelong craving to see that pearl of the Adriatic, directly up the coast from San Lorenzo yet unimaginably strange, like a city on the moon. After the wedding they took the night train from Rome, slicing across the peninsula through the tawny light of dusk, into the sunset, into the vast canopy of night, so that they arrived in Venice by darkness, snatching their first sight of the Grand Canal under the moon, that celestial lighting adding powerfully to the city's unreality. They felt they were stepping onto a stage set when their gondola deposited them at the Grand Hotel.

Francesco had kept himself, throughout the trip, from offering her anything more audacious than a kiss. However bold Teresa seemed the day they met, no caresses more intimate had been exchanged, so he had no idea how she would react to their wedding night, having heard tales of brides reduced to tears by the sight of an aroused and undressed man. In their suite they undressed separately and slipped into the wide antique bed reserved for newlyweds by the light of a single gas-jet. Teresa extinguished it and then lay stiffly next to her husband without a word.

"Are you tired, darling?"

"It doesn't matter."

Francesco kissed her, sliding her negligee down with one hand and nuzzling her breasts. Teresa did not respond until he stroked her loins, grazing her with expert fingers until she gasped suddenly. And then she seized his head with both hands and began kissing him, in a frenzy, deep kisses such as they had never shared, until he broke loose to replace his fingers with his mouth. Teresa was startled at first, until her pleasure began, and she could feel herself melting with a liquid flame, and she reached her climax with a cry like one of pain.

The week they stayed in Venice blurred into a single night. All day long they both trembled in anticipation of sundown, as though only darkness could sanction such transports of the flesh. They saw, of course, the famous churches, paintings, oddities; each day they exhausted themselves gazing at Bellinis and Tiepolos and the palazzi where dead geniuses had lived, they raced from sight to sight as though in penance for the night before, guidebooks in hand, feet sore, never speaking of what they did in the dark out of mutual delicacy. But they held hands incessantly and kissed everywhere, in the Ca' D'Oro, on the Bridge of Sighs, in Saint Mark's Square, provoking tolerant smiles even from Venetians hardened to honeymoon bliss.

One evening they walked back to the hotel from a trattoria where they ate a fishermen's rice, which reminded Francesco irritatingly of Rosita and her food. He tried not to think of how he would break with her once he and Teresa arrived in Philadelphia. They turned onto a walkway beside a narrow canal where their steps echoed, talking about tomorrow's sightseeing until Teresa announced, "I think we took the wrong turn." Under a streetlight she consulted her guidebook map and announced joyfully, "We're lost!" Francesco groaned theatrically and reversed course, claiming their waiter could set them straight.

When they reached the trattoria they saw a gang of blackshirts hurling tables, glasses, plates into the street, kicking them into the canal with jackbooted feet. Three of them administered castor oil to the owner, banging his head against a stucco wall while they poured the fluid down his throat. The waiters stood by, arms crossed, watching anxiously. Francesco shouted at the blackshirts to stop, but Teresa grabbed his arm to shut him up. When the blackshirts finished their task of destruction, not a wine bottle, not a table remained intact. They marched out of the trattoria, arms linked, laughing, singing patriotic songs from the War.

One waiter said to the vomiting owner, "Why didn't you pay? Was it worth all this—to stand up to *them?*"

"Fascisti," the same waiter said to Francesco. "If you don't pay ten thousand lira every month, they redecorate your restaurant." The other waiters laughed bitterly, while the owner, hugging his belly and groaning, ran in to the toilet, where he slammed the seat so loudly everyone heard it in the street.

"That goddamn castor oil," the waiter said. "He'll be shitting for four days, the fool. All he had to do was pay like everybody else, who cares if he's a goddamn Socialist? We're workers too, but what about our tips?"

Mutely the waiters began sweeping up debris. Francesco didn't have the heart to ask directions, so they hired a water taxi back to the hotel, both too stunned to finish their sentences:

" . . . . cowardly scum, that's all . . . ."
" . . . . now I see what your father meant when . . . ."
" . . . . not sorry to leave Italy, honestly, not now . . . ."
" . . . . if I'd had a gun I would have . . . ."

Francesco asked the concierge at the Grand Hotel if the Fascisti menaced his establishment.

"We pay them and they leave us alone. They are nothing, Signore, boys still playing soldiers though the War's over for years. That is all."

"But aren't you afraid of them?"

"Everyone is. A little bit. But in Milan the Fascisti *kill* people—Socialists, of course. What is a little castor oil compared to that?"

"The government should do something."

The concierge smiled. "And make martyrs of those thugs? If they ever cause real trouble the Prime Minister will crush them like lice."

"Yes, I suppose." Francesco didn't know what to say. "I suppose you're right."

They met Vittorio in Genoa, where all three boarded a liner to America. After revisiting his student haunts in Rome he told tales of the rich beauties he'd swept off their feet. Teresa rolled her eyes at her brother-in-law's vanity, kicking Francesco under the table when his stories grew more improbable, like when he met a married Countess on the Pincio and had to fend off her attentions night and day.

Now, on shipboard, they had no distractions during the day, and so they made love after breakfast and before lunch, arriving flushed in the first-class dining room with the vague suspicion that the other passengers all knew what they had just done.

Halfway to America, past the Azores, a steward handed Teresa a telegram. FATHER DIED THREE TEN A.M. THIS MORNING MAY GOD WING HIS SOUL TO PARADISE. Teresa staggered as if struck, began weeping, and did not stop until the boat hit stormy seas in the horse latitudes. After that she lay numbly in bed, staring out the cabin window at the swollen waves, listening to the sound of rain lashing the Atlantic. Francesco arranged for her to get sleeping pills. They did her no good, absolutely no good at all.

PART THREE

ONE

The wedding of Bellina and Vittorio Monti crowned Philadelphia's Italian-American social season. The bride was known to be rich, while the groom was quite unknown to the guests who converged first on the Cathedral of Saints Peter and Paul and then on the Rose Ballroom of the Bellevue Stratford Hotel, the very same room where, each year, the city's Protestant aristocrats staged a coming out party for their daughters. Some guests suspected Doctor Gioia of asserting his daughter's parity with those taffeta-sheathed debutantes by choosing the Rose Ballroom, since everyone knew how keenly the doctor resented his exclusion from those medical societies which systematically blackballed not only Italians but Jews, along with those Irish ambitious enough to apply.

The real interest of the reception lay in the chance it offered to inspect Bellina Monti, nee Gioia, more closely than in the echoing vastness of the Cathedral. She was, all agreed, a girl transformed. In the weeks before her wedding Bellina travelled to a ladies' spa in Arizona named Desert D'Or, where masseurs pounded flesh, waiters served cottage cheese, and instructors led calisthenics. Bellina would never be svelte, of course, but Desert D'Or had pared sixty pounds from her large bones, bringing her dress size down to a six. The Gioias tried to keep her trip secret, impossible since their own servants boasted of how lovely the young mistress had become. Lovely she perhaps was not—the standards of the day demanded emaciation as beauty's price—yet even the most evil-minded guest, watching her smile shyly, couldn't deny that Bellina had tidied the mess Nature had made of her. "That girl," went the collective verdict of her guests, "looks fit for a war hero."

Vittorio looked unmistakably heroic because instead of the traditional cutaway or frock coat he wore his Army uniform, his chest gleaming with the King's medals. Though in San Lorenzo his gesture would have seemed vainglorious, few Italians gathered in the Rose Ballroom had seen a veteran of the Great War; to most it seemed unimaginably remote, something Italy suffered blindly, the way it endured earthquakes, famines, floods. So Vittorio's gesture made the guests feel closer to the War, and perhaps to Italy, than newsprint or photographs had done for the past seven years. He stood with conscious elegance in the receiving line, bowing to the men and brushing the women's hands with the bold kiss no American dared.

Beside him Bellina flashed her timid smile, raking in the guests' envelopes of cash as a croupier rakes in chips, while Doctor and Mrs. Gioia greeted guests with the relieved grins of parents who defied long odds to marry off their daughter. Francesco and Teresa shook hands in the American style at the end of the receiving line, Teresa wearing a black armband to indicate she still mourned her father, Francesco pouring out a stream of jokes, business propositions, one-liners, his dryly amused tone floating, since he alone spoke English, over the Italian formalities everyone else carefully mouthed. The guests observed him critically. Francesco Monti seemed too pleased with himself, and some—especially the older women, who clung to superstition in this America dedicated to scientific cause and effect—predicted trouble ahead for such conceit. Already owners of his Garibaldi Homes complained of shoddy roofs that leaked rain, of toilets they had to unstop on hands and knees. Though nobody called Francesco a thief, the murmur was growing that he'd profited too much from the Italians who wanted to flee their tenements. More irritating still, he seemed to know all that and not give a damn.

I'm smarter than you and don't you forget it, his cool eyes told the assembled guests, *I'm more of a success than you and always will be.*

Teresa couldn't tolerate the heat and noise and crowds, and fled to the pink-marbled ladies room where she sat in a stall placing wet cloths on her hectically flushed brow. The whole day seemed monstrously unreal to her. She despised social pretension of the sort that dictated a reception for six hundred guests and, though she would have died rather than tell her husband, she disliked Vittorio. Thank God, Teresa thought, *she* hadn't married a petty tyrant who expected his bride to heed every self-infatuated syllable that fell from his lips. Francesco had such moments, true, yet he seemed the mildest of tyrants, consulting her about everything from their new car to the thickness of the mattress on which she wished to sleep. Anyone could see what different men the brothers were.

To begin with politics, the Italians' favorite debate no matter where they lived: Vittorio supported a strongman, even the thug Mussolini, as the alternative to chaos. "But Italy's freedom, its liberties!" Teresa protested, to which her brother-in-law savagely replied that there could be no liberties without law and order. When Teresa mentioned the Fascisti in Venice with their casual brutality, Vittorio told her not to exaggerate, seeming to regard discussing politics with a mere woman as beneath his dignity. From then on Teresa kept a scrapbook of Fascist crimes clipped from the American papers, which improved her English mightily, but Vittorio refused to look. "Newspapers lie," he told her angrily, "they lied about the War and now they lie about the peace!" Always in her head she heard her father's voice, declaring that without the rule of law men would massacre each other worse than animals, that the progress of history depended on the Rights of Man . . . . Vittorio laughed sardonically. "The strong have rights, because they dare greatly—the rest are cattle, haven't you learned that yet?"

Forget politics: Vittorio displeased her because he was so selfish. He expected Teresa to wait on him with the same devotion his mother had. Teresa should collect his dirty linens, socks, and shirts and return them to him clean by nightfall, she should cook him dinner and overlook his late arrivals at her table. The Italian male, she thought, expects to be babied until the grave; good thing I married Francesco, who's used to taking care of himself; how sorry I feel for Bellina, because nobody can ever satisfy a spoiled child, and a spoiled child can never love anyone.

Worst of all, Vittorio visited brothels before his wedding. Teresa knew because she overheard Francesco warn his brother he might be caught in a raid; the anti-vice societies were on the warpath, now that they'd closed the saloons. Vittorio laughed. "Tell me you never went to one yourself," he taunted his brother. She sucked in her breath, waiting for Francesco's reply, but he parried the point by saying Doctor Gioia might cancel the wedding if he knew how his future son-in-law liked to amuse himself. "Then you can bargain for me once again," Vittorio grinned, leaving the house for another harlot's romp. Teresa knew the Calabrian proverbs about not interfering between brothers and so she avoided the subject, knowing or rather sensing that Francesco would defend Vittorio as he always did. Still, Vittorio's idea of manhood—freedom for himself, slavery for his virgin bride—made her tremble with outrage. It seemed a harsh punishment for Bellina Gioia to wed a man as old-fashioned as Vittorio.

Not that Teresa didn't feel old-fashioned herself; how could she not, catapulted from San Lorenzo into this America as bizarre as a city on the moon? Not one thing seemed familiar save the human element, and even there America made her gape in awe, with its mad whirl of Negroes, Chinamen, forelocked Jews; the Americans looked as alien as their country did. At first the Philadelphia Francesco tried to show off frightened her, especially when she reflected that she had married it in marrying him; the thought of never returning to San Lorenzo made her chest ache exactly as though she were being crushed. Whenever she rode in the Packard with her husband, and bit by bit he was showing her his colorless, sprawling city, from the Negro slums to the "French" mansions of Chestnut Hill, she saw the New Women, mannish and jaunty, their very bodies (thin, unwomanly, legs like giraffes) declaring their independence from servitude. They looked at men as coolly and appraisingly as men looked at them. They were startling, they were appalling, and Teresa knew they were the future.

But her fear passed. She grew greedily curious about this city on the moon, insisting Francesco show her all Philadelphia, high and low. So began their journeys in the wan winter light, navigating point to point so carefully that Teresa saw what Francesco took years to grasp: each neighborhood in Philadelphia was a world within a world, the city in miniature. Each had as little contact with the rest as possible: the Negroes filled a thousand churches their white neighbors never saw, the Jews retreated into their insular pride after a day of pushcart peddling, while the Italians scarcely left their quarter at all, as ignorant of the city encircling them as San Lorenzo was of Italy.

Somehow Francesco escaped. He spoke English all day at the brickyard, so that even his thoughts flowed differently from theirs, for was not language both bearer and creator of consciousness? She would never equal his fluency, she knew, yet already she could guess the meanings of American voices, more from inflection and pitch than from the words. In their neighborhood of course she heard Italian: barbarous immigrant speech, clumsy with dialect and bad grammar, yet recognizably the language of her heart. Teresa herself spoke the pure Italian her parents used at home, strange to the ears of Sicilians or Neapolitans, who took her for a welfare inspector who'd learned *la bella lingua* in America.

There they sat, yawning behind fans, the stout matrons spooning spumoni or cajoling their husbands into one more rumba on the glittering black dance floor of the Rose Ballroom. Teresa felt a certain weariness when she thought of spending her life with them. What narrow horizons her fellow daughters of Italy had! Their lives consisted of the bed and the kitchen, as the saying went; for recreation they scrubbed their marble steps each week or dragged their husbands to the Italian music hall, where comedians improvised doggerel and babies squalled despite the hisses of prowling managers. The women avoided moving pictures, scandalized by kissing faces fifty feet high; they also shunned the Opera, in Italy the people's opiate but here in Philadelphia patronized, oddly enough, by rich Protestants. Most laughable was the hybrid Italian women spoke: 'ausa' for house, 'bisiniss' and 'grosseria' and 'La Merica.'

What a strange life they all led, what a fearful one! Unwilling to abandon Italy and terrified of the meatgrinder America, the men lived suspended in between, like tightrope walkers high over the earth. They were just American enough to work, to join the tailor's union, to drive garbage trucks, yet as soon as they reached Ritner or Mifflin Street they re-entered their hometowns once again. Young men lounged, played cards, flirted with virgins exactly as they would at home; even the smell of red wine and espresso recalled them to that simpler life, whose rituals assuaged all fears. The monthly religious feasts with their crowds of chanting women following plaster saints, dollar bills fluttering from their painted skin, electrified the crowded Masses ending each procession in incense and thundering homilies. Yes, these people were afraid. Through some perverse fate they found themselves trapped in barbarous America, determined to remain untainted by its ways. No flappers strode brazenly through South Philadelphia, not one speakeasy dared open; even the Negroes respected an invisible barricade between their streets and these blocks ruled by nostalgia, clannishness, and dread.

She tried to tell Francesco that. He listened, bored. They're wops, that's all. He paused. So am I. His voice sounded like lead. Teresa, I am a wop and I will always be a wop. At least to the kind of people who send their sons to Princeton University. You'll say I'm feeling sorry for myself but I'm not, I swear. The One Hundred Percent Americans, they hate us. They hate the Jews like Greenglass and the Irish like Carney too but they will *always* hate us. The only Italian they know is Al Capone. Read the papers. All we're good for, all *they* think we're good for, is shooting tommy guns and maybe singing opera. So I'll always be a wop, and it won't make any damn difference if I die as rich as Greenglass. That's why I want our son to go to Princeton. I want him to feel like *one of them*. I want him to feel he's as good as any shitbrain from Rittenhouse Square, because maybe then he won't think of himself as a wop.

You have such rage in you! I think you hate America worse than Vittorio does!

I understand it, that's all. That doesn't mean I accept it or approve of it but . . . . I had to, just to survive this long. You see, Teresa?

All I see is an angry face, and that frightens me.

I'll try one last time, but you won't understand . . . . alone, I can only rise so high. I don't mean money, I mean—well, look at Carney. He wants to be Mayor of Philadelphia, isn't that ridiculous? Except he could make it. I never could.

You're right. I *don't* understand. It sounds to me like you're eaten up with envy and pride.

Pride, maybe. Not envy. Oh, sure, there was a time I envied Carney and Greenglass, a long, long time ago. Before I got the point.

What point?

I keep telling you, I'm a wop. I'm a rich man and I don't sound like I fell off the boat, but I'm always going to be a wop no matter what I do—

You repeat yourself, Francesco. It isn't like you. Say something amusing.

God bless America!

You must be drunk, she said, turning her back firmly against him for the first time in their married life. And then she fell asleep, dreaming of a Tiepolo sunset over the San Lorenzo beach.

TWO

On sunny mornings that spring, spring 1924, the Year Two of Mussolini's regime, Leonora took her son Carlo far from the walkup she and Lampa rented on Via Margutta, Rome's parody of Bohemian Paris. Despite or perhaps because of her years in that convent near the Vatican, she knew the city scarcely at all; each turn disclosed an unfamiliar street, and even the Margutta seemed alien on those torchlit nights when their artist neighbors, ardent Futurists all, dressed up like Jules Verne astronauts, bumping and thumping their motorcycles up the Spanish Steps.

She would take Carlo to the Capitoline Museum, which perched inconveniently atop two hundred stairs. Its galleries held cool marble calm; even the busts of Roman generals looked serene. Best of all she liked the small statues of unknown provenance, like the child worshipper of Isis identified with a question mark. His round cherubic face resembled Carlo's. He always recognized that white marble smile and smiled back at it.

In the Museum Leonora could forget what year it was, who ruled Italy. Lampa had gotten elected as a Socialist Deputy from the northern town of Bressanone; that put him on the dictator's list of enemies, who'd be arrested when the moment came. Gramsci, now leading the Communist Deputies, shouted himself hoarse above the Fascists' jeers. Blackshirts glowered on every street corner, arrogantly young, like juvenile delinquents whose gang improbably ruled Italy. Almost two years ago the renegade ex-Socialist, Benito Mussolini, by invitation from their craven King, arrived peacefully in a sleeping car, an event now grandly dubbed the March on Rome. His power, still incomplete, grew every month, this newspaper taken over, that Ministry falling into line. Leonora found it hard to believe the fat clown ruled at all, this fugitive from a silent comedy, who deserved only a pie hurled in his face. Except there was nothing comic in what the Fascists did: the beatings, the castor oil, the midnight knock followed by arrest for "conspiracy against the State." The State meaning Mussolini, of course, even if he didn't have total power yet . . . .

Carlo helped her forget all that. At not quite three, her son regarded the world with quiet merriment, though soon, she knew, the screaming and squalling would begin. When Lampa came home from Parliament he played with the child until his bedtime. Then he bolted dinner before racing out again to jabber in the cafes with Socialists. Everyone expected Mussolini to fall any day now; surely the King would tire of this slovenly regime. Surely, once the workers and the peasants rose, the Fascists would collapse . . . .

At five one afternoon in late May, Carlo startled her from a nap with throaty cries. Already the sky was darkening over the Borghese Gardens, smearing the azaleas and umbrella pines with the opulent gold of Roman dusk. From the Pincio came the shouts of racetrack spectators, while nearer her window tinkled the laughter of girls letting themselves be chased by boys. Lampa liked to cite the Gardens as a perfect instance of Roman decadence, the leisure class enjoying its money mindlessly; Leonora could not agree. The aimless, playful life reassured her that no matter what bully boys ruled the streets, the Romans would chase the same girls, bet on the same horses, oblivious and therefore superior to the new regime.

The postman knocked with the day's second delivery. The only mail was for Leonora, a letter on lavender paper scented faintly with cologne:

Come for tea tomorrow at four. No politics, I
swear! Let me show you the small marble bust I have
been working on. I still miss Paris painfully!
The Duchess Bondini

Leonora smiled, rocking a still bawling Carlo uselessly. His weeping died into a string of sobs like hiccups before surging into noise once again. The Duchess was in Rome to learn marble sculpture, since, as she said, "Anyone can sculpt by addition, but only a true sculptor shapes marble as easily as clay." She lived in a small palazzo on Via Della Croce, surrounded, when not sculpting, by Jesuits eager to capture her wealth for their order. The Duchess spent her days studying the Vatican's antique portrait busts or taking lessons from artists certain of their genius. In the evenings she sat up debating theology, amused, she told Leonora, by the way the Jesuits whipsawed between greed and their ingrained habit of chastising error. Just now she was baffling them with Kierkegaard, whose arguments reduced her Jesuits to stammering St. Pelagius' name like an abracadabra which would make the great Dane disappear.

Leonora fed Carlo pastina with butter and egg, and little by little he slid into sleep. She stared at her son, wondering why she could feel no more for him than harassed tolerance. Wasn't having a child supposed to transform her, make her kinder, tenderer? More often than she dared confess she resented him, dreaded his unpredictable cries, wishing she could leave him on the steps of her old convent and then flee into the night. Leonora followed the steps of motherhood but never knew the dance, never allowed herself to bend as all mothers, even her own, surely must. Worst of all, Carlo resembled Lampa, not her, with his red hair, his green eyes that shaded unpredictably between laughter and tears: A Monti he would never be. He would grow into an alien man, a stranger-son, no kin to her or her brothers now vanished to America.

Yet she hid such thoughts from Lampa, no matter how much

she wanted to scream them at him when they lay in bed. She knew he would call her mad, and she half-suspected he'd be right. So that night, when he returned from the Chamber, she made his favorite risotto with fresh peas, while he rattled on about the afternoon debates. That is his life, Leonora told herself, and little Carlo is mine, and what in God's name has one got to do with the other? Nothing at all? Then, she asked whatever power she still prayed to, let me be a double agent in my house, my life . . .

That night Lampa bolted his dinner and left, explaining he had to attend a meeting at Comrade Matteotti's house. Too tired to rinse dishes, she let them sit dirty in the sink and, after checking on Carlo, fell asleep even before night had spilled its ink across the Roman sky. She dreamed: vivid dreams she could not remember when she woke in the cold hour before dawn with Lampa beside her, and since they frightened her she drew close to him, breathing in the smell of tobacco and coffee that clung to him. In his sleep Lampa looked harmless, even young, his face unwrinkled by anxiety, his mouth moving in a dreaming smile. Now he laughed aloud, and his laughter comforted her. Leonora drew closer to him, nestling in the warmth of his body, its male musk and roughness.

"Come to the Chamber today," Lampa said the next morning, glancing up from the papers, "if you want to see history being made." Leonora asked why she should, but Lampa smiled and said nothing, piquing her interest all the more. She knew he wanted her there but wouldn't beg her to come; typical of his stubborn pride. At times she prayed their son would not grow up to resemble his father or, for that matter, her.

In that year of our Lord 1924 the Roman spring, lush and fragrant, seemed to mock those who lived among its azaleas, its poppies, its palms. You could almost smell the fear, Leonora thought, walking quickly down the Corso to the Aventine. Mussolini was a cocked and loaded gun, certain to fire, or so it seemed since the election of last month. His Fascists ruled most of Italy thanks to faked ballots and bribes and, the last resort, brutalizing Opposition candidates. Only Northern Italy held out.

There, Lampa's Reform Socialists elected deputies, as did the old Socialist Party and even the Communists, who sent Gramsci as envoy to the mysterious Soviets. He'd returned to Rome without calling on Leonora, no surprise since Lampa's party and his traded insults almost as fiercely as they attacked their common enemy, the bandit, the terrorist, this strutting Duce who still, oddly, attended debates in the Chamber every day: this cross, said Lampa, between Julius Caesar and a bickering housewife.

And here he was today, his face mobile like an actor's, his laughter overloud, his grimaces worthy of a silent film. A frock coat concealed his corpulence. In its buttonhole, the eternal rose; on his fingers the rings his admirers sent—too many rings, lapis and diamond and sapphire, they made his butcher's hands too noticeable.

Watching him from the balcony, Leonora saw a look cloud his gaze, the frown of a child who feared mockery, and she felt strangely touched that their dictator had the same insecurities as other men. Nothing else explained his conduct. He sat in the Chamber every day and argued with the Opposition like a schoolboy; he might keep his enemies alive merely to shout them down. At such moments the Duce seemed too puny for his chosen role, no Caesar but a village crank who'd deny it was raining while his clothes got soaked. That was one face, childish and nearly reassuring. Then, when he drew himself up in rage and waved his fist he reminded her of opera baritones who hurled arpeggios of villainy. The drama of their lives now, the painful suspense, consisted of waiting anxiously for his mask to reveal a face. Great clown, great criminal, which would he be?

Just now the Duce had his clown mask on, flashing large white teeth as he greeted the Fascist Deputies toadying up to pay him homage. When the Chamber came to order he sat down like a child reluctantly confined to school, resting his bulbous chin against his palm, twiddling his fingers impatiently on the desk.

You could say anything about the Duce, and it would be true. Also its opposite.

He entered politics as a militant Socialist. Now he served big business, the aristocrats, the King.

He was a vulgar peasant, barely literate. He surrounded himself with poets, artists, architects.

He took power after revolution, the march on Rome. The King handed over power and he arrived by first-class train.

He was a fierce patriot. He would ruin Italy on a whim.

In the flesh Mussolini looked unreal, counterfeit, not the noble figure projected by newsreels and photographs. He was most himself when he posed—Leonora often thought—because then he surrendered to his own illusion, embodied it, acted it. The newsreels made him heroic because he stood alone, the strongman, he gestured from the heights. Here in the Chamber he was, instead, one more politician, and far from the most brilliant or most eloquent. Etched into his face was the uneasy knowledge that without troops he would never command these men. Elsewhere Mussolini could tell himself he ruled, like a king, by divine right or perhaps destiny; not here, not when he faced the cool scorn of a Matteotti, Lampa's party leader, who gracefully strolled to the podium, feigning ease. The chattering stopped at once.

Matteotti spoke the elegantly pure Italian of Florence, the tongue of Dante and Galileo. In itself this seemed a rebuke to the Duce, who like his followers spoke crudely, commonly. How you spoke indicated your class, and Matteotti's accent, limpidly clear, his tone as perfectly rounded as a Brunelleschi dome, suggested the cultivated gentry, not the gutter from which so many Fascists sprang. They proclaimed that proudly, as though their base origins somehow entitled them to rule.

His voice steady, Matteotti began reading a long list of Fascist crimes. His fellow Socialists held their breath: their leader was tightwalking over the abyss. Everyone knew the last election was corrupt, that the Duce's majority was fraudulent, but the gap between what everyone knew and what anyone dared say grew wider by the day.

The Fascists, Matteotti said, were stealing public money to

pay off big business for its support. He had dates, numbers, names. He recited them calmly, his indictment all the more forceful for his detached tone.

The Duce's staff was conspiring to grant an oil monopoly to an American company, which would give them millions in kickbacks. The Duce pretended to be surprised.

Academic freedom had vanished from the universities. Mussolini gave a stagy shrug, drawing titters from his deputies.

Then came the real attack: the Fascists used violence all over Italy to steal the elections of last month: "The government, having declared it intended to remain in power, implemented this declaration by using its armed militia to bully the people."

"Enough!" Mussolini interrupted, his voice trembling.

"The honorable president perhaps did not hear me," Matteotti said. "I am speaking of the elections. An armed militia exists whose sole purpose is to prop up a certain chief of government, a certain Duce of Fascism. We saw that all over Italy—"

Farinacci, the Duce's chief flunky, interrupted. Matteotti kept reading, his voice rising over the cries of 'liar' and 'prove it' from the Fascist deputies. Fifty interruptions, seventy, a Babel of voices in the gilded room.

"Conclude!" Mussolini roared. "Honorable Matteotti, stop making a scene."

"I protest. It is the others who are making scenes . . . ."

"Well, then—speak."

"The Honorable Piccinini was assassinated in his own home because he opposed a Fascist candidate . . . ." And the list of murders and beatings went on, in total silence now, ending with a description of the Fascist terror on Election Day. "And so," Matteotti continued, smiling sardonically, "only a small minority of the Italian people was allowed to vote, which makes the election a fraud, and makes the Fascist majority in this Chamber null and void."

Now Mussolini couldn't hide his rage. He smashed both fists down on his desk, the noise thundering through the enormous hall. At once Fascist deputies, like little boys, started vying loudly for the honor of refuting the Socialist. Leonora felt flushed and dizzy. She made her way downstairs. Matteotti stood smoking calmly, surrounded by his Socialists, receiving their praise with a wry smile, the ironic smile of powerlessness. She saw Lampa beside him and waved; he didn't catch her eye. At that moment she heard Matteotti say: "And now, comrades, you may prepare my funeral oration."

"His funeral oration!" The Duchess Bondini cackled sardonically, startling Leonora out of her anxious trance. "Grand opera, my dear, grand opera! Don't you know every Italian thinks he's a Verdi tenor saving the heroine?"

"Only Matteotti had the courage to sing at all."

The Duchess shrugged. "He knew he was safe. Who will touch him after his aria?"

Not wanting to argue, Leonora walked toward a marble bust in the corner of the Duchess's atelier. A young man's head, face unfinished, eyes expressionless.

"I think I will leave his eyes like that," the Duchess said. "The Greeks sculpted eyes that way. None of our damned nonsense about the soul. They were unsentimental—they exposed ugly babies rather than tolerate what wasn't beautiful."

"Horrible," Leonora said reflexively, thinking of Carlo.

"But we cannot be Greeks, I fear. We're cursed with Christian souls and we cannot shed them, ever."

"Is that what Kierkegaard says?"

"Don't mention that man to me! He has poisoned my peace of mind. All these years I thought I believed in God! But now . . . . now I know what absolute faith is, and I know I'll never have it. You can't imagine how much that hurts . . . ."

"That's how I feel about Socialism. I'll never believe enough to satisfy Lampa or anyone else who does."

"I am weary of it all," the Duchess sighed. "We live so barrenly, all of us. Testing ourselves constantly, doubting what we most desire. It wearies me. Is there no end to the questions I ask myself? What would I not give to *be*, merely to *be*, like a medieval peasant, to be and not to think."

"Even those peasants had doubts. Why did they follow every heretic who came along?"

"But what do any of us believe? We are Catholics in Church and nowhere else. Can you tell a believer from an atheist from the way both of them behave? We have banished God, I tell you, exiled him to some galaxy our telescopes cannot detect; he is no longer here, with us. And in his place we put man, man's intellect, man's power, as though we hadn't just butchered fourteen million in a senseless war."

"You expect too much," Leonora said. "How can you or I believe the way our ancestors did, when we do nothing else the way they did? Man changes and his image of God changes. How could it be otherwise?"

"And if we slaughter fifty million in the next war? Will our faith grow even weaker than it is today? What if we wipe out an entire race, will we say there is no God because God remained silent? No, we must have absolute faith or we have none at all."

"Duchess, I am no Kierkegaard but I love God. I feel certain that is good enough for Him. He is not a torturer, he only wants us to have love in our hearts."

"But God *is* a torturer! He is! You haven't lived long enough to know—life is pain and loss and breaking down. And if I can't love the God who wounds me, who kills my brother and my son in a meaningless war, then I love something else, a lie, a kindly face I substitute for the God of Abraham."

"Yes, that's what your Kierkegaard says. But he also admits no Christian with such faith exists anywhere. It's an ideal, Duchess, a mountaintop, not the valley where all of us live. And you can't blame yourself for not living on a mountain peak."

Tears began to stream suddenly down the Duchess's face. "No, no, you are right . . . . oh, if only you had known me before the war! I was clever then, and I was amusing, people said I was good company. I never wasted time on morbid thoughts, the way I do now. I torment myself all day with things I cannot accept or understand. And every night I pray to God to kill me in my sleep."

Leonora moved to embrace the Duchess, but the other woman brushed her sympathy brusquely away. "Somehow I must learn to love my torturer," she said, to herself. Then she collected herself behind her cool aristocrat's mask and said, quite calmly, "My driver will take you home now."

Matteotti's body turned up a week after his speech to Parliament. His throat and torso brutalized, his face recognizable, he became the regime's first martyr-saint. Though Lampa resisted, his party and the other Socialist Deputies walked out of Parliament and "left the Aventine." She and Lampa debated leaving Italy, always coming back to the fact that, though the Duce's henchman Dumini was in jail, which tied the murder to Mussolini himself, the predicted uprising had not begun. Roman summer cooled into a fall more temperate than usual. Day and night, the sidewalk cafes teemed with jabbering Socialists trying to guess history's trajectory.

By Christmas all agreed: Mussolini dreaded imposing a Fascist terror, for fear of dismissal by the King. They took Carlo to Bressanone, where he played merrily in the snowbanks and Lampa taught Leonora how to ski. They got fat on the region's rich stews and buttery Austrian cuisine, and they were making love every day for the first time in years—Leonora thought she hadn't seen Lampa so relaxed since he'd courted her. He made even his taciturn constituents laugh.

On New Year's Day 1925, the Duce played the cards he'd been clutching tightly to his breast. He seduced the King into outlawing Parliament—except for his hand-picked thugs—and that very day boasted that he and he alone was responsible for Matteotti's death: "If this regime is criminal, then I am its chief criminal! The solution to our problems is force! History has never known any other means!"

Leonora and Lampa listened, stunned, to the bellowing bull's voice. Lampa got up to switch off the radio.

"He'll arrest us all, now."

"He's all talk."

"Tell it to Matteotti! He'll arrest us all. He has no choice."

"Darling, he won't, you're safe, you'll see. You're safe."

"Your Duchess could help."

"With money?"

"With influence. She knows Margherita Sarfatti, the Duce's whore. They move in the same circles, you know that."

"And then?"

"I don't know, dammit! I'm thinking out loud! You want to sit here counting raindrops until the cops show up?"

"I could ask her."

"Tonight." Lampa stopped pacing, stared at her. "You could go see the Duchess tonight, couldn't you?"

"You don't drop in on your friends unannounced! *And* I haven't been there for a month. She keeps saying she's ill."

"Oh for Christ's sake, Leonora, forget the manners those asinine parents of yours taught you. We need her help, we need it tonight!"

"Then give me cab fare, I'm not walking down the Corso in this rain . . . ."

Lampa relaxed into something like a smile. "I love you, did I tell you that today? I love you, Leonora."

"Is that what love means? Making your wife obey you like a slave?"

"We're saving ourselves, you fool! All over Rome, tonight, people like us are making plans—yes, even your beloved Gramsci too. Why the hell shouldn't *we*?"

It took nearly an hour to reach the Duchess's palazzo, and when she got there she had to stand in the rain waiting for someone to answer the bell. A middle-aged man, his face taut and etched with deep lines, answered the door. When she asked if she could see the Duchess, tears, startling tears, began coursing down his cheeks.

"Not tonight. No. No. No."

"Then when, Signore?"

"I am the Duke of Bondini, Madame," he said with weary *hauteur*.

"When can I see her, Signor Duke? I am an old friend . . . ."

"I think never, Signora."

"Never?" Leonora nearly reeled backward with the shock. "Do you mean she's dead?"

The Duke of Bondini nodded slowly. His look became opaque. "Suicide . . . . and now the Church won't bury her in consecrated ground . . . . what a disgrace for my family . . . ."

"But she said—"

"Signora, I am still in mourning." Leonora noticed his black armband, his black suit. "I can do nothing for you now."

And the Duke shut the street door of the palazzo in her face, leaving Leonora to stand helplessly in the rain. I should have known, she told herself, walking away, I should have known, I should have . . . .

When she reached Piazza Santa Maria Della Pace, the rain was letting up a little, and she glimpsed a wine shop down an alley, approaching it thankfully. Leonora had just enough in her pocket to buy a cup of mulled red wine, spicy with cloves and cinnamon. She knew her old convent was nearby, because she remembered the shop and even, she thought, the red-faced man who served her now. But what earthly good would it do to find her convent now? At that moment her youth seemed as blurred and distant as a half-forgotten dream.

No. She would never destroy herself, she would never feel such despair. She never had. And waiting for her in the apartment were Carlo and Lampa, her men, as she liked to call them; they needed her, didn't they? She might have sinned, if love outside the Church was truly sin, though she did everything she did out of love. And so weren't her sins, as Dante promised, weighed by God on a different scale? She glimpsed a copy of the Socialist paper under the counter and gave the man the party salute. He shrugged, feigning indifference as Romans always did. Leonora pushed the glass door open, avoiding a puddle, and walked briskly home to her two men.

THREE

Thanks to what Vittorio called the devil's pact between his brother and Doctor Gioia, he owned a modern, modestly impressive house on South Broad Street. In fine weather he walked home from Gioia's clinic twelve blocks to the north, in the Sicilian pocket of South Philadelphia. Even on sunny days Vittorio came home irritated, not to say enraged.

Most afternoons Gioia vanished without a word, paying calls on his broker or his bank and leaving his patients in Vittorio's startled hands. Since Gioia kept their files locked in his memory, Vittorio had to waste time extracting them, in broken dialect, from immigrants who visibly mistrusted this young unknown. On those days, inevitably, he worked twice as hard, often telephoning Bellina to put dinner in the oven until he arrived. The rage he felt, walking home dog-tired, could lead—he knew it—to apoplexy, so scalding was the heat sizzling his nerves. God damn it, Gioia was treating him—a University of Rome doctor, a war hero—like a serf! True, he could diagnose the sick and prescribe remedies, even work the random magic of a cure; nevertheless he was, seemingly always would be, Gioia's slave.

The greedy old prick didn't even have the courtesy, after disappearing uptown, to offer an apology or an excuse. Which left Vittorio handcuffed to his rage: Bellina was so loyal she never believed her father guilty of any wrong, while Francesco disliked hearing his complaints. Vittorio contemplated various tactics—

refusing to treat Gioia's patients, for one, or confronting the old bastard at Sunday dinner—yet in the end chose to do nothing, and dream of Italy instead. Perhaps the feelings he had for Bellina made him lose his nerve.

She was his unexpected reward in this devil's bargain, not that he ever told her so: speak endearments to a woman and she grew, as all Italian men knew, too confident of her power . . . . still, after a year of marriage Bellina knew she made Vittorio happy. She hadn't, luckily, become an entirely American girl; she didn't believe marriage was one long swoon in which every day (as the silly song said) was *a holiday because you're married to me.*

Of course she'd been a virgin, and he recalled the proverb that virgins are more wanton than any whore. Each night she timidly (or not so timidly) asked him for sex, until by weekend his balls ached and he had to feign weariness. Worse, Bellina became so fascinated by positions he taught her that their marriage bed became a circus. Sometimes he thought she spent all day dreaming about what they would do that night, so that by the time he flicked off the bedside lamp (Bellina was only a harlot in the dark) she resembled those succubae who drained men of their life, killing them in the most delicious way imaginable. Somewhere Bellina found an American marriage manual which taught her about orgasms, and then whatever tranquillity Vittorio found disappeared. My days, he thought, my days are too busy because of Gioia, and now my nights are worse thanks to his daughter who was a virgin two months ago!

Yet he felt tenderness for her, not merely the itch of sex. She did love him, he sensed it despite her banal formulas; she wanted nothing more than to raise his children, serve him dinner, and spend his salary. What else did a good wife do? She and Teresa even became fast friends, were always in each other's houses gossiping—Bellina even took Francesco's bride shopping at Strawbridge's and Wanamaker's, initiating her into the American bliss of installment plans and credit cards and layaways.

"Teresa says you were the terror of your town, what was it called?"

'San Lorenzo," Vittorio replied, annoyed, "and I wish I'd never left."

"You don't mean that!"

"This life I lead, what good is it? Slaving for your father in a country where I don't belong? Am I some Old Testament Jew, to suffer such a fate?"

"You aren't suffering. You have me, darling, think of that."

Vittorio grunted. "I would have you in Italy far more happily."

"And what would I do in Italy? My family is here, my friends—"

"You'd be my wife. You'd help me build a great country."

"Oh, darling, you aren't serious?" she cried.

"I'd leave tomorrow," he said grimly, "if I could."

"But my father's clinic, this house, our life?"

"Our life, yes, what is it after all? I work like a cafone and you go shopping with my brother's wife. Nothing noble or heroic about that."

"I'm happy here with you," Bellina said, beginning to cry, "why aren't you happy with me?"

"It isn't you."

"You want to be a hero, is that it? You're talking like a boy, darling. There are no heroes nowadays. Being a good doctor and a good husband is enough for anyone."

"That isn't life. It's—paralysis."

"Of course that's life, a good life too! What did you expect, another war, more medals from the King?"

"I can't accept it. I won't. This drudgery is killing me."

"Your brother Francesco doesn't complain. He does what he has to do."

"He does what he wants! He doesn't have a father-in-law kicking him in the ass every day!"

"Don't you dare speak of Papa that way!"

Vittorio laughed. "Someday your darling Papa is going to lose his precious money. I only hope I'm around to see that day."

"You are wicked, Vittorio, you are cruel! He has been so kind to you," Bellina said, sobbing loudly now.

"So kind. He pays me like a serf. Which reminds me—you're spending too damn much in all those stores you and Teresa haunt. I'm going to have to put a stop to it."

"I'll go to my father, he will pay my bills!"

"You'll embarrass me and yourself. No, from now on you spend less, much less, and remember, please, we aren't rich."

"Francesco never talks to Teresa this way."

"Has it escaped your notice how much richer he is? You want me to be a good doctor, then live like a doctor's wife, modestly."

"Ask Francesco," she stammered, "for a loan . . . ."

"Never! Are you mad? Women have no notion of honor, not a glimmer of what honor means! Francesco helps me in other ways, and that's enough."

Francesco advised Vittorio on how much money to save, where to invest, the mysteries of finance which had always bored Vittorio. Now that he had a wife and soon, God willing, a family, he couldn't remain ignorant, as Francesco gently pointed out. And then there were letters almost every week from San Lorenzo, or from Leonora in Rome, letters they pored over like fruit from a garden they would never see again, their lost Eden, the Italy they'd exiled themselves from.

Vittorio saw, with some envy, how important a man his brother was; his Calabrian Bank was central to the life of the colony, between the mortgages it held, the mundane banking it performed, and the new brokerage desk where Francesco sold stocks on margin, ten or fifteen percent down. He had no envy of such success, or told himself he had none, since he had always found their father's greed the quintessence of vulgarity. As far as he could see Francesco resembled the old man little, and thank God for that—he would never wreck his family betting like a madman on one spin of the wheel. No, Francesco was too phlegmatic, so coolly controlled, that the Calabrians joked he was a German posing as one of them. It pleased Vittorio, though he never said it, that Francesco was making the money he made, because he might need to borrow for a clinic he dreamed of opening, to treat the children of the slums. His father-in-law mocked Vittorio every time they talked about his hopes. "Slum children," Gioia liked to declare pompously, "should all die off, young man—better for them and better for us! If you were a veterinarian would you keep rats alive?"

Vittorio stopped arguing after a time, depressed by the knowledge that Gioia was merely parroting America's 'philosophy.' This insane country worshipped Mammon, revered the Golden Calf—every nation did, but here, in this empty continent, no other values had taken hold, not even Christianity; Protestants blamed the poor for not being rich and claimed God had no love for such weaklings. And Gioia was a good American, damn him. Oh, he listened to the homily each Sunday at Saint Nicholas of Tolentine, where the parish priest, Father Brennan, a dour Irishman, dared to preach the social gospel—Gioia listened and heard nothing. Perhaps he was adding up his gold.

"Get used to it," Francesco shrugged when his brother complained. "Because Gioia's not apt to change, and for that matter neither is America."

"How can you stand it here? Doesn't this place make you sick?"

"You're going to tell me Italy is better off? How Mussolini is changing everything?"

"I admire the Duce," Vittorio said. "He has courage, and great ideals. If you'd fought in the War you'd understand—the bastards he kicked out, they slaughtered us like sheep! It was only God's grace I'm not rotting in a common grave."

"Oh, now you believe in God?" Francesco teased. "What happened to our village atheist?"

"A figure of speech. Tell me, little brother, you never think about going home?"

"To Italy? I've been here too long. And why should I go back?"

"Why shouldn't you? I want to, I think about it every day."

Francesco gave him a startled look. "You're unhappy here. I didn't realize."

"Happy or unhappy, this is not my home. Italy is coming

back to life, and here I am trapped in this neon wilderness. The food is appalling, the people are rude, and the climate is fit only for animals."

"You *are* unhappy. Does Bellina know?"

"Not everything. Not that I want to go home."

"Don't tell her, then. Unless you want an explosion in your house."

"If anyone explodes it's going to be me, working for that bastard Gioia, that greedy fool. He's not a doctor, he's a—he's a disgrace! He thinks the Hippocratic Oath is something you use to wipe your ass!"

"Disgrace or not, he thinks you came to America to stay."

"And where did he get that idea? From you?"

"Not is so many words."

"Tell me the truth, did you promise him anything?"

"No, no, no promises. I swear. But have you ever thought, Francesco asked craftily, "of what Bellina will inherit when he dies?"

"She has sisters," Vittorio said bitterly.

"Do the arithmetic, you'll still be rich. And his practice, you'll inherit that."

"You're as bad as Gioia, as greedy as he is! I belong in Italy, not surrounded by morons and misers like Gioia!"

"Bellina won't want to go, you know. She's too American."

"She's my wife and she loves me. What choice does she have?"

Francesco smiled sardonically. "She's an American woman, don't forget. Why do you think I didn't marry one? She isn't at your mercy, you're at hers."

"You promised her father I'd stay in this hellhole, didn't you? Don't lie to me! Didn't you?"

Francesco looked at him uneasily. "I had to. He wouldn't have signed the marriage contract otherwise."

"My own brother, and you chained me hand and foot!"

"I was doing what you asked," Francesco replied testily. "You asked me to find you a rich bride in America."

"And for that mistake I must suffer all my life? Is that what you want?"

"You can't go. Not with Bellina, not with her marriage settlement. Gioia would hire fifty lawyers to keep you here."

"Then I am trapped," Vittorio said slowly, "and thanks to you."

"Not trapped. You have a fine practice and a fine house and a wife who worships you."

"All in the wrong country. All of them wrong."

"A country where you can make money can't be wrong! Would you rather starve in Italy? Because that's what you'll do. Unless your darling Duce gives you a hospital, you'll starve."

"I'd rather starve honorably than eat Gioia's stinking bread."

"You wanted it," Francesco said angrily. "You asked me to get it for you. You chose this fate, Vittorio, accept it gracefully."

"Would you? Would you?"

"I've accepted much worse," Francesco said grimly, "to get both of us this far."

"I accept nothing," Vittorio shot back at him. "You may have imprisoned me, but my spirit is free, I will rebel."

"You're going to take a mistress? Is that it?"

Vittorio grinned. "Is that what you do?"

"I love Teresa," his brother said angrily.

"And I love Italy. And Italy seems very far away from these barbarous streets you like to wallow in."

"You wouldn't be happier there. Have you forgotten? You were miserable, so miserable you wanted to come here."

"When the gods wish to punish us," Vittorio sighed, "they give us what we want . . . ."

FOUR

"Tell me again why we can't go to America."

"America!" Lampa made a disgusted noise.

"That's not an answer. My brothers are there. They can help us. We'll be safe, all of us, Carlo too, doesn't that matter to you!"

"Of course. But we're gamblers. We made a bet, we bet on revolution. We said we would make one."

"Which will never happen in Italy."

"Which hasn't happened *yet*. If we can lead a general strike . . . ."

"The militia will crush you. Mussolini brags he's responsible for killing Matteotti, you think he'll shrink from shooting strikers too?"

"But look at his eyes! He's scared shitless, that fat fuck. Any day now he'll go too far and the workers will rise up, you wait and see. And then we'll win, the way Lenin and Trotsky won, the future will be ours."

"What future? There's Carlo and there's you and me, that's the only future I care about. And you Socialists are marked men, everybody says so. We have to leave Italy before your beloved future crushes you."

"Listen to me—you don't run if you believe in your cause. That's for women and cowards, not Italian men. The people know where we stand, any day they'll bring the tyrant down. That's why that fat bastard is shitting in his pants."

"The people don't care," Leonora said wearily. "All they want is a little order. Six months went by after Matteotti was killed, and what did they do? They pretended nothing was happening. And so nothing did."

"Nothing happened! The Opposition parties walked out of Parliament, the tyrant nearly lost control of his own followers!"

"Lower your voice. Carlo needs his sleep."

"And you, my darling, what do you need?"

"No, stop it—stop touching me, I don't want it now."

"But your cunt's getting wet, feel for yourself."

"My cunt," she sighed, "has a mind of its own. A moronic one. Why else would I have run off with you?"

"What a tongue you have! Like that Fascist snake Farinacci!"

"Why do you bring everything back to politics?"

"Why do you bring everything back to us?"

"And you aren't even worried that your passport's cancelled. You haven't said a word about *that* all night."

"I'm taking care of it."

"What does that mean? What the hell is that?"

"I found someone . . . . somebody who can help."

"Who? How?"

"Don't be such a wife." He rolled onto his side. Leonora began to tickle his back and ribs, knowing that would shatter his reticence.

"Tell me, tell me everything—"

"All right, just stop and I will! God!"

"Who's going to get you new papers? Some Fascist you bribed?"

"Better. A forger in Trastevere."

"A criminal?"

"Yes, my little convent girl, a jailbird with a record as long as your arm."

"But how did you ever find him?"

"I have my ways."

"And I suppose you want me to give you cash."

"Francesco's money—you never touch it, so now's the time."

"How you've corrupted me," Leonora said, but her merry tone belied her words.

"Is your cunt still wet?"

"Taste it and see," she told him, and there was silence in their bedroom for a long time after that.

In the morning he disappeared before she woke up, leaving an address scrawled on butcher paper with the words MEET ME AT 11, WAIT OUTSIDE. Carlo yawned his way through breakfast—the damp Roman winter made him sleepier than usual—and his sloth made Leonora curse the thought of dressing them both, carrying him to the bus, and crossing the near-flooding Tiber to the forger's shop. She had no doubt that was the destination Lampa intended her to reach. Little as she knew Trastevere, she recognized the name of the street; in the old days Lampa and his comrades patronized a seafood trattoria which, they swore, served the best spaghetti with clams in all of Rome. Those nights of laughing and drinking Frascati under the trees seemed a hundred years ago. Was it her imagination, or had time passed more slowly then? In those days they had time for dinners that began at midnight and ended drunkenly in the dawn; they talked about everything as though they thought nothing mattered if you couldn't joke about it, quickly and wittily. Who thought so now? That miserable Duce, he's made us all too serious . . . .

Not knowing how much money the forger required, she went to Trastevere with a checkbook, wondering whether criminals even accepted checks. The address lay on a street, narrow and sunless, bare even of winter trees, three piazzas east of Santa Maria. She wheeled Carlo, who was making unhappy noises over the cobblestones; at that hour few Trasteverese were abroad. The modern city the Duce sought to make of Rome halted here at the statue of Belli, that delicate poet who wrote verse in the dialect of pork butchers and prostitutes. With a smile, she recalled the tale of the Roman watching the Pope crossing Trastevere who lit a pipe, indifferent to such magnificence. When a Swiss Guard chastised him for insolence, replied, "Don't bother me, I'm smoking." So Rome would endure Mussolini as it endured everything, less the Eternal City than the Imperturbable.

She and Carlo turned down the last loop of street, and to her horror she saw a detachment of the Fascist police, the political squad reputed to carry out murders on the Duce's personal command. A Black Maria stood, engine running, blocking the far end of the street. Leonora heard the sounds that only a billyclub makes when it pounds flesh and bone.

Lampa's voice, strangely thickened, spat out: "You stinking murderers!"

"Shut your shit mouth, you Red—" And the club came down on Lampa's skull, making a sickening, dull thud. The police were dragging Lampa out into the street. His left eye was black; his nose was streaming blood like a water faucet onto his threadbare suit. As they wrenched him out the door by his hair Lampa caught sight of her. He was trying to wriggle away from the kicks they were all administering to his ribs, like a demented chorus line. Meantime the cop with the club aimed expert blows at Lampa's head, making him shut his eyes with pain as each one fell.

"A Goddamn police trap," he called out to her, disclosing a mouth bright with blood and broken teeth.

"Jesus God, leave him alone, enough!" she screamed, abandoning Carlo to plunge forward among the men.

"You want the same thing, whore?" demanded one, squeezing her breasts so hard she lost her breath.

"He's a member of Parliament, you bastards, you can't—"

The cop with the truncheon cracked it so hard across Lampa's forehead that even his comrades stared. Lampa's eyes closed and his body sagged in a sort of swoon. "We can treat anybody exactly as we like, you Red whore. We're going to clean all the lice like you and him out of Italy before we're done." The cop raised his club as gracefully as a conductor's baton.

"Jesus no, he'll die, he'll *die* if you hit him like that again!"

"Good thing," another cop said, hoisting Lampa's body into the wagon and hurling him against its bench. "Scum like this don't deserve to live. First we kill Matteotti, then all the other Reds!"

Leonora stood helplessly, tears of shock and rage scorching her cheeks. When Lampa was inside the policemen bolted the wagon shut. She had the presence of mind to ask where they were taking him.

"To prison or maybe a firing squad—why don't you come along?" The cops laughed like schoolboys at the gibe, and then the Black Maria accelerated away, disappearing in a sooty cloud of dust. Leonora sank on her knees into the street, sobbing and weeping with a bitterness she'd never felt, pounding the cobblestones helplessly with her fists. The world had just shown her another face, crueller even than the riots and strikes she'd seen; she tasted the iron flavor of injustice in her mouth, and against her will wished she'd never met Lampa here today, never seen him made the plaything of these thugs, these children in black shirts. With a start she remembered Carlo needed her too. He was lying peaceably in his stroller, as though they were visiting the Zoo.

"Mommy's here," she crooned to him, though he needed no quieting, "Mommy's here, I'll sing you a lullaby . . . ."

The next day she got dressed only to buy the papers, which (unsurprisingly) carried no report of the arrest. For a week, or was it two, she mostly lay in her bed, feeding Carlo but swallowing not a mouthful herself. Leonora half-slept, half-dreamed: she saw Lampa carted away, over and over again, each time with new and more frightening details, a bloody eye, a gun shoved into his mouth. She seemed unable to dream about anything else. Days and nights melted into one another; the color of the sky outside her window made no difference, for she slept in broad daylight and did the housework after dark. Leonora wondered if she was breaking down, the way those soldiers of the Great War did once they were safely behind the lines. Like them she suppressed an urge to scream, to shout and never stop, and like them she couldn't keep her body from shaking with fear when she was awake . . . .

One afternoon a postal messenger knocked with a telegram.

The boy wore the new uniform of the regime, crisp gray and glossy black. Leonora stared at him as she would have a spy, the enemy's secret agent invading her house yet again.

ARRIVE THREE P.M. ROME RAILWAY TERMINAL ROOM AT EXCELSIOR RESERVED.

MOTHER

How could she have forgotten her mother's semi-annual trip to see Carlo and have an audience with the Pope? Luckily, she had a few hours to awaken from her fog.

"But I don't understand—why haven't you visited your husband in prison?"

Leonora sighed, despairing of explaining the lassitude that kept her paralyzed. That was nothing her mother would ever experience, let alone understand. If the plagues of Egypt ever struck San Lorenzo, she would find some use for the frogs and snakes that were falling from the sky.

"I don't even know where he is, Mother . . . ."

"How many prisons can there be? And you must find an attorney, this very day."

"Don't you see? The Fascists set a trap for him, which means they want him convicted, legally or not. It's political, Mother, it has nothing to do with law."

"Oh, nonsense! Things aren't that bad in Italy, whatever you Socialists pretend!"

"They killed Matteotti, didn't they?"

"That's another matter. He attacked the Duce publicly."

"So he deserved what he got, you mean?"

"You always argue with me! What disrespect!"

"I don't know any attorneys. And I couldn't afford one if I did."

"I'll help, I'll help! Good heavens, you think I want to see my grandson's father locked up with murderers?

But the comrade of Lampa's she approached told her it was too late: he'd already been tried in secret session, and awaited sentence in Regina Coeli Prison. So many false charges had been piled atop the original one of soliciting forgery that Lampa's fate now depended on whether or not the Fascists would exile him to an island—the ancient Roman punishment they adopted for politicals—or whether he would rot in an ordinary prison with ordinary criminals. Exile! Leonora heard the word with horror. To a sociable man like Lampa that could be worse than death, that shadow existence on some volcanic isle. She reported it to her mother, who remarked coolly that Fascist judges were surely no less corrupt than the ones her late husband used to bribe . . . .

One sunny March morning, Leonora arrived at Regina Coeli. As soon as its iron doors clanged behind her she felt her spirits sink, as though she too were imprisoned there. A surly guard led her to the visiting room, a huge cellar bisected by a wire screen; on the far side huddled dirty, dejected prisoners. He called out Lampa's name and an unrecognizable figure shuffled toward the screen. Leonora had to bite her lip to stifle a scream; as in her nightmare, one of Lampa's eyes was caked with blood.

"Oh, my poor darling, what have they done to you?"

He smiled crookedly. Half his front teeth had disappeared. "They tortured me, they wanted me to betray my comrades . . . . but they gave up, so I guess they didn't want them that badly after all."

"And your eye?"

"The day they arrested me—don't you remember?"

Waves of revulsion, like nausea, flooded through Leonora. She shook her head.

"My dear, oh my poor, poor dear . . . ."

"No sentiment, please," Lampa said, his voice shaking unsteadily.

"What will they do with you?"

"Exile," Lampa said, trying to sound casual. "The Duce decides all political cases personally."

"It wouldn't help if we . . . . reached the judge?"

"We? That sounds like something your dear mother thought of!"

"She only wants to help."

"Tell her the judge will do whatever the Duce wants. That's what Fascist justice means."

"But how will you live, my dearest? How will you survive?"

"You mean if it's exile? I'll live. It's not terrible."

"You'll go mad with nobody to talk to!"

Lampa laughed bitterly. "Don't underestimate me, Leonora."

"I brought you Carlo's picture, but how—"

"Give the guard a few lira, he'll pass it to me."

An awkward silence fell.

"We're moving to a smaller flat, maybe on Monte Mario . . . ."

"Why the hell are you staying in Rome? Are you insane?"

"You want us to go up to Bressanone, to your people?"

"Shit, no. Leave Italy, there's nothing here for you now." Lampa glanced around him, lowering his voice. "*Paris*, that's the place, the politicals are all there. Or will be, soon. You'll find our friends there. And that's where the revolution will be planned, not Rome."

"You don't think I'm in any danger, do you?"

"No, not if they haven't grabbed you by now."

"Then why should I leave?"

"It may take years for me to get out—what good will you do anyone moping around Rome? I don't want you to throw your life away here, understand? In Paris you'll be part of the cause."

"What if I fall in love with another man?"

Lampa grinned lopsidedly. "Play your cards right, and I'll never know."

"You aren't serious?"

"I want you to live. And I want Carlo to grow up knowing what free men look like, how they behave. You can't give him that in goddamn Italy."

The guard overheard Lampa's last sentence and quick-marched

over to butt him in the ribs with a swagger stick. "Show respect for the Fatherland, you Red scum, show respect!"

Lampa absorbed the sudden blow with a low groan. "I'm talking to my wife—"

"Shit on her, you're going back to the pens, you scum!"

And the guard began kicking Lampa in the back and kidneys, each kick forcing him five paces backward from Leonora. She watched, too horrified to speak. Was this the true face of humanity, this casual cruelty? She refused to believe it. The regime was in a state of sin, that was it, sin that infected even its lowest man, this guard who laughed at Lampa's pained face and staggering walk . . . ."I love you!" she called out, "I love you!" but Lampa disappeared before he could reply.

On the afternoon of the same day Leonora and her mother sat sipping espresso in the Café Greco, an establishment too expensive for her to have patronized in all the years she lived ten blocks away. All around them chirped the young daughters of the Roman bourgeoisie, beautifully dressed in their French frocks and cloche hats. Leonora reflected that her own life could have led her to sit just as indolently, as brainlessly, on those banquettes. She'd spurned the inheritance her parents offered her, a quiet life, an orderly one, for what was quieter or more orderly than the cloister in which an Italian wife of wealth spent her days and nights? Instead she had a husband in prison and a son, an illegitimate son, who might never know him as more than a name without a face.

"Paris," her mother said, in the tone she might have said *Antartica*.

"I think so."

"A dreadful idea! Why must all my children abandon me? Abandon Italy?"

"We are nomads," Leonora said with a false cheerfulness. "Gypsies . . . ."

"At least your brothers are putting down roots. You tear yours up!"

"Oh, mother, please . . . ."

"And what will you do with Carlo? Raising a child costs money, my dear, and in Paris that means a great deal of money, everyone knows how costly life is there . . . ."

"I've got my savings. Francesco's cash."

"In six months you'll be begging me for more. No," her mother said, drawing herself up erect and haughty like a queen in a tapestry, "no, I have a better plan—a far, far better plan. You leave Carlo with me when you go to Paris. I shall raise him in San Lorenzo. That way you can be free, and I can be a grandmother."

"Leave him with you? You aren't serious?"

"Utterly."

"But why now? You never gave a damn about his welfare, you let us live in slums all over Italy—"

"As long as you were a couple I refused to interfere. I knew Carlo would be housed and clothed and fed, and he was."

"Don't you think I can take care of my own son?"

"*I* want to take care of him now." Her voice dropped to an urgent tone, and her face hardened into a determined mask. "What do I have in my old age? Village gossip, family portraits for the maid to dust? I have nothing, Leonora. Do you know how bitter it is to grow old with no family around for comfort, no grandchildren to give you joy? I need someone to love, you forget that, you think that only you need a husband and a child. What should I live on, dusty memories? I have needs too, and I can take much better care of Carlo than you. It will give me great happiness and it will give him a fine home." She stopped, gazing intently at Leonora as though expecting her, like a conquered enemy, to surrender formally: "I'll give you money for Paris if you agree. Go have your fling but let me have your son. He's all I have now, all I'll ever have . . . ."

"I need to think it over, Mother. This is—unexpected."

"Life is unexpected, every bit of it, from the day we're born until the last time we draw breath."

"Perhaps you're right."

"I am right. And I'm right about Carlo too. Her mother gestured for the waiter to bring another round. Her tone changed to that of a frivolous café patron: "I have tickets for the new Pirandello play tonight, can you come?"

"Oh, I adore Pirandello!" And as their talk slid into triviality Leonora could feel her soul surrendering Carlo even before her mind found excuses for doing so. How well her mother knew her, to guess that her pressure today would succeed . . . .

FIVE

By 1925 Carney was at best an absent-minded, at worst an absent partner to Francesco. He had an interest in three speakeasies, one of them the saloon near the brickyard where they used to gobble lunch in what now seemed those impossibly distant days before the War. Carney's three speaks served different clienteles, so that Carney had a foothold in each of the drinking classes Prohibition had made. The old saloon served mostly workmen, who staggered home by dinnertime, plus the cops and firemen who knew they could drink "on the cuff." In that speakeasy, and only there, Carney sold soda pop moon, a Philadelphia specialty so heavily laced with alcohol that devotees (not, of course, in Carney's place) might find themselves vomiting like dogs or wracked with convulsions only morphine could relieve. Carney boasted that his speakeasy served the only "reliable" soda pop moon in town.

His second speak catered to sheiks and shebas, and flaming youth, and flappers and their escorts—moneyed youth burning to drink and smoke and dance in the deliciously illicit aura Prohibition gave such pastimes. Carney swore he would disinherit his daughters if they ever did the same. He was old-fashioned enough to feel disgusted by these well-born daughters of Philadelphia necking with any man who bought them a Manhattan, and who did God knew what in private . . . . whores, he called them, scarlet, shameless whores. He prophesied the ruin of America, while Francesco smiled ironically. They ain't fit to raise children, them flapper girls, they're a generation of swine, like the ones our Lord Jesus had to exorcise!

It was in his third speakeasy that Carney invested his heart. On Sansom Street behind the Democratic Party headquarters, it resembled an expensive brothel: red velvet wallpaper, statues of blackamoors, and palm trees tall enough to scrape the ceiling. Boss Greer and his minions held court there daily, spitting into brass cuspidors and scheming against unslayable Republicans. Carney served them for free, despite Francesco's warnings: bread on the waters, son, he replied, to which Francesco invariably quipped that bread cost less than Haig and Haig. Of course most customers paid—stockbrokers, mostly, celebrating another triumphant day—but Francesco guessed Carney's favorite speak was running at a loss; it had to be.

His partner kept such facts as murky as he could. Francesco knew Carney had investors in all the speakeasies, if only because he overheard him muttering about their earnings on the phone. Still, he didn't know who the men were, and though he admitted to himself it wasn't his affair, he resented Carney's secrecy. Even more he deplored his absences from their brickyard. Carney's withdrawal forced Francesco to waste precious hours he should have been spending at his bank, approving mortgages and supervising stockbrokers. Throughout 1924 and early 1925 his frustration grew steadily, until by the day Carney summoned him to Sansom Street, he felt ready to issue an ultimatum. Teresa's pregnancy only tightened the screws of anxiety, since once the baby came he would have fewer hours for business.

How long his days already were, yet how little they wearied him. He was not a young man now, and still he found the stamina for the brickyard and the bank, even with Carney taking French leave. Teresa made the difference and he knew it; he often told her so. There was a special calm a man carried inside him when he was loved, and only then. He knew because he had never felt it before, certainly not with Laura Warrington. That had been lust, the blind rutting of two animals. He knew the difference.

Teresa, now, Teresa gave him a strength, a joy he'd never felt. The thought of her waiting for him at the end of the day, eager and expectant, made any number of frustrations bearable. And it calmed the anxiety he felt about his fortunes.

Francesco was learning that money, in the quantity he now had it, assumed a life entirely its own. He wasn't a really rich man, not by the standard of 1925, and yet his dollars kept multiplying as fast as cancer cells. To itemize his holdings always astonished him: the number was always greater than he expected it to be. And stock quotes unfurled all day on his tickers (he put one in his brickyard office so that he never missed an hour's trading), US Steel N.Y. Central Radio Telephone Radio Ford Motors Radio; sometimes he even awoke knowing which to buy and which to sell. Each morning he sipped Teresa's strong espresso while dictating his order to his broker, an "old Philadelphian" named Brad Butcher whom Francesco had met once only, the day he hired his services. He kept his business hidden from his own brokers for reasons of security. Some days Butcher had to swallow his bile at being bossed by this immigrant wop, swallowed it audibly when he nearly quarreled with Francesco's puts and sells. He never did. Even in those years of easy money the wop's luck, or foresight, struck Butcher as miraculous, and so he passed it on as tips to his best customers, carrying fifty of them upward on the same wild ride. In 1923 and 1924 there seemed no necessary limit to anyone's wealth and there might never be. Money: it was the music of the age, the jazz band everybody danced to, the siren song. Even the kids selling pretzels on Chestnut Street dabbled in stocks, buying them on margin with ten percent down. Francesco had to laugh at that.

After the Garibaldi Homes he balked at a second venture of that sort; too much trouble, he told himself, remembering the frenzy that had led him to blackmail Gioia. I can make better money, easier, with less heartache . . . . By 1925, impatient for profits, he was shifting his capital into the stock market and the Calabrian Bank. One fed the other: his depositors, like those pretzel boys, borrowed from him to speculate, with ten or twenty percent down, and though Francesco at first discouraged them, his executives warned he would lose their business. And so he did what all the bankers in America claimed loudly was best for them and for the country, and was there even a difference now?

This was the age of publicity, of ballyhoo. In South Philadelphia movie premieres glittered with Hollywood stars blowing kisses at frenzied crowds, while klieg lights made the night sky a second picture show. On the radio constant jingles for soap or lard jangled the nerves; announcers touted a new "celebrity" each week and, mercifully, forgot them by the next. And the business world shone with the same hectic glow. Stocks rose two hundred points on a rumor at breakfast, only to tumble when the market closed. Anyone with the time visited that room on Market Street with its picture window where boys ceaselessly scribbled and erased, erased and scribbled stock prices on a blackboard the size of a trolley car. The crowd watched open-mouthed, shouting lustily when Radio spurted up fifteen points.

Teresa believed it all. She listened to the radio for hours each day, which improved her English if not her sense of American reality. She knew all the latest jokes but couldn't tell you what their punch lines meant. Francesco tried to teach her, he made her study an atlas and a primer of English grammar, but after a month gave up, defeated by her willfulness. Teresa did know America's geography better than he ever had; English she swore she would never learn, it was so illogical that it gave her a migraine. "All the words with the same spelling that sound different! Like *though* and *tough*! A language fit only for the mad!"

At such moments Francesco marvelled at how little he knew her. In San Lorenzo Teresa seemed spoiled, kittenish, Amabile's petted youngest child: a piece of china too fine for everyday use. Now she was changing, or had she always secreted this second self under the mask that he'd fallen in love with? Teresa, in America, unmoored from the shelter of family, revealed a character quite as determined as his own, able to choose what she wanted and did not want, as when he casually suggested changing his last name to Hill, one night in bed. The force of her reaction jolted him awake.

"Is our son going to be a Monti or a Hill? Did you even think of that?"

"He will be an American," Francesco replied in a tone meant to quell all argument.

"And what is that?" Teresa asked angrily. "Please tell me, I'm just a dumb Italian girl, what is this wonderful thing you want our child to be when he grows up?"

"You have the devil in you tonight."

"That is not an answer!" Teresa cried triumphantly.

"It's nothing shameful. Abe Greenglass did it too."

"I'm not married to him! I'm your wife and I won't permit it."

"You won't permit it?"

"No. Let our son change his name if he wants to. Let him decide."

And so it went every night for the next three weeks. How did I forget she was a lawyer's daughter, Francesco asked himself? Teresa disposed of his argument that the new name would help his business by pointing to his previous success as Francesco Monti, quoting Scripture about rich men entering Heaven and that notorious needle's eye, and naming all the Italian tycoons who kept their names, like A.P Giannini in California. After that he fought a rear-guard action defending what even he now suspected was a poor idea. To clinch her victory Teresa mentioned his plan to Bellina—the two sisters-in-law saw one another each afternoon—who, as she hoped, told Vittorio. He came personally to the Calabrian Bank to denounce his younger brother as a traitor to Italy. That ended his fantasy.

Though Teresa kept her worries to herself, Francesco could see his business puzzled or frightened her, sometimes, the way the owner of that mythical golden-egged goose must have feared his mysterious good luck. He tried to explain his doings so she'd understand them, trying not to keep his life shrouded as his father had, wanting her to be his partner in spirit if not in fact. She listened to him patiently, asking the sharp question which invariably exposed a flaw in his designs. In the end he fell back, always, on his luck—the Monti luck, the Italians were calling it, that tangible sign of grace which would (he hoped) persuade her of the wisdom of even a risk like loaning margin money to the speculators in stock.

"What are you afraid of?" he mocked her. "Would you prefer a poor husband who digs ditches, a *cafone?*"

"I'm not afraid." She was two months pregnant and already nauseated; a basin covered the night table beside her head.

"Oh, you are. Listen to yourself sometime."

"Maybe . . ." Teresa nestled against the hollow of his arm. "Do you ever think about your father?"

"Him? Why?"

"You're very like him, you know."

"I'm nothing like my father, don't be a fool."

"Oh yes, you are. He wanted a fortune too. Leonora says—"

"You only quote her when you want to vex me! Anyway she's a Red—she thinks people like me should be shot."

"She knows *you*," said Teresa, sweetly stubborn.

"All right, she knows me. *You* know me. You want me to stop making money, for Christ's sakes? You want to eat bread and onions? You're a lucky woman, you don't even know how lucky you are . . . ."

He was thinking of their words as he strolled through the spring evening to Carney's Sansom Street speakeasy. Puddles of rainwater reflected the sunset, giving the streets a coppery glow. On every tree dogwood and flowering judas bloomed, electric white, perfuming the evening air. Francesco bought a persimmon, no doubt shipped from California in the new refrigerated cars; he stood eating it at Broad and Walnut, watching the tangle of taxis and streetcars and roadsters speeding and nearly colliding in their frenzy to reach the next light. If he closed his eyes he could recall, just barely, the way the city looked to him ten years earlier; he could recover the infinite sense of promise, the magic it held then. Now he saw only Whitman's hectic glow, and now, of course, he was part of it, hectic if not incandescent: his reflection in a shop window told him as much, a saturnine man of business, eyes narrowed in perpetual calculation. He had arrived. It was his city now, just as he'd told Senator Penrose, he wore the face the city demanded that he wear. That was his true and lasting assimilation, not the crude shorthand of changing his name. That was the measure of this city and this country whose uncountable hills and valleys rolled west to the Pacific: it had the power to alter a man's face.

Out in the street the stench of garbage filled his head. For three weeks the city workers had been on strike, though the mountains of refuse seemed the result of three years instead: crates of rotting vegetables, newspapers fanned on the sidewalk like playing cards, mattresses propped against fire hydrants, sofas stripped of fabric and stuffing and reduced to the spine of springs, even the occasional suit of clothes, so shiny with age no charity would want it, draped absent-mindedly atop a pile of ripped picture magazines, the celebrity on the cover missing nose and mouth. The New World, Francesco thought ironically: this goddamn America. The country was growing up too fast, it was rushing from innocence to decadence while bypassing maturity. The garbage made him think of Italy, Italian thrift, the bastard child of poverty: never would you see such wastefulness at home. Here, the entire country was in the business of manufacturing waste. Wastefulness was virtuous, it signified you had money to burn, as the saying went. When fashions changed, the women, even in his neighborhood, threw out closetsful of dresses, pumps, cloche hats, frenzied to keep up with the style. Every few months a new radio went on sale, a little larger or better engineered, and grown men ran to buy one. You couldn't have prosperity without waste, any more than you could have desire without—but what was the opposite of desire? Boredom, he guesses, or maybe disillusionment. America told you to satisfy every desire, as though you could buy happiness on the installment plan, easy credit, reduced terms, anyone can pay. Waste and desire, Francesco thought, two terms in the same equation, two faces of one coin.

This mad country with its hectic glow would race on forever, always reaching for the dream it was doomed to betray.

And he remembered his parents. Strange how he thought of his mother, even now, not as she was today but as she looked in his childhood, smiling, serene, very much in his father's shadow. Even Vittorio, hellion that he was, couldn't ruffle her, though God knows he tried. There was the time the brothers captured summer honeybees in their schoolcaps and brought them home, where Vittorio released the creatures during Sunday dinner. It was their father who made them pull down their pants and burned their asses with his belt. And then he caught himself up short. Why do I make excuses for her, why do I justify what she did? If not for her I could have grown up in San Lorenzo with all the other boys. The thought struck him as childish, but there it was, the eternal reproach, eternally unvoiced. Another part of his mind interrupted, as it always did, to say that his mother hadn't had any choice, that she had to send him away for the sake of the family. The family! The altar at which he sacrificed, at which he worshipped even now. The first reality which was also the last refuge, the only haven in this heartless world. And heartless it was. He'd travelled far since 1905 but not far enough to expunge the imprint those years in the mines made, those anxious years spent largely, he saw now, in fear, though he couldn't have said then or now precisely what he feared. Italy might have frightened him equally, though he doubted it. He could have gone to Turin or Milan, he could have worked in the Italian factories. Francesco often wondered what his life would have been like if he had. That would have scared him, surely, but immeasurably less. It was the combination of America and leaving home so young and, of course, working like an animal underground that terrified him. Still, he'd learned to conceal his fear; he scarcely ever let his mask slip, even now. The mask that had become his face: this face, calm-eyed, tight-mouthed, a man of respect, as the Italians said, meaning a man to be respected. Even Teresa seemed fooled. Someday he would tell her what lay locked in his heart, what feelings: but not today. Today, he had to pretend he was stronger, surer of himself than he sometimes felt, for if America had taught him any lesson it was that you had to play the man you needed others to believe you were. You played that man and they believed; and believing, they made you the man you played.

"She's due any day now, your Teresa, ain't she?" Carney asked when the two men were sitting over cocktails in the mahogany-panelled office behind his speakeasy.

"Any day. My brother is taking good care of her."

"Nothin' like seein' your first child's face. It's like touchin' God, almost."

Francesco smiled impatiently, as though to say, let's drop all this small talk.

"Well, ye probably know what I have in mind, Frank. Nobody ever put one over on Frank Monti yet."

"I'm no good at mind reading. What do you want from me?"

Carney gestured grandly in the direction of the bar. "Ye got any idea what this place brings in? Even with the drinks I give Boss Greer and his men gratis for nothing?"

"A thousand a week?"

"*Four* thousand a week, Frank. And that's after I pay protection to the local cops and the Feds. Four thousand. You didn't think I was playin' with myself, did you?"

"What about the other two?"

"All of them together, a steady nine-ten grand a week. If I owned them all myself, that is . . . ."

"You don't want me to loan you the cash to buy?"

"Cash . . . ." Carney looked glum as he said the word. "I want to sell my share of the business to you, Frank. A straight business proposition, not a friggin' loan."

"Sell the brickyard? You aren't serious?"

"Never more fuckin' serious in my life. You know I want to run for office, maybe State Senator, maybe Mayor. And that takes money. It's the Philadelphia way. Boss Greer's no different from the Republicans, he don't give you nothin' for free."

"And this is how you want to earn it?"

"Don't sound like a preacher, Frank. Sellin' liquor don't hurt nobody, for Christ's sake, it ain't the white slave trade! And where else can a man like me earn half a million a year, cold cash, no tax? How many years would it take me to do that sellin' goddamn bricks short of another war?"

"You have a point there," Francesco admitted reluctantly.

"Look at you, you bought that bank, you knew you needed to make money faster than we were. This ain't no different."

"The bank is legal."

"I'll tell you what's legal in America, gettin' rich, that's what. And when you get there nobody asks how you done it, they only ask how rich you are. I told you about Joe Kennedy, that Harvard mick. Don't you know he's the biggest bootlegger in New York? Smart as he is, you think he cares about the law? He told me, Carney, the law is whatever a strong man gets away with, otherwise we'd all be shittin' our britches fearin' damnation when we bang the parlor maid. And he's goin' to be President someday, Joe Kennedy, you bet he will!"

"I don't care about this Kennedy, I care about you. Listen, you helped me, you gave me a chance when nobody in this city would—"

"Ye helped yourself, and that's the truth. Only the strong survive, Frank, and ye know I'm right. And you would have gone just as far without my help. Don't get sentimental on me now."

"All right, dollars and cents. I can't buy you out all at once, not this year."

"Shit, I know that." Carney produced a sheet of accountant's ledger paper. "I had my fellas work out the arithmetic. Two even payments, Frank, that you can afford. I know."

"I'd rather pay you in Calabrian Bank stock, at least part of the price."

"No good. My partners in this business want cash, or they don't sell."

"You're making a mistake," Francesco said. "What if they crack down on these speakeasies? What if the business disappears?"

Carney grinned. "How can the booze business disappear? Things are good, people celebrate, things go bad, people cry into their beer. It's like sellin' oxygen, that's how folks drink nowadays, even the dames, you've seen' em, shameless hussies as they are."

"There's nothing I can say to make you change your mind?"

"I need the money to run for office, Frank. We both know the brickyard ain't makin' enough for either of us now. Simple as that."

"Nothing is simple," Francesco smiled. "Nothing about money, anyway. I need to think it over, Carney. I can't decide tonight."

"Remember, I can sell my share to a stranger, and how would you like that?"

An agitated rapping came from the office door. Carney twisted the key in its lock and stepped back to admit Enrico, who was panting and sweaty as though he'd run all the way from South Philadelphia. He addressed Francesco in breathless Italian:

"Your wife . . . . she has given birth . . . . in the hospital."

"Why wasn't I told earlier?"

"We couldn't find you . . . . I looked all over town . . . ."

"Is she healthy? Is the baby all right?"

"Everyone is fine," Enrico allowed himself to grin. "Signora Teresa is waiting for you to come."

"Is my brother with her?"

"He went home to take a nap."

"Is that what I sent him to medical school for? To sleep like an animal? Let's go." He turned to Carney and explained tersely in English. His partner handed him a fistful of Havanas, slapped him on the back, and offered his car and driver to take them to the hospital.

The corridors breathed the sickly smell of disinfectant, and Francesco strode down them almost at a run, ignoring the nuns who insisted he had to wait. When he reached a door labelled TERESA MONTI he halted outside, suddenly paralyzed. He heard his child wail—his child!—and pushed the door open to disclose a pale, red-faced Teresa rocking a white bundle on her lap.

"A boy?"

She nodded, smiling like a Quattrocento Madonna. He approached the bed slowly, timidly. He smelled new life as he neared the white bundle, an aroma compounded of yeast, urine, and feces, yet strangely sweet. Teresa handed the boy up to him. He grasped the swaddling clothes carefully, gazing into the wrinkled red face; his son seemed quite unaware of him, wailing intermittently and absently.

"Did it . . . . hurt?" he asked Teresa diffidently, shifting his attention from their child to her.

"It doesn't matter," she answered. "I'm alive and so is he, and he's all that matters now." She smiled at him, a hint of the old Teresa peeping through her new guise. "Why don't you kiss me? I'm not made of porcelain, I won't break . . . ."

As he bent down to press his lips to hers, their son began to howl, a sudden sound that made him step back, startled. Teresa rocked and cradled the boy to her breast, murmuring nonsense syllables, offering her nipple for him to suck. After a time the child's cries lost their plagency, dwindling into intermittent wails.

"You want to name him after your father, I suppose?"

"Only if you agree. I don't want to quarrel over our firstborn the way so many couples do . . . ."

She shrugged. "He won't be our only child. We'll name our next one after an Amabile." Her gaze narrowed suspiciously. "Where were you? We couldn't find you, when Vittorio brought me here."

"With Carney."

Teresa made a face. "Talking business, like an American!"

"He asked to see me. He wants to sell me his share of the brickyard."

"What did you say?"

"I said maybe, that's what I said. What does it matter?"

"I don't," Teresa said as sharply as she could, "want him to have a bankrupt for a father."

"Oh, for Christ's sake! I had one, and I did fine, didn't I?"

Teresa looked down. "Leone Monti—you like your name,

my little jewel?"

For answer the infant resumed his furious, helpless cries.

SIX

"**What** happened to our automobile?" Leonora asked her mother, climbing into a horsedrawn cart at the San Lorenzo station. She handed Carlo, miraculously still asleep despite the shrill whistle, into his grandmother's outstretched hands.

"I decided to sell it. With gasoline so high . . . ."

"Don't criticize the Duce," Leonora said sardonically. "He made the trains run on time, didn't he?"

"He also tripled the gasoline tax, like the thief he is," her mother sighed. "Soon it'll cost as much to live here as America." Signora Monti rapped the drowsing driver on his knee. With a lurch the cart rumbled off, awakening Carlo, who began to bawl.

"You should have given him to me in Rome. You always muddle everything!"

"Please, Mother . . . . I had to consult Lampa before I did anything."

"Lampa! He forfeited his rights long ago, if you ask me! And how could you ask that jailbird anything, he's incommunicado, isn't he?"

"A comrade carried my message to Regina Coeli, then carried his answer back. We have friends even in Mussolini's jails, thank God . . . ."

"At least Lampa had the good sense to agree with me," Signora Monti sniffed.

Hoping to avert a quarrel, Leonora kept still, watching the landscape of her memory unfold as the cart clattered lazily downhill. In the distance, sunlight glittered so sharply on the azure her eyes hurt when she glanced at it. It was high summer: the olive trees hummed with blackbirds hopping from branch to branch while from the eucalyptus rose the choral buzz of cicadas. The town's thoroughfare looked as rutted as it had ten years before, so that the coachman had to maneuver around potholes she'd played in as a child. Was it true what the Socialists claimed, that the South hadn't embraced the Duce yet? Surely he would reward loyalty with an asphalt road. And then the Prince's palace slid into view, gaudy with Fascist flags and posters of Mussolini strutting in uniform.

"Party headquarters," her mother said, following Leonora's game. "The police station, too. You'll have to register there, it's the law."

"You mean the Fascists stole it from the Prince?"

"Why not?" Signora Monti shrugged with all the fatalism of the South. "They made that thief Brunetti police chief, can you imagine? All the years he tried to rob the Prince, it took Mussolini to finish the job."

"Brunetti came back from America?"

"I doubt he ever went, the dirty dog. The scum of the town follows him, even that whore Carmela who takes her customers to the graveyard. And then the Blackshirts complain that San Lorenzo doesn't love them!"

As she spoke she was rocking Carlo to hush his cries. Leonora watched her handle him with the calm acceptance of a woman who'd raised children of her own, a back-of-the-hand ease she herself would never share. God help me, she thought, my mother might raise him better than I ever could. The cart halted abruptly in front of the Monti house, which looked dingier than Leonora would have dreamed possible.

"I let my housemaid go," her mother said, defensively. "It was wasteful to keep two servants, just for me."

"But doesn't Francesco send you money any more?"

"I save your brother's dollars for myself—and for my grandson, now."

"None of this makes any—" Leonora began, but her mother cut her off:

"What kind of Socialist needs servants to take care of her?"

They walked into the mercifully cool drawing room. The driver carried in luggage and waited for Signora Monti's cash. Leonora gave him a gleaming new ten-lira piece; he bit it, that ancient peasant gesture, to make sure it was good, then grinned his thank-you with discolored teeth.

"I don't need them," Leonora shot back, "I always thought you did."

"Don't argue with me! Be grateful I've closed my eyes to your folly all these years."

"My folly? And what do you mean by that?"

"I mean Lampa. You tried to deceive me, and I let you think you had."

"I must be going mad! Deceive you, how?"

"That you were married, that your child is legitimate. A stupid lie, even Vittorio saw through that! And now my grandson is a bastard, a jailbird's son—thanks to your so-called principles!"

Leonora began to tremble uncontrollably. "Lampa is in jail because of *his* principles, because he won't kiss the boot that's crushing Italy . . . ."

"Only a fool would not! A real man, an *Italian* man, would say whatever he had to say and do whatever he had to do to care for his family. But your precious hero has no love for you and no love for Carlo, that's obvious! He'd rather rot in a stinking jail than be a good father to your son!"

"You mean like my father, who ruined all of us with his greed?"

"Enough!" her mother shouted, "I forbid such disrespect!"

And like all women unable to enforce an absurd command, Signora Monti had no choice but to storm out of the room. With a sigh of relief Leonora picked up Carlo, who again slept happily, smiling like the statue she loved in the Capitoline Museum of the child worshipper of Isis, and sank into the Second

Empire settee cradling him in her arms. In five minutes she fell asleep, wrapped in the Southern heat fatigue which drives even natives indoors every noon. Leonora dozed lightly until night was falling, until the churchbells began calling the faithful to early Mass. She woke with a smile, thinking, I'd know those cracked, tuneless bells anywhere, even in the cacophony of Rome's thousand churchbells awakening the city at Sunday dawn . . . .

Signora Monti strode regally into the room. Leonora could tell from her stiff back and her hands crossed like an executioner's, that her mother's wrath hadn't disappeared.

"How dare you speak of your poor father so scornfully! While he was alive you still acted like a woman of good family, at least."

"Good family, yes—until he wrecked it with his avarice. Are you proud of sending Francesco to America? That's what you both did, sentenced your son to hard labor, did you forget?"

"*I* made the decision," her mother said with icy dignity. "Blame me, not him—blame me that Francesco's a millionaire today."

"You robbed him of his youth. There aren't enough dollars in the world to buy that back!"

Signora Monti gazed at her, shocked. "I never knew you hated me so much."

"I don't hate you, Mother, I don't—only we have to live with truth, not dreams, and the truth is my father was a greedy fool."

"What do you know about it?" her mother jeered. "Let me enlighten you—the Prince ruined him, the Prince and that viper of a priest. Oh yes! They plotted and schemed to ruin him, and they did. The whole town knows he fell into the pit they dug for him, like Joseph in the hands of his enemies."

"I know all that," Leonora snapped impatiently.

"You know nothing. You hate Leone in your heart, but have you ever tried to understand *his* heart? He wanted this family to rise in the world, he did what he did for all of us. Yes, yes," she said quickly, seeing Leonora about to reply, "he failed. How many men do not? Do you sneer at your Lampa because he failed too?"

"We aren't talking about him."

"You know what Lampa dreamed of and so you forgive, because his dream was beautiful. So was your father's. Maybe someday you'll forgive *him*."

Leonora felt stifled by her mother's voice, by the heat, by the dust floating in the air. "I think I'll go to the police station now," she said. "I might as well . . . ."

She trudged up to her old room, where she began changing out of her travelling dress into clothes that didn't reek of cigarettes and railroad smoke. Her mother knocked—an old formality—then sat on the bed watching her with sad eyes.

"What did I ever do to make you hate me?"

"You know that's not true." She gave her mother a quick hug.

"Then why must we wound each other like this?"

"It's how we show our love."

"You think so?" Signora Monti forced herself to smile.

"Is Carlo asleep?"

"I cut up a peach, he swallowed it and started to snore. He'll be a happy boy—he smiles at everything."

"Was I like that, Mother?"

"Oh, you were so serious! You looked at your father and me with such big eyes . . . ."

"That must have been," Leonora said wryly, stepping into her shoes, "the last time I gave you any happiness."

"No! I was happy to see you on the train platform, just now."

"You think I've thrown my life away, I know. Even when you don't say so, I know you're thinking it."

"But you're still young! People your age don't know how unpredictable life is. We zigzag, Leonora, we aren't arrows flying straight through the sky."

"You mean I wrecked my life, but I can still redeem myself?"

"Oh, you see everything in the harshest light possible! Did I say anything of the sort?" Signora Monti grasped her daughter's hands in hers, bony and overlong like a Giotto saint's. "The only thing we can't repair is death. You have a son, you have your health. Who knows what's awaiting you in Paris? Perhaps a miracle."

"The age of miracles ended long ago."

"If your brother believed that, he'd still be digging coal."

"I'll try hoping, Mother, if that's what you want me to do. Only it isn't easy with Lampa chained to a latrine."

"Let me tell you something." Signora Lampa's voice dropped to a confidential tone. "The Duce will not rule Italy forever. His kind are like fireworks—they rise up fast and furious and they come down just as fast in the dark . . . ."

"I'll pray for that." Leonora gave herself a quick inspection in the cheval glass. "But mind who you say that to—one subversive in the family is enough."

As she approached the Prince's palace, she saw the Fascist flag, not the King's, flying from a high window in sight of half the town. That didn't surprise her, though her anxiety increased. The Duce still hadn't won his battle to subordinate the Fascists to his authority; all over Italy rogue militias were refusing to lay down their guns. Worse: Farinacci, Part Secretary and the Party's brain, shouted that Fascism must replace the state—to hell with the King and his bureaucrats. Perhaps Brunetti was making San Lorenzo a breakaway town where he ruled unhampered by the King and his laws.

Three boys were playing soldiers in the unpaved dirt that faced the palace gate. Though they wore the black shirts and shorts of the Fascist Youth, she heard no menace in their harsh shouts, their frenzied wrestling that stirred up clouds of dust; they resembled her own brothers at the age when puberty charged them with aimless energy. When the boys saw Leonora they scrambled to attention, presenting a sloppy copy of the Fascist salute. She smiled at them and walked into the dark anteroom.

Leonora tiptoed through dusty salons, calling out for Brunetti, getting no response. Sheets covered the ancestral portraits still jutting from the walls, the sole whiteness lightening the palace gloom. But doors stood open and windows looked wetly washed: someone had been here, and certainly not the indolent Prince's

ghost. When Leonora reached the scallop staircase, she called out
Brunetti's name louder than before, then froze: a peasant girl
stood staring suspiciously down at her.

"You're shouting like a crazy woman." The girl grinned,
stepping down the stairs to the marble floor where Leonora stood.
As she approached, her features swam into focus despite the
gloom: overripe breasts that nearly burst her brassiere, short stocky
legs that bespoke peasant blood, cheeks pocked with smallpox,
badly camouflaged by rouge. A sharp ammoniac smell of
unwashed flesh rose from her clothes. Leonora must have made
a face, because the girl immediately snarled:

"Who the fuck are *you* to look down on *me*—the Goddamn
Queen?"

"I wasn't, but if you thought so, I apologize."

"Tell me your name. You're not from San Lorenzo, I know
that."

"Oh but I am. I was born here, same as you." She extended
her hand, which the girl refused to touch. "I'm Leonora Monti—
Leonora Lampa, now."

The girl's face twisted into a mirthless smile. "Vittorio Monti's
sister?"

"You know my brother?"

"I worked for your stinking family," the girl said venomously.
"Until Vittorio had his way with me and threw me into the
street, the way you eat an orange and throw away the peel. After
that nobody would marry me, so naturally I had to earn my
living on my back."

"I'm very sorry for you. Truly, I am."

"Sure, you call yourself a Socialist, don't you? You and your
Red husband that the Duce threw in jail. Why aren't *you* there,
that's what I want to know?"

"It might happen yet," Leonora tried to joke.

"And what's your goddamn business here? Trying to get
arrested too?"

"I came to present my papers to the police."

The girl tilted her head toward the second floor and yelled

for Chief of Police Brunetti to come down quick. Desolate silence answered her. Then came the sound of a door slamming and boots clattering across a floor. "What the fuck is it now?" a man's tipsy voice called down raucously.

"I've got a Red for you," the girl cried excitedly.

"And I've got a stiff prick for you," the voice drawled.

"Oh, please come down and see her for yourself! She's an enemy of the State!"

The boots began descending reluctantly, in lazy steps that audibly lacked all urgency. She and the girl kept their eyes fixed on the staircase as though a ghost was descending on them. Yes, a ghost, Leonora thought, the proprietor of this haunted house . . . .

Brunetti appeared. He wore the Blackshirt, a dirty one, with Garibaldian cartridge belts slung across his chest. His billyclub, essential to the good Fascist's uniform, swung from a loop in his thick leather belt. Even his haircut mimicked the Duce's, though without success. Vexation filled his eyes, the annoyance of a drinker interrupted before he's had his first glass of the day.

"Signor Brunetti—" Leonora began.

"Colonel Brunetti," he cut in, still idling down the steps. "That's who I am, but who the fuck are *you*?"

"She's the Monti whore," the girl rattled on excitedly, "the one who ran off with that Red the Duce put in jail."

"A Monti," Brunetti said. "Well, well, I thought we cleaned this town of all you shits."

"My name is Leonora Lampa now," she said with all the composure she could summon. She told herself it was shameful to feel the fear that was tightening her chest.

"Haven't you heard the radio?" Brunetti smirked. "The Duce exiled your shitheel husband. To the island of Ponza, wherever the fuck that is. Me, I'd have shot the Red bastard against the nearest wall."

"Ponza?" Leonora repeated, her mind numb with shock. How absurd, she thought, to learn his fate from this Fascist scum five hundred miles from Rome . . .

"Lock the bitch up too, she's an accomplish," the girl cried.

"The word's *accomplice*, you dumb slut. No. That's not Fascist justice."

"You aren't going to let her go?" Carmela shrieked.

"Don't tell me my fucking job." He grinned sourly at Leonora, extending one dirty-nailed hand. "Your papers better be in shape . . . ."

Brunetti examined them, squinting in the weak light filtering down from the small oval windows above the stairs. It seemed he had trouble reading, judging from the time he took over every word. Carmela walked close to Leonora and looked her up and down with contempt, as though she were already a prisoner. Leonora caught the foxy odor of menstruation mingled with her scent of unwashed flesh. At last Brunetti lifted his head, scratching his unshaved chin, to ask:

"What brings you to San Lorenzo when Lampa's in Rome?"

"Family business, Colonel."

He grinned at Carmela and then at her. "Socialist business, you mean," he said, heavily sarcastic. "Your shitheel husband's in jail and you're taking his place—admit it, bitch, admit you're a Socialist courier!"

Leonora began stammering: "No, I swear, it isn't so, I swear . . . ."

"Prove it, you bitch. Prove you're not an enemy of the State."

"But how?" Leonora wailed. "How can I prove I'm not what you want me to be?"

"Strip the whore naked," Carmela yelled. "Strip the whore stark naked!"

Brunetti pretended to reflect. "Yes. Good. Take off your clothes."

"You can't be serious."

Brunetti jerked the billyclub from his belt loop and slapped it against his palm. "You want me to beat the truth out of you instead? I can. Look at this club—the Duce calls it the sacred club of Fascism. I call it the Holy Ghost," he grinned, "because it descends mysteriously . . . ."

He cracked it across her knees, sharply and suddenly, so hard that Leonora buckled, and nearly fell. "How do you like the Holy Ghost, you Socialist bitch?"

"No, no, *hurt* her," Carmela implored. "Her bastard of a brother raped me! I want you to hurt her like he hurt me."

"Strip, bitch, and you, Carmela, keep quiet. We aren't animals like those Reds, you know. We're Italians, civilized, heirs of the Roman Empire like the Duce says."

Leonora undressed, at first slowly, then with increasing speed, hoping that would lighten the shame she felt. It did not. Carmela scowled at her.

"Jesus, what tits," Brunetti sighed. "Why did God waste them on a Socialist?"

"Mine are just as good," Carmela sniffed.

"Her legs are better, and her ass . . . ." Brunetti murmured, walking around Leonora to study her. Carmela grew suddenly enraged and grabbed the billyclub from his belt.

"Now I'm going to hurt you, whore," she announced. "Bend over and spread your legs."

Leonora glanced at Brunetti. He shrugged indifferently. After a moment's hesitation she obeyed. Slowly, insolently, Carmela walked behind her and slapped her buttocks with the club so hard that the room echoed with the blow. Leonora nearly lost her balance then.

"Stay on your feet," Carmela warned her, "I'm not finished with you, bitch."

Brunetti laughed. "What a good Fascist you make. You have got no pity, no pity at all."

Without warning she thrust the billyclub into Leonora with such force that she blacked out from the pain. When she came to, she began to cry, to scream, quite uselessly now that Carmela was shoving and twisting the club into her even more violently, panting all the while.

"You like her ass," she said to Brunetti. "Take a look at it now."

Carmela plunged the club into Leonora's rear, sending a searing fire through her that scorched her stomach, her kidneys, even her spine. Carmela's panting grew louder, huskier. She kept plunging the club until Brunetti noticed blood trickling out of Leonora's backside.

"That's enough, Carmela, don't kill the bitch! You'll get me in trouble with Rome, stupid cow!"

Carmela obeyed, every muscle in her body protesting visibly. She walked around to face Leonora and then slowly, deliberately spat in her face.

"Get dressed and get out," Brunetti said. "And leave San Lorenzo on the morning train. Unless you want to feel the Holy Ghost descend again." He laughed and walked back up the stairs.

Leonora never knew how she managed to dress and walk home to her mother's house, though somehow she did. The council of mother and daughter that night was remarkably brief: Leonora announced she wanted a ticket to America. It seemed Paris wasn't far enough from San Lorenzo to suit her now.

SEVEN

In 1926 a prosperous Philadelphian of the immigrant class displayed certain signs of his success, signs as rigidly fixed and clearly understood as those medieval costumes identifying whoever wore them as a serf or a cleric. The first, most exciting one was your motorcar. Not only did you drive a late-model Franklin or Packard (never a vulgar Ford), you had to install every feature, from running boards to a car radio to the new air-cooling plants. Your motorcar testified infallibly to last year's gains and this year's hopes. So did your house: your wife had to cook on a glittering new range the food she plucked from her equally new, equally glittering Frigidaire. But the most concrete sign that you had arrived, that your success was permanent, was a seashore house.

Before the Boom the Jersey shore looked as it had for fifty years—a scattering of saltboxes, separated by sand and grass, ending in the gaudy splendor of Atlantic City, that neon Versailles of gamblers and fast women noisily alien to the towns approaching it. Now those miles of sand and grass were subdivided, and subdivided again, so that Philadelphia money might better display itself. The one hundred percent Americans sneered at this frenzy, while privately cursing themselves for not buying lots before the War. Anyone with foresight found himself effortlessly rich, for the new houses, matchboxes of wood and glue certain to be splintered by the first good storm, were now fetching prices high even for those giddy days of the Boom.

Francesco knew better than to buy. He built himself and Vittorio two good, small houses on adjacent lots. And he quietly registered Carney and Monti as a Jersey company, which let him write off their construction as a business expense. Carney smiled at his shrewdness but chose to buy a beachfront showplace, where he could entertain his best customers and his friends in politics. "Good will, Frank," he explained. "The best goddamn investment of all."

Thinking he'd freed Teresa from the sooty humidity of city summer, Francesco was shocked when she complained that now she had to run two households, thank you very much. Plainly there was no pleasing a wife with a young child, except perhaps in bed where their marriage remained splendidly unchanged. In the end, thankfully, Teresa took to spending weeks at a time in their Ventnor house; thankfully, because despite her complaints the salt air and the crisp light did soothe her nerves. Francesco would run down for a night or a weekend—run was perhaps not the word, given the miserably rutted Jersey roads—and return to the city as fresh as though he'd dallied for a week. Alone in the city on a summer night he would find his eye straying to a toothsome pair of buttocks or of legs; how easy it would be, he thought, and how many men he knew parked their wives in the sand for exactly that . . . . he never did, of course, ruefully thinking that Carney was right, he was the only husband in Philadelphia who didn't play around. Wondering, too, if that made him somehow less of a man than all the rest . . . .

It was the last weekend in July. He arrived late Friday night, too late to play with his son. Teresa served him cold veal cutlets and tomato salad, slices of those perfect Jersey tomatoes that grew in the sandy soil so well they were the only American food as tasty as their Italian counterpart.

Always he felt a certain vertigo at the end of the day, the week. Vertigo, not weariness, not the honest fatigue of a workman digging ditches or laying subway track from dawn to dark.

Francesco tried to start his days calmly wearing a quiet smile, until something sprang to ferocious life inside him, some beast tearing at his nerves, tugging at his skin as though to burst it: the beast of his ambition. It tasted like old pennies in his mouth, it filled his lungs like liquid fire. Whether the numbers on the ticker tape cheered him or chilled him the beast breathed hot and hard into his ear. This beast didn't want money, didn't want success or fame. It wanted his blood as surely as his mother had, as the coal mine had, except from this beast there was no deliverance and no escape.

"You had company tonight?"

"Bellina. I'll tell you about it later."

Next to the demitasse cups Teresa set out a salver of biscotti, a modest offering for her guests. She herself was dieting ruthlessly, determined not to become "one of these gross Mamma Marias that has to wear black to hide her fat," as she always said, which meant she kept no sweets or snacks in her kitchen; even bread she bought and served in precisely the amount each day required. Francesco teased her about acting like an American, and even worse, a flapper girl. "You should have married your sister-in-law," she'd say, smiling and unperturbed. They both understood the dig: Bellina's pantry resembled a Ninth Street bakery, where cannolis and rum babas and sfogliatelle appeared as if by magic, always fresh, always in such quantity that Francesco found himself eating two of each simply to be polite. Bellina's svelte figure was slowly thickening; her trip to Desert D'Or was vanishing into the chamber of memory reserved for excursions without consequence. She pressed, too, on her guests, Italian brandy, which made even Italians shudder, along with French bonbons and English cheese sticks, pressed them all at once and so insistently that only a heart as hard as Vittorio's could refuse this affection disguised as food.

"You think about home much, darling?" Teresa asked.

It galled him that she still called Italy *home*. "Not much nowadays. And especially," he grinned, "not when you serve me those tomatoes."

"You're so coarse," she complained. "You have no soul, I swear. You don't . . . ."

"If God made San Lorenzo he made these tomatoes too, didn't He?"

"Don't talk about God. You're no better than a pagan," she said, a slight smile lifting the corners of her mouth.

"No, that's Vittorio. He doesn't believe in anything."

"Oh, I know. Bellina says it, she's afraid he'll burn in Hell."

"Maybe. But not for that."

"He was here tonight, they both were. Then he took her home and drove to the city. Isn't that strange?"

"He must have patients in the hospital."

"No he doesn't," Teresa said triumphantly. "He has a meeting. And Bellina didn't want him to, they argued right up to when he drove off, what do you think about that?"

"I think I married a snoop, that's what I think. Why would you spy on them?"

"I wasn't spying! They were arguing so loud I couldn't help hearing it."

"You were spying. You care too much about other people, dear."

"What do you mean by that? I certainly do not. Who do you mean?"

"Oh, those Italian women you had over here the other night," he said, "the ones who said you weren't breast feeding Leone the right way."

"That's *not* what they *said!* They said I should breast feed him until he was five and I said that was bad for both of us, because he'd be impossible to wean. And I asked your brother tonight and he told me I *was* right!"

"That's my point," he said gently, "you shouldn't care."

"You care about Vittorio," she said, smiling again.

"That's different," Francesco declared, standing up with a yawn.

"You're a good brother."

"Well, and you write to your sisters and your mother every week, don't you?"

She reached up to tousle his hair. "It's not the same. You're good to me . . . . it scares me sometimes, thinking what would have happened to me if I hadn't met you."

"Your father would have found you some mangy old aristocrat."

"Don't tease, I'm serious! We'd never have loved each other, we'd have wandered in Limbo like lost souls!"

"You worry too much about foolishness," he laughed, lifting her out of her chair, into his arms. "Let's go lie down . . . ."

"And who's going to clean my kitchen? You?"

"Why not?" he smiled, covering her mouth with a kiss before she could reply.

And then about an hour later, when they were lying entwined and almost melting into each other's flesh:

"It's so cool and breezy in here, I should bring the baby in to sleep with us."

"Go ahead."

"You've had your fill of me? You don't want any more?"

"Good thing I love you, idiot, or I'd—"

"It is a good thing. And you're a good husband, not like Vittorio. To hear Bellina tell it, that is."

"And I bet you just love hearing her complain. Makes you feel fine, doesn't it?"

"Don't be so smart," Teresa laughed. "I'll get Leone now."

After the baby was tucked in with them in bed they lay self-consciously, trying to recover the sweetness that trickled after their lovemaking. Teresa sang a folk tune from San Lorenzo that went:

'All the fathers and their sons
Went out to hunt, hunt, hunt the wild boar
And all the fathers and all their sons
Came back, back, back with empty hands!'

"Oh, that makes me homesick!" she exclaimed. "Some days, everything does . . . ."

"Ah, I was like that too. I didn't dare walk through my neighborhood for fear I'd hear our dialect."

"You know what I mean, then."

"Why else do you think I came back to Italy?"

"God willed it! So you could marry me."

"You believe God cares who Calabrian girls make babies with?"

"God cares about everything, everything."

"Maybe he *cares*, but . . . ."

"Keep talking and I'll swear I married an atheist. That's what Bellina says, you know, Vittorio makes fun of her every time she prays."

"He could do worse," Francesco said. "He could make fun of her every time she strips."

"You're terrible! Though it's true, she's getting fat again. Maybe that's why Vittorio stays away from her."

"What do you mean, stays away? He's got no mistress, I can tell you that."

"As if you'd admit it if he did! No, he's always at meetings, you know, the Sons of Italy, all that cafone crowd that brags they're really nobles who got born on the wrong side of the bed."

"He doesn't have time for meetings. Gioia works him like a horse."

"Don't you know anything? That's why he went back to town tonight. He wants to start a Fascio with that Sons of Italy crowd. The Duce wants to spread his gospel in America, he says we immigrants deserve him as much as his Italians do. *His* Italians! What airs that hoodlum gives himself!"

"Nothing new there, he set up Overseas Propaganda years ago. It doesn't mean a thing."

"It'll mean something when your brother starts his own Fascio," Teresa said acidly.

"A *Fascio*? A Fascist society? He'd damn well better not, he could lose his visa. And why the hell didn't I hear this earlier?"

"You're always telling me not to gossip," Teresa said with a tart edge of mockery. "Besides, I thought you knew."

Francesco sat up and fumbled for a Lucky Strike. "He didn't

tell me, he knew I'd say no. That stubborn idiot! He always had a head like a rock when he made up his mind . . . ."

"When you wanted to marry me, you were just like that—and thank God you were! Even after my poor father asked you for a loan—" Teresa broke off, embarrassed at the words.

After a moment Francesco said: "I always wondered if you knew."

"I knew. He was a good man, really and truly, even if he seemed like a thief to you then. He was desperate. You see, my father was a patriot," Teresa said firmly, pleased to have found a word that summed him up.

"I never thought he was a bad man—a bit foolish, maybe . . . ."

"No more foolish than your darling Vittorio," Teresa shot back. "Your brother wrote a big speech, Bellina says he practiced it every night this week, and for what? To make a bunch of cafoni who can't even afford a good cigar agree to create a Fascist club! Honestly, what good will that do anyone?"

"Probably none," Francesco replied wearily. "They'll sing Fascist songs, they'll argue, they'll drink dago red."

"What cafonita."

"Vittorio wants to lead them, I suppose?"

"Of course—why else would he talk to those peasants when he doesn't even invite them to his home . . . ."

"My brother," Francesco sighed. "He used to make me march up and down San Lorenzo with him, playing soldiers, and guess who always got to be general?"

"He couldn't really lose his visa, do you think?"

"Who knows? Things change fast in America. Friends become enemies and enemies become friends, and overnight. I saw it during the Great War, that's why I had to stop them from deporting Enrico—have I told you that story?"

"Many times," Teresa said, but she said it lovingly.

Teresa kissed Francesco lightly on the lips, nestling into the crook of his arm. Long after she plunged into sleep he remained awake, adding another cigarette butt every few minutes to the pile in the bedside tray. He kept thinking of the last time he'd seen Vittorio, two weekends ago . . . .

"Just think," Francesco said, leaning on the rail of the Atlantic City boardwalk in the cool of a summer evening, "somewhere out there is Europe. If you sailed straight ahead you'd run aground, wouldn't you?" Clouds the shape of galleons tacked across a Della Robbia blue twilight sky. "Look at them, like a mirage."

Vittorio gave his unamused bark of a laugh. "*This* is the mirage," he replied, indicating with a contemptuous sweep of his hand the bathers in their striped suits, the Boardwalk strollers, the neon-pink pleasure domes. "Those clouds are realer than this. Not to mention *you*, dressed up like a one hundred percent American."

"And why shouldn't I look prosperous? You want me to go around in rags like our paisans, afraid God will take their money away if they let anyone see they have it?"

"Be like my father-in-law," Vittorio told him with a crooked grin. "Pretend you're dead broke so nobody will beg from you."

"Your clinic?"

Vittorio nodded. "He's breaking his word, but the old bastard doesn't care. I think someone told him he could take his dollars to the afterlife."

"He said what exactly?"

"Young man," Vittorio mimicked Doctor Gioia with malicious glee, "You'll have to earn that money yourself, the same way I did . . . . as if I *could*! He doesn't even pay me enough to buy Bellina her own car!"

"But I had an understanding with Gioia all along . . . ."

"You did, he didn't. Anyway I'm trapped. I can't leave his practice, Bellina would scream her head off. And I'd still need money for my clinic . . . . it's like the Prince of San Lorenzo all over again."

"For Christ's sake, it's not as bad as that! At least you're in America!"

"Oh yes—and *that* makes it even worse."

Francesco stared at Vittorio, forcing himself to stay calm. "What will you do?"

"I don't know . . . . I want to change everything, but I don't know how."

"Change your life? For what? You have a profession, and a wife . . . ."

"You know they offered me a battlefield commission after Caporetto? I should have taken it, little brother. At least I would have had some honor in that." And Vittorio glanced away, at the invisible Italy they could both see across the waves.

EIGHT

My dearest love, my life, my heart of hearts—

I never stop thinking of you, not even in my dreams. I see your face before me always and it inspires me, it gives me a bit of your courage and your hope, in spite of everything. What a strange destiny keeps us apart, or is it just the hard hearts of our enemies and not really fate at all? I looked up the island of Ponza in my schoolgirl atlas: population 53, not counting political prisoners of course; used also by Emperor Nero as a place of banishment . . . . and I, in my infinitely less heroic way, am banished too. To the land of Whitman's "hectic glow," as Francesco likes to say!

You always said I was unobservant, saw nothing, lived in a dream. And maybe I was, once. No more.

America is overpowering, overwhelming, not easily described—I say America when I mean New York and Philadelphia, these gigantic cages of steel, iron, glass. The people move like automatons, so stiff you'd swear they have lead inside, until a lightning bolt like Valentino's death hits them, and grown men and women gape like shocked children watching the news flash past on electric signs. He was one of ours, the Great Lover, an Italian immigrant. In death he seems too gorgeous for such grubby facts. Women still weep for him, weeks later, when they see the Sheik of Araby's face on the screen two stories high.

But most of the time they look asleep, unformed, behind

their greedy eyes. Even the men. Any Italian kid has a thousand times more cunning than the baby-faced killers slaughtering each other on the Stock Exchange. Children, that's what they are, a race of lucky children who've inherited the earth. I hope they lose their innocence soon—it's dangerous, it cheats them of what you and I were born knowing, the underside of things, *the dark*!

The great Professor Salvemini, like you an enemy of the Duce, though luckier since he escaped to England, sent me a list of sympathizers in New York who might give me work. By now I don't care what kind, even scrubbing floors has dignity—you taught me that, didn't you? So I corresponded with three of them and naturally I got no reply. Two weeks passed. I paced up and down my furnished room in Greenwich Village—a kind of bohemian quarter filled with Italians and 'artists' and God knows what sort of 'rebels,' men in dresses and girls in business suits. America has gone from barbarism to decadence without a period of civilization in between.

There's a big piazza called Washington Square. I go there in the afternoons, now that the summer light is growing pale and the greenery of the trees is getting that coppery look, especially when the sunset paints everything with a rusty light. From a distance I can hear someone playing a Chopin etude or the new song on every radio, "Over There Where Europe Used To Be."

You'll want the reasons why I'm staying away from my family. They're simple—

One, I would loathe being beholden to my brother after all these years on my own. Francesco has made himself into something of a king, or at least a feudal lord. The other Italians either resent his success or beg his help, even at streetcorners, in the most embarrassing way. He's got his fingers in a hundred businesses, the brickyard he started out with, a bank, stock speculations and loaning money so others can do the same—he even confessed he's a silent partner in some saloons (illegal here). But none of this tells you what sort of man he is. All capitalists are *not* alike, my dear, no matter what your beloved Marx and Engels say—at least not in their souls, and yes, they do have souls; Francesco has one, anyway.

He speaks quietly and unassumingly yet he's acquired the habit of command, he expects obedience. When I told him I preferred living in New York he gazed at me as though I were a dimwitted clerk whose sums didn't add up. Then when he saw I was determined, and wouldn't be swayed by silly arguments like how lonely I would be, his face lost its calm and his eyes flashed, exactly the way our father's did when he played the autocrat of the dining room. I must not leave, our family was scattered far too long, he said, to separate again now after so many years. And who would protect me in New York? Then he shifted from fear to hope: in Philadelphia I could live in luxury, in my own house, even drive my own little car. Money went further here, whereas Manhattan . . . . he grimaced, to indicate the thousand economies I would have to make. Why, he said hotly, you'll live like the cafoni do! Did you leave Italy and come to America to keep making sacrifices endlessly? And Teresa will miss you, and of course (he added hastily) so will I. And our little Leone can take the place of the son you left behind.

I'll admit some of his arguments hit home, yet the longer he talked the more stubborn I became. At last I said, Francesco, please, let me go, and if I'm unhappy I'll come back, all right? You haven't changed, he smiled, still stubborn after all these years! You and Vittorio, you're impossible to persuade, you're like donkeys that refuse to pull the cart!

Two, Vittorio is organizing a Fascio; yes, he's become a Blackshirt. Which means we'll be squabbling constantly. He says *you* must be a criminal or the Duce would never have exiled you. My blood boiled! Was he always a cretin, or is he lost in America and following the first banner that offers him peace of mind? Whichever, I don't want to be drawn into arguments of the kind he loves to start. Why defend Socialism? Let *him* defend the bastard who slaughtered Matteotti ("a frame up by the Duce's enemies, for which he nobly took the blame") and banished you to Ponza . . . .

"The Duce will restore Italy's greatness and redeem our honor," he says.

"And how can a thug surrounded by rapists and murderers do that?"

"We were cheated," he answers bitterly, "cheated of the lands our so-called Allies promised us: the Tyrol, Dalmatia, and new colonies in Africa! They even snatched Trieste back from us, as though the blood we shed defeating Austria was a joke. Italy was tricked into war, too. Our blood, my sister, must be repaid— and the Duce will force Europe to repay us, wait and see!"

"Those men didn't die for Italy, they died because our politicians and our generals led them into battles they couldn't win."

"Who's taught you this seditious shit? Lampa?"

"Even children know your war was a bloody farce."

"A farce!" Vittorio jumped to his feet, eyes blazing, lips trembling with rage. "Traitors like you and Lampa should be shot, the way mad dogs are shot. The Duce is right to quarantine Socialist scum far from patriots!"

Somehow Bellina, his wife, the only subject of his realm, managed to get my brother back into his chair and even calm him down. He finally apologized for speaking violently and said I should read his speech to the Fascio, if I wanted to understand what the Duce means to a man like him. Now do you understand?

Third reason: New York is a center of protest, especially against the terrible case of Sacco and Vanzetti. Here I may be of some use organizing the Italians; in Philadelphia, it's like shouting through cotton wool.

It's strange, my darling, as soon as I step inside this house on Cornelia Street where I rent a room, I'm back in Italy . . . . the smell of Italian coffee bought fresh roasted on Mulberry Street, Puccini on the Victrola, pictures of Saint Anne and the Blessed Mother in gaudy mezzotints, a tripe casserole sizzling in the oven beside a dozen stuffed eggplants. Outside we're called WOPs, meaning Without Papers; in here we dwell in snug coziness, like Jonah in the belly of his whale.

I'm boarding with a Sicilian family, the Vergas, who've made a fortress to shield their customs from this America which amazes and repulses them. Preziosa, the wife, complains to me: "In Sicily everyone followed the rules, we had to, because we'd had the same rules for hundreds of years and so they were written on our hearts. Even the criminals respected the rules, you follow me? But in this insane place nobody follows any rule, nobody respects anything! And if we don't keep ourselves separate, their disrespect will ruin us too. Our children will get married without their parents' consent—imagine such a thing in Italy! (I kept my mouth shut about *us*.) And my husband won't be master in his house, once our children leave home and marry anyone they please—and that's anarchy, isn't it? You're an educated woman, don't you think so too? Now d'you see why we all curse this country and grumble 'Managia l'America!'"

But what a fool I am, leaving the story of my job hanging!

Two nights ago I went to Cooper Union, a lecture hall where people like us gather, to hear a free talk on 'The God of the Gnostics and Our Living Faith.' I need to improve my English, understanding as well as speaking. I'm better off than the peasants who (after ten years) know only a few broken words, but if I want to stay here I know I need to learn. Unfortunately, esoteric theology wasn't the ideal choice!

Did you know that the Catholic Church was created to battle the Manichean heresy? Before then nobody knew what orthodoxy was. (There's your beloved dialectic in action again!) Marcion, the Manichees' anti-Pope, claimed there were two Gods ruling Creation, and that the Evil God, the one the Old Testament calls Yahweh, actually made this world. The Good God sent Christ to destroy the Evil God, so that His Passion and Crucifixion were a sort of magic act without anguish or agony. Christ took human form only to deceive the Evil God, not to redeem mankind—what a curious theology!

But what's happened to you, and even in a strange way to Vittorio, makes me wonder if there isn't something to these heresies. It does seem that the Evil God rules this world, punishing anyone pure of heart, like you, and dazzling the weak and vainglorious, like my brother, that fool. Maybe the evil God truly does reign now. And that thought frightens me, because what can possibly follow except we're his puppets now, and the whole world will be too—don't you ever fear the bloody farce has only *begun* in Italy, in Europe? Oh, I know you'll mock me and call me superstitious, tell me the nuns ruined my capacity for logic and dialectical argument—but I've thought this, one way or another, ever since that day I watched Matteotti—I've thought, God help me, that Satan is enthroned now, and our struggle is doomed, because more innocent blood must flow before the evil is swept away. And so what difference, I sometimes ask myself, does my struggle make when all of Europe will be purged with fire? But I don't let myself think that for long, it's too close to despair.

(Which is what killed my friend the Duchess, in the end. Like all of us she was born into one world and then found herself living in a totally different one, morally, socially, even spiritually. Our parents felt emotions we shall never feel, they're extinct, they're as dead as the planet Jupiter. And we feel things they never dreamed of—look at my despair, or the Duchess's. Think of how certain *they* all were that the world made sense and always would! Will any of us ever feel that sure of anything again? They were spoiled, our parents, because their world *did* make sense—even its injustices were reasonable compared to ours. Now we inhabit nightmare terrain. And I fear we'll never awaken without bloodletting. The Great War showed that even quiet men, placid men, secretly long for one.)

Anyway, I was leaving the hall when I overheard a beautifully well-dressed woman, an American, speaking Italian to the young girl who accompanied her. I froze, as I do whenever I hear la bella lingua anywhere outside my house, and the woman noticed; she asked me, using the formal address, if I were an Italian myself. Now here's the strange part—she was one of Salvemini's contacts. I'd already written to her!

Her name is Laura Warrington and she is quite rich and, I'm afraid, beautiful. She must be older than me, but these American women have a thousand tricks—creams, unguents, powder of

course—so she looks at least five years younger than I do. Her
husband lives in London most of the year, and her son goes to a
boarding school far away (the name sounds like Eggseter) so she
is alone in New York, like me. Except she has millions to cushion
her! She gave me her card and insisted I call on her next morning
without fail, which I did.

Laura Warrington lives in a townhouse in the best part of
Manhattan, the East Seventies. It's similar, I suppose, to Parioli
in Rome only with more charm, since the houses have that air of
old money the Roman nouveaux riches so desperately covet. She
greeted me warmly, my letter in her hand, though she didn't
refer to it until we'd wasted half an hour eulogizing Salvemini.
When that topic died a natural death I told her about your troubles,
and her blue eyes filled with (I think) genuine tears. But how
will you support yourself, she cried! I mentioned Francesco's bank
draft, and his offer of Philadelphia, at which Laura gave me a
pitying smile. No, my dear, no, no, you must stay here! You
cannot bury yourself in the provinces! Her hand gripped my knee.
She looked me up and down, an uncomfortable feeling, almost
the way a strange man would have in the street. At that moment
the girl from last night sauntered in, and Laura became businesslike
again: she offered to hire me as a translator, pamphlets like
Salvemini's, and a play or two by Pirandello—she yearns to direct
a shocking, modern play, and nobody has shocked New York
with Pirandello yet.

She pressed some silver certificates into my hand. We'll start
in two days, she said, be here at the same time prepared to work
hard! Leonora, she said, what a noble name you have, like that
lovely Beethoven overture . . . . the other girl gave me a sour
smile and then I found myself on the sidewalk, the money in my
hand. Now is that good fortune or not, my dear? And doesn't
this stroke of luck solve the dilemmas that were besetting me?
When I called Francesco, he sounded too stunned even to
congratulate me. But never mind! Today I am a real New Yorker
and a woman of independent means . . . .

I see I haven't yet told you what this mad whirligig of a city feels like to me. New York is everything we heard it was, and even more: it's the capital of this century, the way Paris must have been the capital of the last. Imagine a city without history or real pride in the past, where every five minutes, it seems, a new skyscraper or a new subway line appears as if by magic. And the people, most of them, look anxious, even frenzied, they rush like insects through the canyons between the glittering towers. Insects, because they move not as individuals but as a mass of drones, or worker ants, heading for cubicles high above the mob. How hard they all try to look alike, the same shirts and collars and neckties on the men, the same skirts and shirtwaists on the girls, as though one deviation from the insect pattern would mean some dreadful fall! And yet this New York madness exhilarates me, it quickens my pulse as I haven't felt it quicken since those wild days in Turin . . . .

I think of those days more than you know. Some wise man or woman once said that happiness isn't a state of being, it's a memory of what was—and if that's so then I was happy, profoundly happy, with you then. Even with the strikes and the lockouts and the riots and all! I often think of our trips to the "country" at the end of the tram line, how we used to lie on the grass and read poetry aloud and embrace, shamelessly, for anyone to see. If there is any *greater* joy than making love with the man of your heart, it must be strong enough to kill any woman who feels it. Yes, you're my only man and you always will be—no matter what nonsense you talked in jail. I think of you and I dream of you—write me soon, dearest, so I can have a tiny sliver of your soul for myself.

NINE

How ridiculous, Francesco thought, when I need an undistracted hour so I can think, I have to ride the Camden ferry back and forth.

Though it was late March, winter still smothered the city with its gray felt damp. Out on the river dirty chips of ice bobbed lazily downstream, remnants of the last storm with its freezing rain that, frozen abruptly solid, paralyzed even the trolley cars. Francesco stood on the deck watching two crows, cawing and crying, wheel in lopsided circles above the boat. He wondered whether this was the scene Whitman had glimpsed from the same ferry, fifty or sixty years ago. Except for the gleaming towers of midtown it must have been: Camden—feckless and humble, a poor relation even then—must have displayed the same tumble-down houses and rotting wharves as it did today. Whitman. He had to strain to remember what his words once meant to him. In those first days of fear and struggle, they'd guided him like a melody, and soothed him too. But the Whitman he remembered wasn't the shameless bard of selfishness who roared his defiance into the national deaf ear; now he kept thinking of the Walt who damned his neighbors for greed and soullessness in prose. Yes, Francesco thought, these are my own specimen days, and goddamn every one of them!

He'd overextended himself; it was as simple and inescapable as that. Carney hadn't paid for his share of the brickyard, in fact

after the first installment he'd given Francesco a laughably small
fraction of what remained. By then, of course, his bank and his
brokerage were making demands for cash he had to meet. He
could give up the brickyard, he guessed, but not until it was
paying for itself. And that was a year or maybe even more away.
Until then Francesco was counting on his mortgage business and
the money he loaned out to buy stocks. He'd raised his charges as
much as he dared, which helped a bit, if not enough: for now, he
was going to have to bleed.

I'll never, Francesco raged silently, do another son-of-a-bitch
a favor like I did for Carney, not as long as I live. And no more
partners to drag me down the way he did, never . . . . look at
Abe, he's a lone wolf, he has investors, sure, but nobody who can
force him into an asshole move. That bastard Carney, he ought
to kiss my ass, he wouldn't even have a business if I hadn't caught
those firebugs, years ago. That's gratitude for you, Francesco
thought bitterly, sucking the sore tooth of his grievances.

His memory retrieved the film of the night he'd saved the
brickyard, and Carney too. He saw the distorted faces of those
thugs, setting fire to the property with noisy glee, he heard his
voice crying out for them to stop. It all started that night, he
mused, my good luck and my bad. Because Laura and he began
soon after, and that was one fire he couldn't keep from ravaging
his life. Laura's face floated back to him down the aquarium of
memory; that pale, delicate skin of hers, that flushed whenever
he took her to bed. He wondered if she still had her looks; that
was something else he'd never know. Leonora hadn't said. And
wasn't that a damn strange thing, his sister translating Italian plays
for her, her, the woman who broke his goddamn heart . . . .

What he had with Teresa was better, wasn't it? Not that you
could compare two women so incommensurately different as
they were. But Teresa loved him back, didn't she, and that was
the whole difference. She made his life into something precious
merely by inhabiting one of its rooms. Whatever he'd seen that
day in San Lorenzo, when she stood framed by those wild roses,
whatever he saw in her mischievous eyes, heard in her sweet girlish

voice, had grown and ripened until he knew he would never leave her because he knew he would never want to: never leave, and never betray her. He was nothing like Vittorio. Already his older brother was eyeing South Philadelphia widows covetously. Francesco felt half-afraid he would find Rosita Parenti, his old mistress, and what would stop either of them from coupling, if only to ridicule *him*? He didn't have the heart to tell his brother to stop prowling: he prayed Dr. Gioia or Bellina would.

But what use was there preening himself on how much better a husband he was? His troubles lay elsewhere than his marriage bed. He'd made the one mistake America didn't forgive, and now he would have to pay the price. Carney had made him and Carney, it seemed, would shortly ruin him. No: he was ruining himself. Why on earth, Francesco demanded angrily, did I think the universal rules didn't apply to me?

Always he had defied the odds, all his life in America, and like a reckless gambler he'd dreamed his streak of good fortune would never end. And now it had, and what a fool he felt, what an idiot to believe otherwise. He'd been full of illusions, he'd truly expected his whole life to defy gravity just because his early successes had, those petty triumphs that tasted, now, like ashes in his mouth. Francesco tried not to remember his father in any detail but found himself hypnotized. He saw again his face on that terrible day when his parents announced the facts to Vittorio and Leonora and himself, his father's white, stunned, disbelieving face. Was that how he would look by the time the gods had finished mocking his presumption? Francesco believed intermittently in Christ yet he never doubted the old gods, who tormented humans for their sport, still reigned somehow as well. The old gods, the true gods of Calabria, of San Lorenzo: they ensured a fine harvest or they scorched your fields, they raised you high or punished you for—what was that word Lampa always used?—your hubris, your overweening pride.

Now the ferry was sliding back into Philadelphia's wharf. A small figure in a rust-black suit was waving, calling to him: Enrico. It took Francesco a minute to force himself back into the world.

He stepped onto the dock, where Enrico was all but twitching with impatience.

"I found out what's fucking up Carney so bad," he announced without preamble.

"And what is that," Francesco said, mournful and uninterested.

"That Jew Lansky up in New York—his boys collect thirty percent a week protection money from the speaks. The big profitable ones anyway."

Francesco was starting to snap out of his funk. "And you're sure of this?"

"Carney admitted it himself."

"Why wouldn't he tell me himself, the goddamn fool? I'd have understood."

"Who knows?" Enrico ran his thumb up his cheek, the ancient Italian expression signifying mystery. "Maybe he's too proud."

"Ah, but what the hell can I do? Lansky's a gangster, isn't he, what am I supposed to do?"

"You wanted me to find out and I found out," Enrico replied, annoyed that Francesco hadn't praised his detective work. "It's your business, thank God, not mine."

"Thank God? What the hell do you mean by that?"

"Nothing. Nothing. I mean, Carney owes you, not me."

"Sometimes I think we were better off working those fucking mines."

"Stop feeling sorry for yourself," Enrico grinned. "You'll find a way out, you always do." And he trotted off quickly to catch a clanging trolley pulling up across the street with a shower of sparks and a grinding metallic sound.

"I am an acme of things accomplished, and an encloser of things to be,
My feet strike the apex of the stairs,
All below duly travel'd, and still I mount and mount . . . ."

Now he was a man and he dealt in the squalor of manhood, the practicality all men clung to, the rock face they had to climb. Francesco wanted to keep climbing and never stop, to mount and mount, and so he would have to do what was necessary:

whatever he decided was necessary he would have to do. That was the way the game was played, wasn't it? Or else he would have to retreat, would have to grow smaller and meaner and weaker, poorer too of course but even that wouldn't ache like the loss of manhood; he would become a lesser man who led a lesser life. Look at him, the Italians would say, he tried to fly too high and he crashed into the ground, poor fool, poor failure that he is! Francesco knew he would do anything to avoid that. He might as well kill himself, he kept thinking grimly, over and over until he heard a knock.

"Signor Monti, excuse me, I took the liberty of coming straight in," said the head that peeped around the corner of Francesco's door. It belonged to a gaunt man with a wispy gray beard, whose eyes still burned with the dogmatic fire of youth. He strode into Francesco's sanctum and stood with his hands gripping a leather chair.

"No ceremony, Signor Giovannitti, no ceremony for an old friend like yourself."

"I find you flourishing—your bank is jammed with customers! You will control the East Coast banks as our brilliant friend Giannini does in the West!"

"Hardly, hardly," Francesco said, involuntarily flattered, as Giovannitti intended him to be.

"Your sister Leonora asked me to give you her special love. I see her often in New York, you know—she does fine work for our martyrs in the Bronx and Greenwich Village, of course, since she lives down there herself. She's carried Vanzetti's writings to thousands of our people, and collected money for the defense as well."

This eulogy annoyed Francesco, who asked curtly: "I was expecting you nearly two hours ago, was your train late?"

"I called at your brickyard, thinking I would find you there. It seems half of Philadelphia is under scaffolding."

"No more than New York, surely?"

"But we have nothing as huge as this Chinese Wall your railroad has just built. Incredible—a bridge wide enough for sixteen trains at once! You must have sold them a hell of a lot of bricks?"

Francesco smiled to conceal his embarrassment. The man was altogether too blunt for anyone seeking to fund Sacco and Vanzetti's new appeal, which seemed as doomed as all their previous maneuvers.

"Our company was outbid by an upstate firm," Francesco told him in his driest tone. "By a strange coincidence, two railroad directors happened to own its stock."

"O tempora, o mores!" declaimed Giovannitti. "What a sink of corruption America has become! In a country of honest men, would Sacco and Vanzetti be fighting for their lives?"

"But you somehow got justice, and in the very same state that convicted them. How do you account for the difference?"

"Ah, my dear friend," sighed Giovannitti, spreading his hands in a gesture of despair, "have you any idea of the vicious frame-up those men are suffering? The prosecutors manufactured evidence, suppressed all inconvenient facts—as bad as what the French did to Dreyfus, no, even worse! Here the judges are part of the plot, even the Governor is baying for their blood. And do you know that last year eighteen Italians were attacked or lynched?"

"They lynch the colored too," Francesco shrugged. "In this country, everyone hates and fears everybody else. Especially the one hundred percent Americans."

"Then we must fight them until our dying breath. We must fight!"

"You're wrong, that's not how they'll change their minds. When they see Italians like me, respectable, hardworking, with businesses like any good American, they'll respect us—not if we march up and down carrying signs."

"What about our brothers in Massachusetts? They could be railroaded into the electric chair—they would have been already if people like me hadn't carried signs. What good does your respectability do *them*?"

"What good will anything do?" Francesco shot back. "Nothing will save them, not even if the real murderers confessed."

"Ah, Signor Monti, you think like an American—not a brave son of Italy I knew who fought for his success, and won. Remember who you are, my friend, remember the odds—" Giovannitti gestured grandly at the panelled office, the massive desk, "against all of this twenty years ago."

"I succeeded, yes. What has that to do with Sacco or Vanzetti or, frankly, you?"

"Let *me* speak frankly, Signor Monti—you succeeded because our people, our blood, supported you. As they do still—I saw those beautiful Italian faces in your waiting room. They are loyal to you, and so you must be loyal to the cause that burns in all their hearts."

"I used to be afraid of you," Francesco said quietly, "I used to think you were my conscience. That I'd have a bad conscience if I didn't give you everything you asked. But that was long ago. Now I see that you're trying to stir my guilt, the way you always do. And I have nothing to feel guilty for. I gave you money last year and the year before that. And now it's too late for money to help. Whether they live or die, it's out of my control—or yours. As much as whether my bricks ended up in that Chinese Wall."

Giovannitti rose and stood staring down at him with cold righteousness, like a priest excommunicating a sinner from his church.

"I hope your money can help you sleep at night," he said, and then he left.

Enrico drove him uptown, the two men riding in silence through a chill, light rain. This weather makes the city look decayed, Francesco thought, a ruin, like one of those Roman towns lost in the Italian woods, not a marble temple dedicated to Progress, the American deity. Rain smeared the white facades of banks and skyscrapers, rain blurred the sharp edges of commerce's altars so that they looked as though their builders had abandoned them before finishing. Here and there at streetcorners men in flapping slickers broadjumped from curb to curb, trying vainly to miss the mud cars and trolleys were sluicing up. All sounds were muffled by the rain. Even the City Hall clock chimed faintly, dismally, through the lead-colored sky.

Abner Greenglass kept an office in the Girard Bank and Trust, since his real-estate consortium owned a mysteriously vague amount of Girard stock. Francesco and Enrico climbed a winding brass stair to the mezzanine which overlooked a quiet beehive of cashiers. Above them loomed a vast marble dome topped with a small skylight through which, today, a mere trickle of daylight filtered in.

"An exact replica of the Pantheon in Rome," Francesco remarked. "Every people builds temples to the thing it longs for most. Americans build banks."

"You think our ancestors were different?" Enrico grinned. "They were better architects, that's all . . . ."

A pink marble walkway hugged the edge of the dome, leading them past desks manned by blank-eyed executives tapping steel pencils, and finally to Greenglass's suite of offices. Here men and a few women were yelling, wheedling, bullying into their telephones. Francesco could smell the rich fragrance of pickles and delicatessen spread before them like Homeric feasts.

"Now why the fuck would I want your lousy brickyard?" Greenglass was saying to Carney when they walked in. Francesco recognized the furniture, down to the ratty carpet under Greenglass's desk; the one new touch was a wall of photographs, Greenglass shaking hands with dignitaries and movie stars, most prominent his assault on a sour-faced President Coolidge's right arm. "It ain't worth shit to me *or* anybody else, after you dumb schmucks couldn't even sell bricks to the railroad boys. It's a loss leader, is what it is. A loss leader—Baron Rothschild himself couldn't make that shithole pay."

"It's all I've got, Abe," Francesco said, trying to sound unfazed. He couldn't be sure if Greenglass was speaking bluntly or trying to cut his price.

"Not true, not true. Think hard, Frank, you useta be able to think like a Jew when you wanted to. What else you got I'd like to buy?"

"My bank?" Francesco forced himself to laugh. "You're sitting here in this palace and you want my little Calabrian bank?"

"Don't sell yourself short, Frank," Carney said. "You've done a grand job buildin' up that thing and the whole city knows it. Why, my customers say you could grow as big as your countryman A.P. Giannini's gettin' out there in California, you catch some lucky breaks."

"No wonder you're broke," Greenglass smiled. "You two ain't business partners, you're a goddamn vaudeville act. 'Lawsy, lawsy, Mr. Bones, how'd you ever get to be so smart!'" he mimicked. "You're jerkin' each other off, boys, and it might feel good but it sure ain't good business."

"You don't *seriously* want to buy my bank?"

"Not altogether, no. I'm gettin' into mortgages, they're a hell of a lot safer an investment than this bull market. And you got mortgages, Frank, you got mortgages out your goddamn ass."

Francesco's mind was racing. "I sell them to you, I might as well sell the bank, Abe. You'd be in control, not me."

"Stop thinkin' like a putz," Greenglass barked. "I took all Girard's home equities, and you think they worried about control? It's good business, Frank—I thought you were smart enough to see that far ahead of your goddamn face."

"These are my people. My customers, they've been dealing with me, for Christ's sake. What would I tell them?"

"You say, fellas, you ain't got any choice. You say, fellas, welcome to America."

"I don't know," Francesco said. "My people wouldn't like it if I sold to you."

"Because I'm a Jew, you mean? A Christ-killer, isn't that what you wops call us?"

"No, no, no. They need someone who speaks Italian to explain things to them. That's all."

There was an awkward silence in the room. All four men managed to avoid meeting each other's eyes.

"I came to sell the brickyard, Abe," Francesco said finally. "Nothing else."

"Let me tell you a story," Greenglass said expansively. "I started out in business with a guy named Onions Abromowitz. *He* was a putz. Christ, he was always *shtupping* taxi dancers when he shoulda been takin' care of business. And finally it caught up with the dumb putz. He comes to me one day, Onions does, and he says to me, 'I got a business I gotta sell except nobody wants to buy the goddamn thing!'"

"What business?" Carney asked.

"Jesus, Carney, you interrupt like a hopped-up whore! No wonder you ain't payin' Frank back like you're supposed to!"

"Go on with your story," Francesco said quickly.

"So I says to him, Onions, ain't you ever heard of Jewish lightening? And he says shit no, what in the fuck is that? Onions, I says, that's what hits your place of business when your insurance is all paid up and the goddamn thing is goin' down the shitter. And Onions looks at me with these big eyes and says, *Gottenyu*—that's Jewish for Christ Almighty. And sure enough, the next night, Onions Abromowitz loses his business in a fire, and the insurance takes care of everything."

"What business was he in?"

"I think he was in the brickyard business, come to think of it. Yeah. Onions Abromowitz was in the brickyard business."

"And he never—I mean, nothing happened to him?"

"Nothin' bad, if that's what you mean. Married a nice Jewish girl and moved to Pittsburgh."

Greenglass stared at Francesco, to make his meaning unmistakable. Francesco couldn't help wondering whether Abe was leading him into a trap.

"I ain't settin' you up, if that's what's eatin' you," Greenglass said as though able to read his thoughts.

"A very interesting discussion," Francesco said, standing up.

"Yeah, yeah," Greenglass said dismissively. "You call me if you decide to unload those mortgages, Frank, okay?"

Outside on the street Francesco, Carney, and Enrico stood making small talk until Carney asked: "You ain't really thinkin' about *doin'* what that kike said?"

Francesco laughed. "Don't you know me after all these years? Besides, didn't I save the yard from arson when it was yours?"

"That does my heart good, Frank, truly it does. Now I'll leave you gentlemen alone. I have my lunch customers . . . ."

When Carney was a safe distance away, Francesco told Enrico in Italian, "See what it will take to make a fire. I want nobody injured, and I want the hook and ladder called before the flames can spread."

Enrico looked surprised. "You aren't asking me to do this myself?"

"I don't want to know anything, not who does it, not when the place will burn."

"And you're absolutely sure it's what you want?"

"Are you going to help me or not, dammit?"

"I'll help you," Enrico muttered, as though each word were a painfully extracted tooth.

"Good," Francesco said, lighting a cigarette. "Now be so good as to drive me back downtown."

TEN

On the train down to Philadelphia Leonora sat up, uncomfortably, in the parlor car which stank of dead cigars and whisky and asked herself: In the year of Our Lord 1930 has anything really changed?

Lampa was still exiled to the island of Ponza, likely until he died.

Carlo was living in San Lorenzo, by now no doubt a member of the Fascist Youth. And no doubt drinking in all the false consciousness her mother could dispense, as poisonously intoxicating as the whisky her fellow passengers drank from their flasks.

And she was still living in New York, sleeping in the Village and working on the Upper East Side, or in whatever theater Laura could afford to rent. In truth, she was drifting. Her life was sliding like a melting icicle, skittering as it lost gravity, direction, aim. What frightened her most was the prospect of drifting along forever: how easy that would be, how painless too. She didn't even have a lover to give her days purpose or shape: she had only her translating job for Laura Warrington which bore the occasional, dazzling fruit of actors reciting her words to an audience of bond salesmen posing as Bohemians. That made an existence, she knew, though not a life, not one she could in good conscience drag on another more year. She was drifting; she knew it; she despised herself for it. Without Lampa she was lost, much as she loathed admitting that to herself; without Carlo and Lampa she was not only lost but damned—if not to hell, then to triviality, a fate perhaps even more anguishing.

Over her desk in Laura Warrington's townhouse Leonora tacked reproductions of paintings and lithographs. She guessed the images disclosed her soul or, to be absolutely modern and Freudian, her unconscious, assuming that wasn't another Viennese concoction like Sacher Torte.

The Degas ballerinas of her first year in America vanished, replaced by Goya etchings, those nightmares of reason: winged devils, priests with pig's snouts, dungeons filled with shrieking prisoners. My God, Laura would cry, I can't bear to look at them, how can you? And in fact she didn't, not truly, she didn't stare; those etchings protected her, in some way she could never have explained.

And then after a time they lost their potency, they no longer inoculated her. And so Leonora turned to Hieronymous Bosch, whose work made Laura nearly faint. Still, she let her hang "The Death of the Miser," though in a reproduction small enough to blur details. What Leonora saw looked chilling enough: devils jumping joyously out of pits, or peeping through windows, sinners bled white by Satan, a sermon against evil so loving that Bosch was paying homage to the forces he condemned. There was no need, she saw, to accept the evil God the Gnostics used to explain the world; not even her childhood's God, that potent patriarch, could contain the energy evil was flooding her life with, let alone vanquish it.

A masher sat down across from her, hoping to make time. One frigid glance sent him reeling, stammering, into another car. Laura had taught her long ago how to deal with the American men who circled her, circled any woman not a hag or a hunchback. Think of a piece of shit, she told Leonora, yes, right down to the smell. Then look at him. Pretend he's a turd, oh, trust me, it works every time! Laura's laugh tinkled, silvery, witchy, the laugh of a woman who's now far beyond such coarse overtures. You don't know how glad I am to be a Sapphic . . . .

She said that with particular conviction not, as one might have expected, when she and Leonora and her 'little friend of my heart'—whose identity and hence her youthfulness, changed twice a year—were leaving a theatrical soiree, cocktails for three hundred compliments of the Theater Guild, say, when every man had, it seemed, three hands: one for the cocktails, one for the canapes, and one for the passes that ended only when the women fled into the Fifth Avenue night. Instead she said it when she and Leonora returned from a Communist Party meeting—indoors or outdoors, it made no difference to the comrades' lust—where village radicals mingled with electricians from the Bronx, and everyone sang the Russian anthem and the Internationale and tried to look idealistic while they pinched Laura's fashionably bony ass. Thankfully, Leonora had no Sapphic tendencies herself. Laura dangled in front of her any number of unattached lesbians in any number of styles—the girlish femme, the mannish executive, the street-wise, tough-talking butch who could drink any mere man under the table, and often did. These women all worshipped Dietrich and Garbo, whom they claimed as fellow daughters of Bilitis ("Just look at these snaps of Garbo in slacks!" Laura crowed, studying *Vanity Fair*). They longed to join the lesbian mecca on the Left Bank of Paris, where deep-voiced Sapphics walked the streets in men's suits and a kiss between two of Les Girls was too routine to raise the eyebrow of any passer-by. So they considered themselves marooned in Manhattan, just as Leonora did.

Not even the freest woman in Laura's circle, though, would trot off with her to the Party meetings, dour covens in dingy halls near Union Square, where invariably a wino would roll in midway through the reading of the Politburo line against Japanese aggression ("The peace-loving People's Republic of Soviet States condemns in the strongest possible terms the recent Japanese incursion into Manchuria, and deplores the indifference towards this act of blatant aggression shown by all capitalist states"), shouting for the price of a drink, comrades, one measly drink for the love of God! God was unmentionable, but the drunk, after all, belonged to the proletariat, and so, after a whispered collection of nickels and dimes, the man got his drink.

Leonora wondered, as the train lurched out of Princeton, why she attended those meetings with Laura. Not conviction, certainly: the small sum of her knowledge about Russia failed to inspire her with any enthusiasm for the New Jerusalem. Why do I let myself drift into these entanglements, she asked herself irritably, thinking of the pattern her life made, considered with detachment: one drift after another, yes; even her love for Lampa had been a sort of drift, hadn't it? Not a decision, not anything she'd reasoned her way to. Perhaps love was always a leaf skittering down a river, floating this way and that, miraculously surviving the rushing force of the water that bore it along.

If she had gone to live with her brothers, perhaps then she would not drift, perhaps then her life would make a sort of sense like anyone else's, logical, and reasonable: a San Lorenzo kind of sense. But no—she pinballed around Manhattan, while Francesco and Vittorio were raising families in Philadelphia. Francesco still sent her *bustarelle*, envelopes, though she told him she no longer needed him, she could support herself. Perhaps she could use that money now, now that the stock market had crashed two months earlier—a cataclysm she found baffling, inexplicable, like the eruption of a volcano or some other natural disaster, frightening precisely because its causes were invisible.

Laura's last show opened in October, a saccharine creampuff by Maeterlinck, and when Leonora reached the theater she noticed a silent, sullen audience trickling in. It wasn't until she saw the headlines proclaiming the Wall Street Crash that she understood. And now Laura confessed she might not be able to raise funds for next season, all German plays: Buchner, Hauptmann, Kleist, somber tragedians surely distasteful to any millionaires who hadn't jumped out of their windows. Since the crash Laura had lost six of her patrons to suicide.

When Leonora came to her house, on her last workday before Easter, she found Laura striding nervously up and down the

Aubusson. Not even a cup of tea and a madeleine from the French bakery managed, as they always did, to calm her nerves.

"We need a miracle," Laura announced. "I don't know where to get one, Nora, do you?"

"It's not really as bad as that?"

"Oh yes." Laura smiled grimly, like a coroner specifying a cause of death. "We don't have sufficient funds to open next season, let alone see it through."

"Ask your husband, then."

"You know that's impossible, I've told you a thousand times."

In fact Leonora had never before broached the subject of the invisible Mr. Warrington and his evidently substantial wealth. She kept quiet, while Laura mounted a tirade against the philistines who cared more for the Gold and Silver Ball—tickets, one thousand dollars per head, to benefit unmarried seamstresses!—than for culture, art, theater . . . . Leonora had heard the aria before. At last Laura asked:

"When will you see your brother Frank?"

"Francesco? As soon as I reach Philadelphia—but why—"

"I want you to give him a letter from me. I'll tell you why, so don't bother reading it."

"You don't have to tell me anything."

"You may as well know." Memory veiled her eyes for a moment. "We were lovers, years ago. Frank and I." She smiled. "Back when I still liked men, fool that I was."

"In New York?" Leonora babbled stupidly. "I never knew Francesco lived up here—"

"In Philadelphia. I was separated from Teddy then, and when he heard about Frank he—oh, it was awful, he made me swear never to see him as long as I lived, he threatened me horribly."

"What was he like then?" Leonora was fascinated despite herself.

"Young. Brash. He didn't suffer fools. I'm amazed," Laura said with a wondering smile, "that he ever suffered *me*. I didn't know what I wanted in those days, not in any way that mattered, and I caused him quite a lot of pain. Yes, I'm afraid I did."

"Was he handsome then?"

"My dear, he was forbidden fruit. Can you possibly understand? There I was, a well brought-up little fool from Windsor, Connecticut—the only Italians I'd ever seen were organ grinders or chimney sweeps! And by then I was ready to rebel. That's what Frank was, poor, dear man. My rebellion."

You didn't love him one little bit, did you, Leonora thought. She said: "I'll carry your letter. You needn't tell me any more . . . ."

"This beastly money," Laura exclaimed. "It rules everything, everything! Why didn't anyone teach me that before it was too late!"

When she returned, an hour later, letter in hand, she showed Leonora an old photo of Francesco and herself, posed before a screen painted with turtledoves and overweight Cupids poised to fire their darts. Her tale wasn't real until Leonora saw the framed and faded image of her brother, shockingly young, his eyes burning, linking hands for the camera, gravely and decorously, with Mrs. Theodore Warrington. Did Teresa know, she wondered; and in the next instant vowed never to say a word to her sister-in-law, knowing how the revelation would wound her uncalloused heart. She glanced up at Laura to catch the afterimage of that passion in her eyes; instead Laura was staring vacantly out at Fifth Avenue.

She loves nothing, Leonora thought with a chill, not even her son, banished to New Hampshire just as surely as Lampa was banished to Ponza; not even those little friends of her heart, considering how often their faces changed. Was it any wonder she sat staring at the eastern edge of Central Park, as though she were staring into an open grave? Leonora's mouth filled with a resentment that tasted like bile. She, Leonora, had no choice: her man and her son were oceans distant from her, and she refused to take a lover, no matter how Laura mocked her prudishness and told her she needed a good lay. So she had nobody to love except her brothers and Teresa and her brothers' sons, Leone and the newborn Bellina delivered last Christmas week, Vittorio Secondo, or Junior as the Americans said; and they might as well have been in Europe for all the contact she had with them. Teresa wrote and telephoned, Francesco enclosed a few scribbled lines with his monthly check, Vittorio ignored her entirely. No fool he: he knew what his sister thought of him, or at least of his Blackshirt and his band of ilicits. Yet even that didn't explain her repulsion. She hated to think of San Lorenzo, of that hideous day, that was the truth. In dreams she still saw Brunetti, saw that slutty girl, and awoke with nearly as much terror as she'd felt in the Prince's palace that awful afternoon. In dreams nothing died, time never passed, or so the fashionable Dr. Freud declared. And looking at herself Leonora saw that it was so. Only asleep, only in her dreams—good or bad, it made no difference—did her shadow life assume color and sound, her memories becoming realer, clearer, than the new sound movies she watched in picture palaces, astonished, a bit afraid that so much life could unspool like a silk ribbon, seamlessly, time passing into silvery light just as it germinated dreams, in her case, as full of demons as a Bosch eggshell. Perhaps there was no time: not in the soul, at least. Everything you knew or suffered was present, perfectly available if out of reach, waiting to be threaded onto the reel and projected onto the screen of consciousness. So nothing died, not ever, so long as the soul and its treacherous ally, mind, could throw the switch and begin running the film, that unbroken record stored somewhere below (above?) the treadmill you trudged every waking day . . . .

The train was hurtling into Philadelphia. On all sides, factory smokestacks grew as thick as the cedars of Lebanon. Leonora caught glimpses of red brick rowhouses in red brick, as primly proper as little girls dressed up for Mass. Some of those houses Francesco must have built, she thought, or at least sold the builders the bricks I see . . . . the slight melancholy Philadelphia always caused her to feel was chilling her blood. Such a stolid city, so proud of its propriety, almost defiantly dull! After the reckless energy of Manhattan, this city fell upon her like a shroud. If San Lorenzo could have grown a hundred times larger, it would have become Philadelphia: no wonder Teresa and her brothers found it congenial. Leonora knew she was unjust, and she reminded herself to keep from annoying Francesco with what he called her absurd misunderstandings of America. New York was a city on the moon, he claimed. Philadelphia, earthy and welcoming, a place where men could work, was a city in America. And if you can't see the difference, he always added, you might as well be blind . . . .

They all wanted her to move down here. Teresa, especially: as though being an aunt could assuage her guilt at leaving Carlo. And perhaps they're right, she startled herself by thinking, as the train screeched to a halt and she carried her Gladstone bag into the passageway. Whatever happiness is I haven't found it by exiling myself from my family. Ah, what an American I've become, thinking of happiness, that substance rarer than radium!

To her surprise Teresa met her with Francesco's car. As soon as Leonora got in, Teresa tootled her horn—a silvery arpeggio of three notes—and slid the Packard into the swift river of traffic west on Market Street, towards the setting sun.

"Francesco taught me to drive," Teresa told her merrily. "He found a big empty lot and made me practice two hours every day." She sounded the horn again, scattering pushcarts from her path.

"What a fine American wife you are!"

"No sarcasm, please! It's not practical for me to sit home all day, I have a household to run. And if you move down here I'm sure you could have a car of your own, too."

"A car! Just taking the subway in Manhattan shatters my nerves!"

"I thought you were a modern woman, brave as any man . . . ." Teresa scowled.

"No sarcasm, please!" And they both had to laugh. After another mile Teresa was driving through South Philadelphia. In this quarter, the wives sat on stoops chatting and watching over children in short pants who ran up and down the narrow streets.

"You like it here?" Teresa asked as she slowed the engine to a crawl.

"It's like Greenwich Village, without the women dressed as men."

"How you can live in that Sodom and Gomorrah, I'll never know."

She parked the Packard, with much backing and filling that finally yielded a perfect fit, in front of a four-story house that sat on a corner lot. An iron gate separated it from the adjacent property; through its bars peeped the tendrils of a flowering vine. In the middle distance, a cherry tree was blossoming behind the house, and daffodils pushed up through the slushy soil.

"How do you like it?"

"It's so big—you never see single houses like that where I live. And the garden, well . . . ."

"How would you like to live there yourself?"

"Me? You're joking!" Leonora gave a startled laugh. "That huge place? Don't tell me Francesco wants to give it to me?"

"In a way," Teresa replied mysteriously, and then would say nothing else. They drove another few blocks to Francesco and Teresa's house, where—more mystery—Francesco was waiting on the sidewalk, pacing and smoking until he heard Teresa blow her horn. He threw his cigarette into the street and half-walked, half-ran to open Leonora's door. When they embraced she smelled a French cologne which reminded her of one their father wore thirty years before. She thought, is he trying to become Leone Monti, without the foolishness that brought our father down?

"My bag," she began, but Francesco cut her off. "Let it wait. Come inside, now." His eyes sought out Teresa's. "You didn't tell her, did you?"

"Didn't I swear I wouldn't say a word?"

"Tell me what? What are you two up to? What's happening?"

"Step through my door," Francesco said in a deep charlatan's voice, "and all will be revealed."

The door flew open at her touch. She stepped inside, smelling the rich fragrance of a roasting lamb. Voices speaking Italian, la bella lingua, voices she knew (whose?) floated towards her. A little boy was gazing up at her, wearing short pants and a sweater of European weave, Venetian blue, with blue leather elbow patches. He smiled up at her curiously.

"Hello," the young boy said in Italian, his accent neither San Lorenzo's or Rome's. At that moment Signora Monti surged into sight, resting her weight on a malacca cane.

"What is the matter with you," she smiled, "you don't even recognize your own son?"

"Carlo! Oh my God, Carlo—come give your mother a kiss!"

The reunion, begun in astonishment, passed through showers of tears and much, much laughter, warming all of them with such a fierce flame that by the end of the evening Leonora agreed to dwell in that big house with its daffodils and its cherry tree, in the company of her mother and her smiling, silent son. She knew that she had nowhere else to go.

ELEVEN

The Montis soon fell into the custom of meeting for Friday dinner, cooked by her mother, who completed her facsimile of San Lorenzo by serving dishes suitable for the Prince himself. Vittorio insisted on eating exactly the same meal each week— linguini with butter and veal cutlets—thereby annoying his mother thoroughly; she served him with disdainful speeches about what a monomaniac and a bore he had become. The others gratefully dissected roast lambs, partridges, even soft-shelled crabs, the single American food Signora Monti saw fit to include in her repertoire.

Dr. Gioia often dined with them, accompanied by his wife whose airs now rivalled that of the screen star Nazimova. Mrs. Gioia liked to gesture grandly, one arm raised sadly while her eyes glittered from under dyed lashes. The doctor looked genuinely sad. In April the stock market began sliding downward, quickly slipping back to the level of the Crash. Businesses kept failing, unemployment rose, and no surge in wasteful (euphemistically called private) spending would reverse the trend. Like everyone, Dr. Gioia wanted to believe otherwise, wanted to believe the cheery chirps that passed for Presidential statements; yet by June he was observing sourly that every time Hoover said how good business was, the market dropped another fifty points.

Like a veteran obsessively reliving his war, Gioia kept telling and retelling the tale of October 29, the day his money's melody changed from hot jazz to a slow dirge: "The ticker kept running

until midnight, dammit, midnight! That's how far behind the
trading we were, we didn't know anything! All the brokers
stopped answering their phones, believe you me. But those
bastards made money, dammit, they made a fortune in
commissions because every fool was selling like it was Judgment
Day! *I* knew what was going on, believe you me—those bastards
with their stock pools were selling short, driving prices down,
and panicking everyone. But I didn't panic! I stood firm! And all
the time those cannibals in New York were dumping, dumping,
dumping. My God, it made me furious to be at the mercy of
those bloodsuckers!"

He cursed his luck, he cursed America, he cursed Hoover,
and he even cursed money too. "What is it," Gioia liked to say,
"bits of paper, bits of metal, a charade, a farce, a confidence trick
to bleed a man of his life blood and leave him with his hands full
of shit! Yes, shit, because even if stocks are good they're worth
pennies on the dollar! A ruse, an illusion, a confidence trick!"

Vittorio encouraged his father-in-law to rage, hoping to enlist
him out of disgust in the Fascio. Dr. Gioia neatly sidestepped
that trap. "What the hell is Mussolini but another liar, another
whore? Could he rescue us from the Wall Street wolves? No, no,
this country is solid, thank God, solid," and then he'd bang on
any surface available to indicate the soundness of America, on
this point agreeing entirely with President Hoover. "We have
now passed the worst and will shortly recover," the red-faced
man in the White House cried. "All shit," Gioia replied. "Look
at those men on the streetcorners, laid off from factories. If that's
recovery, Herbert Hoover can kiss my ass!"

At last Gioia subsided into gloom. He sat in a dark room for
hours, reckoning his losses, without even the radio to keep him
company. His wife would flutter by and ask in her swooping
tones if he was all right, and then, ignoring the silence that
answered her, would continue on her way. Vittorio expected his
father-in-law to suffer melancholia, deeming it normal now in
one so attached to his worldly goods; yet even he grew alarmed
when the doctor took to pacing all night in his bathrobe, moving

from room to room as the fancy seized him, so that at three in the morning Gioia's house, once as dark as the deep woods, now blazed with light, and passers-by often paused to watch the spectacle of Dr. Gioia marching back and forth like an automaton.

Gioia seemed not to notice, or not to care. He sat each afternoon, listening to the radio announce closing prices, eyes vacant, lips twisting convulsively whenever one of his stocks plunged. Because he ate only toast and coffee, his face grew sallow and hollow-cheeked, his neck too thin for any of his shirts. When Bellina begged Vittorio to act, he replied her father would have to run the course of melancholia just as a man with a fever must.

Francesco said he knew how the old miser felt. His own businesses were tottering over the abyss, thanks to the thousands he'd had to spend on covering his clients' margin calls when their stocks began to fall. He now owned those securities, but what earthly good did they do him now? Even the insurance money from his brickyard ended up financing his gamble that the stocks would soar, as they always had before. Yet nobody could say when that would happen or if it would happen at all. Francesco reluctantly inclined to pessimism as the wisest theology. Even if, say, by 1931 securities began to rise again, he'd drained most of his cash to buy U.S. Steel, down to 22 from 262 just before the Crash, or Ford, or Radio . . . . strong, sound companies, but like him no longer the masters of their fate; like him they were helplessly bobbing in the same shipwreck. Now Francesco would be hated, since he would have to foreclose on his Italians' mortgages; his bank couldn't afford to act charitably. They'll lynch me, he thought ironically, and why? I'll have houses nobody wants along with stock nobody buys. I've escaped the fire only to drown in the hurricane . . . .

He spent his afternoons in Carney's poshest speak, not drinking, listening to investors exchanging hunches, gossip, jokes. None of them knew any more than he did, though they still pretended to. A pall hung over the men by five o'clock that no amount of whiskey could dispel. Only Carney could smile, since the more unnerved his customers became, the more excuses they found for another drink. *His* wealth was tangible, not bits of paper embossed with mocking words; it sat beneath his feet in wooden crates. When one of the men would bleat about suicide (*I'll blow my brains out and I'll shoot any bastard that gets in my way*), Carney would dunk the drunk's head into the ice bucket, then feed him corned beef and talk common sense into him, what Philadelphia called common sense that year: going on despite the hopelessness of going on.

One afternoon in June 1930, when the humidity defeated Carney's system of electric fans and blocks of ice, Francesco sat with a few regulars rolling dice to see who'd buy the scotch. The sound of high heels tap-tap-tapping down the stairs made them sit up, surprised. If women came at all they came there after dark: no decent Philadelphia girl dared invade the men's club all speakeasies were until sundown.

The woman—she was thirty, at most thirty-five—wore a green cloche hat and a linen suit the color of seawater. Her long hands displayed no rings, and she wore no jewelry except a silver pin. She walked toward the men at the bar, her eyes meeting theirs, her shoulders thrown back defiantly.

"Is Francesco Monti here?"

As soon as he heard her voice he knew for certain it was Laura Warrington. He rose to greet her, taking the cool hand she extended while forgetting, in his confusion, to shake; Laura laughed. He led her to a side table, gesturing for Carney to send over the boy. Laura placed a Turkish cigarette in an ebony holder and beckoned him to light it.

"Your office sent me," she began. "I told them I had to see you urgently."

"Your letter, I'm sorry, I forgot to answer—"

"Please don't tell lies. We loved each other once."

"Yes, you said so in your letter."

She exhaled slowly, scanning his face for traces of irony, sarcasm, wrath.

"I also told you Teddy has cut me off. I'll have to sell my Manhattan house if I don't go back to him. Thank God, I made him put *that* in my name . . . ."

"This is a bad time for business, Laura, I'm sure you know . . . ."

"Everybody knows that." Her tone was sharp even as she ordered a Planter's Punch. "That's not the real reason, Frank. You're still angry at me, aren't you?"

"Of course not," he said quickly. He dreaded examining his feelings about anyone, let alone his feelings about Laura Warrington.

"Listen to me." She leaned forward, clasping his fingers between her thin bony ones. "I know Teddy gave you money. Five thousand dollars, wasn't it?" When Francesco said nothing, she added: "Really, I was the making of you, Frank. Wasn't I?"

"You should go on the stage yourself," he said. "The way you act, you almost make me think you did love me once."

"My house in Manhattan won't fetch twenty percent of what I paid for it, and what can I live on once that money's gone?"

"Divorce Teddy. Marry another millionaire."

"Impossible," she grinned. "Didn't Leonora tell you? I only love women now."

He sat back in surprise. A sly smile twitched the corners of Laura's mouth.

"Then find a rich woman who shares your tastes," he said finally.

"They're all either in Paris or uglier than sin. But look, Frank, why can't you give me that five thousand back? I'll take it in stocks or bonds if you don't have cash."

He laughed at her. 'Stocks and bonds! You'll take it in stocks and bonds!"

"And why shouldn't I?"

"Stocks and bonds are all I have now, Laura. Me and every banker in the country, we paid in blood, we covered those margin calls last October in our blood."

Her drink arrived; Laura took a long swallow. "I'd forgotten how horribly hot it gets down here. I could drink that whole glass in one gulp, I swear."

"Laura—do you hear what I'm telling you?"

"Yes. You can't, or won't, give me a single dime."

"I'm sorry," Francesco said mechanically.

"No you're not. You've waited fifteen years to pay me back and now you have and you're glad, I can see it in your eyes. You've changed, Frank, but not so much that I can't see that much."

"You're wrong," he told her. "Believe me, I—"

"You used to believe in honor—you thought it was the most important thing of all. Now honor means paying me Teddy's money back."

"What about *your* honor that night?" he asked her quietly. "You sent me off to pack for Atlantic City and all the time you knew you would never see me again, don't you even remember that?"

She avoided his eyes: "I didn't have any choice that night."

"What if I tell you I have no choice today?"

"A man, a real man, always has a choice."

He grinned. "You've been sleeping with women too long, you forgot what a prick is like."

Before the last syllable escaped his lips she threw the Planters Punch into Francesco's face. He was still blinking with surprise when she leaned close to him and said, "You stink of garlic, you dirty little wop."

"That's money you're smelling, Mrs. Warrington," he replied, but Laura was already striding toward the door.

TWELVE

Then began the time in Vittorio's life he would recall as a blur of activity—as frenzied as the war, if less perilous. Now that Dr. Gioia had let his practice go entirely, Vittorio treated his patients and his own, along with those Italians who came because he led the Fascio. He appreciated the trust they showed in him, and he liked the new freedom from Gioia a larger income brought. But new servitude replaced the old: up before dawn for hospital rounds, then twelve hours at the clinic with ten minutes to gobble down lunch and an antacid, followed by coffee with the Italian Consul to talk over plans for the Fascio or a second visit to the hospital, then dinner with Bellina and his child, after which he either convened the Fascio or collapsed into a dreamless daze.

But I never see you now, Bellina cried.

Bring in a young doctor just out of school, Francesco advised.

You're acting like an American, Teresa teased.

Your wife and your child will suffer, Signora Monti warned.

You'll die before I do, idiot; Gioia yelled.

They were all right, he knew, but so was he. There was a time in your life when you built the future and this was his time to build. When Gioia died he would have the best practice in South Philadelphia; his Fascio would be the largest in America, the richest and best uniformed. Even now, when his men marched down Broad Street or held a torchlight ritual, they inspired awe. The Consul told him that his was but one of a hundred groups coast to coast; listening, Vittorio vowed silently to make it the most glittering jewel in the tiara America would offer the Fatherland. And then, he told himself, the Duce will win the Empire Italy deserves, and nobody will dare call us cowards again, not even the English scum who stabbed us in the back . . . .

He still treated a few patients for free, and that few could have swelled to ten times as many now that the factories were laying off South Philadelphians. The mills by the river, those long windowless boxes emitting a low roar and a dull whirr even at three a.m., let go so many that the men he passed in the streets looked lost, like sailors tossed overboard by a storm. Even during the War he'd never seen such faces, not even during the great retreat. And when the smaller factories began to fold, and when the city, pleading poverty, fired the streetsweepers and trashmen and gardeners, Vittorio could have sworn he saw more Italians hour after hour in the streets, gray as ghosts, than ever have left his neighborhood two years earlier, each morning, lunch pails in hand. To make the pill bitterer, nobody knew when these "conditions" would ever end; even Francesco shrugged and talked vaguely of history, how no panic or crash had ever lasted longer than two years, three at the most. That seemed strange reasoning to Vittorio. The War had lasted years longer than anyone guessed, had killed ten million, and toppled dynasties. The past meant nothing. Now; history, as Henry Ford once said, was bunk.

Still, he saw to it that the Fascio organized relief. Some members, like the persnickety Pisano, objected, saying the neighborhood was too big, but in the end Vittorio persuaded all of them. And so they collected food—chickens about to spoil, vegetables, day-old bread—and handed it out at the Calabrian Club. It made Vittorio nearly weep to see the line of men, dressed in their best clothes to preserve a shred of dignity while they took charity, stand in the cold drizzle of Catherine Street until they reached the head of the line. They took their food, mumbling thanks, and vanished into the blocks of brick and brownstone like the ghosts they had become, ghosts burdened with human appetites; and that night, the kitchen windows on every street glowed with the leaping light of stoves.

Some of those men begged to join the Fascio: "You do more for us than that Irish bastard of a priest," they told Vittorio, who tried to conceal his joy. For the unemployed he waived all fees, assigning them instead duties like sweeping the club or passing out handbills during a march. That earned him the name he thought a good Fascist should have, generous yet tough. Even the Consul seemed impressed, offering to buy the poor men Fascist uniforms. Bellina, as she had more and more since giving birth, yelled:

"Stop acting like a Christian, when you don't even believe! Please tell me why you help those riffraff, these cafoni you wouldn't *talk* to a year ago! The scum of the earth, is that who you want marching beside you now? They're using you, my darling, and you can't even see! All they want is your food, they don't care about the Duce or Italy or the Treaty of Versailles! Illiterates, animals, that's who you choose to help—isn't it enough to treat these stinking peasants for nothing in Daddy's clinic? Why do any more for them?"

"What snobbery," he mocked her. "I didn't know I married an aristocrat."

"Yes, I'm a snob! Our class makes the money and you throw it away on fools who refuse to work! Without my father, where would you be, I'd like to know! You wouldn't have the money for your Fascio at all!"

Vittorio laughed mirthlessly. "Money? What money? I work harder than any of those cafoni now that your dear father's in mourning for his stocks!"

"That's your *duty*. Your loyalty is to your blood. You owe us your loyalty, not any tramp who comes begging a loaf of bread. And our son, you never even see him now, for all you know he could have two heads."

"Enough! I am a man and my duty is to myself."

"Who said that, your blessed Duce with his parade of whores? You want to find a whore, I know that's it—you want those

cafoni to pimp for you. And what will happen to me then?"
Bellina began to weep; her tears turned pink as they rolled down
her powdered cheeks. Vittorio was torn between the desire to
laugh and the impulse to comfort her.

The telephone rang. Bellina snatched it away from him.

"Yes, Mamma, yes, I understand . . . . what? How long ago?
Why didn't you call sooner? Yes, I'll send him out right now . . . ."

"What is it," Vittorio asked, "your mother needs olive oil?"

"My father's disappeared, idiot! He's been gone since lunch,
she wants you to find him."

"For Christ's sake, he could be anywhere!"

"Vittorio!" She was ready to weep again. "Just go! And find
him quickly, he's been gone hours by now . . . ."

Vittorio decided to seize the chance and visit his new girl, a
bookkeeper who lived in a Washington Square flat so tiny that
she had to move furniture every time she unlatched the Murphy
bed. Not to mention her cats: Caresse took in every stray between
Broad Street and the Delaware, so that he was too afraid, after a
few assaults, to mount her as he mounted Bellina, and so had to
satisfy himself with Caresse's timid efforts to straddle him as a
good New Woman should.

Caresse unlocked the door, a surprised look in her myopic
eyes; Vittorio hadn't bothered to call her in advance, and she
wore a nightgown embroidered with enough flowers for a baby's
grave. He jammed his mouth onto hers, tasting the bathtub gin
Caresse sipped "to break the monotony," she said. Trying to be
dexterous, he let down the Murphy bed, which landed with a
sickening crash, arousing her cats, those insolent toms, to howl
contrapuntally at the intruder. Vittorio ignored the animals,
backing her onto the bed—unmade, he noted with distaste—
and running his hands impatiently up Caresse's thighs. He
unzipped and, without even tugging his trousers down, thrust
himself into her. At that instant two of the cats leapt onto his
buttocks—how, how could he have forgotten them?—each one
biting and scratching, emitting a piercing, high-pitched yowlp.
Vittorio waggled his ass as hard as he could without losing his

place in her; the cats only dug their claws in deeper. Determined not to surrender, he thrust in and out of her like a madman, while Caresse began making little rhythmic cries, until at last he managed to shake off the cats and, feeling the blood on his buttocks, brought both of them to the supreme pleasure.

"Oh, boy, you do things to me," she breathed into his ear as he lay motionless.

"I'll pay you to drown those cats, Caresse, any goddamn price you want . . . ."

She pouted prettily. "You're terrible! I couldn't ever, you know that! My babies!"

"I swear, Caresse, you drown 'em or you'll never see me in this bed again."

"Divorce your wife and marry me, and I'll get rid of my babies then."

"You're crazy," Vittorio said, sitting up and rubbing his eyes as though awakening.

"They really scared you tonight," Caresse laughed. "Your poor ass looks like it's been through the wars!"

"Thank God I'm a doctor and I know what to do."

"Then what about not having a baby? I wasn't wearing nothing and neither were you."

"That bottle of Salvocet I bought you? Go douche with that, right now."

She pouted again. "It stings . . . ."

"Having a baby stings a hell of a lot worse."

He watched through the bathroom door to make sure she obeyed. Oh, Vittorio knew the rules of this game: you had a mistress, you gave her money every month and maybe you even took her out, but you didn't make a baby with her. Rosita Parenti had taught him that much. Tonight, if he hadn't felt such lust, he would have made Caresse wear the pessary he'd ordered from the Margaret Sanger Clinic in New York. Never again, Vittorio swore, never again this heedless, needless lust—

"What do ya say, Doc?"

"Very good. Very clean."

"You know I'm afraid to have a baby . . . ."

"And you won't. Next time we'll use the pessary."

"You mean that rubber cup?" Caresse smiled. "The cats chewed it up while I was out yesterday."

"That's it! Goodbye! Goodnight!" Vittorio clapped on his fedora and fled.

Francesco was double-parked outside Caresse's flat. Vittorio pretended not to notice until his brother sounded the horn.

"How did you find me?"

"Get in, get in," Francesco grimaced. "They found your father-in-law. He died of a stroke."

"What? How?"

"He walked over to the bocce courts on Eleventh Street. After lunch, I guess." Francesco put the Packard into gear and slowly rounded Washington Square. "His eyes were closed, they all thought he fell asleep, even the poor guy sitting next to him."

"I've seen worse ways to die."

"I'm sure you have," Francesco said. "Now nobody knows where you were, so don't worry—"

"How did *you* know?"

"You're my brother, Vittorio. You think you can fuck around in this town and I won't find out?"

Vittorio tried to look dignified. "Is everyone at the family house?"

"Sure. But there's just one thing. Signora Gioia says he never made out a will. What do *you* say?"

"I never saw one, personally. But even after the stock market fell he was a rich man, properties all over town . . . ."

"If there's no will, his widow gets everything." Francesco spoke slowly so as to make his meaning clear.

"I can't help that."

"Think again. You want to go to your mother-in-law for handouts all her life?"

"I refuse to forge a will!"

"Who said forge? I bet Gioia left a real will in that office of yours. I bet you could find it, if you looked hard enough."

"I suppose you've got your angle figured out, you always

do."

"My angle!" Francesco laughed joylessly. "I choked down coal dust for seven years to make you a doctor, what was my angle then? I found you a rich wife, I set you up in her father's practice. Did I ever ask for a crumb from their table? Now I need Gioia's money. Make my bank the trustee of his estate, that's all I want. Nothing illegal, Vittorio. It's done every day of the week."

"You're serious," Vittorio said. "You really want this."

"I'll tell you how serious I am—you read the papers, did you read about the Bank of the United States? Bigger than my bank, and ruined by depositors when they pulled their money out. I read that and I swore that isn't going to happen to me. I'm not going to wind up flat on my ass."

"You aren't thinking of telling Bellina about—" Vittorio gestured towards Caresse's flat.

"Relax," Francesco said, forcing himself to laugh. "What kind of brother would I be if I did that?"

"But what if I can't find a will?"

"You'll find one, you'll find one. You know Italians—they play with their wills the way Americans play with dogs."

Vittorio looked at Francesco with a wondering smile.

"You always win, don't you? You never lose."

"Nobody does," Francesco told him. "Not even God."

THIRTEEN

Like Zeus appearing from a cloud, the locomotive pulling the train of prisoners parted thick shrouds of vapor and smoke before grinding, with the sickening crunch of metal on metal, to a halt. Italian soldiers prevented the men inside from rushing to the windows; instead, in the best Fascist style, a pointless order was ostentatiously maintained. The crowd waiting on the platform let out a moan. Leonora stood twisting a handkerchief to shreds, nearly unable to bear the anxiety of knowing that Lampa was hidden somewhere behind those glittering windows bedecked with tricolor flags.

In the year Ten of the Duce's rule, he had decided to amnesty, all at once, one hundred prisoners: thieves, pimps, politicals. The regime was declaring its unshakable hold on Italy's heart, and what better way to prove it deserved that love than clemency? 1932 would begin the Duce's real glory, his propaganda blared; the decade past was no more than the keystone of the arch, the foundation for unimaginably brilliant deeds. Now that the Roman Empire was reborn, in the style of the Emperor Augustus, the Duce would pardon his enemies, a gesture that showed his greatness of soul and freedom from petty fear, just as Augustus had.

Thieves and pimps remained in Italy; not so politicals, for whom internal exile became exile for life from the Fatherland. Unspoken threats circulated everywhere: wherever the traitors went, the Duce would watch them as closely as prisoners. Leonora didn't believe these threats nor did she disbelieve them. She refused to fear the future when the present, their present, was unfolding like fairy tale. How many times had she given up hope of ever seeing Lampa alive again, how many times had she despaired of ever again kissing those lips that were still the only ones she'd ever known?

A cold spring was stripping Nice of its flowers, that famous azalea tricolor declaring that here France began. Instead, a few limp pansies, faded as old laundry, fluttered in the wind the train seemed to have brought from Italy. No matter, Leonora thought, we'll be in Paris soon, eating caviar . . . . she pictured them eating and drinking vodka in one of those Russian cabarets, served by dispossessed Grand Dukes; the image made her smile.

Now the prisoners began descending, one by one, onto the platform. There should be thirty-three, Leonora thought, counting the grizzled men with disoriented eyes who, some of them, kissed the soil of France, land sacred to liberty and revolt . . . . she saw a man who might be Lampa and moved closer to examine him. He was the proper height, except that over his right eye he wore a patch stitched from worn-out leather bits. Then she saw him grimace, scanning the platform for her, and she knew . . . .

There were no words when he caught sight of her, not because they had nothing to say but because at that moment they felt the emptiness, the shallowness of words. He embraced her, holding her so tight she thought he would crush her breasts to his chest, and yet she said nothing, she clung to his neck and kissed his face. She felt hot liquid drop onto her face and, looking up, saw that Lampa was weeping. How strange to see tears roll down from his blind eye.

"Our boy," he finally said, "why didn't you bring our boy to me?"

"He's fine, he's in America. You'll see him, darling, soon enough."

"Stubborn as ever," he laughed hoarsely, through his tears. "You haven't changed." Before she could answer he said in a strange voice, "Swear to me you haven't changed."

"No, no . . . . and you? Are you—" she faltered, unable to ask about his eye.

"Yes, blind. It's fine now. They did the best they could, they even sent me to a clinic in Rome for the surgery."

"That's good, you aren't bitter . . . ."

"It's the least of their crimes," Lampa grinned. "*Your* crime is you didn't bring Carlo. What is he like, does he speak English now? Is he tall, or is he—"

"I brought his photograph," Leonora said. "Now let's eat breakfast. You're going to have three hot meals a day, every day, from now on, my dear."

He was still crushing her to his chest, and he gave no sign of ever letting her go.

"Leonora, Leonora," he said as though to himself. "I didn't think you'd still be beautiful."

"I'm not," she laughed. "You've forgotten me, that's all . . . ."

"You remember when I told you to have an affair?" She smiled until she saw Lampa's mouth twist with remembered pain.

"I thought about that . . . . every night, sometimes. So—if you did, I don't want to hear a word, understand, not one word? None of your Catholic confessional, understand?"

"There hasn't been anyone. I swear on Carlo's head, I swear."

"Good," Lampa said more calmly, relaxing his grip on her body so that she slipped from his arms. "So this is freedom," he said, glancing at the limp pansies, the sooty soil. "God help me, I'd rather be in Italy."

FOURTEEN

The sound of high-pitched wailing sliced through humid August air. It was that keening sound no Italian had been driven to make since reaching America, that ai-ai-ai of helpless despair reminiscent of old women mourning their dead in forgotten villages, forgotten towns. Now that the banks were foreclosing on mortgages, the wailing meant something different, as everyone in South Philadelphia knew nowadays. Francesco's car was a block or two from the wailing when he heard the wail. His radio was singing:

> "Life is just a bowl of cherries,
> Don't make it serious,
> Life's too mysterious,
> You work, you save, you worry so,
> But you can't take your dough when you go-go-
> go . . . ."

He swiftly turned the corner, scanning the streets for the usual tableau. And there it was: sheriff, family, furniture piled on the sidewalk for an instant sheriff's sale. Now even the husband was crying out, his basso roar supporting soprano shrieks. A few scavengers stood poised to purchase lamps, tables, a radio for five cents on a buck; the sheriff kept them apart from a daughter who stood spitting curses at the purchasers.

I should go home and forget it, Francesco told himself, as he always did. Why should I help, what sins am I atoning for? In lieu of answering his own question he jumped out of his car and half-walked, half-ran to the noisy knot on the opposite sidewalk.

"Stay back, bub," the sheriff warned, fingering his billy club. "We don't want more trouble here than we already got."

"I'll buy this furniture." The family regarded him with wary looks. He said in Italian, "I own apartments, you'll live in one of mine until you can pay, understand?"

"You got the cash, bub, you can have the whole shebang," the sheriff said wearily. "Christ knows why though, just look at it!" He kicked a spindly end table, which wobbled crazily.

"And who are *you*?" demanded the man suspiciously.

"Francesco Monti. I own the Calabrian Bank. If you'd come to *me* for your mortgage, friend, you'd still have your house. I foreclose on nobody."

"I've heard of you," the man allowed.

"Your brother delivered our children," his wife said joyfully. "What a fine doctor, what a fine man he is!"

"You really have a place for us?" the man asked, timidly. "Knowing we cannot pay?"

"Of course, come by the bank in an hour for the key."

They stared at him with empty, mistrustful eyes.

"But I want you to help me in return," Francesco said, knowing these peasants would trust him only if he stated his terms crassly, as a cafone would.

"Ah, I knew it!" the man said with something that might once have been a smile. "Nothing for nothing, Signor Monti, not even in Paradise . . . ."

"You know Franklin Roosevelt, our next President? He asked me to get him Italian votes so he can end your suffering. If we elect him, he will end this cursed Depression, and put you back to work!"

"And you want me to help you?" the man shrugged. "What can I do for Roosevelt?"

"Do you know how to drive?"

"What kind of cafone do you take me for?"

"You'll drive a truck with Roosevelt's signs and Roosevelt's voice on a recording, every day until Election Day. You—what's your name, anyway?"

"Bastone, Vincenzo Bastone—"

"OK, Bastone, does that sound fair to you? And a free apartment and your old furniture until you get a salary?"

"Eh, Signor Monti, you talk fast like an American. But you have a heart like one of us, thank God." Bastone pumped Francesco's hand gratefully. "Thank God for you!"

"Don't make me fuckin' cry," the sheriff jeered. "Give me the money and you can have this greaseball's shit."

"When Roosevelt gets elected," Francesco told the sheriff, counting out money into his greasy palm, "he'll take care of all you bastards, mark my words . . . ."

In the nearly three years since the Crash, South Philadelphia became a village again, cut off from the city by poverty and insularity and a miasma of dread. Since nobody believed the papers, not even the Italian ones, all facts were now rumors and all rumors were now facts. Men sitting on their stoops exchanged gossip that travelled simultaneously through the neighborhood: *Fumo committed suicide, Carlucci's bankrupt, Donato's kids stole the church's silver plate* . . . . that it all might be demonstrably false troubled nobody. The Crash taught everyone the same lesson: America was now as rabid as a mad dog you had to shoot, it would bite you in the ass and send you into convulsions to die in an anguish. Which meant that anything was possible, anyone was capable of the most implausible degeneracy and crime; anyone might be telling you the truth, even when he told you your best friend was stealing cars and selling them in Jersey, because even the truth was no longer plausible these days.

The shouting reached him as soon as he turned onto Christian Street. It was the sort of windless summer day when sound travels with startling clarity. Words grew distinct as he drove on, speeding up when he realized at last that the noise was emanating from his bank.

—Let us in, bastards, we want our fucking cash, let us in, you criminals!

—Where's that prick Monti, I'll boil him in oil, I swear!

—He won't steal my money, I'll kill him first, see if I don't!

In front of the bank a crowd surged back and forth convulsively to the locked front door, as though executing some chaotic dance. Some of the men—there wasn't a woman in sight—pounded rhythmically on the steel bars, making a dull noise like cannonfire heard from far away. As the crowd moved forward the men grunted and cursed, straining to break down the door even though they were cooperating not at all. Their faces were reddened, twisted with rage, nearly animal. A lynch mob, Francesco thought. Carefully he drove past, slouching in his seat so that nobody would spot him going by, then parked in the next street, running to the private entrance only his employees, thankfully, knew about. He noticed his hands were shaking when he let himself into the bank.

Enrico and the tellers huddled together, white-faced, as far from the front door and they could get without bumping into a wall. Just as Francesco walked up to them, a brick smashed through the oval window above the door. It soared through the dusty air and crashed against the safe, which echoed like a kettle drum. That set off the fusillade: more bricks followed, aimed so randomly that they kept landing all over the bank. The crowd began smashing the other windows, which were too small to give them entry into the bank. Without a word, Francesco went to his desk and rummaged until he found a small, blue .32. He'd bought it on a whim, never thinking he would need it, so many years before that he wondered crazily if the bullets still even worked.

"No, no," Enrico said. "Put that away, you'll end up shooting somebody."

"I'll fire a warning shot. That's all." His voice sounded unsteady to his own ear.

"Don't be foolish," Enrico said, trying to sound self-possessed. "They've been out there ever since we shut the bank. They want *you*, they think the bank's swallowed their funds."

"But why? What the hell started this?"

Enrico shrugged, affecting calm. "Rumors. Gossip. Banks fail all over the city, why not here?"

"Those fucking shit for brains! They'll ruin me before they're through!"

"That's the paradox. Bank panics make the very thing happen that customers most fear . . . ."

"Spare me the lecture, for Christ's sake! What are we going to do?"

Enrico drew in his breath. "I will go out and talk to them."

"You think you can? Shit, listen to those apes!"

"*You* want to try instead? They'll murder you, they think you're swindling them . . . ."

"I wish I were! I've done everything I could to save this goddamn bank! I wish I never heard of it, I swear to God!"

Outside the crowd's shouts were turning, slowly, slowly, to the ordinary chat. Enrico and Francesco listened closely; was it possible the rage was burning out? Even the ambuscade of bricks had stopped. They might have been an ordinary crowd, Francesco thought, waiting for the bank to open for payday. But a crowd was a fool, and unpredictable . . . .

"I'll go," Enrico said. "I can handle them."

"Then take the fucking gun. In case you can't."

Enrico smiled. "You forgot, anarchists don't believe in guns."

"Look at it. It exists. It's not like believing in Jesus Christ."

"Listen to me," Enrico said patiently. "If I shoot someone it'll ruin both of us."

"Then we both go and I hold the goddamn gun!"

"No, that's worse. They're after you. I'll go, I'll *reason* with those men."

Francesco laughed. "Go ahead, things can't possibly get any worse."

Enrico slipped out the back door. Francesco could hear the moment when he reached the front, because the noise instantly rose to screams, like a radio whose volume was suddenly raised. Enrico was trying to make himself heard, saying over and over,

"Friends, no need for panic, friends, calm yourselves, friends, please . . . ." Then the crowd, like a hundredfooted beast, let out a terrible roar. The sickening sound of Enrico's body slamming into the door came next, and then his screams, and then silence. That was the most disturbing sound of all.

Francesco listened to it until he couldn't take it any more. He and the tellers got the front door open and he ran out of the bank.

The crowd was gone. There was only Enrico now, lying on his back, his limbs flung out like a broken doll. Someone had stabbed him in the chest, so that a strangely beautiful half moon of blood covered his shirt. Francesco sank to his knees beside him and cried out, a word, a syllable, taking his friend into his arms and cradling him in his lap. He didn't stop until the ambulance came, though he knew perfectly well after the first minute that Enrico was gone. The ambulance crew had to separate them forcibly.

PART FOUR

ONE

Your life won't change, Leonora thought, if you refuse to admit it has; look how Teresa kept flying the proud flag of affluence long after Francesco could afford a pole. By 1938 he owned only his bank. To keep it liquid he'd sold the mortgages to Abe Greenglass, and without them a small savings and loan like his barely survived. Nobody used stockbrokers nowadays, so he closed that sideline, cursing his loans of margin money for nearly bankrupting him, yet nostalgic, Leonora guessed, for those flush days of the Boom when, on paper anyway, Francesco was a millionaire. Now he would have sold his seashore house if anyone could buy, not that Teresa would tolerate losing it; the house stayed open all summer, never rented out for cash.

Francesco still housed their mother separately, so Teresa wouldn't have to wait on her, even hiring a maid who dusted and gossiped and cooked meals Signora Monti invariably criticized and invariably gobbled down. She was growing stout, their mother, perhaps from all the days she spent sitting beside the radio. Outside her window Philadelphia sang and joked, but she preferred Tommy Dorsey and Jimmy Durante and the Mystery Theater of the Air. She came to Francesco's for Sunday dinner, though most weeks she rarely went anywhere else. She's become an old woman, thought Leonora after a call from her mother cursing the neighbors for putting out trash sloppily. An old woman, and how did that happen to her?

Characteristically, Teresa announced a party for Carlo's graduation. When Leonora demurred, discreetly mentioning the cost, Teresa laughed.

"Carlo's the first one of us to finish school in America. It's a big deal."

"You just want to have a party and he's your excuse."

"Don't be a bitch. Don't you want Carlo to have the presents our guests will bring?"

"Now you're bribing me."

"Well, we can't all be Communists like your husband."

"Lampa's a Socialist, I've told you a thousand times!"

"Don't Socialists give parties too?"

"As long as you don't invite Rockefeller or Henry Ford."

"Spoilsport. I already did."

"Tell them they're our class enemies."

"You're crazy," Teresa sighed. "I'd love to be Rockefeller's wife. I'd wear a different gown every night. I'd cruise the Riviera on a yacht full of movie stars!"

"And *I'm* crazy? What movie stars would you invite?"

"Gary Cooper and Cary Grant and Charles Boyer."

"Together?"

"If I were rich enough, I could do anything I want! Money buys freedom, haven't you learned that yet? Money *is* freedom. We'll have the party at the seashore house, isn't that a good idea?"

When she told Lampa she presented the party as a fait accompli. She knew how little he relished seeing her family now, least of all Vittorio. After his session with the House Un-American Activities Committee, six weeks ago, Lampa had no taste for talking politics, even with their Village friends; confronting Vittorio must have seemed insane. Yet he surprised her. He merely asked what day Teresa had in mind, noted it in his daybook, and summoned Carlo, their dreamy Carlo who spent his spare time reading every physics book he could find. Carlo received the news as he received everything unscientific, neutrally as a cat greeting a strange guest. Leonora felt again that helpless sensation of facing a stranger, not her son at all, a stranger who had the secret power to kill her, wound her, break her heart. You make a child, she thought, you make an enemy.

So on a bright June Saturday they fled sooty Manhattan and took the train to Atlantic City, where Francesco met them with his car. Cry of gulls, shout of crowds, sugary smell of fudge. The Atlantic spread out like a carpet, a greenish rug on which sprinkled points of brilliant light. They chatted about nonsense while Francesco shot down the long straight boulevard beside the waves. After a time they left the district of lush lawns and gardeners and reached middle class streets, where houses clumped in pairs, like overripe fruit fallen from the trees.

Teresa was waiting on the porch, smoking a cigarette, a habit she'd acquired since her husband's troubles in 1932. She still seemed awkward holding her Chesterfield, a young girl posing as an adult. When she saw her husband's car pull up she raced down to embrace first Carlo and then his parents; she hugged them with surprising force, given her sparrow's frame.

"Over there," said Francesco, "is Europe, think of that." He pointed east.

"Surely not," Lampa replied like the pedant he sometimes seemed. "North Africa, perhaps."

"We're lucky we live here," Teresa said, crossing herself. "Will there be war?"

"Inevitably," Lampa replied with the grin of one pleased by dire prophecies.

War seemed very far away, farther than Europe, Leonora decided, gazing down at the glittering white carpet between Francesco's house and the indolent waves. Even the sand looked different in America, newer somehow, and fresh as though no human foot had yet disturbed its virgin cleanliness.

She glanced over at Carlo. He was an American kid, not one of them at all, a stickball in the street at twilight kid, a jitterbug, as close to one hundred percent American as the Montis could produce. But there was a light in his eyes, a cunning glint, that told her he didn't trust anyone. This is a boy who keeps secrets, Leonora thought, and what could be more natural given the life

I've made him lead? A scientist, a man in a white coat hunched silently over a microscope—that's what he wants to be. A physicist, not a doctor like Vittorio, tainted by everyday unhappiness, by pain. Carlo longed to study atoms and molecules, those invisible foundation stones. He used to come home from Stuyvesant High School complaining: Mom, nobody even knows what an atom *is*!

He was the future and he knew it, his mother could see that in his eyes. Nature will disclose her secrets one by one and Carlo will be one of the elect, the new priesthood hunched over microscopes. Science, that's my son's church. Not God, not Stalin, a dreamy dropout named Albert Einstein who with a few scribbled equations changed the world, that's who my son worships. Equations so abstruse only six men in the whole world comprehend them!

She wondered what Carlo would give to be one of those six men. Or just to meet Einstein, who looks to her like Harpo Marx, to walk with him through the leafy lanes of Princeton, where the great man scribbles new and possibly more ominous equations.

Carlo will go to Columbia instead. He will live at home, no question of plunging him into dormitory life with boys who swilled gin along with their mother's milk. Let him not be transformed, she prayed, while Lampa thundered that no son of his would join a fraternity that kept out Jews, the way the Fascists did. Carlo agreed to everything, mysteriously affable as usual, a boy who hid his feelings until he spoke of science and his words rushed out, tumbling over one another like jewels spilling from his hands, *isotopes* and *atomic weight* and *the uncertainty effect* . . . . all he believed in—and this has struck her before—is clarity, impeccable proofs, solutions he calls "elegant." What cannibals these scientists were, eating each other's brains to make something newly elegant. Carlo wanted to be a cannibal too, didn't he? Forget people, too tricky, forget politics, too illogical: science offered absolute faith, and isn't that what Leonora wanted once? She wanted it so long ago, in her convent days, that even the desire has faded into memory by now. Yet she knew her son must find the same absolution in science that she once thought she found in God.

"The guests will come at six," Teresa said to her. "Two hours left for one of your famous naps."

"I slept on the train, so don't make fun of me."

"I made your favorite appetizer, stuffed olives, I'll bet you never make them yourself."

"Now I'm a rotten housewife because I don't cook all day long?"

"You *are* a rotten housewife, look at your husband's suit, more dandruff than starch!"

Lampa looked out of place, but then, she decided, he was condemned to look out of place anywhere outside a city, outside a room. His features had hardened into an urbane mask, so that even his glass eye, acquired after a few years in America, seemed to smile with dry irony at everything not-Lampa, anything not urbane. Even his socialism remained quaintly free of bitterness; Lampa was the least sectarian of men, listening politely even to Stalinists he loathed. And his whole face, his whole being radiated a sort of amused patience or tolerance, especially at this instant when Teresa was handing him a zinc plate pyramided with stuffed olives. Here I am, he seemed to say, I may as well amuse myself among these curious beings!

"Delicious," he told Teresa. "Better than Italy."

"You're making fun of me—he's making fun, Leonora, isn't he?"

"Not a bit. Food is too serious to joke about," Lampa smiled.

"Now I know you are. Leonora, how can you *stand* such a clever man?"

"Am I a blockhead?" Francesco demanded, feigning wrath.

"Yes, but you're my blockhead," she sweetly replied.

"I read your testimony," Francesco told his brother-in-law. "You must have been frightened, you should have let me hire counsel for you."

Lampa shrugged as though the subject were trivial. "I testified. There was nothing else to do."

"There is nothing else to do," Leonora told him. "Refuse and you could go back to Italy, think of that."

"I escaped Fascism only to be victimized by democracy!"

Husband and wife stared at each other as coldly as they ever had, both aware that Carlo lay reading ten feet away. They could not quarrel, if they quarreled at all, until he was asleep; he knew nothing about the subpoena, stiff and ominous, on Lampa's desk: THE COMMITTEE ON UN-AMERICAN ACTIVITIES OF THE HOUSE OF REPRESENTATIVES REQUESTS . . . .

At last Leonora forced herself to laugh. "The Duchess was right."

"That lunatic? What did she say?"

"That all Italian men think they're Verdi tenors singing heroically. In your case I'd say Puccini, you sound more like Cavaradossi in Tosca actually . . . ."

"I'm glad you can laugh at me," Lampa said bitterly.

"Oh, darling, I'm not, only when you call yourself a victim—"

"Aren't we both victims? You especially?"

"I don't care if I am. I've loved my life with you so much. I never felt like a real mother before, not even a real wife."

"You were always my wife, why say such a stupid thing?"

"Before now I never felt it in the marrow of my bones."

"And as my wife you tell me to testify? Put on a suit and smile at those monkeys in Washington?"

"You won't go alone, Francesco can hire you an attorney."

"No! I go alone, or not at all."

"Don't be a fool. Nobody testifies to Congressmen alone."

Lampa silenced her with the same gesture her father used to end discussion with her mother, an imperious slice of the hand upward through the air still vibrating with the force of their syllables. We will talk later, she told herself, and went out for a walk in the spring dusk, across Washington Square to Patchin Place, where a blues record blared from a Victrola:

"If I take a notion
To jump right in the ocean
Taint nobody's business if I do,
If I give a man my last nickel
And he leaves me in a pickle
Taint nobody's business if I do . . . ."

The trees were shooting forth electric green, electric white flowers. Their fragrance filled the darkening air, that oversweet perfume. In the Square itself the seasons never changed. Winter and summer soapbox orators stood at every gate, rattling off the names Trotsky, Stalin, Hitler, like so many bullets sprayed at the passersby. Threadbare lovers held hands or necked, their bodies wriggling against each other painfully. Only the trees knew it was spring, and the robins darting from branch to branch, and the grass which looked as fresh as Manhattan grass ever could. Washington Square was her piazza, Leonora thought, and as in San Lorenzo she greeted and was greeted by a dozen neighbors, not all of whose names she could recall. I won't give all this up, she told herself, I won't, I love this life . . . .

In New York Lampa led the restless existence of a refugee, teaching at the New School in its grimly modern building which mimicked a factory, in this case an assembly line where European exiles, usually Communists, stamped their pessimism onto the shiny tin of American students who sat, mouths gaping, while their entire mental universe was tilted to one side. He sailed a cautious, tacking course between the other refugees, a majority of one, allied to no faction, least of all the rich Stalinists, who raised money for Spain in Beekman Place apartments where Picassos hung, and presumably oppressed servants passed canapes and cocktails between speeches by Hemingway or Lillian Hellman. "A dreadful woman," Lampa said, "good thing she's not a commissar, she'd send her own family to the camps."

He distrusted American intellectuals, complaining their Marxism was second-hand and so unreal that they swallowed

Stalin's lies like wonder drugs. After the Moscow trials began Lampa distanced himself from everyone political. He told Leonora it was impossible to believe that men who made the Revolution were selling Russia out to foreigners, though it was dangerous to say that openly; the Stalinists, like spiders, lived in a web whose threads touched everything. Leonora disliked his caution but agreed. And then came Spain, their passion play, the proof that Mussolini and Hitler, his evil twin, could launch a war any time they chose. Spain, the country of their hearts, of La Pasionaria hurling defiance on the radio—*they shall not pass!*—of children carrying machine guns, of desperate bravery. Spain tested Lampa's need to remain aloof. He attended those Beekman Place parties, he and Leonora, they danced at Tangos For Teruel in Union Square, they sang the Internationale side by side with Communists whose hands they wouldn't shake.

By day Lampa taught history to those few students affluent enough to pay his fees; at night he gave lectures, there and at Cooper Union, where Leonora had met Laura Warrington, indeed anywhere in the five boroughs that he could, always the same lecture: What Does Fascism Mean To You? And in his pitifully sparse free time Lampa worked on committees, so many committees Leonora forgot most of them, denouncing them as packed with rich Stalinist fools like Laura, yet continuing to attend. In that fashion they passed the years. Lampa claimed he was writing a book but never did, instead publishing articles about his prison years or the twin ogres who would, any day now, drag the world into another war. These Leonora translated into English, haltingly since Lampa insisted on checking every word. She would have complained had she not known a dozen refugee wives, Germans especially, who accompanied their husbands to all public events to serve as interpreters. Lampa, at least, had bothered to learn English. It was a good life, she told herself, and of course there was Carlo to give them joy when nothing else could— Carlo, who lost his red hair at puberty and now sported wavy black Monti locks, resembling his uncle Francesco at the same age. He was a model son, so much that Leonora wondered what secret mischief sizzled in his brain. Coolly polite to his elders, coolly dutiful at home, the boy seemed to have no rebelliousness at all. When she asked Lampa who their son could possibly take after he laughed and said, *you, of course.*

And so what could be less objectionable than the Lampas' life? What could be more comforting, more cozy, than the existence these three led in their Village walkup, parents and child, dining each evening while the radio crackled and Carlo asked Lampa where Barcelona or Ethiopia was, and Leonora looked at her two men with a contentment deeper than happiness, a serenity like grace. And yet Lampa did not love their life. She felt sure of that. He would have preferred to fight in Spain than live peacefully in America, the fool, the heroic fool. Hadn't he lost enough for the cause, wearing a glass eye now in the hollow socket that marked his martyrdom?

In bed that night, with Carlo presumably asleep, she said: "This is no time for heroics. I want you to get a lawyer."

"No. No. No. And we can't discuss this again, because I'm going to say something I'll regret. You made your point, I heard you, we don't agree."

"I married a fool! God help me but I did!"

Lampa smiled sardonically. "Don't tell me you just found that out?"

They arranged for Carlo to stay with a Stuyvesant friend in the Bronx. He wanted to know why and Leonora said she would explain another time, an answer he accepted icily. The night before the hearing, she and Lampa reached Washington, exhausted more by not speaking to one another than by the heat and dust. They slept in a fleabag on 14th Street, awakened all night by streetwalkers and drunken sailors shouting in the hall. In the morning Lampa surprised her by removing his glass eye and donning his eyepatch for the first time in years.

"I want to show them the face of a radical man," he said, taking her arm.

She said nothing, in fact kept silent throughout the taxi ride to Capitol Hill. Leonora prayed her childhood petitions along with what she called panic prayers, improvised deals with the Almighty such as: spare Lampa trouble and I'll go back to scrubbing floors in a convent, I swear I will, I swear . . . . as they approached the Capitol its white marble seemed to shimmer in the heat, like a mirage beckoning them. There were few cars; here and there a lone figure in a gray suit could be seen climbing gray steps. Capitol Hill was nearly asleep, not at all like the Parliament in Rome; the dull millstones of democracy ground noiselessly, without fanfare or fuss.

Photographers waited inside the lobby. Thankfully, they let Lampa pass undisturbed. Leonora realized she was shaking and forced herself to freeze her muscles into something resembling calm.

"Do you smell him here?"

"Smell who? Straighten your tie, the wind blew it."

"Your devil who rules the world. Your Evil God."

"All I smell," said Leonora truthfully, "is the stink of cheap cigars. What are you going to say?"

"As little as I have to and as much as my conscience allows."

"You rehearsed that, admit it, I could tell."

"I won't lie and say I'm not a Socialist."

"Just as long as you say you're definitely not a Communist."

"What a smart wife I have!" He kissed her quickly on the lips.

The House Un-American Activities Committee was evidently deemed unimportant, not to say trivial, since it met in a small windowless coffin of a room. A few Congressmen sat on a dais no larger than a car; below, on the dirty red carpet stained by tobacco juice, a stenographer faced the witness table, a wedge of cheap wood like the coffins poor people were buried in. In the back of the room three reporters were playing cards.

The air, motionless and musty with ancient smoke, made Leonora's eyes water. She sat behind Lampa, who after refusing to swear to God and settling on the formula that he would 'affirm,' slouched casually in the witness chair. His demeanor visibly displeased the Chairman, Martin Dies, whose small, porcine eyes narrowed as he began the questioning: how old was the witness, when did he arrive in America—

Soon enough their real attack appeared. Lampa had to list every organization he belonged to in New York, say whether each was a Communist Front, and what proportion of Communists made up its membership. Leonora saw his back stiffen.

"Let me say something, Congressman," he began.

"Answer the question, sir. Is the Peace League backed by Communists?"

"It has some Communist members, Congressman, but I—"

"According to the testimony of Sam Baron, the Peace League is a Communist Front organization. Is that correct?"

"Perhaps he has information I do not have."

"Mr. Lampa, you belong to a great number of organizations that this Committee knows are, in fact, financed and run and directed by Moscow. Agents of the Comintern here in America are infiltrating peace groups, Spanish relief groups, and diverting them to the Communist side. Do you have an opinion about that, Mr. Lampa?"

"All I can say is that I am not a Communist, and so the people you are talking about aren't likely to—"

"But if you're not a Communist you should cooperate with the Committee to the fullest extent possible. You should tell us what you know about Communist subversion. You should tell us exactly how the Communists recruit their members, the tricks they use, the lies."

"Congressman, they've never recruited me. Do you want me to tell you hearsay that might be wrong?"

"Are you saying the Communists never tried to recruit you?"

"That is right."

"Never?"

"My record in Italy is too well known, Congressman. I was an independent Socialist and Stalin says we're just as much the enemy as the Fascists are. In Spain, the Communists shoot people like me."

"We're not in Spain. I repeat my question. No Communist has ever tried to recruit you to their cause?"

"To the Communist cause? No, my record is too well known."

"All right. Do you consider the Communists a subversive force in this country?"

"I don't know what you mean, Congressman. Subversive of what?"

"They are infiltrating schools, colleges, universities, trade unions, even Hollywood, as Miss Dorothy Parker testified."

"I am unaware of any such activity, Congressman."

"Mr. Lampa, do you know this Committee has the power to cite you for contempt?"

"Let me say—I think there are Communists in unions, in colleges, but I don't think they are subverting anything. Their numbers are too small, Congressman, and people don't like them very much. I don't like them very much myself."

This last remark detonated a bark of laughter from the reporters playing cards.

"Their numbers were small in Russia too, weren't they, at first?" The question came from a different Congressman, who looked like a nervous stork. "And the world saw there what a few fanatics can do."

"If you don't like the Communists why do you work side by side with them in every group you join?" Chairman Dies asked pleasantly.

"Because they are willing to do the work—get their hands dirty, as you say in America."

"So you don't like them but you'll work side by side with them?"

"I don't like what they stand for. Some of them I like as people, the way *you* might make friends with a *Democrat*, Congressman."

More laughter. Dies pounded his gavel, which sounded like a gunshot in the closed room.

"And you refuse to admit that the Communists are a subversive force?"

"I didn't say yes or no, I said I just don't know. They could be. But they would work secretly if they were subversives, wouldn't they?"

"So the Communists are secret subversives, is that your claim?"

"No, no, no, I was talking—what is the word—hypothetically. I don't know that anything like that is going on."

"Would you tell the legal authorities if you did?"

Lampa shifted uneasily in his chair. "If I had definite proof, perhaps."

"You mean you wouldn't report Communist subversion to the FBI?"

"I don't know of any for sure, Congressman."

"Any decent American would report such a conspiracy. Alan Baron, a man who knows what Americanism is, sat in that chair and testified for six hours about what he knew. Why won't you do the same?"

"Congressman, I read his testimony, and I have to say not much of it made sense."

"Are you saying Alan Baron lied?"

"I'm saying he's confused, he's emotional. A lot of people came back from Spain hating the Communists, wanting to get revenge. Your great novelist John Dos Passos told me he'll never shake hands with a Communist again."

"Will he testify in front of this committee?"

Lampa laughed. "If Dos ever testifies, you won't get in a word."

"Why are you so reluctant to attack Communists?" the bird-faced Congressman asked.

"Why don't you ask about the *real* subversives? The Italian Fascists, the Nazi Bund? They wear uniforms and march in parades all over America. They have millions of members. And they take orders from Berlin and Rome and brag about the fact!"

"We're investigating them too," Dies said dismissively.

"Then ask me about them, I'm Italian, for Heaven's sake! My own brother-in-law leads the Fascists in Philadelphia, supported by money from Mussolini, guided by the Italian Consul himself."

Now, standing on Teresa and Francesco's porch with a glass of cool wine in her hand, Leonora could feel her body shudder exactly as it had when Lampa mentioned Vittorio. Goddamn him, she cursed her husband as she had for weeks, why did he have to drag her family into it? He was right, of course, whatever the word meant, and at the same time he was wrong, terribly wrong; Vittorio had never harmed Lampa in any way, and he was no subversive, only an overgrown boy playing soldier with his platoon of idiots.

"Oh, good," Teresa said gaily, "here come Vittorio and Bellina and the boys."

TWO

Teresa made her voice sound light and cheery, the mask of a well bred San Lorenzo girl. Her eyes, though, gave her away as soon as Vittorio approached.

All happiness, all contentment, depends on ignoring some shadow over it. Vittorio was Teresa's shadow and she ignored him fervently, scarcely even complaining to Leonora, since complaining would have meant acknowledging the shadow, the bond between the brothers that seemed so impossible to dissolve. Yet there was one occasion on which she shed her reticence and actually called Leonora in Manhattan, in tears, to sob out a complaint.

That was three years ago; 1935. Mussolini had just launched his war in Ethiopia, Lampa was busy organizing boycotts and protests, while Leonora and Carlo glimpsed it only in newsreels, warplanes bombing mud huts and driving columns of half-naked, weeping natives along unpaved roads. It all seemed somehow unreal. And barbarous, of course, to use planes and machine guns on the villagers, no matter what defeats at Adowa and elsewhere Italy burned to avenge. Leonora thought of the war as little as possible, perhaps because it resembled the Manichean heresy on the march.

One afternoon in October Teresa called. She brushed aside small talk and questions to tell her tale:

The Duce was asking all emigrants to help the war effort, as surely Leonora knew? Well, Vittorio was collecting wedding rings, earrings, bracelets, anything made of gold to send home to Italy: his cry was Gold For Our Fatherland. Teresa was evading him, successfully she thought, until the night before when he arrived unexpectedly, dressed in his blackshirt and his army boots.

Time for you to do your part, he told her. Even Bellina gave me her wedding ring.

You can bully her but you can't bully me, Teresa said. Thank God *I'm* not married to *you*.

Every decent Italian woman will do the same.

I won't give you my wedding ring. I won't. I won't.

Then you're a traitor to our fatherland, Teresa, think of that.

My wedding ring is sacred to me, sacred, do you understand, more sacred to me than our country ever was!

You have no honor, Vittorio said slowly. You are a woman and don't understand these things.

I understand that your Duce needs gold so he can kill more savages. Is that honorable?

The British have colonies all over Africa. They conquered theirs, now we must conquer ours.

I don't care about the British or the Italians or even those poor Africans—I care about Francesco. Francesco is my country now. He is my native land, not Italy.

For shame! You have no loyalty to the land that gave you birth!

My mother gave me birth. And if you think Italy is so splendid, why aren't you there yourself? I'll buy you the steamship ticket so you can go back!

You've never liked me, I know you never have.

That's right. And now you come into my kitchen, demanding my wedding ring, and I don't dislike you now, I hate you in my heart.

Don't talk like a fool. You don't understand these things.

Stop saying that! Tell it to your cow of a wife or one of those sluts you keep company with!

Vittorio stared at her. He gaped, unable to reply, mouth open like a fool. Without a word he jammed on his black cap and marched out, slamming the front door so hard the whole house shook. Teresa sank onto the kitchen table and began to weep, melting her tension in a torrent that did not end when Francesco came home to find her sobbing into a rag.

Leonora listened, startled if not surprised. Vittorio had grown up into the man his youth threatened, a thought that frightened her; what if her actions too were predestined, what if free will was nothing more than an illusion necessary to live at all? Because her brother and she and Francesco had all, in some deep and mysterious fashion, become no more than proofs of a theorem they had demonstrated twenty years before. Leonora less than her brothers, perhaps; her path had twisted and doubled back unpredictably, or so she liked to tell herself, forgetting how she'd vowed not to become a nun and so laid the trap of romance for herself, the trap of Lampa, though to be candid it could have been another man, another trap. How much of life, anyone's life, was blind chance? Your character might be your fate, as the Greeks said, yet how little power you had over the vectors of that fate . . . . inevitably she thought of Brunetti and that hideous day. Was that fate or coincidence? Certainly it shadowed her still, she dreamed of it, she shuddered whenever she saw anyone resembling Brunetti or the girl. But what if she had gone there another day? Would she have walked out unharmed? The randomness of her pain opened an abyss. Was there anything beneath her feet except an earthquake that would not end?

Now Vittorio and Bellina climbed the porch stairs, followed by their two sons, who wore the black uniforms of the balilla, the Fascist Youth Squad their father organized.

Leonora could see at once that Vittorio was pretending he had no quarrel with Lampa, or with her. He rushed to embrace Carlo, who gave him a sheepish smile, and handed the boy a fat envelope filled with cash.

"Our young genius," Vittorio declaimed, "will be a second

Enrico Fermi, I know! May Heaven speed his mind to great discoveries!"

"Thank your uncle for his gift," Leonora told her son.

"Thank you," Carlo said dutifully. "I'll pay you back, Uncle—when I win the Nobel Prize."

His family all laughed, even Lampa who found his son's confidence admirable. Only Vittorio's expression remained serious.

"You must be young to dream great dreams and young, alas, to carry them out. Goethe says the same thing in his dialogues with Eckermann."

"Goethe," Lampa exclaimed, "that turncoat, that lackey of the nobility!"

"He served his Prince, as any loyal citizen would. Without loyalty there can be no peace on earth, no good will between men."

"But what are we loyal to in this life, and what does that say about us?"

"To our principles," Vittorio said calmly. "We are loyal to our beliefs."

"You've been in America so long you talk like a Protestant," Lampa teased. "What about authority, aren't you loyal to that?"

"Authority, yes—provided it serves the people's will."

"Your friend Goethe said injustice was worse than disorder. A typical German. He would have served Hitler with equal zeal."

"Because Hitler embodies the German will as Mussolini does Italy's today. They are both great men—the only great men alive—no matter how people like you may scoff."

"Great men?" Lampa forced himself to laugh. "They are bad actors who believe their own speeches. Liars drunk on their own lies."

"They restored their nation's honor with the whole world trying to beat them down. Let's not quibble about greatness when it stares us in the face!"

"Let me remind you I spent time in your great man's jails."

"Italy had to defend itself against fools like you. Without strength there has never, in history, been greatness anywhere!"

"Greatness!" Lampa laughed derisively. He seemed about to say more, and would have, except that Signora Monti emerged from the shadows of the house wearing an air of regal dignity and—despite the sunlight—a black dress. She paused to receive an embrace from her children, their spouses, and finally her grandchildren, who alone melted the frost veiling her eyes. After she accepted their last kiss she turned to Vittorio, gesturing impatiently, and said, "No politics today, for heaven's sake! You want to ruin my grandson's party too?"

"But my father talks politics everywhere," Carlo said, making everybody laugh.

"Yes," Vittorio added stonily, "especially when he should bite his tongue."

"Please, darling," Bellina warned in her mother's swooping tone. "Let's be happy today, we all see each other too rarely to quarrel when we do . . . ."

"Then Lampa and I will talk privately."

"Come to Manhattan if you want to debate," Lampa smiled. "Stand on a soapbox, you can argue there all night."

"I want to ask you why you named me in Washington. I have a right to know!"

"No arguments, for heaven's sake, no arguments!" Signora Monti cried. "These matters are not for the children, Vittorio!"

"He has betrayed this family, and these children too."

"Why do you always want to fight?" his mother sighed.

"I am a man and it is my nature to fight."

"And I," his mother snapped, "am a woman and it is my nature to keep peace."

"A cowardly peace," Vittorio sneered.

"You want to ruin my grandson's celebration, is that your aim?"

"His father tried to ruin my life—didn't you, Lampa, traitor that you are?"

Bellina placed her hand warningly on Vittorio's arm. He shook it off as he would have shaken off a fly.

"I did not tell that committee one single lie," Lampa said.

"I don't care about truth, I care about this family. You don't."

"But all of it is true—you lead the fascio, the Consul gives you money from Rome, you march up and down wearing blackshirts and guns. All this is public knowledge, isn't it?"

"What is now public knowledge is your desire to hurt your wife's brother. A shame and a disgrace! After this family has clasped you to its bosom, you, like a snake, attack us for no reason at all!"

"I have no reason to attack the blackshirts? Leonora has no grievance with them?"

"Don't tell him," Leonora pleaded. "Darling, don't say a word—"

"You don't know what Brunetti did to your sister in San Lorenzo, you don't know about that?"

"You'll say anything now, to justify yourself."

"Look at your sister's face and see if I am lying! That monster attacked her physically, intimately!"

Vittorio seemed not to hear. "And the damage *you* did her? Making her pregnant without marrying her, with your Socialist free love? This fine son of yours is a bastard, yes, he is a common bastard like the cafoni in the slums!"

Lampa lunged at Vittorio—unable, as the saying went, to see out of his eyes, he was so blinded by rage—until Francesco seized his arms to hold him back.

"You preach morality, you hypocrite, you whoremonger! Brunetti hurt Leonora because of *you*, because of the girl *you* turned into a whore—Carmela, do you even remember her? Or have you had too many sluts since then?"

Bellina went white, though she said not a word. Vittorio's fist cracked audibly against Lampa's mouth, drawing a ribbon of blood from his split lip. Shockingly, Lampa began to laugh.

"Thank you, Vittorio, for showing my son how Fascists fight. What a lousy coward, hitting me when Francesco was holding my arms back!"

Signora Monti placed her body between the men. Her eyes glowed with the phosphorescence of an angry cat.

"For shame, grown men scrapping like boys, for shame, for shame!"

"You are my enemy," Vittorio told Lampa in a cracked voice. "Never forget you are my enemy."

"Enough," Francesco said without raising his voice. "You're my brother and I love you, but you're acting like a fool, Vittorio. Apologize to Lampa at once. Apologize."

For answer Vittorio spat on the wood floor of the porch. He turned away from the others before he spoke:

"He is not my brother-in-law. He is my enemy."

And then, without a backward glance, without a pause, he walked rapidly down the stairs and back to his house. The rest of the family listened to the silence that followed in his wake.

THREE

Though he knew Enrico would have protested violently at the thought, Francesco had his remains buried in a Catholic cemetery underneath a proper stone. The church, in those Depression days, was as impoverished as any other institution, and so Enrico was buried without awkward questions about his piety. Now, five years later, Francesco still drove to Holy Cross monthly to clean the grave and, in season, prop flowers against the granite marker which never failed to fill him with dread. He felt responsible, even now; the years had done nothing to cauterize that wound. In Francesco's mind it was always that afternoon, that hour and that day, and Enrico was always about to step outside and face the mob, and Francesco was always sending him out. That it hadn't happened in quite that way meant nothing at all to him. Your friend died for you, he told himself, you let him die, of course you are responsible.

The alternative was to believe that nonsense Leonora talked. What a notion, the world run by the Devil, God fearful and impotent! No wonder the heretics burned at the stake, whole towns of them, certain that the visible world was the province of Satan. It was the theology of despair. Instead of grace, all that descended from above was evil, and you were plagued no matter how clean your conscience, no matter how many good works you did; the Devil was no respecter of the virtuous. Perhaps that was what Leonora needed to believe, if she believed it at all, given the vicissitudes of her own life, given the pain she knew she hadn't earned through sin. Yet the world was neither evil nor good, but both at once, sometimes at the same instant, and that was what made life difficult: no final judgment seemed possible, damnation and salvation loomed equally distant, equally plausible.

Francesco refused the luxury of despair. He was not helpless, not entirely, and even if he had lost most of his wealth he had not lost it all, which told him that someday he would regain it all tenfold, like Job, whose faith was rewarded with still greater wealth. Now, for the first time since his youth, he was struggling like the rest, he knew he was no better than the ragged men shuffling through the streets.

Driving back from the cemetery he thought: I'm a dumb ox, that's what I am, I plod on the way oxen do, no matter what blows I absorb, no matter what pain. A mental picture of himself on all fours lumbering through his life appeared instantly. What else was there except plodding on? I was a dumb ox when I came to America, I worked like an animal, and now I am one again. I don't work as hard as I did in the mines, thank God; there I stood underground so many hours my shoes would fill with blood. Or the time, God help me, when I pulled my own tooth because I couldn't afford a dentist. Nowadays he dreamed often of the pits, he would wake in the darkness beside Teresa certain he was going to dig coal again. In his dreams he was still young and afraid, so fearful that his heart, as the saying went, was in his mouth. And it took minutes of agony, when he awoke, to feel certain that he was in his own bed, beside his wife, in his own house; sometimes he had to embrace Teresa, who moaned in her sleep when he did, before he knew who he was, and where.

He was a man, first and foremost, with obligations. Now that he had children he was responsible to Teresa and his boys, a joyful burden, one he never resented even when Teresa insisted on living more expensively than they should. Then his brother and his sister stood inside that circle of loyalty, and his mother, and they all constituted his life: what he owed to them and what they meant to him. And since Enrico's death those debts seemed sacred to him. He would never, he swore, let any of those loyalties fall to the ground bleeding as he had his friend. It irked him when Lampa didn't come to him after his subpoena, just as it irked him that Vittorio ignored him about leaving the Fascio. He tried so hard to do his duty to them all and yet he failed; he watched the quarrel that erupted that day at the beach and he failed to do any more than watch. It was hard to recall those years when he lived only for himself, alone in America, sending money back to Italy so distant as to seem mythical beside the steel girders and neon lights of his exile. How young he'd been then, how stupid, how afraid. He was still afraid but now, at least, he knew what he feared for, and it was more than himself, it was all of them. What a fragile shelter his family was! He had been, and he thought it often, stronger when he stood alone.

In the beginning was his end.

Beginnings: the taste of coal dust in his mouth, a taste nothing could wash away. The harsh voices of whores in doorways, vying for customers. Whores wearing nightgowns and boots, hugging themselves against the mountain wind. For weeks he walked by fast, fooling nobody, trying to decide which one deserved the doubtful gift of his virginity. What a schoolboy, Enrico mocked, as if it makes any difference who you choose! A whore is a whore, the world over, choose one who looks clean, that's the important thing . . . .

In the end he chose Sasha, a Russian girl with hair the color of dawn, thin, almost tubercular, yet somehow motherly—she never lifted her voice to shriek with the rest.

Your first time?

How could you tell?

You couldn't look me in the eye, that's how. Now put the dollar on the sink, that's good. Now get undressed.

Sasha vanished behind a paper screen painted gold, cheap factory goods the company sold the whores as they sold the miners spoiled canned food and lanterns that broke underground. Rumor had it that the company took a cut from the whores, but now was not the time to ask. Undressing, Francesco scanned the small room nervously. He spied an icon before which a stubby candle guttered, Christ, he supposed, one hand raised in benediction, both eyes black pools of suffering. Even here, he thought with dismay, even here I can't escape him. He felt like asking Sasha to blow the candle out or turn the icon to the wall.

Come on, undress, she said from behind the screen, we ain't got all fuckin' night.

How old are you, Sasha?

She stepped away from the screen, her skinny legs akimbo, and she laughed.

Listen, wop, I been whoring longer than you been an American.

She undressed him roughly, then shoved him onto the narrow cot. Francesco closed his eyes and savored the texture of her skin, running his fingers in wonder down her breasts, amazed by a silkiness so opposite to his flesh, so unimagined even in fantasies. He reached up to kiss Sasha but she twisted away.

Want me to french you? That's fifty cents extra, you'll love it, everybody does.

Unsure what the word meant, Francesco shook his head, feeling as pitifully ignorant as he had in San Lorenzo, begging Vittorio for the truth. The memory began to cool his heat, so that Sasha grasped him in a remarkably strong hand (calluses, dirt under the fingernails), arousing him all over again. She grinned at him until her labor succeeded, a child's grin, a kids-playing-together-in-the-street grin, as though she were as innocent as he.

You can kiss me now, she said coyly.

He tasted gin and cigarettes. Sasha's tongue slithered around his, a dizzying sensation, not innocent at all. She broke the kiss with a laugh.

Pretty cool for a first timer, ain't you? Now love me up, little boy.

She sank backwards, her legs parted, and Francesco knew he was supposed to do something, but what? He tried to recall Vittorio and the girl Carmela; the memory was no use. Finally Sasha pulled him atop her and guided him impatiently into her, after which Francesco began, at first tentatively, to rock back and forth against her thin body. She locked her legs across his back and wrenched up to meet him, as little grunts escaped her lips and her pale face started to flush. In an instant, or so it seemed, Francesco could feel himself explode, his mind whirling into blackness, far from the girl or the room, until a galaxy seemed to detonate behind his eyes, and he could hear himself panting as though breathless.

Sasha was lying beneath him, a mocking smile on her lips. Let me up, she said, let me up.

Not yet. Francesco pressed his head to her breasts.

Whaddya want, applause? I gotta wash.

And she wrested herself off the cot, leaving Francesco amazed at how fast such potent sensations disappeared. He heard her splash herself vigorously behind the screen.

Without having to be told Enrico knew what he had done. He clapped Francesco on the back.

So tonight you became a man, you feel like one?

It was all over too fast.

She must be a good piece of ass, Enrico laughed. He picked up his harmonica and started blowing chords.

You know, Francesco said, if I'd stayed home I'd be married now, think of that.

Married and fucking every night, is that what you think? Wrong, friend, wrong. Marriage is the end of love, its tomb. That's why we anarchists don't believe in it.

Oh, I thought you were all too ugly to get married. Look at you.

Ugly! You ungrateful bastard, from now on you cook for yourself. Ugly—when I've never paid for a woman in my life.

Five thousand men in this town, Francesco jeered, but *you* don't pay?

I have a Russian girl, Sasha. She does it with me for love.

You lousy liar, Francesco said after he absorbed the blow. What does her room look like?

A cheap screen, a cheap cot, and one of those Russian icons that makes you want to kill yourself.

You saw her room because you paid her, tell the truth.

Enrico smiled. You're so jealous toads and snakes are jumping from your mouth.

You're a liar, Francesco said, lying down to sleep, reflecting that Enrico had managed to ruin his night. It was as bad as being back in San Lorenzo with Vittorio, who never let his brother forget his ignorance. Finally, after the oil lamp and its liquid shadows had disappeared, Enrico said:

Listen, I paid Sasha, she makes everybody pay.

Is that the truth?

Close enough. Now forget it and try to sleep.

After that Francesco was careful to frequent new whores Enrico did not know. With them he learned the gymnastics of love, though each lesson cost him four hours in the mines. Four hours of toil for twenty minutes of bliss: that was the deal America offered him. One of them, a Chinese girl improbably named Monica, decided she wanted him for her fancy man; and so Francesco began a love affair with this yellow cat, so quiet and polite her presence scarcely registered, until he backed her into bed, where she clawed his shoulders and wailed, beating his back with tiny fists until he brought her to release, when she moaned and growled and shuddered in his arms. He came to her weekly, twice weekly, inflamed by her dry tallow skin with that faint perfume that might have been jasmine, or opium.

To torment his friend he disappeared into the night without a word. He tramped the icy streets in hobnailed boots, waving to the whores waiting in doorways for their customers, secure at last in the knowledge he was loved—or if not loved, then at least desired and pampered, like a princeling with his courtesan. Monica loved feeding him sweetmeats, delicately sliding shelled walnuts and candied fruit between his lips—what else did it mean to be a fancy man? Yet she seemed ever more sad and the opium smell grew stronger on her skin. Francesco tried asking her questions, a fruitless exercise. Happy-happy, she would say, you make me happy, Frank. And she cut off all further inquiry with a kiss.

At last one summer night he came to Monica's cabin, where

so many whores stood in silent grief he couldn't enter without shoving them aside. At last her body, draped with a dragon quilt, was carried out to the counterpoint of sobbing whores; perhaps they saw their future in her end. Francesco reached out to touch her body as it passed: dry, cold, lifeless as paper, not the lithe partner of his horizontal dance. Without a word he went to the saloon and drank bourbon until closing time, hoping to get so drunk he couldn't think. He did, of course; he kept thinking how horrible life was, this life he had no choice except to live . . . . after a week, he talked Enrico into leaving the mines for Philadelphia, a different sort of hell, at least.

It occurred to him now that he must have loved Enrico, for he thought of him every day.

You loved people although you knew they were going to die.

You loved people precisely because you knew they would die.

You loved your family because you had no choice. There was no question of not loving them, because they were your blood, flesh of your flesh, and you loved them as you loved yourself. You could kill yourself the way that whore in the coaltown did, but how could you ever rid yourself of your blood?

Now he was passing the Garibaldi Homes. Every time he saw them, no matter how he tried hardening himself in advance, the sight of his handiwork, dilapidated now, dusty and desolate, made his throat close with grief. Some of the owners still lived there, their laundry fluttering limply in the river breeze, their secondhand Fords parked forlornly in driveways spattered with axle grease. Perhaps half of the Homes stood empty now. Razor grass grew knee-high in the yards, and spiderwebs covered the windowpanes.

He accelerated, not wishing to linger there, and in a few moments reached his own block. He glanced into the rear-view mirror to verify his smile; it would never do to look downcast in his neighbors' eyes. When he stepped out of his car their voices barraged him, those ribald jokes and sly greetings that let him know he was home.

Teresa was waiting for him on the steps. When she stood up to greet him he saw an anxious look in her eyes; he started to ask why, but she gestured for him to be silent until they went inside.

"What's wrong? One of the boys?"

"No, no." She drew in a breath as though in shock, like one swimming in water deeper than comfort allows. "They were here. Just now. The government."

"Who was here? Tell me straight out, sweet Jesus, who was here?"

"Two men from the FBI. I wrote down their names," she added helplessly.

"Asking questions about what? No, let me guess, Vittorio?"

"How did you know?"

"Logical, isn't it?" He flopped into the chesterfield and lit a cigarette.

"I tried to keep them out, but they—"

"I'm not angry at you, darling. I'm not angry at you at all."

"Is this because of Lampa?"

"It's because my brother is an idiot," he said grimly. "There'll be a war in Europe any day, and he wants to strut around in his goddamn blackshirt. I should have made him stop long ago."

"Dissolve the fascio?" Vittorio said with a smile. "Now why should I do that?"

"For my sake. So the FBI will leave us all alone."

They were talking in Vittorio's office where every wall blazed with oversized photographs:

Vittorio and the Duce shaking hands in Rome, Vittorio gazing awestruck at his leader who glared belligerently into the camera lens.

Vittorio and his fascio, marching, followed by a thousand children in blackshirts.

Vittorio trying to mimic the Duce's warlike glare.

Vittorio riding a black horse at the head of one more parade, the horse rearing up in either terror or triumph.

"If you won't dissolve this thing, resign, take yourself out of it."

"The coward's way! Is that the kind of man I am?"

"Cowards," Francesco said patiently, "often live longer than idiots."

"Yes, that would make Lampa happy, if I walked away!"

"We are not speaking of him, we are speaking of you and our family."

"And what about my duty to myself?" Vittorio tried to thrust his chin out the way Mussolini did, and failed.

Francesco brought his fist down on the desk, making a hollow thud. "You have a duty to this family! You will dissolve the fascio, and that is all I have to say!"

"I will let my comrades decide," Vittorio replied after a moment's thought. "I will put it to a vote."

"Promise me," Francesco said, calm again, "promise me you are finished with it no matter what."

"I didn't know you scared so easily," Vittorio smiled sardonically.

"I didn't know you were too foolish to scare at all."

"Don't speak to me of fear, little brother, I survived the war. Have respect for my experience."

"Then respect mine. I love this country, do you understand? I will never go back to Italy, this is my homeland now. Yes, mock me if you want, but this is all I want, to watch my sons grow up here, to love my wife and to grow old. You will call that a peasant dream, I know how you love to sneer—and I don't give a damn. And so long as we are both in America we must be loyal, do you understand? We cannot break the vow we took. It is not honorable. And we must be honorable, Vittorio, or we are lost.

His brother clapped ironically. "Bravo, bravo, a touching aria!"

"I want your word on it. You will resign."

"And if I don't?"

"Don't make me blackmail you. Let's agree that you will do it because you must."

"Goddamn you," Vittorio said slowly, "goddamn all of you."

"All of who?"

"You Americans," he said.

FOUR

Leonora slept fitfully in a bed that smelled of the sea and of camphor balls, slept so late that Lampa had already bathed and shaved and set off to eat breakfast—the only edible meal in America, he claimed—on Commercial Street, the sluggish artery of off-season Provincetown. The night before, she'd gotten tipsier than she intended at one of the bottle parties the local literati notoriously gave, fifty intellectuals talking so loud over a Billie Holliday record that nobody noticed it was skipping back over the same song all night. Tipsy she got, not drunk; that door prize for attendance went to their Village neighbor, Edmund Wilson, inexplicably dubbed Bunny despite his dour face, who stood on a table chanting "The Hollow Men" in his wheezing voice. Lampa talked politics—what else?—while Leonora fended off the intelligentsia's groping hands, at one point backed against an icebox by a young Southern Agrarian determined to have her right there and then. Now she was sleeping her hangover off, in the pool of morning sun spilling through the blinds, that Cape Cod light as thick and pure as an egg yolk. She pressed her face into the camphor-scented pillow and she dreamed.

She was flying over Italy, her hands extended to feel the wind rushing past her as she flew. At first she could see nothing on the ground, not even land. Then with a sound like the fabric tearing she descended, and Rome came into view. She was flying in from the ocean, so that she saw first the nondescript suburbs, the highways where a few cars dawdled lazily as ants, and finally the Vatican. Oddly, its great piazza stood empty, unpeopled even by Swiss Guards. The vast ellipse of marble and travertine seemed as dead as the Pyramids; even the Pope's gardens looked sullenly overgrown, choked with weeds. A war, Leonora told herself, there must have been a war. She forced herself to fly on.

When she crossed the Tiber she saw deserted streets, shops shuttered, not even a cat prowling the cobblestones. Astonished, Leonora decided to land. Standing at the dead center of Piazza del Popolo, for the first time she began to feel afraid. She wanted to move, walk in any direction, yet her body was refusing to obey. Leonora stared up at the gardens, which hung sloppy and sodden over the stone terraces; the stink of rot was filling her nostrils. She heard a woman's heels tap-tapping towards her and, glancing up, saw the Duchess Bondini approaching her. Deep, frightful gashes covered her arms and neck, reminding Leonora of a martyred saint, and as the Duchess came closer she saw that blood dripped from every wound.

"My dear Leonora, how kind of you to come."

"What happened? Where has everybody gone?"

"How did *you* get here? You gave me quite a surprise, my dear."

"I flew through the air. Why do you look so—horrible?"

"You flew?" The Duchess laughed in polite mockery. "Now, Leonora, tell the truth."

"I can't stand to look at you like that. I'll take you to the hospital!"

"But what earthly good would that do? It's too late for me, and if you're here it must be too late for you as well."

"What in God's name do you mean? You're going to bleed to death."

The Duchess frowned. "You mean you don't know where you are?"

"In the Piazza del Popolo, of course."

"No, no, my dear. This is the afterlife. I have been dead for years, and now you are dead too."

"I can't possibly be dead, that is insane—"

"But you are. Your body won't move when you command it, isn't that right?"

"That's shock. I'm in shock. It will pass soon enough."

"Raise your arm. I will prove to you we are both dead."

As though by magic, Leonora watched her right arm lift from her side. The Duchess walked up to her and then walked through her arm, her flesh as insubstantial as air. Leonora trembled, terrified.

"Do you believe me now?" the Duchess asked.

"That blood dripping from you? What about that blood?"

"My punishment, so I can never forget what I did. What did you do, my dear?"

"I did nothing! I was flying through the air!"

"But you must have done what I did. You must have killed yourself. This is the zone of the afterlife reserved for suicides."

And again the Duchess brushed Leonora's body with her own, which passed through it as easily as a ray of light through dust.

"I did nothing! For God's sake, let me go!"

"You cannot mention Him here. That is our commandment. You must learn."

"Let me go, let me go, let me go—"

The Duchess laughed at her, a savage laugh.

"You little fool. Did you think to end your pain so easily?"

Leonora began to scream, but no sound issued from her throat. At that precise instant, she woke up.

By the time she found Lampa eating pancakes in a coffee shop, she'd managed to forget her dream, or at least shove it back into her mental lumber room along with all the unused furniture of thought. Bad dreams, of course, meant nothing at all, despite what current fashion claimed; and she knew better than to tell hers to Lampa, who found such self-preoccupation at best laughable, at worst pitifully bourgeois.

"I wonder how Carlo is," she said instead.

"He's grown, he can cook for himself when he gets back at night."

"But maybe we should have been there when he started Columbia."

Lampa smiled. "He wouldn't have noticed. Sometimes I look at him and think, where did he come from, this scholarly monster, this scientific monk?"

"You were quite a scholar once upon a time, yourself."

"In history, yes. A humane subject! I don't think our boy likes people much—prefers atoms and photons and God knows what. I can't blame him," Lampa sighed. "Those particles make more sense than we do, less trouble too."

"Don't judge by those idiots last night, for heaven's sakes . . . ."

"Those idiots, as you call them, are the American intelligentsia! Half of them worship Stalin, the other half worship scotch. If there's ever a revolution in America, it'll be a cocktail party that runs out of booze."

"Then no more parties," Leonora said gaily. "I don't care if I ever see another ice cube in my life."

"You were in your element," Lampa said ironically. "You could have had any man in the room."

"You're jealous, aren't you? After all these years!"

"Not jealous. You're not my property, after all. But you're still beautiful, and you like masculine attention, that's obvious. You ended up in the kitchen with that boy, didn't you?"

"Nothing happened! He was drunk and silly and I fought him off."

"You mean if he hadn't been drunk and silly, you might not have? I saw the boy, he was handsome, wasn't he?"

"Now I know you are jealous. Handsome! He hadn't washed his hair in a month!"

"Oh, you got close enough to tell, did you?"

"He cornered me, for God's sake—if you were watching you must have seen."

"You were laughing, you were enjoying yourself."

"I was not. I was laughing at him to make him feel foolish, that's all."

"Is that how you handle men?"

"Men who make passes, yes—what's gotten into you today?"

"And how many of those men are there? I have no idea."

"I have no idea how many women throw themselves at you when I'm not around. What difference does it make? Why are you doing this?"

"I get frightened sometimes," Lampa said, glancing away. "It's lunatic, I know."

Leonora understood but said nothing. It was impossible to talk that way with Lampa for very long: he mistrusted emotions, mistrusted the formulas denoting them even more. It offended his sense of precision, of life as concrete and palpable, to speculate about those clouds of impulse and shadow the world called sentiments. Sometimes Leonora blamed the Marxist in him for the unexamined life Lampa led, that materialism which led him to suspect all talk of the spirit as pretty evasions, pretty lies, weighed against the terrible truths enacted in Barcelona, Rome, Berlin. And yet she knew better than to blame his politics, which after all were the armor he had chosen long after his skin and nerves were fully grown; except for his politics, he had the same instinct as her brothers, the same reluctance to examine his own soul. Something stoic and bitter survived in Italian men: some sense of the world as an obstacle course won only by the man who kept his soul uncorrupted by its miseries, which meant in practice the man who chose not to ponder his own misery. Man was a poor soul burdened by a corpse, said Marcus Aurelius, misquoting Epictetus. And too: "It is possible to live on earth as you mean to live hereafter. But if men will not let you, quit the house of life." The Stoics valued suicide because they devalued the life of this world, this prison of such brief duration, beside infinity, that the wise man died by his own hand if the prison walls closed too tight. A rational philosophy, she thought, entirely too rational!

Lampa and she rode a jitney to a rock beach where the tide silently rolled in and out, making the gray pebbles green in the sunlight. She swam in the cold dark water, thinking of San Lorenzo, its translucent azure sea through which nosed schools of tiny fish, scales glittering in the sunlight that pierced the waves. She wondered if she would ever see her home again. In a way she never needed to again, so potent were her memories: the sharp perfume of the pines above the town, the orange and lemon trees that clung to the dry soil, the eucalyptus trees with their medicinal odor. What was patriotism except a helpless love for the landscape you knew best?

Lampa lay on the blanket reading newspapers. When she came out of the water, dripping and cold, he smiled and reached up to towel her off.

"How much longer shall we stay?" he asked. They both knew how he hated lazing in the sun.

"Another hour, can you stand that?" she teased.

"Do you remember the time in Turin when we quarreled and I left you behind?"

"Yes," Leonora said, startled, "what made you think of that?"

"I behaved badly. I want to apologize to you."

"Darling, it doesn't matter now . . . ."

"I don't want you to think poorly of me, that's all."

"I've never thought poorly of you, not even then."

Lampa grinned. "Leonora, we used to argue so much our landlord threatened to kick us out."

"I remember how happy we were then. Our picnics on the grass, reading poetry aloud . . . ."

"And fucking on the grass," Lampa said slyly. "Or did you forget that too?"

"Of course not," Leonora blushed.

"My God, you look like a little convent girl!"

"I'm sure *she's* still inside of me somewhere too. You don't think our past selves die, do you, like snakeskin that gets shed?"

"What difference does that make? All we have is this moment anyway."

"I think you're a Stoic, my darling, not a Marxist at all."

"Don't talk nonsense," Lampa grumbled, bending over a headline about the Sudetenland.

Lampa was bathing, that afternoon at their inn, when Leonora happened to knock his briefcase off the desk. The customary mess—newspaper clippings highlighted in angry red, letters, pamphlets—went spilling onto the floor, and she dutifully began to pick it up. And then her eye lit on unsigned letters in Italian, crudely handwritten as though the writer wanted to efface his own identity:

> TRAITOR TO ITALY, TRAITOR TO YOUR
> BLOOD
> KILL YOURSELF, COWARD, AND RID THE
> WORLD OF YOUR SCUM
> STAY OUT OF PHILADELPHIA ON OCTOBER
> 5, YOU WILL NOT LEAVE ALIVE
> STAY AWAY, LAMPA, IF YOU KNOW WHAT
> IS GOOD FOR YOU!!!

Each letter contained the same four lines, except in a different order and a different hand. Only one envelope remained; the postmark, bafflingly, read Newark, New Jersey and not Philadelphia. Leonora glanced at the letters briefly, appalled, then stuffed them back into Lampa's briefcase with the rest.

That night it required all the discipline she had not to blurt out the question sizzling in her brain. Instead she and Lampa went to a cavernous seafood restaurant on the bay, where a dance orchestra played imitation Tommy Dorsey and Glenn Miller. When "String of Pearls," her favorite, began, Lampa ushered her onto the tiny floor for his stiff foreigner's foxtrot, which she danced mechanically, thinking about those letters all the while.

"You remember Gramsci?" he asked her when they sat down again. "No amnesty for him. The Duce said, when they sent him to prison, 'This brain must stop functioning!' Because he was the most brilliant of us all, even if he fell in love with Russia, the fool—he should have known better. I always wanted to go see him in Rome, never did."

"He was kind to me in Turin after you left. Kind and funny, he made me laugh."

"Yes." Lampa frowned. "We all should have been less kind and less funny, do you know, my dear? Maybe then Mussolini would be in our jails instead."

"You did the best you could," Leonora said soothingly.

"Let history judge. I'm not so goddamned sure we did. We talked! My God, we *talked* a good revolution, didn't we?"

"Don't reproach yourself! Weren't you dangerous enough for those bastards to frame?"

"Maybe they overestimated me, who knows?" Lampa grimaced. "There's a wonderful folktale, I heard it on Ponza— what we all should have done when the Fascists came. Shall I tell it to you?"

"How long is it?"

"Oh, am I keeping Madame from a charity ball?"

Leonora laughed. "Go ahead."

"It's called, The Man Who Robbed The Robbers. You don't know it?"

"I don't think so."

"There were six terrible bandits who thrived on murder and robbery, and they all lived together in a big house whose owner they'd massacred. They kept their loot stashed under lock and key, they had so much it filled an entire room, and whenever they left the house they hid the key under a rock next to the steps.

"One day a farmer and his son went out to gather wood. They saw the bandits leaving their house, so they hid. That's how they learned about the hidden key. When the bandits disappeared they grabbed the key, ran into the house, and filled their pockets with silver coins. Then they locked up the house, put back the key, and went home feeling quite pleased with themselves.

"Next day the father and son robbed the bandits, and the next day after that. On the third day, when the son opened the door, he fell into a tar pit the bandits had dug. The father tried and tried but he couldn't pull his son out. Afraid the bandits would return and kill them both, the father had to make a dreadful choice. He cut his son's head off and ran back to his house.

"When the bandits returned, they found a headless corpse. They had no idea whose it was, so they hung it on a tree, keeping watch to see who returned. The boy's father wanted to retrieve his son's corpse but, not knowing how, consulted a sorceress. She told him to do the following: he and his other sons climbed the hill to the tree where the body hung. The other sons made sounds like cattle and the robber, thinking he could steal some cows, ran off, allowing the father to retrieve the corpse.

"Much later, the robbers were in the village on business and heard of a man who'd suddenly gotten rich. This was none other than the father of the boy. That same day, the robbers ordered six large casks, with lids on top, and then, fully armed, each bandit climbed into a cask. They had them delivered to the rich man on the pretext that he must keep them for their owner until he returned. The man agreed and stored the casks in his wine cellar. That night, before bedtime, a servant girl went down there for some wine and heard voices from the casks. One of the bandits was saying, 'Tell me, is it time to kill and rob this rich man yet?' She flew back up the stairs, shaking like a leaf, went to the master and told him everything. He rounded up all his servants and led them to the wine cellar, where they slew the bandits who still hid inside the casks. That was the end of those ruffians, while the man who'd robbed the robbers kept his fortune and lived in peace."

"A bloodthirsty tale!" Leonora sighed.

"If you could kill evil politely, it would have happened long ago."

"Evil? You're starting to sound like me, my hysterical nonsense as you call it . . . ."

"Would you like to dance? I hear 'String of Pearls' again."

"I saw those letters," she said, astonishing herself. "The death threats. Why didn't you say?"

"I've gotten them before," Lampa said coolly. "They don't mean a thing."

"They mean something to me!"

"Words, only words—illiterate words at that. Sent by a cretin. Once he wrote on paper he had used to wipe himself."

"My God! And you never said anything!"

Lampa shrugged. "It's not important, why should I worry you?"

"Just the same, I would prefer you not visit Philadelphia."

He laughed. "Your brothers are there, doesn't that put your mind at ease?"

"I'm not joking, stay in New York, it's safer there—"

"Don't be a child. Those letters came to our house, am I any safer *there*? Whoever wants to kill me can kill me, yes, even here. You think after prison a death threat means a goddamn thing to me?"

"You've always been selfish, you've never once thought of me—"

"Leonora, listen: if you're my wife I expect you to understand. My God, after all this time I'd think you would! I chose this life, it isn't easy, but it's the life I chose. And when you talk about all this you make things harder than they have to be. So please don't talk about it, ever again."

"You want an accomplice," she said softly, "you don't want a wife."

FIVE

Francesco stood waiting outside the morgue, a gray stone cube on Wood Street he'd passed a hundred times without so much as giving it a glance. A blustery fall breeze was shaking half-bare trees, scattering yellow and scarlet leaves onto the damp sidewalk, where they stuck like postage stamps. He shivered in the breeze, chilled by its wintry edge, a foretaste of the cold that would soon dislodge the fall, or was he shivering at what lay inside? Francesco tried to recall whether he'd ever seen a corpse before: in the mines, maybe, when the men carried out someone suffocated by the coal dust? He had the strength to look at a dead stranger, though he doubted he had enough to do his duty now. Wasn't life supposed to get easier, smoother, more predictable, he asked himself, a dance whose steps you mastered with middle age? No, Francesco decided, that was another American lie; nothing got easier, as San Lorenzo monotonously taught; life was a war from the time you suckled your first breast until the moment when you, too, became another empty shell of flesh. Life was a struggle in which fate or chance or Providence dealt you card after card and you, like a gambler unable to leave the game, had no choice but to bet.

And after that? He had no convictions, at least none that made facing death any easier. His nephew Carlo claimed that we all finally became cosmic dust, particles revolving round the sun, since matter could never die nor disappear. Something about that irked Francesco, perhaps its pointlessness. He preferred to believe not in the bodily resurrection Teresa and her priests espoused. He had a simpler, less theological belief. He felt his soul and the souls of everyone on earth went back to God, there not to be judged, for what difference did judgment make, instead to be gathered back into God's body and there absorbed. He could not have argued his case rationally, so he discussed it only with Teresa, whose gentle mockery left him unfazed; he knew his soul would go back to the Lord, who seemed impotent to direct it down the paths of righteousness.

Strange, Francesco mused; what you believed might be the most important choice of all. What you believed shadowed the actions you took or refused to take, and even if your spirit didn't rule, it guided you, a compass in your brain that never failed to point you north or south. You were, finally, what you believed. Poor Lampa lay dead now not because he chose death but because his spirit chose this path . . . .

With a sudden squeal of brakes Carney's Packard pulled up beside the curb. Francesco's partner, grown slow and heavy now, wriggled out from behind the steering wheel.

"Thanks for coming," Francesco said automatically.

"Anything, Frank, anything. It's a dreadful thing you're doin', God will reward ye."

"You really think God cares?"

"God cares about everything, boyo. His eye is on every sparrow that falls from every tree."

"I wish he'd kept this particular sparrow from falling to the ground."

"It's not for us to question the ways of God, infinitely wise as they are."

"When did you get so Catholic, you old hypocrite?"

Carney smiled. "At my age you go back to the Church the way a bad son crawls back to his family. You feel like a reprobate but it's a damn sight better than bein' out in the cold."

"You said you know this coroner?"

"Shake Hands Maloney, used to run a crap game in the

Seventh Ward. Dumb bastard knows less about stiffs than I know
about Singapore." Carney sighed. "God bless patronage, nobody
wanted the job so they gave it to Shake Hands. Makes a nice
living selling corpses to medical students."

"Not this one he won't."

Carney handed him a cheap cigar the color of pitch. "For the
dead room, you'll need it. Light the thing before we go inside."

"You're kidding me."

"You'll wish I were."

Carney rang a bell concealed in the lintel and, after a moment,
a sleepy black attendant admitted them. Shake Hands Maloney,
attired incongruously in a white suit with a red carnation in his
lapel, greeted Carney by squeezing his forearm and hand
simultaneously, the politician's grip, Francesco thought sourly.

"Meet Frank Monti," Carney said as though the men were in
his bar and not the morgue. "My old friend, Shake Hands. Shake,
you got his brother-in-law in there?"

"You guineas oughta stop playin' with knives and guns."

Francesco had to bite his tongue. If he wanted to retrieve the
corpse without applying at length to City Hall, he would need
this bigot in an ice-cream suit with hair the color and texture of
patent leather. He forced himself to smile.

"That's right, Mr. Maloney, everybody should. It's bad for
their health."

"You said it," Shake Hands nodded vigorously. "Niggers,
especially—I got six dinges back there, and Christ, October's
supposed to be my quiet month. But no, the jigaboos got to
keep breakin' bottles on each others' heads—too fuckin' dumb
to use a gun."

"Frank needs to move the body, Shake Hands . . . . like I
said."

Shake Hands looked doubtful. "Shit, I don't want no heat
from the D.A."

"Fuck the D.A.," Carney said pleasantly. "They got no suspect,
they'll make no arrest. Whoever did the killing disappeared into
the crowd. You know that."

"I dunno," Shake Hands said doubtfully, "I gotta think about my career."

"That's why you need a friend like me," Carney replied. "Politics is favors, and the more favors you do the farther you can go."

"I'm willing," Francesco said, "to make a contribution to your favorite charity."

"Cash money?" Shake Hands replied instantly.

Francesco nodded. Shake Hands pretended to deliberate, then nodded gravely at both men, "He ain't covered up, your brother-in-law. Those goddamn niggers took all the drawers I got, I keep askin' the D.A. for more space, this place is a shithouse, I swear to Christ."

"You sure you want to see this?" Carney asked Francesco. "Easier and simpler to let your undertaker take care of it."

"I want to see." Wasn't there, Francesco thought, an old wives' tale that the wounds of a dead man might speak his killer's name? Or was he going mad from chitchatting while his chest pounded and his head swam in and out of a brightly colored mist?

"Let him in there, Shake Hands," Carney ordered the little man.

"I'll give you three minutes," Shake Hands Maloney said nervously.

"That's fine," said Francesco, remembering Lampa in San Lorenzo, with his red hair and his Northern accent, sitting on the wall with Francesco teasing him, that day he and Leonora had first met. There were so many roads to death: the hot dusty roads of war Vittorio had marched; the road that led you to an ordinary sidewalk, like the one Enrico had died clinging to. And Lampa's road. There was a kind of bitter irony in surviving the Fascists only to die in Philadelphia. You could cheat every man on earth, couldn't you, but never death. Someone had wanted Lampa to die so badly that he waited in the crowd at the station for his train, probably for hours without knowing exactly when he would arrive, waited until he saw Lampa, stooped now, red hair fading to gray, and then burst through the crowd until he got close enough to his quarry to sniff his breath.

"And don't touch nothin' in there," Shake Hands warned, unlocking the door.

The room where the Medical Examiner of Philadelphia stored dead men had no windows or chairs or desks. Its walls were, floor to ceiling, ceramic tile, once as bright as the lights glaring down on them, now faded to a dingy color between yellow and gray. But that was not the first thing Francesco noticed, or even the second or the third.

A dozen men, some naked, some half-clothed, hung from hooks connected to pulleys in the ceiling, so that they all dangled from different heights; the men might have been hanging there forever, or for an hour, it was impossible to tell. All at once their smell assaulted Francesco and he reached for Carney's cigar. Lighting it rapidly he said a silent Our Father, and stepped forward six inches to find Lampa's body among the men on the meathooks.

The dead looked so terribly dead when they were dead, beyond absolution or redemption, and no more human, finally, than the lambs the Ninth Street butchers hung in their windows at Eastertime. They had departed for that foreign land from which no immigrants returned.

Lampa hung, stripped to the waist, a grimace of pain twisting his lips. The killer had stabbed near his heart and then dragged the knife blade down diagonally, so that the wound resembled an unfinished X. Francesco could not bring himself to look long. Why should I be here, he thought, why should I have to see this . . . . he tasted bile rising in his throat, glancing against his will back at the slash across Lampa's chest, then found himself lunging for a waste can to empty the vomit filling his mouth.

SIX

Because she'd been living among Village radicals and atheists, it took years for Leonora to hear about the feast of Our Lady of Mount Carmel. A Freudian analyst deplored it to her in his guttural Berlin accent as mass hysteria, more suited to medieval Europe than Manhattan in 1939. She learned the feast took place in July, lasted a week, and drew so many Catholics to noisome East Harlem that it took two processions to include all the faithful, some of whom knelt all day on the hot asphalt.

She knew what Carlo would do if she asked him to come: make a mocking face identical to his father's, and loudly groan. He found her spiritual wanderings—in the past year she had visited a Theosophist Lodge and a Quaker Meeting House—incomprehensible. "We have to get along without God," her son declared, as though the Almighty were an outmoded luxury, like horsedrawn carriages. Leonora wondered sometimes whether she and Lampa had done the wrong thing raising Carlo outside the Church. Her son didn't even know what he disbelieved.

Not that she knew precisely what she believed herself. Yet as soon as she learned about the feast, she marked July 15 on her calendar. It will remind me of Italy, she told herself, take me away from these headlines about Hitler and Danzig and the Polish Corridor. Since Lampa's murder she felt constant anxiety, dimming some days to mere nervousness but, at worst, making her incapable of sleep or even sitting quietly. On nights like that she walked the Village streets, now old friends as familiar as San Lorenzo's cobblestones. She liked the culs-de-sac off Washington Square, the white stone of Patchin Place bright even at midnight; she loved to watch dawn break over the Hudson, however bleak the Jersey flats looked across the black river. She would walk home, soothed, weary, sleep a few hours before she had to wake Carlo, make breakfast, go to work, all of that possible after enough coffee and cigarettes. In a way she was reborn with every dawn she watched.

She moved through her life smoothly, competently, feeling as though she were underwater, as though the summer air were weighing her down that way water would. Carlo was working in the Columbia physics lab, and after work he drank beer at the West End with his friends, so she might not see him from one breakfast to the next. She suspected he had a girl but did not know how to ask; Barnard coeds were notoriously loose, as if so much lust from the Columbia side of Broadway debauched them instantly. Leonora flinched at the thought of Carlo and his Barnard girl. She knew that soon he would leave, would marry, would become a cool stranger in her house just as she had in her mother's, a stranger and an enemy. And then she would have nothing except her family in Philadelphia: the family she chose not to see.

If I were truly strong, she thought, I would have cut them all out of my life. That would have been their punishment for Vittorio, for shielding the murderer—pathetically feeble, but better than her compromise: visiting at Christmas, entertaining Teresa when she came to Manhattan to buy a dress, as though they were still young girls who cared about hemlines and pleated gowns. For Teresa no time had passed, nothing had ever changed. She never mentioned Lampa and Leonora never did, uncertain whether any of the Montis spoke of him after Francesco had retrieved his corpse. He buried him and gave her money for that first winter alone. That was his answer to every awkwardness. He would have offered Hitler cash, she thought sardonically, to leave the Czechs alone. A check instead of Czechoslovakia! That was

Francesco, eternally doing what he thought right, even when their brother had her husband stabbed to death. He must have known Vittorio's hand guided that knife, how could he not have known? Still, she had taken the cash. For Carlo, she told herself, for his books and his clothes and his beer at the West End. And she had been wrong to take it, and she knew it, and she damned her own weakness. If I were truly strong I would have turned my back on all of them . . . .

And so instead she walked underwater through her days, walking across the Village on those bright summer mornings, before humidity caught Manhattan by the throat, to her job booking lectures at Cooper Union. Laura Warrington finagled it for her after Lampa's death, and though they'd had a few polite dinners, she chose not to stir the ashes of a dead friendship. She spent her days on the phone, efficient, dutiful, impersonating perfectly the calm working mother her colleagues took her to be. At lunchtime she prowled the used book stores on Fourth Avenue, or walked to the East River eating a bag of plums, anything to avoid breaking her underwater stride. She knew if she let her thoughts pause they would swerve back like that broken record in Provincetown to a fixed image: the face of her husband in his coffin, skin white as wax, eyes shut, mouth set in a grim line despite the rouge and lipstick the undertaker used. She wanted to wipe all of that shit off, to see his real face one last time, might even have done it if she'd been alone; Francesco and Teresa were hovering beside her, as though she were ill and had to be watched constantly.

And maybe she had been ill, maybe she still was. She avoided parts of Manhattan on the grounds that she and Lampa were happy there, which was particularly awkward since that included every Italian coffee house in the Village, the Museum of Modern Art, and the southern half of Central Park. She also disliked Fifth Avenue at Christmastime, when happy families strolled, laughing, from shop to shop. She liked quiet spots which held no memories: Gramercy Park at twilight, when the townhouses glowed pink, or the monotonous brownstones of Chelsea, where nobody

seemed to live except Victorian ghosts. If it was illness to mourn
Leonora admitted she was still ill.

Browsing on Fourth Avenue in a used bookshop she came
across Lampa's books; he must have sold them without telling
her. An Italian Nietzsche, La Gaia Scienza, The Joyful Wisdom,
and on the flyleaf Lampa's small, meticulous script, his name,
the date—July 1931. The book fell open to a passage Lampa had
marked in red ink:

"Where is God? the madman cried. I will tell you. *We have
killed him*—you and I have. All of us are his murderers. Are we
not straying through an infinite nothing? Do we not feel the
chill of empty space? Has our world not become icier? What are
all these churches now, if not sepulchers and tombs of God?"

Is that what he believed? He never told her so. You could so
easily spend your life with a man and never once glimpse his
soul. Just as he had, likely, never seen hers at all.

If God were alive anywhere—which only meant He was
fervently hoped for, prayed to, and feared the way desert Jews
had feared Yahweh—she imagined it would happen at the feast.
And so, on the hottest day of the year, when police horses were
collapsing in the street, she boarded the Third Avenue El to ride
uptown. It might have been another city she found, a different
planet from the Village where Sidney Bechet's clarinet warbled
in the cafes all night, and Trotskyites hurled mortal insults at
Stalinists. In the Village God was no more an issue than the
divine right of kings; what did God have to do with living on
your nerves, which seemed to define the year 1939 for even
unpolitical Villagers?

The first thing that struck Leonora was the intense fragrance.
Never in America had she smelled so much Italian food: street
vendors sold boiled beans, sausages, fresh fruit, pasta in huge
bowls, fresh nougat, rings of pastry sweating sugar in the heat,
boiled corn, tomato pies slathered with garlic and peppers, even
the tiny doughnuts fried at Christmastime. She had no appetite,

thanks to the scalding heat. In any case the procession was snaking towards her across 115th Street.

The crowd shuffled forward slowly, singing ecstatic hymns to the Virgin, carrying tall, fat candles in both hands. It took two hours for them to reach the Church of Mount Carmel, a surprisingly small building given the number of its parishioners. By the time the crowd arrived they were drunk with penitence, crawling up the steps on their hands and knees, clutching the stone while moaning broken sentences. Many removed their shoes as a sign of devotion to Mary, while others dragged their faces up the stairs, so that they reached the church door bleeding and blinded from the dust of the street.

The priests standing outside made a gesture that stirred the pilgrims into a buzz of noise. Suddenly fireworks exploded over the street, rockets of blue and white, the Virgin's colors. Bands hidden by the crowd burst into sound, cymbals smashing, tubas droning melancholy chords.

The bands began to march west, and as they did a statue of the Madonna ten feet high was carried out of the church by men wearing suits and ties. The crowd of penitents let out a moan all but sexual in its intensity. Leonora stood frozen as the Madonna descended the church steps, where blood still glistened in the sun, and slowly, slowly descended a path reluctantly yielded by the worshippers.

She could feel the terrible sunlight beating on her face as though upon a drum. When the smell of candles and incense rose, Leonora thought she might suffocate, or sneeze, which would be worse; this crowd might expel her for disrespect to Our Lady. Now she could hear women on both sides shouting vows and pleas at the statue, begging the Virgin to spare a sick child or pledging chastity if only Our Lady would . . . . if only, Leonora thought impatiently, yet she too felt the same urgency now.

And then the Madonna of 115th Street was standing in front of Leonora. Those bright eyes, those rosy plaster cheeks . . . . from somewhere a great wind rushed into Leonora's breast, as though a storm were filling her suddenly, and she reached forward to touch the statue before it passed. She raised her arms, her lips forming she knew not what words, and as she did the sunlight blinded her, she heard a roaring in her ears, and darkness filled her eyes so fiercely that she stumbled backward and collapsed.

SEVEN

The black Packard pulled up to the curb facing Teresa's kitchen and parked, slowly and insolently, to proclaim the power that put it there. Eleven days, she thought, startled by her own bookkeeping; they've been watching this house for eleven days. Unaware or uninterested, her sons played chink on the corner with the other boys, tossing a rubber ball against the stoop and shouting whenever one scored a point. Their voices, high-pitched and merry, made the only sound in the entire street.

And if any of my neighbors notices that car, what can I say, Teresa asked herself. My suddenly patriotic neighbors making the gray Philadelphia winter of rowhouses and dirty snow bloom with flags and bunting and pictures of President Roosevelt in their front windows, as garishly tinted as the rotogravure Christs. How desperate these Italians were to demonstrate their loyalty! None of that mattered, of course, to the black car and its driver, invisible through the slats of its drawn window blinds. Pearl Harbor had shown that nobody could be trusted, not even, presumably, immigrants who dotted their front yards with flags the way they planted flowers in the spring. Now that the treacherous Japanese had attacked, every day until America won was a day that would live in infamy . . . .

On that black Sunday she and Francesco were, of all places, comfortably in bed. It was their only time to make love in peace, since the boys went to Sunday School in the afternoon; that bought them two or three hours alone together, and they used them, ruefully aware that the children held their lives hostage now. Teresa had no idea how Leonora and Lampa ever managed it—did they send Carlo off with instructions not to come home before dark? She knew they'd had physical passion right up to the end, and she also knew wives who confessed that if their husbands touched them once a month they counted themselves fortunate. So she felt grateful for her Sundays, though they all ended with dinner at Vittorio and Bellina's house, which meant listening to her brother-in-law deliver a tirade against Roosevelt the warmonger. She could never connect the newsreel President with his jaunty smile and his rakish cigarette holder to the criminal Vittorio described. It was, she thought, like being told that Cary Grant was a pickpocket.

Afterward they lay in bed, talking of nothing as they always did, warmed by each other's bodies and the closeness they'd just shared. Once such moments had been common, before Leone's birth and even after it for a time, and then the marriage changed without either of them changing it, or rather Francesco's fortunes changed and he now had less energy or desire for her. That wounded Teresa but she said nothing, had prayed and consulted Leonora and other women further along the unlit road of married life, and thankfully his mood had passed. So when they lay in bed now she enjoyed that moment almost more than lovemaking, it reassured her, it made her feel loved almost more than the pressure of his body did.

"Almost three o'clock," he said. "Didn't you want to hear the radio?"

"The New York Philharmonic, but only if you do, I don't care."

"What a cultured wife I have," he grinned. "I'll bet you even know the conductor's name."

"Artur Rodzinski and don't make fun of me."

"Sounds Polish," Francesco observed, twiddling the dial. "Another of Hitler's gifts to America."

Static, ethereal noises gave way to an announcer screaming

over the national anthem: the Japanese had attacked Pearl Harbor at 7:30 that morning, their planes had targeted our Pacific Fleet and destroyed at least three ships and an aircraft squadron on the ground, and the President would go before Congress to declare war. They looked at one another, shocked, embarrassed to hear such news naked and concupiscent in their bed. The national anthem resumed, louder than before, and Francesco switched the radio off.

"Those idiots, those goddamn idiots," he exclaimed.

"Who?" asked Teresa, quickly beginning to get dressed.

"The Japs. How can they win? Roosevelt already cut off their oil. It's impossible. They must have gone insane."

"They beat the British and the Chinese, didn't they?"

"They're insane. Look at a map. Look at a goddamn map. Japan is small."

"Japan is big."

"And America is bigger, and richer, and we have oil and factories. No, they must have gone insane."

"Anybody that starts a war is insane, if you ask me."

"Those goddamn Japs," he said, ignoring her, "are going to wish they never heard of America. Those sneaky bastards, bombing us without declaring war!"

"Us?"

"Yeah, us, the United States."

"I didn't know I was married to a patriot. Will you join the Army too?"

Francesco laughed. "Make you a bet, Teresa, every kid in this neighborhood who's old enough will be in line tomorrow morning to join up."

"Then they're all fools. Worse than the Japanese."

"They're Americans, goddamn it, why wouldn't they join up?"

"Why should they fight for a country that calls them dagos, guineas, wops? Are they fighting for their blood?"

"Then you should have given Vittorio your wedding ring when he asked for it. Mussolini is your blood, Roosevelt isn't."

"I don't mean that! You know I don't."

"Then what? You think the Japs will just disappear?"

"No. Only I don't like killing. I didn't like Lampa being killed. And whoever killed him thought he had good reason, too."

"War isn't the same thing," Francesco snapped.

"Now you're the one who doesn't understand," she said, and left the room.

Francesco lit a cigarette and contemplated the empty bed. He wanted to call Carney, but today he had a ward meeting until dinnertime. For some reason he could not sit quietly with this news. Enrico, he decided, and began to dial before it struck him that Enrico had been dead for years. In the end he called Vittorio.

When Teresa came back into the bedroom she overheard the end of the call.

"You honestly believe FDR planned the whole attack?" Francesco was asking. "They wiped out our Pacific Fleet!"

He sat listening to his brother, a quizzical look on his face. "All right, all right, we'll see you for dinner at the usual time. Tell Bellina I'm bringing rum cake, don't make dessert."

He looked up at her. "I'm surrounded by lunatics."

"Does that include me?"

"Yes. No. Get over here, woman."

She took her time crossing the room to his outstretched arms. "No arguments at Vittorio's tonight, promise me?"

"Unless Bellina serves Japanese food." They both laughed at that.

Now she called Francesco at the Calabrian Bank, staring at the black Packard as she dialed, knowing he would have no comfort to offer her. Give them a cup of coffee and some biscotti, he suggested ironically, I'll bet the FBI doesn't have an expense account . . . .

It was the unfairness that twanged her nerves like a pizzicato violin. Why us, she raged, we're the *good* Italians, not Fascists, not criminals, we didn't even make wine in our cellar before Repeal! We're good citizens, damn you to hell, isn't that enough? The black car sat, mocking her silent plea. Go to Vittorio's house if you want to find the criminal, Teresa thought for the eleventh day in a row, shocked at her disloyalty.

And then her doorbell rang. It took her a moment to react. Not Francesco, she knew, not the boys; a traveling salesman, a neighbor perhaps?

Bellina Monti stood on her doorstep, face swollen by tears, hair undone, body trembling and quivering.

"I had to tell somebody," she said. "They came for Vittorio this morning. At the clinic. They arrested him. The FBI." Embracing her, Teresa led her inside and closed the door.

And then the impossible happened, the way things happen in a dream:

Like dancers, the two FBI men leapt from the car in perfect unison, opening and closing its doors with an abrupt sound. They crossed Porter Street, still perfectly in step, their dark blue suits and white shirts and gray snapbrim hats glittering in the winter sun. Not once did they glance at Teresa, though they must have felt her watching them intently through her big picture window. They stepped onto her sidewalk as though stepping onto a football field, square-jawed, square-shouldered, muscular Christians marching forth to war. One moved slightly forward, eyes riveted to the Montis' door. It seemed to Teresa her bell would never ring.

EIGHT

No bells rang in the law offices of Cozen, Cribbage, and Cantwell, not the elevators banked opposite the entranceway, not even the telephone. Francesco thought he had never set foot in a place of business so busily silent. Young lawyers wearing spectacles and anxious frowns strode up and down, their steps muffled by Persian carpets of crimson and gold. Secretaries murmured into telephones with the proud air of servants who knew they were indispensable. Forty stories down, taxis zigzagged crazily along Madison Avenue, in the dark canyon between Grand Central and Vanderbilt Avenue.

If the quiet was meant to soothe him Francesco had to admit that it did. Every inch of the place proclaimed—quietly, of course—that your case would either vanish or win you a fortune in the courts, that no matter how desperate your problem looked, these high priests of litigation, the true religion of America, would turn it to your advantage with the same easy grace that Charles Cozen offered you a Hepplewhite chair and a cigar.

He'd canvassed Greenglass and Carney and everyone he knew in those black weeks, after Vittorio was led out of his clinic, handcuffed like a criminal. Charles Cozen's name came up so often he grew sick of hearing it: everyone agreed he was the only lawyer who could do anything. Cozen was a civil liberties lawyer, not that Francesco knew what that meant or how a man got rich being one; he argued before the Supreme Court so often that his old friends the Roosevelts put him up at the White House. Nobody in Philadelphia like him, Greenglass said, go see Cozen, you got no other choice. He telephoned New York. Cozen told him to bring a check for five thousand, appeals were expensive, the Army might interfere . . . . and so he arranged a second mortgage through Greenglass, not telling Teresa because he knew she would protest, would curse Vittorio and say he was getting what he deserved. What difference did it make if she was right? Loyalty had nothing to do with justice, only blood.

In those defeatist days of January, February 1942, fear crackled through the city like lightning: the Italians would be shipped off with Germans and Japs to Alcatraz; FDR would ransom them to the Duce once we captured some Italian troops; no, the prisoners would be hostages, placed in the front lines. None of it was true, all of it plausible, no more implausible than the Japanese attack. Francesco couldn't even locate Vittorio with any certainty. For five bucks a clerk at Immigration told him he was possibly in Montana, a state Francesco couldn't find on a map, part of the great wasteland between the coasts he never thought about. In that camp Italians and Germans were mixed, the clerk said; how Vittorio will hate that, Francesco smiled, remembering his brother's tirades after he came back from war. It seemed this camp, like the others now filled with aliens, was built long before Pearl Harbor, which suggested that Roosevelt was planning war or that bulldog-faced Hoover had kept lists of "enemies" for years; how else could thousands disappear so completely, so instantly?

Charles Cozen agreed. He shook his elegant head at the President's recklessness. He is my friend, but in this matter he has behaved no better than the enemy, Cozen sighed. Even the authority of Executive Order 9066 was questionable: in California Italians were being relocated away from the coast, harmless fishermen, even Joe DiMaggio's father, yes! They needed a test case, Cozen repeated, confusingly; Francesco wondered who needed it and why? Cozen was pleased to represent Vittorio, though he underlined how difficult justice might be now, now that the simpleminded, scared by the gutter press, thought Axis subs were prowling the Jersey coast. Difficult, not impossible. Cozen spoke impressively of the Bill of Rights, almost mystically, before striking the chord of practicality: he had friends in Washington, and he thought he could arrange a hearing before the spring.

And so it was with rare calm that Francesco stood waiting for the paneled elevator to plunge him forty stories to the street. For the first time in weeks he no longer felt helpless; that alone made the trip worthwhile.

She stood, Leonora Lampa, directly opposite the revolving doors that deposited messenger boys and executives onto Madison Avenue. Francesco saw her before he passed through and stopped to suck in his breath. She looked older, no question, there were lines in her face, the subtle seams bitterness and disappointment etched. She stood in the damp February wind shuffling her feet for warmth, her purse in one hand and a cigarette she had forgotten in the other, gazing through the wrong set of revolving doors. What struck him as most bizarre was how much makeup she now wore, she who had spurned cosmetics all her life; her eyes glittered with mascara, while rouge only emphasized the sallow tint of her cheeks. Even her hair, marcelled and waved in the latest style, seemed stolen from someone else. She wore a black wool coat cut fashionably, just below the knees, so that the only color Leonora displayed was the blood red of her Chanel scarf. He took another breath and pushed through the revolving door.

Leonora tried to smile. "I thought you'd never leave."

"How did you know I'd be here?"

"How do you think? Look, let's go someplace, I'm cold?"

"Not for long, I have a train to catch."

She glared at him. "Don't treat me so high-handedly. I'm not one of those tenants you evict."

"What tenants? I'm the poorest landlord in Philadelphia."

"You're paying Charlie Cozen, aren't you?"

"Charlie? Do you know the man?"

She steered him into a bar on Forty-Fourth. "When I worked for Laura Warrington I did. He's a patron," she said ironically, "of the arts, assuming there are any artists in New York nowadays."

"A very intelligent man. Not apt to be fooled by an artist or anybody else."

"That's what we have to talk about. Cozen and you."

A shirtsleeved waiter appeared; Francesco ordered coffee, Leonora a Stinger.

"You don't drink alcohol," he exclaimed.

"I get headaches. The alcohol makes them go away."

"A bad habit, Leonora, why, my God—"

"If you lived my life you'd be grateful headaches were all you got. What do I have? My silly job a schoolgirl could do, my son who comes and goes like a stranger, I'm lucky to have dinner with him once a week. I'm not living. I survive. Like an animal."

"Move to Philadelphia."

"So you can save on a housekeeper for our mother? No, thank you. I like my freedom far too much. And there's Vittorio . . . ."

"Don't start, Leonora, I can't listen to that again!"

"You have to listen," she said, leaning forward to grasp his hands. "At last he's being punished, thank God! Let them lock him up, Francesco, let them, it's less than he deserves! Let them punish him!"

"You can't prove he had Lampa killed."

"Are you a lawyer too? You were at that party, you heard what our brother said. Saw what he did. He struck Lampa and he called him his enemy. What more proof do you need?"

"You've got no proof he isn't innocent."

"None of us is innocent. But some of us have blood on our hands."

"You aren't thinking logically—you're too emotional."

"Oh yes, a typical woman, irrational, hysterical! You rational men started the worst war in history, so be proud of yourselves."

"What men? Me, Vittorio, who?"

"You know very well," she said majestically, sipping her Stinger and gesturing with her cigarette to consign the guilty to the lowest circle of Hell.

"Leonora, you're not making any sense."

"Cozen's expensive," she said jeeringly. "What did he charge you? And how are you paying him?"

"That's my business."

"It's *my* business! You're hiring Charlie Cozen to get our brother out of jail when you know damn well he had Lampa killed. Isn't that my business too?"

"I took a second mortgage on our house."

She stared at him, amazed. "You didn't tell Teresa, did you? Did you?"

"No, but *you* will. I would have told her," Francesco added, "eventually."

"You did that for Vittorio." She said it as simply as a child would have.

"He's my blood. Your blood. Why should our family be disgraced?"

"Disgraced! When he and his cafoni were marching in the streets, *you* and *I* were disgraced! You didn't care! You thought having a Fascist for a brother was wonderful!"

"Never. I never approved. But you know what a mule he is, he wouldn't have listened to the Pope. When I asked him to stop that, when the war began, he stopped."

"Listen to yourself! He did it because he had to. Not because he had a change of heart. Vittorio has always been what he is, a bastard, and that's all he is. Only *you* are unable to see what he really is."

"A bastard? Our brother? Where is your loyalty to your blood?"

"And where is yours? Have you no feeling for me or my son, with my husband dead? You saw his body, what those animals did to him—"

"Of course I feel for you. I gave you money, I'll give you more—"

"You think money is love, don't you? No, love is love. The love I had for Lampa was real, it was pure, it survived everything except Vittorio and his butcher boy."

"For God's sake, Leonora! What can I do except help him now?"

"You want everyone to love you, that's your weakness, Francesco, honestly! You want to make everyone happy so all of us will love you! What a childish man you are!"

"I don't need," he said coldly, "to hear you dissect my character. I'm not the one drinking cocktails before noon."

"Then I will say it straight out—if you help Vittorio, you no longer have a sister. My mother has no daughter. Consider me dead, light candles, because you'll never see my face again."

"You shouldn't drink," he said jokingly. "It brings out your nasty side."

"I told Teresa the same thing without a drink. I swear, Francesco. If you do this you won't have a sister," she said slowly.

"If I *don't* do it I won't have a family. You want me to support Bellina and her children until God knows when? You want our mother to call me every day and weep, which is what she does?"

"Let her weep for Lampa. Let her weep for me."

"She did. Now she weeps for Vittorio. My God, we don't even know for certain where he is!"

"I know where he deserves to be. Next to Judas Iscariot, rotting in Hell."

"Then let God judge him. I can't, and neither should you. Forgive, Leonora, forgive, you have no proof."

"Forgive? I'd like to kill him but I can't."

They stared at each other stonily.

"You're going to do this? Cozen is going to save that murderer?"

"I paid him," Francesco said, "five thousand dollars to do that very thing."

"Five thousand," Leonora gasped, sagging backward against the booth. "It's real, then, it's happening?"

Francesco nodded. "I did what I had to do," he said proudly. "I did my duty to our blood."

"*I* am your blood. You had a duty to consider me. When we were children, I was kind to you, our mother wasn't, Francesco, but I always was. And when you went to America, who wrote to you every week? I did, not Vittorio, not any of them. But you always helped him, you gave your blood for him in those stinking mines, wasn't that enough? Will you go on giving him your blood to the grave?"

"Both of you," he replied, "I'll help both of you."

"No," she said, standing up, slipping on her coat of mourning black, "today you made your choice once and for all." She started to say something more, then caught herself and walked quickly out of the bar before he could follow her. By the time he reached Madison Avenue she had vanished into the city's promiscuous embrace.

NINE

The first thought Vittorio had every morning was always the same: I will freeze to death in this Godforsaken place. He'd never felt such cold, not even half-naked in Austrian mud during the War. Cold so piercing that even sleeping in his clothes and boots didn't help, so that he woke each morning blue-lipped, teeth chattering, limbs so rigid he could scarcely move them for ten minutes or more.

The interned Italians slept in hastily slapped together barracks sprawling at the side of Fort Missoula, at the western edge of Montana. Not three miles from the fort, ice-capped mountains loomed up from the plain, their foothills covered with scrub and icicles, barren of trees. They encircled the horizon like a prison wall: you had to stand at an oblique angle to avoid seeing the mountains constantly.

The creeks lay under ice crusted so thick Vittorio could walk on them. He walked as far as the end of the fort, where guards shouted from towers to turn back or be shot. In that immense emptiness their voices carried a mile. He would shrug and walk back, his steps measured as he trudged to the ice-blue field where his barracks stood.

Half a mile from the flimsy huts gleamed the railroad siding where the cattle cars bringing them to Montana had emptied out. The cars smelled like straw and cow shit, a comforting fragrance to a country boy like Vittorio. Three days they'd jostled across the continent, stopping in sunlight, inexplicably, while riding breakneck through the night, through fields of winter wheat where scarecrows dangled as though crucified. Once, the cars passed over a frighteningly long bridge over the seething waters of a river swollen with rain. Vittorio stared out, straight down into a maelstrom not even Odysseus could have contemplated without fear. The other men began wailing and moaning, certain they were about to plunge to their deaths. What a miserable pack of cowards, he thought. If they'd been my troops at Caporetto I'd have machine-gunned every one . . . .

With those men he spoke, here in the camp, as little as possible. It grew tedious to listen to them curse America, curse Roosevelt, curse their luck. Too many blamed the evil eye, the malocchio, la jettatura, a curse some enemy had placed on them. Not Vittorio. He disliked his fate, but found it logical enough. Hitler and the Duce were mad enough to declare war after the Japanese attack, so it made perfect sense to round up Italians who might be saboteurs. It was perhaps unjust but wars were not about justice or reason, they were tribal, irrational, Neanderthal. He knew Italy would be dragged into shit by Hitler; the Duce must have been mad not to know it too. Declaring war on America! Didn't the idiots know how huge, how rich this barbarous country was? Huge enough to find a place as impossible to escape from as Fort Missoula where, the men said, the nearest city was three hundred miles distant. Someone should have shown those fools a map.

They heard war news every day on Armed Forces Radio. The men applauded American defeats sardonically; not him. He guessed he would never leave the camp until Italy left the war. He was prepared to wait, if not forever; the bad food and the Arctic nights might kill him before then.

He wrote to each of his sons every day, a short letter according to the military rules which specified the number of words allowed:

Never forget you are Italians, not Americans. Italians have pride, honor, dignity. These are your birthright. You must not squander them.

Remember that your father is a war hero. Through temporary inconvenience I am interned, but never confuse American stupidity with the valor the King of Italy cited me for long ago. I am not a criminal, not an enemy alien. I am loyal to Italy and I have always (he hesitated here) always obeyed the laws of America. Never listen to strangers who will try to poison your mind. Listen to your family, who knows me for the man I am. Even Jesus Christ was falsely accused.

Obey your Uncle Francesco, your mother, and your grandmothers. Until I return home they are your parents, all of them. Work at your studies. Do not neglect them for your games; that is American sloppiness. To be a true son of mine you must be serious, studious, disciplined. In itself discipline accomplishes nothing, yet without it nothing great has been accomplished yet!

My sons, do not feel disgraced or saddened by my internment. It is a small cloud that will soon pass. It means nothing, not even to me who suffers it. Remember, you are the sons of a man the King of Italy decorated personally. I give you permission to take my medals out of their case and look at them.

Respect your mother. Her life is not easy now, do not make it harder still. And respect your uncle. He is your guardian until I come home. Above all, remember who your father is and who you therefore are!!

After a month he got a letter from his brother and one from his wife. Bellina's was incoherent and he put it aside. Francesco wrote that he'd hired a lawyer to appeal the internment, and that Vittorio would likely be free before summer. The news struck him like a blow and he could not catch his breath at first. Am I accused of killing Lampa, he wondered, biting on the past the way a man in pain bites on a broken tooth. Let them accuse me, he thought defiantly, the way my bitch of a sister did. They can't prove a thing, not a goddamn thing, he told himself.

That night he celebrated by joining the men who bought whisky from the soldiers, drinking outside under an enormous tent of stars until the warm wooziness filled his limbs, erasing the cold, erasing the knowledge of where he was. He sang with the men, the good old songs about the King and the Naples girls and sweet Maria and her devilish kisses. Vittorio sang the old songs in a cracked voice until the tower guards shouted down at him to get inside.

TEN

My dearest Carlo:

Do you know what despair is? I am afraid you are still too young to know. And so you will not understand, and that hurts me in my heart.

In the church my parents raised me in, the one your father refused to baptize you in, despair is a sin—a sin against the Holy Spirit. To despair is to rebel, to deny God's Providence and Grace. That is why Dante punished the suicides so horribly. They defied God by rebelling, they became Gods themselves with the power of life and death.

I suppose I am rebelling now, though I have never felt weaker in my life, not even when your poor father died. I sleep twelve hours a day, I never eat, I scarcely even speak to you. I have been drifting into despair, my son, and you must understand that IT HAS NOTHING TO DO WITH YOU.

My brothers have become my mortal enemies. They have betrayed me just as they betrayed your poor father, may he rest in peace. Grief sharp as a stiletto stabs my heart. I dream of murder, blood, revenge. My brain sizzles with anger—useless anger, since how can I avenge your father now? Vittorio has won. Our family traitor has escaped punishment. And I am too weak to punish him. That is my despair.

If I were still a Catholic I could never do what I do now. But if God were a better Catholic perhaps I would be one too. My son, this world is beautiful, and only men are vile. A sunrise can be perfect, or a rose, but the hearts of men are a crooked labyrinth which baffles even them. Trust no man. Fear evil, for it is everywhere. An Evil God rules this world. I feel joy at escaping his viciousness. It will triumph even in this war, I know it will.

You are brilliant and good and wise beyond your years. You are what the Hindus call an old soul, did I ever tell you that? Work hard, be strong, be a second Fermi. Do not squander your gifts. Be a great man, my son.

I shall walk, very soon, down to the Hudson River piers, the place I went so often late at night. I will put bricks in my skirt, so I will sink quickly, quickly under the black water. It will be a painless death, have no fear of that.

You will hate me for a long time, I know. And then, one day, you too will touch the quicksand of despair, and then you will understand why your mother did what she did. Know that I love you, I have always loved you, and try not to hate me if you can.

So long as I walk this earth the Evil God will torture me. I believe that now, in the circle of light, I shall fly home to the True God, and he shall enfold me in seraph's wings, and my torture shall end. I shall finally be at peace. Forgive me, Carlo, please forgive, forgive.

ELEVEN

"**You** are too thin, my child. Let me make you something to eat."

"No, no thank you, Grandmother, I am fine."

She smiled and nodded and sat back in her easy chair. Now there would be silence until she said something else, silence like lead, as though the air of this dark house he barely knew, with its pictures of the bleeding heart of Jesus and its furniture the color of rust, as though its air were an inert gas crushing Carlo's chest. Why did I come here, he thought angrily.

Signora Monti brightened. "Some peppers, you like peppers, they're nearly cooked?"

He could smell their sweet heavy scent through the kitchen door. Carlo tried to remember his last meal, not counting the peanut butter he kept in his locker at Columbia. Two weeks, a month? Not since he'd had to identify his mother's corpse, anyway; not since that night. Her waterlogged body, skin nearly gray, flashed onto his mind's screen and he pushed it back down, down, with all the strength of will he had.

"Maybe later, Grandmother."

Talking Italian felt strange to Carlo now. He imagined sometimes he had two souls, if there were really such a thing, one speaking English, one Italian. With the physics gang at Columbia, those public school aristocrats, he talked baseball stats, movie stars, experiments. What could be more American than

Betty Grable's overripe breasts or DiMaggio's batting average? He blended, speaking English, into the great homogenized continent, an American kid, innocent of history, laughing at the same jokes and lusting after the same pinup as any kid in Omaha. He knew Tommy Dorsey's trombone solos five blocks away from a radio sobbing them out onto Riverside Drive. The crack of a fastball connecting with a bat made his pulse race, and so did John Wayne's stiff-assed walk and Barbara Stanwyck's mouth in the close-up of a kiss. He was American with one soul, and with the other, what?

An orphan of history. When he pitied himself he called him that. All his life he had been free falling through history, a skydiver without a parachute, pushed unwillingly from his plane. His father was a martyr, never mind why, and his mother . . . . yet when he spoke Italian he felt cautious, an old soul as she called him, and most of all he felt afraid.

Why the hell did I come here? To see my grandmother one last time?

"I see my uncle's sign on a lot of houses, he must be getting rich."

"Wait and see," she said with a sly grin, "he thought he was getting rich before."

"Before the Depression? Everybody thought so, didn't they?"

"Francesco wants to be a good American, and the only good Americans are rich Americans." Signora Monti shrugged. "The war is bringing him luck, these Navy Yard fools need houses, so . . . ."

"Is that it?" How strange, to make money from a war against the country where you were born. His poor father would have told him about capitalist greed . . . . when he thought of him now he remembered, and he knew it, only the good, the way his father joked with him or flung his arm across Carlo's shoulders when they crossed Washington Square. There were other memories but he had no key to wherever they were locked away. What good was it to love somebody if you knew you loved them only when they were dead? And did you really love someone if it took death to teach you what you felt? He thought sometimes all that was a lie, the emotions everyone claimed to feel, a mask over the cold face they secretly wore, the face that stared into the mirror when you awakened from a nightmare feeling hurled unwillingly into this world, entirely alone.

"You will see your uncle tonight, won't you?"

Carlo shifted queasily in his chair. He would have to tell her now.

"No, Grandmother. I came to see you, and then I'll go."

She said with a confused look, "But we are your family."

He drew in a breath. "That's what . . . . why I came. To say goodbye to you."

"Goodbye?" Now she was frightened. "Are you going away somewhere?"

"I'll never come back here, that's certain, Grandmother."

"But why? You aren't serious?"

"You're different from them. You were always kind to my mother and you helped raise me. I have no grievance with you."

She sagged in her chair, suddenly ancient now. "You believe what your mother thought? About Vittorio?"

He had to look away before he could say, "Yes. I do."

"She was a fool and now you are a fool! He is your uncle, you have no proof! Are you Our Lord who sees into every heart and soul?"

"They killed my mother. Both of them. They drove her to despair."

"Nonsense! Your mother was weak, she was always weak, why do you think she left you with me? Weak, I tell you, and maybe even mad."

"Grandmother," Carlo exclaimed, "how can you talk like that?"

"Things are what they are. At my age I have no use for hypocrisy. She was weak, your mother. What should I have done when my husband lost every lira? Should I have drowned myself?"

"That was money. My mother lost much more than that."

"I lost a husband, too. I did not fall to the ground cursing

God. I held this family together, just as your mother should have done with *her* family."

"Uncle Vittorio is not innocent—" he began.

"Does that make him guilty? The streets are full of madmen who hated your father, rest in peace. Is he responsible for them all?"

"You were at my party. You saw what he did, heard what he said. And my father was killed here, in this city, is that an accident?"

"All right!" Signora Monti sat up sharply in her seat. "If you want to hate, go ahead and hate. You will live with hate and your heart will be scorched and dead and black like charcoal. That is what hate does."

"I don't hate anyone," Carlo said, only half-believing his own words.

"I pray you don't. Even your poor father, rest in peace, didn't hate that scum that put him in jail."

"But he left Italy, didn't he? The way I want to leave this family."

"My son, my son, you can never leave your family. We are your blood."

"I can never see any of you again. I never will."

"But we are here," Signora Monti tapped her heart grimly, "and we are here," she said, touching her head. "You cannot run away from that."

"I can," Carlo said, "I will."

"But we are inside you, no matter where you go."

"Don't be so sure, Grandmother, of what's inside of me."

"But how can you hate your own family, it's like hating yourself, you will go mad!"

"I don't hate anyone," he replied, "but I will go mad if I stay in this family pretending I don't blame my uncles for killing my parents, both of them. I know," he added hastily, "I know you think she was weak. I don't care. They did what they did, and my mother is dead."

"You do hate all of us. I can tell."

"Yes, I hate you, do you like that better, Grandmother? I

never want to see a Monti again, never, not even you. I will make my own way in the world alone, without your goddamn money, Uncle Francesco's goddamn checks, tell him to stop sending them, they're sitting in a goddamn drawer. My mother was your blood too, did any of you think of her? Did you ever once think of her?"

"You think you can run away from yourself. You can't."

"I'll forget all of you. I will. I will."

"We are the one thing," she said evenly, "that you will never forget."

The leaden air was suffocating Carlo. He had to flee, he had to escape into sunlight. He stood up and, before his grandmother could say a word, kissed her goodbye, smelling her violet toilet water and that scent of dust peculiar to the old, without another word crossing the living room in two bounds, stepping through the doorway with a painful sigh. Tears rushed to his eyes but he forced them back with a sob.

I will forget them, Carlo swore, knowing he never could, I will forget her and this house and this day, knowing he would forget none of it, not the American flag planted awkwardly in the geraniums, not the way the dust trembled in the light, not the smell of peppers frying in his grandmother's kitchen, not the sight of her, standing now on the porch, waving, as he ran towards a trolley, waving as though he were the Montis' favorite son who would soon return to take his place with them, no, he would forget none of that, it would live always in some chamber of his heart, some cellar of his memory, his family's longing so powerful as to erase his own longing, his own escape. And then the trolley began to move west into the sun and Carlo shielded his eyes so that he could stare straight ahead into his future, his longing for an American life without blood or memory, and by the time he glanced back his grandmother's house had disappeared, one more rowhouse in a perspective line to infinity, and he felt a leaden bird rise from his chest and beat its wings fiercely as it flew west into the night. There must be families God regrets he ever made.

AUTHOR'S NOTE

Although THE SECRET FAMILY is not a historical novel in the usual sense, its fictional characters do intersect with real figures and documented events. Boies Penrose, Mussolini, Matteotti, Gramsci, Giovannitti, and Martin Dies were all in the places at the times I indicate, doing what I describe. Even the episode of Fascists terrorizing a Venice trattoria is factual, witnessed by Vincent Sheean. The 115th Street feast, the HUAC hearings in 1938, and above all the internment of Italians after Pearl Harbor belong to history, if not to textbook history.

Since I don't subscribe to the imported French fashion that erases the distinction between history and fiction, I thought it best to state that this novel incorporates fact without, I hope, traducing it. The Monti family, Lampa, the Gioias, Carney, and Greenglass are all inventions, whatever points of departure in life they may have had. In other words, I have put imaginary birds in a real garden; I have not, like certain of my colleagues, twisted the facts for effect. Joyce called history a nightmare from which he was trying to awake. But since we never can awake from it, the novelist's job is to make us feel as if we were dreaming it, even the part we think we know, for the very first time.

Printed in the United States
1310500002B/161